KU-218-679

Graham Joyce wrote his first novel, *Dreamside*, on the Greek island of Lesbos, having given up his job in youth work to write full time. *House of Lost Dreams* takes him back to a Greek island and follows the success of *Dark Sister* ('a compelling tale of terror' Ramsey Campbell) also available from Headline Feature.

He is married and now lives in Leicester.

Also by Graham Joyce

Dreamside
Dark Sister

House of
Lost Dreams

Graham Joyce

HEADLINE
FEATURE

Copyright © 1993 Graham Joyce

The right of Graham Joyce to be identified as the Author
of the Work has been asserted by him in accordance with the
Copyright, Designs and Patents Act 1988.

First published in 1993
by HEADLINE BOOK PUBLISHING

First published in paperback in 1994
by HEADLINE BOOK PUBLISHING

A HEADLINE FEATURE paperback

10 9 8 7 6 5 4 3 2 1

All rights reserved. No part of this publication may be
reproduced, stored in a retrieval system, or transmitted,
in any form or by any means without the prior written
permission of the publisher, nor be otherwise circulated
in any form of binding or cover other than that in which
it is published and without a similar condition being
imposed on the subsequent purchaser.

All characters in this publication are fictitious
and any resemblance to real persons, living or dead,
is purely coincidental.

ISBN 0 7472 4248 8

Typeset by Keyboard Services, Luton

Printed and bound in Great Britain by
HarperCollins Manufacturing, Glasgow

HEADLINE BOOK PUBLISHING
A division of Hodder Headline PLC
Headline House
79 Great Titchfield Street
London W1P 7FN

To Martin and David,
for enduring in such fine style
that most difficult of beings,
an elder brother

ACKNOWLEDGEMENTS

Thanks are due to David Grossman, for professional support and for becoming a friend. To some very fine writers and artists for their encouragement: Molly Brown, Jim Burns, Storm Constantine, Mark Morris, Kim Newman, Nick Royle, Mary Scott & Ian Watson. To my wife Sue Johnsen, who makes it all possible.

Also to the inspirational George Seferis, with apologies for my hamfisted translation of his poem.

Finally to the one who, miraculously, still sits outside my window, and who has brought more.

At the secret cove
white like a dove
we thirsted at noon
but the water was brackish.

In the golden sand
we scratched her name.
But a fine breeze blew
and the writing vanished.

With what heart, what inspiration,
what lust and passion
we lived our life: a mistake!
Therefore we changed our life.

Seferis

(translated from the original Greek by the author)

1

Mike got out of the water quickly. Whatever that thing was, he didn't like the look of it. Underwater goggles magnify vision, but even accounting for any distortion, the creature must have been four feet in length. He sat on the sand of pulverised shells, catching his breath and letting the sun crystallise the salt water on his skin.

Kim had dispatched him to the rock to collect oregano, but he'd spent the afternoon hunting octopus. It was his idea for a surprise supper. He'd studied the macho locals: they snorkelled around for half an hour, dived suddenly and then reappeared holding aloft a grey-pink sack of blubber, eight tentacles coiled around their tanned fore-arms. So far he hadn't even seen an octopus, far less had the opportunity to dive for one.

He'd been swimming for about twenty minutes, before this *thing* had come towards him from out of the deep waters, baring at him what could only be described as fangs.

He sat shivering slightly on the scallop of sand, looking across the moored rowing boat and at the house beyond. He could see Kim's head bobbing in the water. All of this swimming and rowing was tuning them up. They were as lean and fit as Olympians.

The house across the water reflected white and sharp like

light from a blade. The green hills behind climbed to an exposed ridge of lion-coloured rock, outcropping at intervals to resemble the humped back of a gigantic stegosaurus. He had yet to explore those hills. Further along the beach, about half a mile from the house, stood the low-lying village of Kamari. Seven miles further north was the pretty walled town of Limanaki crested by its Genoese castle. Beyond that lay Turkey and the shores of Asia Minor; far enough away – culturally – to signify the Orient; close enough – geographically – to hear the donkeys braying.

Up there the island was heavily militarised. A state of cold war still existed between the nations of Greece and Turkey; a conflict as old as Helen of Troy.

Mike was planning to take a trip to the north side of the island. There were one or two sites he wanted to visit. The black rocks and grey volcanic sands of the north side had given the island its name. Like most Greek islands there was an alternative title available, Tyminos, but the natives invariably referred to their island as Mavros, the black one.

Mavros was vibrant with geothermal energy. The massive centre of the island had been scooped out by some primeval volcano, such that it resembled a gigantic thick-rimmed cauldron. Water seeped into the base of the cauldron where the volcano had blasted an inlet to the south. Most of the towns and villages hugged the coast or nested in the hills constituting the rim, and to drive from one side to the other required either negotiating difficult coastal routes or descending by a precarious zigzagged road into the cauldron itself and up the other side. A journey across the island – which on a straight road would take half an hour – would here mean three hours of constant gear-crunching.

Vibrations, tremors, shocks and the occasional full-scale earthquake were the island's legacy. The earth crust floated on a shifting bed of hot rocks belching steaming thermal waters into the sea at intervals around the coast. 'The black one' was like a gasping, living creature.

'Do you feel the tension?' Mike had once said to Kim.

'What do you mean by the tension?'

'Take off your shoes and feel it through your feet. It's alive. Just feel it.'

So Kim had kicked off her espadrilles and stood flexing her toes in the warm grass of their garden.

'See what I mean? Do you get it?'

Kim had said yes, but Mike wasn't convinced she knew what he was talking about. Whatever *it* was, he could feel it. It was like a delicate shivering; and even though he accepted that the sensation might be some kind of excitable projection on his part, he nonetheless accounted it as real. He would stand with his toes pressed into sand or shingle repeating the Greek word for earth, *gea*. He was almost serious about it.

What shifted under the surface of the island was almost as miraculous as what flourished above ground. The spring wildlife was sensational. Mike was a graphic artist: he received the world visually, his eyes were the presiding organ of sense. And what he saw was shifting colour. This was the 'endless movie' to which he made constant reference; a kaleidoscope of light breaking with the dawn, easing into morning, rolling into day, unfolding into afternoon, spinning into evening, flooding into sunset, leaking out at twilight. An endless panorama, every day changing. And its populations! In the three weeks they'd been there the island had been colonised by three different species of butterfly, each surviving but a week: brimstone-yellow, red-and-black and peacock-blue butterflies he couldn't name.

Wildlife crept or flew or swam across the apron of land and water in front of the house, tortoises and porcupines, goshawks and golden oriels, giant orange starfish and purple jellyfish. Light refracting from the water. Colour bleeding from the land.

A visual intensity that made him drunk with sensation.

And he hadn't liked the place when they'd first arrived; though there seemed a strange sense of destiny in the way the location was offered to them. They had arrived in the *platia* at Kamari during the early evening. Waiters were sweeping up and preparing the tables in the five tavernas surrounding the *platia*. Mike parked their battered Renault behind an old Mercedes taxi and got out. A man was leaning against the taxi reading a newspaper. There was no one else around, so Mike approached him.

'Speak English?'

The paper dipped. The man inclined his head to one side, Greek for yes.

'We want to rent a room.'

'You want a hotel?'

The plan had indeed been to rent a hotel room for a few days, at least until they were able to find somewhere to settle on a permanent basis. But Mike looked at the man and said, 'No. Not a hotel. We want to rent something for a whole year. Not tourist rates. Maybe a small house.'

The man frowned. Then he mustered a rather forced smile. Gold fillings winked in an overcrowded mouth. 'I have a house you can rent. A house on the beach.' He pronounced the last word *bitch* and manipulated his jaw into another simulated smile.

'How much?'

'First come and look.'

'First how much?'

'Follow me.'

The taxi driver got into his car. Mike climbed back in the driving seat. 'He says he's got a house on the bitch.'

'Sounds nice. That was easy.'

'Too easy. I don't much like the look of him. He wouldn't tell me what he wants for it.'

The taxi pulled away and they followed. He drove for half a mile and turned down a dirt track. There was a lonely taverna on the beach, where they parked. Walking a considerable way ahead, he beckoned them to follow him along a trampled grassy path fringing the beach. At last they came to the shuttered house standing fifty feet back from the beach path. A few ducks and chickens scratched at the earth and a donkey was tethered in the far corner of the garden. Ornamental white doves took off at their approach, only to resettle moments later.

The taxi driver was fumbling with a padlock around the gate. Tacked to the gate was a wooden board, on which was crudely lettered the words HAUS DER VERLORENEN TRAUME. The house itself was a primitive building of whitewashed, unplastered breezeblock, its door- and windowframes hastily splashed with bright-turquoise paint. Its best feature was the large concrete patio splendidly canopied with a healthy vine and hung with queer-shaped decorative gourds. The gourds had also been subjected to indiscriminate splatters of the turquoise paint, as had the large earthenware plant pots dotting the edge of the patio, and anything else unequipped to dodge an approaching paintbrush.

Inside, there were only two rooms. The place reeked of

mildew and dust. There was a bed with broken springs and some evil-smelling blankets. Mike looked around for a light-switch.

'No electricity?'

'No need,' said the taxi driver. He indicated an oil lamp on a table. Kim went outside – in disgust, Mike thought. The inner walls were of the same unplastered rough texture as the exterior. He noticed a few bulbous-headed spiders nestling in the crevices. He followed Kim outside, and the taxi driver bounded after him.

'Toilet,' he said, leading Mike to an outbuilding across the garden. He stopped to crank the handle of a waterpump set by the gate. The pump, similarly splashed with turquoise paint, belched and spat out a gob of water.

'No running water. No electricity. I don't think so,' said Mike.

'Tell him we'll take it,' said Kim. She was looking out across the sea.

'But it's a dump! Have you seen it back there?'

'Never mind what's back there,' she said. 'Just look what's out *there*.' And with a sweep of her arm she indicated the whole of the sky and the sea before her.

Mike stepped from out of the shadow of the grim outbuilding and looked across to the west. The sun was setting over the water. It was lavender and peacock blue and lemon and crimson, and the sun lay spilled on a low cloud like a broken egg yolk. Colours dappled the water like the iridescent scales of a Mediterranean fish. The rock opposite the house was a hump of deep purple, a crouched figure in a cowl.

'Tell him we'll have it,' she repeated.

'Right,' Mike had said. 'How much do you want?'

And every day since then had turned over like a page

from an illuminated manuscript. The optical miracle showed no sign of fading. From the rock Mike looked across the water at the house and felt glad for every day.

Then he remembered the oregano he'd been sent to collect. He climbed the rock and found a clump of the herb. He breathed its aroma before cutting a few leaves. Standing on the highest rock he waved at Kim, who was out of the water and making her way back up to the house. She didn't see him.

Yes, it must have been a sea snake, he decided: the thing which had almost attacked him in the water. He'd heard of sea snakes big enough to bite off your hand or your foot. It was strange. They had been talking about snakes – and sea snakes – only the night before as they sat out on the balcony. They'd also been talking about something else as they watched phantom fishermen.

The silent passage of fishermen in the black of night, close into the shore, had been another revelation. As they relaxed on the patio in the late evenings, under light from the oil lamps or from candles, they might see one drift before them at the bottom of their garden. It was an utterly eerie experience. Only the prow of the boat would be made visible by a bright light designed to draw fish to the surface. There would be no engine noise, only the gentle swish of quiet oars gliding the boat though the shallows. The fishermen themselves went unseen in the dark. They were ghosts. It was possible to believe that the boats were uncrewed.

The previous evening had seen the passage of three such boats. They had emptied two bottles of wine. There was no moon on the water and Kim had made a spread from the Tarot deck on the table. The stealthy passage of the boats had distracted them from the cards. Kim drained her glass and pointed to one of the cards on which a snake was emerging from a cup.

'I thought we'd see more snakes around here,' she said.

'I'm sure we will. They must come to the water by the pump. And there are probably sea snakes out there.'

That was all that was said. It was just that this hadn't been the first time something had been mentioned one day only to manifest itself the following day. Tortoises. Mike had read something aloud from a book suggesting that there were many tortoises on the island. Then two very large, old ones had appeared in the garden. A day or two later Kim had been describing a species of bright red anemone she'd once seen on the island of Rhodes. The next day four plants of this description had flowered alongside the house.

Small things. Echoes from a world of miracles.

And it wasn't just wildlife. Mike was already fascinated by the myth of Orpheus, which featured the island of Mavros, before he left England. Indeed it had been the presiding factor in choosing this island above all others. Something in the tale of Orpheus descending to the underworld had fired his imagination, in the way that some people are excited by the gold mask of Tutankhamun or the lost city of Atlantis. He was intelligent enough to realise that this attraction was likely to reveal more about his own psychology than anything about the nature of the island; but for the time being he was content to visit the tiny library in the village in the hope of finding some hint about possible locations.

'Library' was a rather grand word to describe the half-dozen shelves of books in a small, fusty municipal building, where he'd found but a single work in English. It was a small pamphlet outlining the legend of Orpheus and its relationship to the island. He felt a tiny thrill of confirmation when he picked it out.

All these things were mere coincidence, of course. Until they kept happening.

Now there were snakes.

Mike climbed back in the boat, pushed off from the rock and rowed back across to the House of Lost Dreams. He decided not to mention the sea snake to Kim.

2

Eden-bright, a plump, luminous green snake hung from the lower branches of the fig tree behind the house. It regarded Kim with lazy, complacent eyes as she stiffened. She'd mistaken it for a length of dangling plastic hose. Now she retreated slowly, closing the door on her ambition to clear the storehouse.

'You leave me alone, I'll leave you alone,' she said to the snake.

She would not, she'd already decided, mention it to Mike. It was just one more thing in a list, a growing inventory, of minor encounters and cameo experiences not ripe for the telling. She didn't want to worry him.

Not that Mike would be unnerved by the presence of a snake *per se*. On the contrary he would, with boyish enthusiasm, want to see it for himself, or prod it with a long stick, or sketch it. He wasn't afraid of these things, and neither was she. It was just that they'd had that discussion about snakes the previous evening, when they'd sat in the shadows, with the cards spread and the oil lamps flickering, and the boats of the phantom fishermen gliding past.

It was one in a string of odd coincidences she'd got to think about, and for that reason Kim would edit it from her account of the day's events.

She stepped out from under the vine canopy of the patio and went to wash her hands in the sea. A fringe of shingle beach and a low mesh fence divided the water from the bottom of her scrubby garden. Before steeping her hands she looked across to the tiny island opposite. She could see the brightly painted rowing boat, a watercolour splash of blue, orange and white, bobbing where Mike had moored her. Mike himself was out of view, clambering over the rock in search of oregano. Wild oregano! These were the gifts of the Greek islands, wild herbs, oregano and thyme and sage spicing the breeze. Kneeling at the water's edge Kim threw back her head, feeling hot sun on her face, inhaling scented air.

Behind her the whitewashed house nestled at the foot of a steep incline rising into parched hills. Clonking sheep-bells betrayed the invisible flock grazing high up, where the asphalt road climbed from the village to cut a swathe through the lion-coloured rock. The Aegean spring drugged and seduced her. Nothing could dismay her or dislodge her from the narcotic beauty of this new location, where the threat of venomous serpents – all part of the hallucination – was to be given no quarter.

Kim was still entranced. It was their third week at the house on the island, and the enchanted powder had still to be lifted from her eyes. She was not alone in that. Mike was there with her, still blinking every day at his 'endless movie', the unfolding panorama, the everyday miracle and vigour of Creation. *The life!*

How had that happened? To strip the dead scales from their eyes like that? It was as if some voice had approached them one day, saying 'Give it all up! Pack it all in! Sell the house! Go off and find *the life*! And all you have to do, trust me, is step off the edge of this cliff!'

And step off the cliff they had, and they were still in free fall. Occasionally they looked at each other as if one of them would confess it was all a joke, quite a hoax actually, but now time to go home. But no. Mike had given in his notice, to everyone's surprise; Kim had quit, to everyone's disbelief, her job as nursing sister; and they'd unloaded their joint mortgage.

It had all seemed to happen so quickly and with more ease than was decent. They bought a Renault, stuffed it with clothes and books and camping gear, and threw a farewell party for friends. Everyone had blinked at the haste of the thing – so sudden they almost seemed to take offence – and said, 'So that's it? You're just fucking off to Greece?' This question was repeated so often Mike had tickets printed saying 'WE'RE FUCKING OFF TO GREECE – COME TO A PARTY'. A great party it was too, lasting three days. Finally, hungover, they made it to the ferry port and put the white cliffs of Dover behind them.

Malign forces did conspire to try to make them return. In a rented room in a French farmhouse, Kim went sleepwalking and tried to climb out of the window. Mike came to abrupt awareness in a traffic jam on a German autobahn and started panicking about work left undone. They both endured nightmares and ridiculous arguments in Austria. But when they crossed the snowy Grossglockner, Europe's highest road, they plunged into the Austrian Canton with a sense of having also crossed a psychological mountain pass.

Weird incidents happened in Croatia and Serbia. At the coastal town of Split as they wandered near the Roman ruins, an old woman in Mediterranean widow's black approached them, wagging her finger in their faces. She spoke incomprehensibly to them, presumably in Serbo-Croat. Then she walked off, leaving them bewildered. A waiter from a nearby restaurant had overheard.

'She says you will come to know,' he laughed.

'Come to know? Come to know what?'

The waiter shrugged and turned away. 'That's all she said. You will come to know.'

In Kosovo, while they slept in a hotel, their car was broken into by a tidy thief who removed only a few tape cassettes, leaving a pepper-sausage in exchange. All these episodes were dismissed as mere grist for their travelogue, and Greece was finally achieved.

Across the border, the road curved into mythological distance, and the sky was as blue as legend. In every sense Greece was otherworld, its fables unfolding at odd intervals. Like the place where a motorway terminated abruptly in a cloud of grazing sheep; or the toll booth where a silent attendant issued them with a ticket and then advanced them five yards before taking the ticket back and tearing it up. They actually stopped and waited for the next car, to confirm that this action was routine.

'Greece,' they said happily. 'These are the Greeks.'

And here they were, three weeks later, on the island of Mavros, living like gypsies in a primitive beach house and already wondering if it would ever be possible to return to the life they had left behind. Kim stripped off her T-shirt and waded into the water. The sea was still a little cool; it would heat up with the advance of the Mediterranean summer. She waded carefully to avoid the spines of black sea urchins lying among the weeds on the sea bed, but the water was clear as glass.

She swam halfway to the rock where Mike had moored the rowing boat, and floated on her back. She was still thinking about the snake as she tilted her head to look back at the whitewashed house. But if even paradise had to have its serpent, then, she considered, she should allow the House of Lost Dreams to have one too.

3

Who were they, these brave young *Anglica?* What purpose had brought them here? And by what right had they chosen to live in that house?

That house!

Every day he had watched them. Now they were settled, and already they were dropping their guard. The man was leaving the woman for longer periods, either to make a visit to the village or to row, for some mysterious purpose, back and forth between the island and the rock. And every day he watched them carefully. He could crouch in the hills behind the house and they would not know he was watching them.

It was not clear to him why anyone would choose to live in such a house. Surely they had better dwellings in England. He knew a little about England: they had electricity, piped water and all modern conveniences. Why then live in a house infested with scorpions and lit only by oil lamp? It made no sense. It was *trellos.* Crazy.

Perhaps they were a kind of gypsy couple. Driven out of their homes in England. He should feel sorry for them. Some scandal must have driven them away.

Or maybe they were like those Matala people. Some years ago children from the West had arrived in Crete to live in the caves at Matala. They fucked on the beach and ate only salads, those children. Then the local population got tired of them, and had them gassed from the caves by the police.

The woman was beautiful. She was dark, but not as the Greek women were dark. Her hair fell in a single wave, the light upon it like the water from the tap at the Church of the Virgin. Her skin was pale – this was what they meant by an English rose, he saw it now – skin which would need a damp climate to preserve its moist, fresh petals. Large breasts. They would be of the same creamy complexion as her face, He would like to place his cracked, dry hands on those breasts. Yes, a beautiful woman, only a little strayed beyond the bloom of youth. She was like a fruit gently touched by the shadow of overripeness. He would like to taste the fruit and flower of such a woman.

Why should she come to this house?

He had not noticed them arrive. One morning he had made a path across the hill and had seen them below. They were cleaning the house, incinerating rubbish in the garden. He had watched. Did they know the house crawled with scorpions? Well they would find out soon enough.

Then Lakis the taxi driver had arrived with a gift of something, maybe a transistor radio. He had wanted to stand up and call to them: watch out for Lakis! Watch out for the biggest scorpion of them all! He hated Lakis. The gift-bearer had stayed for a coffee, twiddling with the radio until he found a station. Then after he had gone they had switched off the radio and put it away.

When he saw them do that, when he saw them turn their backs on Lakis' gift, he thought there might be hope. He had enough English. He could go down there and say, 'Don't stay in this house, don't take Lakis' gifts.' But what good would it do? They would ask Lakis, and Lakis would say,

'Don't listen to that madman.' No, it was sealed. They had not chosen the house. The house had chosen them.

He spat out an olive stone and bit into a piece of soft cheese as he crouched in the bushes. He supposed that now they were there he wouldn't be able to steal the eggs. For some time now he had vexed Lakis by stealing the duck and chicken eggs. He'd had some fun watching Lakis sticking his head under the coop and scouring the bushes to find where the fowl were laying. Occasionally he'd left a broken shell or two to suggest animal thieves. Lakis was stupid as well as dangerous.

Swimming. The two were always swimming, like a pair of dolphins. In the morning, at noon, in the afternoon. It was still early spring and he himself was wearing two layers of clothes, yet they disported and played almost in no clothes. The man was brazen. He would stand naked under the outdoor shower contraption, water running off the hard muscles of his wiry physique. There was something ape-like about the Englishman. He was also dark like the woman, but hirsute all over, and he allowed his powerful shoulders to droop, as if he was always pretending to be off guard. Yes it was that: ape-like but intelligent, and somehow adversarial.

The woman had yet to stand naked under the shower. He thought she might, if he watched long enough.

He admired the young English. But he shook his head sadly to think of them living in that house. It had history. It had drawn the evil eye. And they too, by living there, would draw the evil eye.

The water there was no good. He knew that the sea leaked into the sweet-water well at certain tides. This too they would find out for themselves. All in all, these young English had not chosen a good place to live.

19

4

'I think the water from the pump is salty,' said Mike.

Kim nodded. 'I thought so a couple of days ago.'

They were sitting under the vine eating a lunch of black olives and cheese and salad. 'Why didn't you mention it?' Mike wanted to know.

'I didn't want to put the thought in your head. Then everything starts to taste of salt.'

Mike looked at her. It was Kim's way of protecting him, almost like a mother's love, this not wanting to worry him with things. One day he would admit to her that he had been close to a breakdown before they left London, but not yet. Perhaps when he was stronger. Meanwhile he knew that she knew, and that was enough. He loved her. She loved the life here. Already her skin was tanning to a deep shade of peach.

'You know what this means? We can use the pump for washing, but we'll have to carry drinking water from the taverna. Or from the church in the village.'

'Is that a problem?'

'Not really. We've got the car. And after that we've got the boat, and the donkey.'

'And we've got the time.' Kim smiled and stripped an olive to the stone with her teeth.

Mike collected up the plates, and Kim followed him to the pump. He pumped, she rinsed.

He set the plates to dry, straightened his back, and something caught his eye in the distance. 'It's there again.'

'What is?'

'By the monastery.'

She followed the line of his pointing finger due west to the edge of a cliff. A small monastery – abandoned, they'd been told – perched on a grassy promontory looking over the sea. At the very edge of the cliff was a grey pillar, so Mike had originally thought, or some kind of obelisk. But then he'd noticed that some days the obelisk had moved, only to reappear another day.

'It can't be a person standing there, can it?' said Kim.

'If it is, he must stand there for hours on end without moving.'

'Maybe it's some kind of shipping signal, taken down and put up depending on the weather.'

'That would explain it.' He sounded unconvinced. 'How about a short expedition?'

'Today? I thought you were going to start your painting?'

Mike pulled a face. There had been some vague pretext of coming to Greece to paint, to clear his head of fifteen years' commercial graphics. The acrylics and the water-colours were still in a box in the boot of the car.

'*Avrio*,' he said lazily, after the Greek fashion. 'Tomorrow.'

The walk took them almost two hours. They dawdled along the way, wandering along the shingle beach for a distance, negotiating slippery rocks dripping emerald weed until they found their route blocked. They backtracked and made their way inland, along a path through quince trees and olive groves. A ferocious black dog hurled itself at them, snapping and dragging itself back on the steel chain at its throat.

They were forced further inland to go round an inlet, and then to follow a red dust track up the hillside to gain the high ground on which the monastery was built. The sun beat down and lizards skittered at their approach between the baked rocks. Crickets the size of greenfinches crouched in the middle of the path and refused to budge.

The once whitewashed walls of the tiny monastery had flaked mustard yellow under the onslaught of the sun and the corrosive sea air. It was like some rotting fragment of a papier mâché dream. Six cells comprised the seaward wall, standing open and doorless. A seventh cell had preserved its woodwormed door, which was locked shut. The small courtyard had obviously once been a garden. A sheet of rusted metal half covered a deep well, and over it a pulley mechanism waited uselessly, its moving parts welded into one by oxidation. Every bit of metal in the courtyard was ringed by a dark-red rust stain, as though the earth was in the business of reclaiming, slowly sucking back minerals only temporarily loaned.

A miniature church in the corner was shaded by a giant fig tree. Mike tried the door. It too was locked against tourist looters. They sat on a bench, enjoying the shade of the tree. From one of its branches hung a bell, not rusting like everything else. Its clapper was missing, but it tolled the silence, resonating with the sense of decay about the place. The muted bell conjured ghosts in the empty courtyard, and marked the slip of time.

From where they sat they could see the headland sometimes characterised by the obelisk Mike had pointed out to Kim from the house.

'It's gone again.'

They sat, wordless, for some time. The sun moved in the sky and flashed from the bell. The courtyard rippled with heat. The lizards became still. After half an hour an old woman appeared, dressed in the black of the Mediterranean widow. She carried a small bundle under her arm, and showed no surprise at finding the two sitting outside the church.

'*Kali Mera! Kali Mera!*' she shouted, chattering away in Greek with no apparent expectation of a reply. She unlocked the church door and beckoned them inside.

The whitewashed interior was a cool, shadowy vault reeking of mastic incense. A single lamp flickered beneath a silver icon. The floor was meticulously swept and a rickety wooden table bore candles, incense and oil-filled retsina bottles. A fragmenting Byzantine mural had almost faded on one wall; a single religious painting hung on the other.

The woman cheerfully busied herself, refilling the lamp and lighting a candle. She jabbed a finger at various objects, smiling at Kim and directing her attention here and there. Then she noticed Mike studying the painting.

Mike recognised it as a Byzantine representation of the monastery, but it was surrounded by a huge garden and exotic animals: tigers, monkeys, rare birds and other creatures not native to Greece. A skirmish of monks was depicted with bows and arrows drawn, and were shooting them into a wretched human figure thieving from an orchard at the corner of the painting.

'*Iannos*,' cackled the old woman, nodding approvingly. '*Erimitis. Erimitis.*'

'What does she say?'

'I don't know,' said Kim, 'but she keeps squeezing my hand.'

Back outside the bright sunlight made them blink. They made for the strip of headland. The old woman was still chattering to them, or to herself, from within the church. From the cliff edge they could identify their own house and the rock opposite, and they could make out the dot of the rowing boat on the calm water. Beyond that stood the castle of Limanaki and the misted shores of Turkey.

'It's a person,' said Mike.

'What?'

'It's not an obelisk. It's someone who comes and stands here, every day.'

'But they'd have to be here for hours!'

'Yes. Perfectly still.' Mike was almost hypnotised by the unearthly beauty of the view. From somewhere below came the bubbling sound of water running from the rock. Together with the water lapping at the shingle beach it fashioned a sound like a whispering, but a whispering of pressing intimacy. Mike listened, entranced.

'Did you hear me?' said Kim. She was looking at him strangely. 'I said let's go down for a swim.'

A path descended to the beach. Halfway down they passed a gaping cave. Mike wanted to explore, but Kim was in too much of a hurry to throw herself into the sea. She peeled off her clothes and plunged in naked. Mike followed. Light starburst ecstatically on the waters as they splashed each other. Then Kim swam out while Mike lay basking in the shallows. He lay on his back looking up at the rock, and at the water bubbling from just below the cave.

Kim came swimming underwater, grabbing him from below. Mike yelped.

'What are you thinking?'

'I thought this might be a potential site for the oracle.'

'Oracle?'

'The Orpheus myth. I've been reading about it. The women of Thrace, called Maenads, tore Orpheus limb from limb at one of their orgies. They were sex-crazed, like you are. They were drugged and delirious.'

Kim squeezed his balls under the water.

'They chucked his head in the sea, and it was said to have washed up on this island and lodged in a rock, where it continued to speak oracles. One of the possible sites is around here somewhere. I was thinking this might have made a good spot.'

Kim was smiling, bright beads of water glistening on her breasts. She was hardly listening. She was stroking his cock.

'I don't think we should. Someone is watching us from the cave.'

Kim spun around and looked up. An arm went instinctively across her breasts as she squinted back at the gaping cavern. 'I don't see anyone.'

'No. It was just a flicker of movement earlier. I felt it as much as saw it.'

'Surely not the old woman?'

'No. Time to go, I think.'

That evening there was a heat storm. The sky fused red before turning yellow, then lavender, all as if it was in a hurry to get the end of the day over with. Then the lightning came. Unaccompanied by thunder, it lit the Genoese castle at Limanaki like the backdrop to an opera. The silent flickering went on for an hour, and Mike and Kim sat in the boat at the edge of the water just watching the castle coming up in eerie relief, like a negative of a photograph.

'It's not like a British storm,' Kim said.

And then as if to answer her, a great jagged fork of

lightning ripped across the water and touched the rock island opposite, like a finger of God. The rock turned diamond white for a second, and the lightning was followed by an immediate crack of deafening thunder. They spilled wine and scrambled out of the boat. '*That*'s like a British storm,' said Mike, and the downpour started. They were soaked before they'd got halfway back to the house.

Mike stood under the dripping vine canopy but Kim showed no sign of wanting to get out of the torrential rain. She was loving it.

'It feels so good! I don't want to go in!' She put her hands up in the air as if she was reaching for the heart of the storm. Then she came under the canopy.

'There's three types of lightning,' said Mike. 'Sheet lightning; forked lightning, like that last jab . . .' Kim wasn't listening to him. She was taking off her wet clothes and making whooping noises. 'And the extremely rare . . .'

He didn't get time to finish his sentence. A giant wheel of white-hot light rolled across the sky from behind the castle to explode over the rock, accompanied by an instantaneous detonation of thunder.

'. . . ball lightning,' Mike whispered, almost to himself. Jesus! *And sometimes the thing manifests itself before it's even spoken.*

The downpour grew heavier. What in God's name was it about this place? thought Mike. And how do I know there is more to come?

Mike stared hard at his wife. The rain lashed down. Kim had given herself over to the power of the elements. She had one arm wrapped around a patio canopy pillar, and was leaning out from the concrete platform into the rain. She had an arm and a leg stretched out into the darkness, as if the house was a boat sailing through warm winds and churning waters. She was naked. The rain glistened on her wet body. The flicker of sheet lightning painted her skin quicksilver against the blackness. Mike noted an unfamiliar ecstasy in her eyes, and for some moments he was more afraid of his wife than he was of the storm.

5

Kim woke the next morning feeling strangely depressed after her night of elation in the storm. Mike had got up early to go fishing from the rowing boat. She put her hand on the sheet where he'd been sleeping, and was unable to account for these feelings.

In the night they'd made love with the sound of the thunder rolling in from the sea. She'd insisted on leaving the window open. Later the roof started to leak, so they'd had to find a bucket to place under the drip. She'd awoken with the fresh, cool after-storm air coming in through the window. She nibbled at Mike's ear lobes to rouse him again. He'd smiled sleepily. It was a luxury the alarm clock had killed when they'd worked in England.

It had been a mysterious night, of energy and power and lovemaking, so why had she woken to these feelings? This melancholy was alien to her, out of character, ill-fitting. It was like waking to find oneself wearing someone else's clothes.

She dressed and filled a plastic bowl with water from the pump. Before she'd finished washing herself, Lakis arrived with another gift. Kim sighed when she saw him coming along the beach path.

As the owner of the property, Lakis seemed to think it was either his duty or his prerogative to visit the place almost daily. At first he'd been welcomed and offered coffee, or wine and a bite to eat in the fashion of hospitality Mike and Kim had quickly learned from the Greek villagers. But the frequency of his visits proved tedious, and the geniality with which hospitality was at first offered had to cool. Perhaps seeing this, Lakis had taken to bringing small gifts; and Mike and Kim had taken to feeling guilty about being frugal with their company.

However, Lakis' English was restricted to what he needed for his taxi business; and their Greek was more limited still. Conversation always turned on the same subjects.

'No taxi today, Lakis?'

'No enough tourist.'

He had also come for his rent. For what the place was, he was considerably overcharging them. They were living on savings, and though Kim never said anything, she resented what they had to pay Lakis. They figured they could survive for about a year if they supplemented their savings with a little income from olive-picking or teaching English. Until winter, however, they had agreed that all work was suspended. Meanwhile the rent on the house was a drain on resources.

Today Lakis had brought a bag of giant-sized tomatoes, which she accepted from him with slightly less than gratitude. He sat under the vine, sipping his coffee and wiping blisters of sweat from his brow. His forehead seemed permanently corrugated with anxiety, and his sweat glands were, even for such a climate, permanently hyperactive.

'Strong storm last night.'

'Very strong.' He waved a hand through the air.

Conversation faltered. Kim thought about mentioning the leaking roof, but she guessed she had probably seen the last rainfall of spring. She suddenly felt uncomfortable sitting in her T-shirt and bikini pants, so went inside to put on some trousers. As she did so she noticed that Lakis was watching her through the open window. She moved to the shutter and banged it to with unnecessary force.

When she came out again Lakis was lighting a cigarette and avoiding her eyes.

'Lakis, why did you call this place the House of Lost Dreams?'

He wiped a bead of sweat from his brow and acted as though he hadn't heard her.

'*Haus der Verlorenen Traume*,' she tried again. 'Why?'

He got up. 'No understand,' he said, and busied himself with watering some of the plants in the garden. Lakis seemed to have a hundred and one essential tasks around the place to be used as a pretext for his visits.

She was being ignored. It annoyed Kim the way Greek men would do that to women: suddenly grow bored with a conversation, and get up and go somewhere else in a way they would never do with other men. Or if they were talking to a couple, they would address only the man and effortlessly resist any interaction with the woman.

She decided to leave Lakis alone. She collected her purse and locked up the house. Then she walked into the village.

The baker's wife stood in the doorway of the bakery, covered from head to foot with fine white flour. She was taking a breather. Kim didn't know why she was thought of as the baker's wife, since she did all the work. The bakery was no more than a shelf for stacking the bread, a pile of logs taking up most of the room, and the oven itself. There was also a chair where the fat baker rested his ample buttocks, sipping ouzo and supervising his wife's labours.

The villagers were becoming familiar with Kim. The baker's wife nodded in recognition. The flour made her look ghostly and mournful, and pink-eyed. Kim often thought she would like to prod the baker's wife, to see if a cloud of white dust would be released into the air.

She missed out the tomato lady, who had greenhouses behind her house, because Lakis had brought her tomatoes that morning. The fruit lady, who always seemed slightly moist and sticky like her fruit, continued to try to teach her a new phrase every day. The sweet butcher's wife leaned over her counter to pat Kim on the cheek, as she did every morning. And the lady in the dress shop, whose name was Maria and who spoke some English, gave her something to drink while gossiping about the butcher's wife, the fruit lady and the tomato lady; and she never seemed to expect Kim to buy any of her stock.

Thus a shopping expedition to collect but a few items in the tiny village of Kamari could easily take three or four hours.

Maria was a strikingly beautiful woman in her mid-forties. She had raven-black hair and alert, flirtatious eyes, plus a habit of swinging her hips even if she was only crossing the room to make coffee. And as if to advertise her physical attributes she made a habit of trying out all of her new stock, if only for a day. This she justified by claiming to be testing the clothes, as if they were electrical appliances, which in her case they almost were. She crackled sexuality. She was recently widowed. Her businessman husband had been killed in a motoring accident in Athens, and she had returned to her native village, where she had family, to set up shop.

'They expected me to take the widow's black. I said

you're joking, that's not for me. Have you seen those old crows? But I'm still a girl, I told them.'

'I wouldn't like to wear it,' said Kim. They were eating cake in the shop. Kim didn't mind Maria's company, but her gossip had too sharp an edge.

'It's traditional. Kim, you don't know how backward these people are. A hundred years out of date.' Maria picked a crumb from the sequins of a new dress. 'I scandalise them by wearing these things. I like it.'

Kim had once asked Maria why the House of Lost Dreams was so named, but hadn't received an answer. She tried again now.

'Look,' said Maria. 'I have to make some telephone calls. Stay in the shop if you want.'

Kim declined by getting up to leave. 'There's a new store opened behind the church. I want to go and look at it.'

'Yes; Kati's shop. She is opening for the season. Go and meet her. A good woman.'

Whether people were actually avoiding telling her about the House of Lost Dreams, or whether it was simply that they didn't know, Kim couldn't tell. She walked along the cobbled streets of the village, under the decaying timbers of the splendid Turkish House and along to the Church of the Virgin. Here she stopped to wash her hands under the tap, if only for the pleasure of seeing the crystal water damp the dusty earth. The pure mountain water was piped from a spring in the hills not far away.

The new shop sold pottery and ceramics – not the usual tourist tat of fake Corinthian urns – and paintings, plus a couple of racks of dresses in competition with Maria. Kim suspected the shop-owner of superior taste. The woman was on the telephone as Kim went in. She smiled in a friendly way and put down the receiver. She was about the same age as Maria, but much slighter, with short hair and a vaguely patrician air. Kim felt the woman's eyes tracking her as she moved around the shop touching pipette vases and slender items of pottery.

Kim had to break the silence. 'Who makes these?'

The answer came in impeccable English. 'I get them from the mainland. All hand-made.'

'They're very fine pieces.'

The woman inclined her head as if accepting it as a personal compliment. She produced something from behind the counter. 'Try this.'

It was what Kim would have called Turkish Delight. The Greeks never feel comfortable unless they've offered something, she thought. The woman found a seat from behind the counter. 'I'm Kati.'

'I'm Kim.'

'I know. Your husband is Mike. He is a painter. You are a nurse. You're English. I can't sell you anything because you are not a tourist. You're very beautiful.'

Kim blushed. 'You seem to know a lot about us.'

'That was Maria on the phone as you came in. You should know that the people refer to her place as Reuters.'

Sometimes, thought Kim, it is possible to meet someone, and to know immediately and instinctively that here is a friend. Kati smiled at her with kind, rather lazy eyes. Kim said, 'Mike and I are living at . . .'

'I know where you're living,' Kati interrupted. 'I know that house.'

'I keep asking people why it's called the House of Lost Dreams, but no one will tell me.'

Kati looked slightly pained. 'Look.' Kim would find out that Kati prefixed much of what she said with the word, and was always sure to give her audience time to take her literally and look at her. 'Look. Greek people. They only like to tell a person what they want to hear. They don't want to tell a person what they don't want to hear.'

'Is there something bad about the place?'

'Not about the place. But something happened there. Why do you want to know? Are you happy there?'

'Yes.'

'Good. So why must you know? It's not important to you. Stay there. Be happy.'

'I'm just curious about the name.'

Kati lit a cigarette and when she blew out the smoke she looked hard at Kim. She seemed to make some kind of a decision. 'Look. There was a German woman living there. Her name was Eva. She was with Lakis, the owner. When Lakis' wife found out, he wanted to end the affair and this woman tried to kill herself at the house. That's it.'

'When was this?'

'Twenty years ago. Twenty-five. And Lakis named the house; Eva used to call it the House of Dreams, so he called it the House of Lost Dreams. The sign is still there only because Lakis' wife doesn't know any German and after all this time she still thinks it means "House for Rent".'

'Lakis is a romantic?'

'I've heard other words for him.'

When Kim got up to leave, Kati invited them to have dinner at a taverna with her and her husband. 'Come to the shop at any time. For anything.'

'Thanks. I will.'

'Look, about this story. There's no need to mention what I told you to anyone else in the village. It's in the past. It was a bad time for everyone. They don't like talking about it.'

'I understand. Bye, Kati.'

It was the middle of the day when she left the village. Despite the storm of the previous evening, the temperature was higher than before. She decided to take a short cut across the rock to the beach path. Normally she avoided the route because she was shy about the soldiers on the crest of the rock.

There was a lonely outpost up there where one or two conscripts were stationed, supposedly to look over the sea for signs of the Turkish invasion. They were just boys, bored out of their helmets. *Not* to stare after a passing woman would have been a noteworthy incident. Sometimes they smiled, or the more confident ones might beg a cigarette. The monthly wage for a conscript was a bar of soap, a packet of razors and enough money for four beers; or two beers if they drank with the tourists.

One such soldier was slumped with his back against a water barrel, tossing pebbles into his helmet a few yards away. On seeing Kim he scrambled to his feet and came over, making smoking signs at his mouth. She had some cigarettes so she gave him one. The boy grinned stupidly. He also wanted a light and she didn't have one. He said something in Greek, still smiling. He had no English, only a little German.

She proceeded along the path. '*Danke*,' he managed, waving after her. She felt the lonely eyes of the conscript drilling her buttocks and her shoulders as she descended the slope. She was grateful when she'd dropped out of his sight, knowing that he could go back to not watching for the Turks.

6

Life at the house began to settle into an inescapably slow tempo. The sun rose and fell in the sky. The rhythms of island life regulated the pulse and adjusted the heartbeat with the command of a hypnotist swinging a gold watch before their eyes. Mike and Kim succumbed to it exactly.

There was the metronomic roll of the waves forever whispering in the ear, and to further order the sleeping pattern there were demonstration sunrises and exhibition sunsets. Life without electricity is fundamentally different, they noted. Some primitive affection for the authority of night and day was quickly relearned. Candles and oil lamps offered weak light almost by way of negotiation; and it became possible in some cases to see electrical light as a kind of slashing violence done to some naive force within the darkness. Unless they made a celebratory night of things at one of the tavernas, they began to go to bed at nightfall, and to rise early when the light became too bright for them to sleep further.

In this way they discovered a routine passing under their noses of which they'd been hitherto unaware. Earliest of all, while the air was still cool from the night, came the spear-fishing man. Miraculously silent, he waded through the shallows, hunting for octopus or squid or crabs.

Wearing nothing but a pair of shorts, he carried a bucket in his left hand and swept his spear across the water with his free arm. He was unusually thin for a Greek, tanned and fit. If he saw something, the movement of his spear was invisible. The first you would see of it would be his prey impaled on the weapon's point.

In this way he passed near the bottom of the garden each morning. Mike tried once or twice to imitate his soundless progress through the water. It was hopeless. Even his best efforts could be heard by Kim listening on the patio twenty yards away.

Within the hour the shepherd passed by, driving his flock along the beach. It was part of an everyday cycle of moving the sheep from one grazing spot to another. The shepherd had a way of muttering to his animals to keep them on course and out of the garden as he herded them along the water's edge and down the dust track that eventually wound up to the hills behind the house. The shepherd, in his bright knotted headscarf, never spoke and never once looked up at the house, passing by with a curious, swaying gait, almost deliberately averting his eyes.

Later came the yoghurt man on his donkey. His appearance would be anticipated by his low cry, 'Heeyyya! Heeyyya!', as he flicked at his donkey with a switch. The yoghurt man was a great burly figure in a straw hat. Two twenty-litre plastic barrels – empty at this time of the day – were lashed to the donkey. The man sat well back in his high-frame donkey-chair, advertising the great bulk of his belly as he passed. He took to tipping his panama and calling good morning if he saw Mike and Kim up and about.

'*Kali Mera Sas! Kali Mera!*'

For Kim, this was the best time of the day.

Then later the more adventurous tourists would pass by the fence on their way from Kamari to the quieter beach of Lefkas further on. Most would stop and look at the house. The collection of animals in the garden, the fluttering ornamental white doves, and the couple relaxing on the patio would be a source of fascination. If the tourists were French they would gawp unashamedly at the house. If British and caught staring, they would look away guiltily and hurry on. If German, they would make their way up the path and demand to know how much rent Mike and Kim were paying.

They became expert in identifying nationalities at the gate.

Then the tourist boat trips to the furthermost rock out in the water would start up. Blaring bazouki music, the boats would dump their passengers on the rock for basting and snorkelling before collecting them a few hours later, pink and hungry and primed for the night ahead.

After the last boat had returned, the heat of the day would begin to lift. The yoghurt man would pass on his return journey, walking now and leading his burdened donkey. The sun would dip and colour would be restored to the island's bleached brilliance. Something distilled out at this time, a quiet on the land that seemed to have been drawn from the sea bed. The clay had been sucked dry of all moisture, the sage bushes left their scent on the breeze and the earth smelled like seasoned, baked bread.

This was Mike's time. Every evening he would remember to look across at the high promontory by the abandoned monastery, and almost every evening there would be the mysterious figure standing erect on the edge and looking out to sea.

Sunset followed, and then there were the lamplit

evenings spent on the patio under the dark vine. And if the waters were calm enough, the phantom fishing boats would come.

These were the days, they knew, and this was the life they had come to find. The view out to sea, with the same figures passing at set intervals, could easily be seen as a magic lantern or optical glass, or as some enchanting clockwork toy. They sat on their illuminated patio, sipping ouzo or retsina, and thought it was not possible to be happier. Although they'd said they'd come to get away from it, they'd realised it was not after all routine which was the enemy, but want of peace.

Peace and the time to appreciate. The time to notice things. Mike poured himself another glass of ouzo and he *noticed* Kim worrying about something. Would he have seen that at home? Would that shadow, that flickering lizard tongue of anxiety, have been detectable before? Or would it have happened too fast? Something was happening between them now, a magnification, a heightened sensitivity. A sneeze, a sigh, a shiver ran to earth through the other. Their relationship was deepening, but was this merely a product of available time? Could simply having the time to look have such a bearing on the entwining of souls, or was it more? Perhaps it was a product both of time and of place.

This place. The thought seemed to come out of nowhere, someone else's words. It made him shiver. He shifted uneasily in his chair and asked her what she was thinking about.

'I found out today how the house got its name. I didn't want to mention it.'

'You'd better!'

So she told him, and he wondered why she thought she

couldn't mention things like that to him, but said nothing. He shrugged. 'Did she succeed in killing herself?'

'I forgot to ask that. I assumed she didn't.'

'So Lakis is an old lover boy. Better watch out.'

'You'd better watch out too.'

'Why?'

'You're getting a bit lazy. Wanting me to do everything for you. Lazy and chauvinistic, like a Greek man.'

Mike showed her the back of his hand. 'Shut your mouth or I break-a your face.'

'Carry me to bed,' said Kim.

In the morning Kim was woken by what she thought was Mike shaking the bed. But Mike was sitting upright with a smile on his face. The bed was trembling. The lamp and the radio on the table were rattling. So was the wardrobe in the corner of the room; then one of its doors flew open. The whole house was vibrating, and one of the shutters came loose.

'What is it?' said Kim.

'Amazing!'

'What's happening?'

Kim peered outside, where the white doves were flapping and trying to settle, then taking off again. The tethered donkey was braying and chasing around in circles. The vibrations got stronger and a pencil rolled off the table. Then they receded, and everything went calm again.

Mike leapt out of bed. 'Wow! An earthquake! Brilliant! That was a fucking earthquake!' He rushed outside.

Kim pulled some clothes on and followed him out. 'You mean there was an earthquake? And we sat calmly in bed?' She was appalled.

'Yes!'

'Don't you think it would have been more intelligent to

have got out of the house rather than sit there waiting for it to fall on our heads?'

'My first earthquake! Our first earthquake! Wow!'

'Wow? How can you say wow!' She rushed over to free the donkey, which had almost strangled itself with its tether.

'It was only a little one!' Mike was running barefoot in the garden, performing what he imagined to be an earthquake dance.

Kim regarded him steadily. Sometimes she loved his recklessness, and sometimes she questioned his sanity. She looked back at the flimsy breeze-block structure of the house. 'Thank God,' she said, 'it was only a little one.'

Mike didn't stop dancing.

7

They had stayed inside the house, the stupid English! Though the tremor had only lasted for half a minute, they hadn't come running outside until after it was all over. They were crazy, this young couple. He couldn't figure out anything about them.

They did no work. They swam like fishes. They took long walks for no apparent purpose. What kind of people walk, with no purpose in mind? What an extraordinary waste of effort and energy. At first he had thought they must be going somewhere, that they knew something, that they had some secret. Perhaps they were archaeologists with a knowledge of some treasure. He had heard of archaeologists coming from Paris and Stockholm and Frankfurt to unearth some stones in an olive grove along the coast.

He had followed them once, on one of their walks, for almost an hour, in order to detect their secret. They'd simply turned around and come back again. Nothing made any kind of sense. It was against all reason. Certainly they'd shown no great interest in poking around in the earth. He no longer thought they were archaeologists.

He'd felt the approach of the earth tremor some moments before it came. He'd been crouched in the hills, watching the house, knowing the couple would soon be awake. He knew their routine by now: every morning they walked straight from the house like zombies – he usually naked, she in a swimsuit – directly into the water. There they would swim for twenty minutes before returning to rinse off under the shower. Then they would make breakfast.

But not that morning. The first he knew of the coming of the earthquake had been the shaking of the bells. The sheep grazing around him knew what was coming. At first it was one or two bells clonking. Then four or five. Then several until the entire flock was running back and forth in confusion, first this way then that, and then the first way again, unable to stay still yet too puzzled to make progress.

Then he'd not felt it exactly, but smelled it. Or that was how it had seemed to him. As if the earth was giving off some kind of gas. There was nowhere he could go, he knew. He had no great fear, though it did occur to him that one of the rocks behind him might tear itself loose and roll down the hill.

But it was over in moments. A relatively small tremor. He had experienced many quakes over the years, though never anything again like the earthquake of 1957 in which he'd lost half of his family.

But these English, they had waited inside until the tremor had passed. Then they had rushed outside: she to unharness that unspeakably stupid ass, he to perform some inferior kind of an English dance on the grass. He had to shake his head at such unfathomable behaviour.

He knew they had been up to the old monastery. He knew because Ireni who looked after the old church had told him. She seemed to think that they were merely visiting, in the way that tourists will visit simply anything without motivation. He regarded all this pointless visiting as a form of mental illness. Perhaps Ireni was right. Perhaps these English were simply inveterate visitors of places. That was what happened to people, he considered, who didn't have any work.

It was an unhealthy condition, he decided, not to have work.

In some ways they were like children. They lacked awareness. In the night a fox had come and taken one of the chickens, and they didn't even seem to know. He had noticed immediately. Of course, they were Lakis' chickens, but still they should at least notice such an event. If they were *his* chickens he would register every missing feather.

How much did they know about Eva? he wondered. He suspected that someone in the village might have told them some story or other. No one would like to mention it, and even if they did he was certain they would not be told the full story. As certain as the fox is certain of the darkness.

Eva had been beautiful, and desirable like the English woman. It had been a long time ago; he could barely recall her face. He only remembered her desirability. The German woman's colouring had been much lighter, her brow broader. She was not so tall, and less womanly. Though still beautiful. And with a laugh that was like the sun on the water. Had it been that laugh which had sealed her fate? A laugh which made her irresistible? Fate, he knew, turned on such small personal details. Had she had a laugh like a drain – like Lakis' wife – then perhaps fate would have propelled her in a different direction.

It was appalling to think about. Every moment, each personal detail was like a flint striking on fate. A new path was lit every second, glancing off at a marginally new angle, like a fan opening, a fan of flame, where some paths died and some flared, until the fan spreads out to meet itself and start again.

A laugh which made her irresistible, that was all it took. And here now was this lovely Englishwoman with the supreme complexion.

But no, this time it was different. She had a husband with her. The German woman had no such protector. It couldn't happen again. There was no reason why it should happen again.

He watched them come out of the sea and watched them shower. This time the woman rolled down her swimsuit to reveal her breasts. She caught the water between her breasts, rinsing the salt from her lovely skin. Then she went back indoors.

He sighed heavily to himself, and got up when he knew he wouldn't be seen. He couldn't stay here watching all day. He had work to do.

8

Mike woke in the middle of the night bathed in sweat. He sat bolt upright in the dark. Kim turned over beside him.

'What is it?' she murmured.

'Scorpions.'

'Uh?'

'Scorpions. There are scorpions in the room. They come out at night.'

Kim sat up suddenly. She'd been dreaming about scorpions. She said nothing of this. 'How do you know?'

'I can't say. I just woke up with it shouting in my head.'

'You're imagining it because of that conversation we had with Kati.'

The previous evening had been spent at a taverna with Kati and her husband Vassillis. They'd driven to Limanaki and a beautiful garden restaurant, hedged with gardenias and oleander bushes. There was live bazouki music, and the singer sang a verse likening his love to a scorpion. It was the Greek idea of a comic song. Vassillis translated.

Vassillis then asked if they were bothered much by scorpions, because that particular stretch of beach was infested with the creatures. They liked to go into buildings, he said. When they looked blank, Kati shut him up, and tried to make light of it.

'There are probably none where you are,' she said.

'Yes,' Vassillis added, flatly refusing to accept any contribution to the bill, 'there are probably none where you are.'

But on the way home Kati insisted they stop off at her house, from where she fetched a small bottle of ammonia. 'There are probably no scorpions where you are, but if you did get stung you should use this.'

They'd walked back along the beach path in the dark, Mike clutching the small bottle of ammonia, and neither said any more about it.

'No. I'm not imagining it. They're out there.'

'Can you see one?' said Kim, casting around in the blackness of the room. Suddenly every shadow seemed to extend a pair of legs.

'No. But I can *feel* them. They're out there.'

'Light the lamp.'

'I thought about that. But it would mean putting my bare feet on the floor. The torch is on your side.'

'I thought about that, too. It would mean having to grope around with my hands.'

They sat in the darkness as if the floor was a seething mass of venom. Finally Mike got out of bed and lit an oil lamp.

The shadows cast by the lamp were less than comforting. Mike had a good hunt round the floor and under the bed. He checked in all the corners, and on the bed legs and the table legs. Kim had thrown the bedclothes back and was shining the torch on the sheets at the foot of the bed. She'd heard they liked to get into bed with you.

Mike checked their shoes. 'They like warm, moist places.'

'Yes.' Kim was thinking about her warmest, most moist places.

'No,' said Mike bringing the lamp over to the bed. 'There are no scorpions. You were right. It's just that around here, if you talk about something, it has a habit of . . .'

Kim looked up at him. It was the first time he'd said anything about this phenomenon of unconscious prophecy. 'What's the matter?' she said.

He was staring at the wall above her head. He brought the lamp over. Six inches from her nose were three fine, large examples of the species, clinging to the wall, utterly still.

'Ugh!' She leapt out of bed, throwing a blanket around her. She marched outside, and down the garden path.

Mike followed her a few moments later. He found her sitting in the boat. He returned to pick up a bottle of wine and two plastic cups.

'I know I'm being stupid.'

'No, you're not.' He splashed her a generous measure of red wine. 'I don't like the buggers either.'

It was a warm night. The sea was calm like oil, and silver under a bright moon. Kim shivered. She didn't want to have to leave the place. 'People back in England have ceramic flying ducks on their walls. We've got a formation of scorpions.'

'What are we going to do about it?'

They couldn't be driven out of their lodgings, they concurred, by an insect. They agreed the sound thing to do would be to trap the scorpions inside a glass and set them free; but that the inevitable solution was to blowtorch the creatures into oblivion. In the end Mike settled for flattening them with the underside of the frying pan. Kim held the lamp while Mike flattened.

The frying pan rang against the wall like a cracked monastery bell, catching two with one blow. The sting dropped from one of the scorpions and proceeded to skitter round the floor at their feet. They watched with horrified fascination until the reflex died. Then the third scorpion dropped from the wall and took up a defiant position against Mike, the six-foot height disadvantage notwithstanding. It displayed its ugly sting and waved its pincers provocatively in the air at him, like an English football supporter.

Mike again showed it the underside of the frying pan. The slimy bits of carapace would crackle in the gas cooking flame for a day or two afterwards.

But they got accustomed to scorpions being around. They simply became more circumspect, careful with their clothes. Lakis, when challenged, gave them some filthy powder which discouraged the scorpions but which never drove them away entirely. A semblance of order was restored.

But what nagged at both of them more than any anxiety about scorpions was the habit of unconscious prophecy. It had seemed odd enough that some mysterious signal had alerted them to the menace of venomous insects in the night; but once again a devil talked about had, quite disconcertingly, come up. It was happening often enough to unnerve them.

'Tomorrow, dolphins will appear in the bay.'

'What?' said Mike. He was rowing the boat back from the rock where they'd spent an idyllic afternoon.

'I'm trying to make it happen consciously. Instead of it happening accidentally.'

'Make what happen? What are you talking about, Kim?'

'Why do you do that?'

'Uh?'

'Why do you pretend something's not happening, when you know perfectly well that it is? It seems a very *male* thing to do. To deliberately ignore something under your nose. And I know it bothers you as much as it bothers me.'

Mike stopped rowing. He let the oar blades float in the water. 'I don't know. I don't even want to talk about it, in case it triggers another bout. When it happens – when something appears after we've mentioned it – I feel slightly dizzy with the strangeness of it.'

'It's not just in our heads, is it? Is it, Mike?'

'When you put it into words, it doesn't sound much. So what? We mentioned scorpions, snakes, bolts of lightning . . .'

'And about half a dozen other things.'

'. . . but those things were there anyway.'

'Don't fool yourself. It's happening. It keeps happening.'

Mike dipped the oars and began to row again, back to the house. Kim sat on the prow of the boat, hugging her knees and looking around her. 'It's this place,' she said softly to herself. 'This place.'

But no dolphins were spotted the following day. They would have denied it, but both of them were alert to the possibility and were watching. After darkness had closed in, they sat on the patio with cicadas chittering excitedly in the grassy hills behind them. It was the only sound.

Finally, almost formally, Mike declared that no dolphins had been seen to appear in the bay.

'No,' Kim agreed. 'Today, no dolphins appeared in the bay.'

'Does this place frighten you?'

'Yes. But I wouldn't want to leave here.'

'No.'

After this statement they sat in silence. But the chitter of the cicadas seemed to crescendo, and to achieve a wild and ecstatic note.

One day Mike announced that he wanted to drive to the other side of the island. He was still tracking down possible sites for the Orphic oracle and finding other excuses to avoid starting to paint. There were one or two places he wanted to see, and he proposed a picnic. Kim however had promised to mind Kati's shop for a couple of hours on the day in question; and anyway she was becoming a little tired of charging around seeing the sites. She encouraged Mike to go alone. It was the first time in two months they were to be out of each other's company for more than a couple of hours.

'Drive carefully,' she shouted after him. 'Don't scratch the car.'

Mike drove the car up into the mountains and followed the road inside the rim of the volcanic hollow. He didn't have to plunge into the cauldron and up the other side; he was able to drive partially around its circumference before finding a rough road back down to the sea.

The road at the top of the mountains along the cauldron's edge was strewn with massive boulders, lumps of rock blasted out of the hollow when the volcano blew in prehistory. They lay where they'd fallen millions of years ago. Motoring around the rim, Mike stopped the car. A large tortoise was on its back in the middle of the road, its legs waving in the air. The legs retracted as Mike approached. He picked it up and set it down properly at the side of the road. He'd no idea how the thing had got to be in that position: perhaps some predator had been disturbed by the sound of the car engine, and had dumped it. At least, he mused, no one had mentioned tortoises in the last twenty-four hours.

He paused to look across the cauldron. The ribbon of road wound down the side of the bowl in sharp zigzags until it plunged out of sight and skirted the inlet, and could just be distinguished as it laboured its way up to the mountains on the other side. It was hot standing there inside the rim. Heat distortion rippled from the rocks. But for strange, deformed shrubs and diseased-looking mosses, nothing grew. The boulders were alternately black or rust-ochre, sucked dry of all memory of moisture, jagged, flaking and brittle and each one of them looking ready to explode into gaseous dust, like burned-out stars. It was an alien and inhuman place.

Mike was disappointed with the site he'd gone to see. He'd been following the recommendations of the pamphlet discovered in the Kamari library. There was a hot spring there, and the ruins of Roman baths built around it, but the beach was scrubby and unattractive. He had to concede he didn't know what he was looking for exactly, but he remained fascinated by the Orpheus myth.

This was not an archaeologist's fantasy. There was no dream of unearthing another mask of Agamemnon or the jewels of Helen. The compulsion lay buried deeper than a few inches below the soil. The myth spoke to him across the centuries. Orpheus tried to cheat death to recover his lost love. He failed but became wise beyond measure. They dismembered him, but his head continued to speak oracles, here, on this very island.

He took the literal meaning of the story of the butchery by the Maenad women and the location of the head to suggest that after the cult of Orpheus had been suppressed on the mainland, it continued to flourish on the island of Mavros. The location of the head would represent a temple which would continue to speak authoritatively on behalf of the cult.

Perhaps it was after all a speaking tongue Mike was looking for. A voice, any voice that would shape words inside his own mouth. Because he felt his own life was something of an inarticulated experience, and unspoken a thing might or might not be. Once spoken, Mike believed, a thing existed; even if it existed as a lie or as an illusion; or as a perfect realisation of the truth. Lies exist. Illusions exist. They *exist*, but on another plane, on a different shelf. So it was by coming here, by making a kind of quest for himself, he hoped finally to make sense of the chaos of the world.

And he believed in the historicity of the myth. There had to be a physical place. Whatever historical nugget lay inside the myth, Mike knew that the site, wherever it was, would have atmosphere and presence. The cult followers would have chosen a site with at least some natural resonance as a focus for the oracle, and that particular place was not it. At least not for him. He crossed it from his list.

He spent little time there, and drove instead to the great monastery of St Mikalis, where exhibited in the beautiful church were significant works of Byzantine art. This was no abandoned monastery, but a thriving ecclesiastical college. A monk offered him hospitality in the form of a glass of raki and a few dried figs. The church itself was four times as large as the tiny abandoned monastery on the clifftop near his house. Mike found himself spending over two hours there.

In addition to the display of Byzantine art the church was full of curios. Mike was drawn to a macabre death mask set on the wall. It was a lifelike representation of a face, said to have been fashioned from clay and the fresh blood of monks butchered by pirates. The single monk who had survived the raid had spontaneously created the mask, and had succeeded in preserving a moment of terror and grief.

Heads which speak.

There were also shoes which claimed to speak: the shoes of the saint. Mike had noticed offerings of metal shoes all over the church, and now he understood why. A pair of silver shoes inlaid with gold were encased and displayed for all to see. As far as Mike could understand, these represented the footwear of the warrior saint himself. The faithful brought to the church pairs of metal shoes which they offered up to Michael, the angel-militant, with their prayers. If the saint showed special favour, it was said, he returned at night and wore some of the shoes.

In case Mike had any doubt about the story, an old lady who was polishing the floor of the church got off her knees and reached down a pair of metal shoes from a shelf near the altar. She upturned them for him to see. Sure enough, the soles were scuff-marked, proof positive that the saint had returned and walked in those shoes. The old woman took Mike's hand and made him feel the striations in the soles. He nodded politely at the old woman's stupidity and moved on.

Mike was a confirmed atheist, but he paid for a candle and lit it for his wife. He didn't believe in God, but he did believe in his love for her, and he always thought that love was worth lighting a candle for anywhere. He turned from the candle and saw the old woman nodding approvingly, and it irritated the hell out of him.

He disliked the ferocious dark power of the Greek

Orthodox church, just as he detested the Catholic church. For him they were religions of nightmare. They both favoured dark, candlelit shrines and temples emulating caves and caverns; and these caverns were daubed with the icons and effigies of torture and pain. He'd once visited a church in Tuscany, a chamber of horrors with a lighted tableau of the Virgin, seven vicious daggers plunged into her spine, blood curdling on her blue robes. Claustrophobic caverns of nightmare, sickly with the scent of incense, dried blood and old sin. He'd had to rush out into the bright sunlight of the Tuscan mid-afternoon. Kim had mocked him and characterised him as an evil spirit, but nothing evil he knew would trade darkness for daylight.

Here too, in the Greek Orthodox church, the atmosphere of devotion whipped on by guilt and fear under the dark eye of the angel-militant was as overwhelming as the cloying reek of incense. But it was the primitive and woeful pathos of the offerings which dismayed him. Silver icons everywhere in the church were hung with tawdry silver-plate wafers of metal stamped with a crude representation of an arm or a leg or a heart – whatever the supplicant wanted healing, and an American dollar sign in one case. These things hung from the icons by ribbons, along with plastic rosaries or photographs or items of jewellery. No progress had been made in religious terms since the votive offerings made to the priests in the temples of Ancient Greece, and rubbish pits of such discarded offerings were still being turned up by modern archaeologists.

Then there were the shoes. Dozens and dozens of pairs of factory-made copper and aluminium shoes knocked out in medieval style, all for the restless saint to prowl in at night. Mike had had enough. He ignored a box asking for visitors to make a contribution, and left.

He had lunch at a taverna nearby, a dish of stifado washed down by a couple of beers. There was only one other customer, an elderly Greek with cropped grey hair and a huge salt-and-pepper moustache. He greeted Mike when he sat down, and waited until the meal was over before plying him with questions, via the taverna owner, in the normal Greek fashion.

Who are you? Why are you here? Are you married? Where is your wife? Any children? What brings you to this part of the island? The taverna owner, whose English was only a little better than Mike's Greek, did his best, but enjoyed the exercise enough to want to draw a chair up to Mike's table. He poured a complimentary glass of ouzo for both Mike and the old man, and a glass for himself.

Mike answered the catechism of questions happily. The old man insisted on refilling Mike's glass. 'How is it in England?' they asked. 'Crazy. Many people crazy,' he answered, himself slipping into pigeon English. 'Mikalis,' he said when they asked his name. 'Michael.'

'He also Mikalis,' the taverna owner said of the old man. 'He say good luck for this name.'

'Is it?'

This question produced much conversation between the two Greeks, which reduced to, 'Because it is the saint name. Mikalis. He asks if you see the miracle of the shoes?'

'Yes. I saw.' He asked for the old man's glass to be replenished, and saw his own refilled too. Then he made some remark about St Michael making a good football player, which made the taverna owner laugh. The old man was given a very long translation of the joke. He didn't laugh. He seemed offended. He began to speak loudly and passionately.

'What's he say?'

'Ignore him. I tell him this football thing, and then I say the shoes is for fools.'

'But that's not what I said!'

'You are right. It's for simple people.'

'But now he thinks I called him a fool!'

'Don't worry.'

But the old man had got to his feet. He was pointing his finger at Mike and wouldn't be placated by the taverna owner. He was far more upset than the remark merited, and Mike wondered what else had been added to the translation. Now Mike wanted to know what the old man was saying. The taverna owner listened carefully to the old man before talking across him. 'He tell the story of a mens who was drunk in this taverna, and who laugh at St Mikalis. Then the mens he has to walk home, and on his way home, the saint waits for him in a bush and jump out and beat him. So now this mens is a believer. He wants you to know this.'

'Tell him I didn't mean to offend him.'

But it was too late. The old man had left the table and was hobbling away on a stick, still shouting. Mike's round of ouzo stood untouched in the old man's glass.

'Aw shit!' said Mike.

'Don't worry. No problem.' The taverna owner poured them both another measure of ouzo.

Mike was a little light-headed before he got into the car. If this had been England, he wouldn't have thought of driving, but everyone on the island shared a callous disregard for drink-driving laws, since apart from side-saddle on a donkey hardly any other form of transport existed. In any event the road back would be almost traffic-free.

Mike drove through the smothering heat of late

afternoon, the sun dazzling through the windscreen and heat ripples dissolving the road ahead. There was not a breath of wind to relieve the blanket dryness. Movement itself seemed an offence against Nature. The air was no fresher by the time he reached the rim of the cauldron. He felt himself dozing at the wheel.

Mike stopped the car and got out to stretch his legs. The desert dryness was eerie. The only sound was that of his shoes scraping the dust. The absolute stillness made dry boulders seem like sleeping things, animate but hibernating. The air was suffocating. He got back into his car and drove down into the cauldron, carefully negotiating the gradient and the hairpin bends.

Utterly without warning and from around a corner came a huge brown shadow, engulfing his windscreen and obliterating his vision. He stamped on his brakes, still unable to see, but felt the loss of control at the wheel. There was a sensation of spinning, followed by a roll and two massive, heavy jolts that whiplashed his neck.

It was a few moments before his vision cleared. When it did he realised he was upside down in his driving seat. His safety belt was holding him in, and the car's engine was still racing. Groping for the ignition, he managed to switch off the motor. There was a gentle ticking sound, like that of dust settling softly on the car. He was unable to open his door more than a fraction of an inch, but by releasing his belt he found he could scramble out through the passenger door.

The car lay inverted on a rocky platform at the side of the road. Ten or twenty yards either way and it would have plunged down the steep embankment. Mike climbed back into the road and looked at the vehicle, its wheels still spinning. It occurred to him how much it looked like a stranded tortoise. *I've walked away without a scratch*, he thought. *Lucky lucky lucky.*

There was nothing and no one around, and no sign of what might have caused his momentary blackout. It occurred to him that he might have fallen asleep at the wheel, but he felt certain that something had rushed at him from around the corner. But what? It was certainly no other vehicle. Even if they hadn't stopped he would still be able to see them on the winding road for another half an hour. He thought about large birds or big animals, but it didn't seem possible.

He was still dazed and staring at his car. The air quivered with heat. The strange-shaped boulders seemed poised to unbalance. Mike heard a shuffling in the dust behind him.

He turned to find three men standing not two yards away. His first impression was that they were monks, perhaps from the monastery. But they were not like any Greek Orthodox monks he had seen. The figure nearest to him wore a habit of very rough cloth, tied at the waist with a rope of hemp. He was leaning on a long stave. His hair and beard were grey-black and cropped very short. His eyes were deep-set, swimming black pools. They gazed at Mike in a manner not at all friendly. The two monks standing behind the first man to right and left had their faces almost completely masked by cowls. They also each carried a long staff, on which they were leaning.

'Speak English?' said Mike. Then, stupidly, 'I crashed my car.'

The three men failed to respond. '*Kamari*,' he said, forcing a smile and waving across the mountain in what he hoped was the direction of his house.

Again there was no response. The eyes of the uncowled monk burned into him. Then Mike noticed he was wearing metal shoes: shoes made of some heavy grey metal, but pointed and otherwise similar to those he had seen in the monastery. They had cut into the man's feet, and he could see blisters and sores and traces of dried blood. Mike was suddenly very frightened. He stepped back. '*Kamari*,' he tried again, lamely.

The uncowled figure said nothing, drew back his stave and jabbed it sharply into Mike's teeth. Mike jumped back in astonishment. 'What the fuck?' He spat out blood and a piece of broken tooth. The man advanced on him, ready with a second jab, but Mike grabbed the end of the wooden stave and twisted it. The two other men sprang into action, bringing their own staves hard down on Mike's arm, deadening his muscles. Then one of the staves impacted on his skull with a loud crack.

Mike went blind for a moment and doubled over. He opened his eyes to see the sole of one of the metal shoes levelled at his face. He was kicked hard on the jaw. Then a second kick from the metal shoe smashed his kneecap and he sank to the dusty road. The other men began raining hard blows on him with their staves. The pain seemed slight compared with the continuing kicks from the metal shoes which impacted on his body like a dirty heat. He felt vomit rising in his mouth as he tried to lift up his head. Then another blow from a stave caught him on the back of the head and he passed out.

9

Kim watched the sun drop burning red behind the furthermost rock in the sea before she began to get worried. Supper was ready for Mike, garlic tanged the evening air, a bottle of wine stood open. She'd had a deliciously uneventful day, interrupted only when two young Germans had come to her for help after stepping on sea urchins. She'd shown them the Greek remedy of applying toothpaste to draw the spines before pulling them with tweezers. The two were thankful, but left with expressions suggesting they thought it might have been legs, and not just spines, that were being pulled.

Clouds filtered red light on the horizon, and the sky began to darken. For the first time it occurred to Kim to think what she might do if Mike didn't appear. She was about to light an oil lamp when she saw Kati hurrying along the beach path towards her. Kati hesitated at the gate.

It was unusual to see Kati away from her shop. Kim had invited her to the house on more than one occasion, but this was the first time the offer had been taken up.

'Kati! Come on in; don't wait at the gate!'

But Kati seemed unwilling to approach any further. She looked rather serious. A flick of the head indicated she wanted Kim to go to her.

'Look,' said Kati. 'There has been an accident. Mike is in the hospital at Potami. I'm going to take you there.'

'What's happened? What did he do? Is he all right?'

'Be calm. You must bring some things for him. A shirt and some things.'

Kim suddenly felt very clear. She collected together some of Mike's clothes, a towel and his toiletries. She turned off the gas heating their supper and locked the door behind her. Kati had parked her car at the taverna, and she drove Kim to the hospital. She knew very little. Mike had given Kati's name and the hospital had telephoned to say he was there. On the way, Kati stopped at her own house to collect a few things.

When they got to the hospital Mike was sleeping. His head was bandaged across his skull and under his chin. His face was badly bruised. Kim was dismayed at the primitive condition of the hospital. It was unhygienic and neglected. Staff were difficult to locate.

Finally a doctor was able to talk to her. 'He has cracked a rib or two. And he has a broken arm. Lots of cuts and bruises. He'll be OK. I gave him a shot.'

It was only then that Kim started crying.

'I didn't say he's dying. I said he's OK.'

'Yes. Yes. Thank you. Yes. Can I take him home?'

'Not yet. I'm waiting for X-rays.'

'But he can't stay here!'

'Why not?'

Kim looked around her. She didn't want to insult the doctor. He was being very kind. 'Well, can I stay with him?'

The doctor spoke to Kati in Greek, and then left them alone. 'There's nowhere for you to stay here,' said Kati. 'And anyway, you can do nothing. We'll come again tomorrow.'

Kim went to Mike's bed and stood holding his limp hand. He didn't wake up. Kati gave the bag she'd brought with her to a nurse. Outside the hospital Kim started to weep again. 'I'm sorry. I know I'm being stupid.'

Kati looked puzzled. 'Why do you say that?'

'Crying.' And then Kim remembered she was speaking to a Greek, and not an English woman.

'You'll stay at my place,' said Kati. 'I don't want you to spend tonight in that awful house.'

Kim didn't hear Kati's words exactly, but she was grateful not to have to go home alone.

In the morning Kati told her they would need to take some food for Mike. She had left some things the previous evening for his breakfast; Greek hospitals provided little beyond what was supplied by a patient's relatives.

Mike was still doped. He opened one eye. ''Im.'

'Yes it's me. What have you been doing?'

''Rashed the 'ar.'

'So I hear.'

''Ree 'ig 'lokes. 'Eat me up.'

Kim couldn't understand any of it, and wasn't particularly listening. She was too moved by the swelling and bruises to his face, and trying not to show it. She organised a yoghurt and honey breakfast for him and sat with him for an hour. Kati had travelled on to Palioskala, the island capital, and would return later. Kim went to find out what she could about the accident. The same doctor from the previous evening was still around.

'You work long hours.'

'Yes. It's too much.' He looked as though he meant it.

'Can you tell me anything about what happened?'

'A farmer found your husband lying by the side of the road up in the mountains. He'd turned his car over and he'd been thrown clear. So the farmer brought him here.'

'You must let me know who he is. I want to thank him.'

The doctor laughed. 'We're Greeks. Do you think we leave a man to die in the road? Yes, I can give you his address.'

'And the car. I'm going to need it to come here.'

'I'm only going to keep your husband in for a couple of days. He's still concussed. The farmer who found your husband has a brother who is a mechanic, and he's already had the car taken back to Palioskala. You'll have to pay him.'

'How was my husband when he was brought in?'

'Raving. Does he speak Greek?'

'Not very well. Why?'

'He was speaking fluent Greek when he was brought here. But since then, not a word.'

'What was he saying?'

'It was fluent, but it was all nonsense.'

After Kati had collected her from the hospital, Kim insisted on returning to the house. Locked and shuttered as she had left it, it looked strangely sullen in the heat of the afternoon. Once inside she suspected that someone – probably Lakis – had been in while she was away. She thought she could detect a faint trace of hair oil in the air. She was drawn to examining the drawer containing her underwear, but nothing had been moved or disturbed in any way.

She threw open the shutters and the room received the sunlight like a set of lungs accepting oxygen. Then she busied herself with cleaning the place. She scrubbed the floor and the table top; she made the glass in the oil lamps sparkle. She swept the patio, wiped down the stove and mopped the floor of the outhouse. Then she burned the rubbish in the garden, throwing a couple of Lakis' filthy, spidery old rugs on to the bonfire for good measure.

It was as if by setting her house in order, she could somehow insulate herself against this visit by misfortune.

The drinking-water container was almost empty. She would have to take it to the village and replenish it from the tap outside the Church of the Virgin. Even with the use of the car this involved lugging the heavy load along the path to the house. With a full drum even Mike struggled over that distance. There was a second option they'd considered before but never exploited.

The soldiers' lookout post on the hill had water. It was on the short cut to the road, the route she generally avoided. The alternative of a trip to the village would be sticky and tiring. The heat of the afternoon had begun to subside, but there was no breeze to offer relief. 'Make it work for you for a change,' she said aloud, and decided to beg water from the soldiers.

She changed out of her shorts and T-shirt into a pair of trousers and a long-sleeved blouse. Wearing sunglasses and a straw panama, she collected some cigarettes for the soldiers and set off with the plastic water container.

White dust settled on her shoes as she climbed the winding path through the rock. The dry boulders to either side were tufted with sage and saxifrage. Halfway to the lookout post she stopped and turned towards the promontory behind her. The mysterious watcher was there again, a tiny erect figure gazing out to sea from the edge of the cliff.

The ridge of stones through which she had to pass looked like a set of decaying dentures, splintering in the arid heat. At the post two young sentries sat with their backs to huge drums marked *Ammo*, sand, and *Nero*, water. Their legs were splayed open, and their helmets rested on the yellow dirt between their boots. They scrambled to their feet when they saw Kim approaching.

The soldiers were only eighteen or so, boys with huge smiles. They blinked at her as if she was a film star or a pop celebrity just stepped out of a helicopter.

'*Yia!*' she said, offering a cigarette to each of them. '*Yia!*'

They took the cigarettes and a light gratefully, inhaling deeply and blowing the smoke vertically into the air. They were still blushing and smiling, when Kim held up her container. '*Thelo nero*. I want water.'

'You speak Greek!' said one of the boys, in English.

'Not much. Only enough to ask for what I want.'

'It's very good! Very good Greek!' He grabbed the water container and jogged to a hose. Kim sensed that by speaking English the first soldier could exclude the second. 'Where do you live?'

'In the white house on the beach.'

'I've seen it. I've seen you living there.'

'Please! Don't fill it! I can't carry it!'

Kim realised her mistake too late. The boy waved away her complaint. 'No problem. I take it for you.' He was already speaking in rapid Greek to his smiling, nodding comrade. Despite her protests, the young soldier insisted on carrying the water down the hill to the house.

He had underestimated the weight of the thing, and though he kept up a barrage of questions on the way down, he was struggling, breathing heavily and switching the container from hand to hand. Huge oval sweatstains darkened his fatigues around the armpits, but he refused to take a break. When he reached the house he dumped the container and sat down on the concrete patio, wiping sweat from his eyes and demanding another cigarette.

Kim obliged and poured him some of the water he had carried down the hill. She sat with him until he had recovered.

'Where is your husband?' he asked.

'Inside. Sleeping.'

The boy tried to look through the window. It was open. She hoped he was unable to see. He seemed reluctant to return to his post.

'Well,' said Kim, standing up and offering to shake his hand, 'we wouldn't want you to miss the Turks.'

The irony was lost on him, but he got up to leave. Kim followed him to the gate and watched him walk swiftly back up the path. Then she turned towards the promontory, where the obsessive watcher was still gazing out to sea.

The following morning Kim awoke and felt again that same inexplicable sense of depression she'd experienced before. She blinked open her eyes and put her hand on the bed where Mike's warm body should have been, and couldn't seem to remember what had happened to him. Then it flooded back. She pulled on a T-shirt and padded out on to the patio, squinting into the bedazzling light. For all the sharpness of the day, she felt uncomfortably shrouded in a greasy film, some hazy, milky substance. Light settled in indecisive tones on the vine, and tinted the blue sea at the foot of the garden. It was like a photograph fixed with poor chemicals, where the colour had distorted through age.

Nonsense. You don't want to kill yourself.

The stray thought was in and out of her head as quick as a lizard. Where had it come from? It was almost like someone else's thought, cuckoo-laid inside her own head; and it was actually a second thought, a reply prompted by what sentiment? Instinctively her hand clutched her belly, and her fingers splayed to cover her pubis. An unaccountable deep yearning swept through her, a loneliness like a hunger. It felt alien, but it was of her; it used her. It was like something leaking from her, draining her. It seemed to begrudge having surrendered her from her dreams, it wanted to drag her back there.

She ran down to the beach, stripped off her T-shirt and plunged into the chilly water. The sea was as fresh as a lime. It effervesced around her. Her skin burned with the early morning chill of it. She kept her head under the water for as long as possible, and when she came up again, the sea had cleansed her, woken her, peeled back the dreams that had clung like dirty weeds.

She stood in the water holding her hands to her mouth, shivering slightly and looking back at the house. The cuckoo sentiments had gone.

Later, the tomato lady's husband gave her a lift to the hospital. Mike was up and about and itching to leave. He was badly bruised, but his injuries were clearly nothing compared with the suffering endured by confinement to a Greek hospital. At least he was joking about his misery. One more day, said the doctor. One more day.

Kim said nothing about what had happened to her that morning.

The doctor took an opportunity to speak privately with her. 'Look, the wounds are healing. But you know your husband. If he starts – you know . . .' Here he waved his arms in the air.

'What do you mean?'

'If he starts saying crazy things, he's your husband, you know he doesn't mean what he says.'

'Is he all right?'

'I've checked him over. It's a bit of delayed concussion. Just one more day.'

Back at the house that afternoon, Kim put on her bikini and stretched out in the garden with a paperback thriller. After a while she took off her top, and, absorbed by the novel she was reading, unconsciously stroked her breast with a forefinger. She turned a page and became aware of someone standing at the gate.

It was the young soldier who had carried the water for her only yesterday. He grinned in a foolish, simian manner, and waved. She sat up, but made no attempt to cover herself.

'Maybe a cigarette?'

She looked at him coolly. She could hardly refuse him. 'On the table. Help yourself.'

He opened the gate and walked self-consciously up to the patio, averting his eyes from her breasts as if they were on display to him every day. He brought the cigarettes from the table and sat down on the grass four feet away. He was still grinning. He lit a cigarette and asked if she would like one.

'Yes, I will.'

She reached for the packet but instead he gave her the one he had lit for himself, and proceeded to light another one. She could taste the sweat of his lip on the filter. He was still smiling and pretending to look around the garden. He looked relaxed, but she noticed his fist was clenched tight.

She should cover herself, she knew, but for the moment she was unable to resist sampling the delicious sense of power she felt over the youth.

He nodded at the house. 'Is your husband sleeping again?'

'Yes.'

'No. I looked in. There is no one.' He laughed.

'You're right. I lied.'

This time he allowed his gaze to fall on her breasts. He was a handsome boy with a strong wiry body; but his twitching movements and flickering glances made him seem like an insect caught in molasses. Men initiate, thought Kim, but women – unless some violence forces the issue – always stand at the mysterious gate determining whether or not it shall swing open. Sometimes the exercise of this power was more delicious than the pleasures latent within it.

She had never been unfaithful to Mike. She had come close, but had always prized her fidelity enough to draw back at the crucial moment. Now as she looked at this grinning boy from behind her sunglasses, she appreciated how quickly an act of infidelity could be realised. It might only take a minute, less. The impulse was there before it was realised; the act could be accomplished before conscience had even arrived. All she had to do was to smile at him, perhaps lightly brush the back of his evenly tanned arm. The rest would fasten on in quick succession, like the links in the gold chain he wore around his neck.

Let him.

The words surprised her by popping into her head. They seemed not her own, cuckoo-laid again. Suddenly she felt uncomfortable. The same greasy film, the lacquer of dreams, seemed to settle on the boy and on the cloying air around him.

Let him.

Her hand went instinctively to her breast. She was confused. The boy soldier was reaching for a bottle of sun lotion. 'Shall I put this on for you?'

Let him.

Suddenly there was a movement at the gate, and the narrow spit of beach was busy with sheep. The shepherd! It was the shepherd, varying his routine, coming down early from the hills. He who normally passed by without acknowledging their existence at the house was now standing at the gate. '*Kali Mera*,' he shouted.

The soldier shifted uncomfortably. Kim got up, pulling on a blouse, but already the shepherd was moving on further down the beach, taking his flock with him. Yet his unexpected greeting had a crucial timing; it had broken some mischievous spell.

'You must go now,' Kim told the soldier.

'Yes?'

'Yes, goodbye.'

The soldier looked baffled. 'I will come again.'

'No. Don't come here again. Goodbye.'

She marched up to the house and slammed the door behind her. She watched the soldier through the slats in the wooden shutters, watched him scratch his head and slowly get to his feet. Then he vaulted the gate. He was striding back to his lookout post, where he was commanded to watch for phantom enemies from across the water.

10

That had indeed been worth the wait! All of this watching
and waiting! He would gladly have sat here for another year
to witness the spectacle of Lakis being chased from his own
house. He'd had to tear off his neckerchief and stuff it into
his mouth just to prevent himself from laughing out loud.
He'd almost betrayed his presence, rolling around in the
bushes and thumping the earth. Run, Lakis, fool! Run,
Lakis, you ridiculous old bastard!

It still made him laugh. How had it come about?

First something bad had happened to the man. Some
kind of accident. That explained why he had been away.
The Englishwoman had stayed away for one night; then she
had spent the second night alone. It was not good for her to
sleep in that house alone. In the village they said it was a
motoring accident. The Englishman was drunk and he had
smashed his car. But there would be more to it. There was
always more to it than that.

And in the night while they were away, the fox had
returned and had taken another chicken. So, since they
were Lakis' chickens, he had followed the fox and taken
another for himself. He had cooked it that same night. A
tough old broiler, but at least the fox would be blamed.

Now the woman was without protection.

He had seen her invite a soldier into the garden, and that,

he considered, was not a wise thing. This, he said to the sheep around him – as if advising a classroom of young people not otherwise equipped to recognise good counsel – is where the trouble begins. He shook his head and drew a greasy, wrinkled package from his pocket. Wrapped in the slimy brown paper was a wedge of feta cheese and a handful of black olives. He cut himself a slice of the cheese and tossed an olive into his mouth.

All women, he conjectured, incline to this trouble. The female is more susceptible to the dance. She may only have accepted the soldier's offer to carry the water, and that was understandable. But thereby she incurred a debt. Now she may have tried to meet the debt with a cigarette or two, but beyond that a small commerce had been set up. And in that commerce an engine had been set in motion. And these engines of commerce between human beings were not like the mechanical contraptions of technology: they were different in that once set in motion they required greater energy to stop than they had to start.

He cut himself another slice of cheese. Far better, he observed, to avoid commerce of any kind. Far better to lead a simple life uncomplicated by these relationships.

Take the complication of Lakis, for example. He might just as well have paid Lakis for one of those old broiler chickens. But then he would have had to pretend to have forgotten old animosities; and Lakis would have had to pretend too; and more words than were spoken would be hidden away under whatever was said, and what a whore and a confusion of a misunderstanding that would provoke. This way there was no commerce, and no debt, except to the fox, which he had paid before with a newborn lamb, and would again, no doubt.

And the young soldier, passing by that way the next day,

and thinking himself a fine and quite irresistible fellow, had chanced his arm. A call on the debt was made, and a moment and a blink and a look and a glance, and that other more complicated commerce had been suggested.

But there was something extra. Something had for a moment frightened him by its very unexpectedness, frightened Manoussos the shepherd who watched the house. Some slow wave had rolled over the scene, like a milky mist forming before his eyes, as the soldier sat uneasily with the Englishwoman. The earth had given off a subtle scent, a yeasty odour identifiable with women but difficult to name. It was an odour he had experienced before, and that was its most terrifying character. His stomach had turned. There was a thrumming in the air, a vibration, and Manoussos had known he must act quickly.

At the risk of revealing his habit, he had gathered his sheep and had driven them down to the gate of the house, and by calling from the gate he had been able to arrest the moment. He had punctured the swelling scene like a balloon. The milky mist had rolled back, had withdrawn almost angrily, like childish fingers from a flame.

He had made an intervention. He had saved her, not from the soldier but from herself; or perhaps not even from herself but from the unnatural summons of that dangerous place.

He had not seen that mist form for many years. Since the first time when the thing had happened, he had perhaps seen it twice. Now the Englishwoman was in his debt. He knew she was glad he had appeared at that moment. He'd seen it in the surprise that had stiffened her mouth. A commerce had now started between them, but she could not guess at the currency. She would not know. He prayed she would not have to know.

But another astonishing thing had happened. It was after he had moved on, after he had shepherded his flock back up the hill. Manoussos had turned to look back at the house, and had seen Lakis crouched in the olive grove a short distance away. How long had he been there? He too must have seen the entire incident – or lack of it – involving the soldier. So he too must have seen the opaque mist forming, and similarly felt its unruly summons.

Did the others see it as a mist? Smell the unmistakable scent? Was it also available to other people, like Lakis? Manoussos would never know the answer to that question. He'd never discussed it with anyone, so how would he know a single thing about what they saw or how anything appeared to them?

Lakis had approached the house from the landward slope of the olive grove before breaking through the hedge, a curious way for anyone to reach the property. Manoussos had heard the pig-like squeak of his greeting and had seen the Englishwoman emerge from the house, this time more modestly attired. Lakis had asked for a coffee and his request appeared to be ignored. The woman was smoking and clearly still in a state of some distress from the recent encounter. Lakis failed to notice this, and suddenly began counting the chickens. Manoussos had been unable to discern everything that was said, but could hear Lakis trying to make himself understood by raising his voice. Perhaps she had stolen his chickens? Yes? No? Ha ha! Did you steal my chickens?

Then the donkey had started to bray. Lakis, as if taking this message from the ass as a signal or prompt, moved up behind the woman, reached around and pinched her breast! It was the most extraordinarily inept advance

Manoussos had ever seen. Astonished, the Englishwoman leapt back.

Lakis laughed gaily and reached out, perhaps to placate her by stroking her wrist. She coolly took a draw on her cigarette before stubbing it out on his tanned forearm. Howling, Lakis had moved forward to stop her by roughly grabbing her arm, but she picked up a heavy hurricane lamp from the table and swung it by its hook. Manoussos had seen the lamp flash in the sunlight as it cut an arc through the air. There was a hollow clonk as it connected with the bone above Lakis' left eye, loud enough to resound dully from the dry boulders at the top of the hill. It was wonderful to behold! On witnessing all of this Manoussos actually bit into his own fingers!

A red crescent gash had appeared instantly above Lakis' brow. Even from a distance the wound looked the size of a ripe plum. Lakis had staggered back, and seeing the woman swinging the lamp for a second blow had charged at the gate. Then the thing had become farcical as he was unable to open the catch on the gate. Lakis was squealing in his high-pitched voice, like a piglet. The lamp was thrown at him and he vaulted the gate and landed on his bottom before scrambling to his feet and running along the path. She pursued him for a few metres, tearing up stones from the beach to hurl at him.

Manoussos was still laughing when he saw the woman return in a rage. He saw her pick up one of the oars from the rowing boat and crack it down on the rowlocks, twice, three times, as if the boat had been the source of the offence. Then he saw her climb inside the boat and sit down and weep; and that stopped his mirth, for further laughter would have been inappropriate.

11

Kim stepped out of the boat, stooping to rinse her eyes with sea water. Weeds the colour of stewed tea tangled between her toes as she walked up the beach. She halted when she realised the shepherd was standing in the shade of the broad-trunked fig tree by the hedgerow. His sheep grazed the slope behind the house.

'Excuse me,' he said formally. 'You have right.'

'Pardon?' Kim stroked her eyes with the ball of a hand, wondering if the tears still showed.

'You have right. This thing with Lakis; I saw from the hill.'

His English was good, but larded with accent. He spoke English like many Greeks, as if through a mouthful of olives. It dawned on her that the man was offering some kind of approval for what had just happened. She was embarrassed not at what he'd seen, but that he might have seen her crying afterwards. She didn't care that the shepherd would tell the whole village. Perhaps Lakis' wife would get to hear about it.

The shepherd stepped out of the shade. 'Are you all right?'

'I'm perfectly all right.' Kim felt her throat tighten, and her lips clamped too hard over her words; but she had no intention of elaborating the fiasco for this man's entertainment. The shepherd suddenly looked bewildered, as though he thought he might have made some terrible mistake in showing concern. He shuffled uneasily, fingering a monstrous and unruly iron-grey moustache.

Kim was surprised at how much younger he looked than she'd suspected. The man who crossed the beach path twice a day with his grey cloud of sheep was perhaps in his mid-forties. His grey hair was mostly hidden by a blue headscarf knotted over his brow. Daily exposure to the sun had tooled his face like a piece of fabulously soft leather. A peasant's face, it was bruised and puffy with toil, though not without dignity. The chin was uplifted sharply, the eyes quick and intelligent. Yet there was something brooding and ferocious in the deep blackness of his eyes. His stare was cold and intimidating, and socially inept.

Intimidating, yes, but she was not frightened by the man. He wore at least three layers of woollens, and rubber boots. Kim wondered how he could breathe. Something in the unravelling wool of his clothes made her soften.

'Yes, I'm fine. Thank you for being concerned.'

He looked enormously relieved. 'Only to say, we are not all like Lakis, we Greeks.'

'I know that.'

'He is not a good man.'

'As I found out today.'

He turned and looked up the hill. Then his eyes seemed to fix on the distant promontory, where the lonely figure continued to watch from the clifftop. He turned back to Kim. Creases of agitation returned to his brow. He seemed to be waiting for something, some invitation, some recognition. By now Kim knew enough of Greek culture to understand that the moment was right to exhibit the courtesy of *philoxenia*, that unique hospitality to strangers which offers a glass, a modest dish of something. But today she'd had enough interaction with Greek men. What wasn't felt wasn't about to be offered.

The shepherd seemed to have reached resolution. He nodded his head. 'So, then. *Yia!*' he cried, holding up a hand in farewell and turning on his heel. '*Yia!*'

He was already halfway up the hill when Kim reciprocated. '*Yia soo!*'

That evening Kim sat on the beach in her bathing suit. She was watching the sunset. The calming miracle was enacted every single evening, ordinary and spectacular, varying slightly each time with kaleidoscopic invention. The sun pulsed above the horizon like a human organ, the sky fluttered lavender and was streaked cerise. Out in the water yellow rock veined with black volcanic strata flared briefly.

Kim's bottom made a hollow in the warm sand. She inhaled the warm scent of her own tanned skin as she watched the show as if from a gallery. The dependability of these electrifying sunsets was precious. It was cinema and transcendental meditation in one package. It offered moments which mythologised themselves at each passing breath.

'Beautiful,' whispered a voice behind her.

The shepherd had returned. He had changed his clothes, and was wearing a black shirt and a rough pair of trousers rolled up halfway to his knees. The rubber boots had been traded in for a pair of sandals, and he carried a large metal container.

Kim blinked at him.

'This is for you.'

She stood up and he handed her the tin. Kim didn't know what to do with it. He took it back from her, set it on the ground and removed the lid. Inside was an enormous block of feta cheese, swimming in a lake of olive oil.

'It's a cheese,' he said unnecessarily.

Kim felt both gratified and irritated. 'That's kind. Very kind. Look, can I offer you some coffee?'

'No. I have something to show you.'

'What?'

'It's special. Come with me?'

What, now? she thought. Why don't they just leave me alone? 'Where? What is it? Where do you want me to go?'

'Just along the beach. Not far.'

'It's not convenient. Really . . .'

'Please. For me.'

He pressed the palm of his hand to his chest and looked at her with sad spaniel eyes. Clearly it was important to him. She couldn't understand why he was doing this. She conceded.

'I'll put some shoes on.'

He watched her intently as she returned to the patio to pull on a pair of jeans and a sweatshirt.

'Bring a towel,' he called.

'A towel?'

'Yes,' he replied as if she were slightly dim-witted, 'a towel.'

Kim was already questioning the wisdom of this venture as she was locking the door. Twilight had darkened the water and was stealing over the hedgerow. They'd gone some way along the beach before she broke the silence.

'Where are we going?'

'You will see.'

They were heading in the direction of the promontory. The watcher had gone again.

'You speak good English,' said Kim.

'You are wrong. It's not good. Before, I had good English. Now not.'

'Better than my Greek.'

They came to a rock slippery with moss luminous green in the dusk. He gently steered her by the elbow to help her over it. 'I was not always a shepherd. When I was young I was a mercantile seaman. I learned some English. But then some things happened. My father had this flock, and he died. I went back. I don't use my English too much.' There was a mixture of regret and resignation in his voice. 'Now we must get our feet wet.'

They had reached the point where Kim and Mike always diverted along the inland pathway, believing further access along the beach to be impossible. But the shepherd kicked off his sandals and waited for Kim to do the same. Paddling round a black outcrop of jagged rock, they reached a dark, dank recess with dripping walls. The shepherd stopped. Something suddenly occurred to him.

'I am Manoussos,' he said.

'I'm Kim.'

He held up a hand. 'Kim. Now be careful, Kim.'

He made directly for the rock face, and Kim realised there was a fissure in the rock. Manoussos stroked a finger on the rock to alert her to its scythe-sharpness, offering a nod of encouragement before slipping nimbly through the fissure. She followed, emerging with some surprise on to a small, scallop-shaped beach on the other side.

The sea slapped against the rock and sucked intimately at the shingle. In the gloaming Kim could discern a steep path suspended above a sudden drop twelve feet above her head: the rock had crumbled some time ago, leaving the path hanging desolate and useless. Kim saw why people used to come here. At the other end of the beach – where the broken path would have led – was a curious building.

This small construction was built into the rock itself. Nearest the ground were neat layers of thin red brickwork, characteristically Roman. At shoulder height these had fallen irregularly, and had been repaired by concrete infill at some later, but still ancient time. The roof of the building was a rather crude dome with two small apertures.

Kim hesitated. The sea slapped and sucked. Manoussos beckoned her on.

The doorway was concrete with a boulder lintel. As she approached, Kim got a strong whiff of sulphur. Water gurgled from the rock near the concrete doorway of the structure releasing an occasional light puff of vapour.

They ducked inside to pitch darkness. The smell of sulphur was fetid and overpowering. She heard Manoussos' feet scraping on the concrete floor. Then a match flared as he lit a small candle stub. He placed it in a recess in the wall, and produced a fistful of thin candles of different lengths; brown votive candles, as if he'd raided a church to get them.

A culvert ran at their feet, carrying steaming water from the rock through a cervix-like gap into a generous trough the size of the dome itself. Manoussos stepped though the gap and lit more candles, placing them around the trough. Kim watched from the anteroom. Light fizzed on the trembling black mirror of water. A geothermal spring trickled in at one end of the trough and drained at the same rate at the other. Steam rose in visible coils, unwinding to escape through the two tiny roof apertures. Every slight shifting or scrape of feet echoed eerily in the chamber.

'It's a—'

'Yes,' said Manoussos. 'A Turkish bath. The Turks made this roof. Long time ago.'

'And before them, the Romans?' Kim was enthralled.

'Yes. Why not?' Manoussos tested the water with his finger. 'Water comes here; goes out there. Temperature stays the same, always. Once every week I make a bath here. Then swim. Long life. Good health.'

She stepped into the chamber. Stooping to test the water, she found it barely tolerable to the hand.

'You want to try?'

'You're joking. I couldn't stand the heat!'

'Excuse me. I will wait out here if you want to bathe.'

'No, it's not that. It's just too hot.'

So Manoussos showed her. He stripped down to a pair of baggy swimming trunks he was wearing under his trousers and eased himself in. 'The trick is not to disturb the water. To make no splash.'

He was in, basking in the heat and the steam, his coarse brown skin reflecting orange light from the candles and the plaster walls.

'Mike – my husband – would love to see this place.'

He smiled from the water. 'I would be very happy if you brought him here.'

'But perhaps you can bring us both, another time?'

'That too would make me happy.' After a moment he said, 'Now I will get out so you can try.'

'There's no need.'

It was not fear of Manoussos that kept her from the bath, but the suggestion of intense heat. Indeed she felt safe enough with the man, even though his motivation was still unclear. His gentle, reassuring manner encouraged confidence; plus there was a modesty about his movements, a certain shyness which made her lower her guard.

He stepped back through to the antechamber. 'I will wait here. But you needn't fear; no one will come. And I will not watch.'

Though somewhat clumsy in his formality, he was trying to behave correctly. She also guessed that this place was special to him. His hushed tones betrayed almost a reverence for the place. It was a secret place, and for some reason he had decided to share it with her. It was a gift. She could see it would disappoint him if she showed distrust, or even if she refused to avail herself of the bath.

Yes, you can trust him.

She heard the words spoken clearly inside her own head, so clearly that she looked to Manoussos in astonishment. But he was in the antechamber on the other side of the dripping wall, unaware of what had startled her. The words were at once her own, and not her own. It was like the voice she had heard in the garden when she had been alone with the soldier; familiar, intimate, and yet frightening her by intruding out of nowhere. Schizophrenics hear voices, she told herself: you're going insane. Yet the voice had insisted she could trust him.

She still had her bathing suit on under her clothes. Making a decision, she peeled off her jeans and sweatshirt and inched into the water as Manoussos had demonstrated. It was so hot it didn't seem safe.

'Ahhhhhhhhhh!!!!'

'No splash!' His voice echoed from the anteroom.

'Ahhhhhhh!!!'

The heat immediately penetrated her. She even felt her bones absorbing the temperature as she slid along the bath, immersed up to her chin. The sulphurous fumes relaxed her, made her feel vague. The heat exercised exotic fingers massaging her muscles, probing her body; a deep sensuous ripple chased along her spine, forcing a sigh of pleasure.

'Good?' Manoussos called gently from the darkness.

'Uhhhhhhh.'

The water stroked her thighs and her arms with a light chafing action, almost as if it was delicately erasing dead skin, old cells, stripping the body down, making ready the bright, clean new creature underneath. Blisters of sweat began to appear on her brow, and soon her face was streaked with perspiration. She felt a pleasurable ripple pass across her brain, like the closing down of old tired cells and the awakening of new ones. It was possible to imagine every toxic waste from the body being discharged into the water. Food poisons, pollutants, spent adrenaline, wasted pheromones, dead thoughts, bad memories, useless ideas, unproductive waves and spirals all seemed to leak out and dissolve in the heat and the steam and the sulphur of the water as it sprang from the rock still burning with primal energy.

It was like being back inside the womb. The plaster was still oxide red with some ancient, flaking Turkish paint. The candles flickered and reflected orange and red, and the water gurgled with intestinal, digestive delight. Even the entrance to the chamber was like the neck of the womb. Once in, you did not feel inclined to get out.

Ten minutes passed unmarked.

'Not too long,' Manoussos called softly but patiently from the anteroom.

Kim reluctantly obeyed his dictum. As she eased herself out, an inadvertent splash reminded her of the searing heat. As she stepped through the gap, the antechamber seemed as cold as a tomb.

'Now I suggest a swim,' said Manoussos.

'In the sea?'

'Where else?'

So she stepped out of the building and on to the shingle beach. Moonlit, the surrounding rocks were like vast chunks of gleaming obsidian. The sky was operatic, star-painted, and the sea was a calm pool. She splashed in without hesitation. It was not cold; the inner heat from the bath seemed to insulate her. The sea chilled the outer skin, but failed to penetrate her internal warmth, her deep heat. Ripples of cold and heat passed through her, deep in her belly.

She got out feeling deliriously happy. The effect was like a drug. Manoussos was waiting on the beach, holding her clothes and her towel at the ready. He was studying her closely, and the sight of him made her throw her wet hair back and shriek. Her laughter ricocheted from the rocks. She ran around the shingle with her arms outstretched like an aeroplane.

'You see?' said Manoussos. 'You see?'

'Yes! Yes!'

'Special place. Very special place. Put on your clothes. Don't get cold.' They walked back to the house, Kim in a dreamy, euphoric state. Manoussos remained silent most of the way, but when they drew close to the house, he suddenly burst out with surprising fierceness: 'But how do you find this house? How do you find it?'

Kim was taken aback. 'Well, I like it.'

'Like it? You like it?'

She was obviously expected to find fault. 'It can be a little strange.'

'Strange? How, strange?'

Rather than answer, she recounted what Kati had told her about the fate of the German woman, Eva.

He listened and then shook his head. 'There's more to it,' he said. Then he resumed walking, his arms hanging limp at his sides.

'What more is there?'

But he wouldn't be drawn, and even though Kim tried to press him, he shook his head and gazed at the ground in front of him.

Manoussos pulled up short at the gate and gazed at the house. He was lost in his own thoughts.

'Would you like a coffee? Or perhaps a glass of something?'

'No. Another time when your husband is here. Then I will take a coffee.'

'Manoussos, thank you for showing me the Turkish bath.' He made a sweet gesture of pressing his chest and closing his eyes, as if to indicate the pleasure was his. 'But why? Why did you show me?'

He looked embarrassed for a moment. Recovering, he said, 'Why not?'

'Thank you again. Good night.'

'*Kali Nikta!*' he shouted. He had his back turned already, but one arm was held aloft in a farewell salute. '*Kali Nikta!*'

But she knew why he had taken her to the Turkish bath. It was the best gift he could offer her. He had arrived burdened with a sense of debt, and all because of Lakis' actions, for which Manoussos had somehow made himself accountable. He had witnessed the event and had felt the need to discharge a dishonour.

Well, he had accomplished that. Kim felt a sense of gratitude and affection. The profound relaxation of the hot spring bath stayed with her. It was deeply satisfying, even sexual in character. She remained outside on the patio for a while, gazing at the eel-like shivers of moonlight on the still sea and the stars set above the coastline of Asia Minor. Then she retired for a night of untroubled dreamless sleep.

12

Mike had discovered a new Greek word while he was in hospital.

'*Trellos*. They all think I'm *trellos*. The doctor thinks I'm crazy, the nurse with the moustache thinks I'm crazy. The other patients and their relatives: they kept looking at me with this terrible expression of sympathy.'

Kim had collected the Renault from Palioskala. Most of the dents had been hammered out and repainted in a shade of cream which didn't exactly match the original white. Mike had been so keen to leave the hospital he'd been waiting at the door in anticipation of Kim's arrival, sitting on the step with his things. He cheered when she arrived and waved his plaster cast at her. All the other patients had autographed the cast: Mike had used it to learn the Greek alphabet.

'So who was it? Who do you think did it?'

'I don't know,' said Mike. 'The crazy thing was they didn't steal anything. My wallet was in my pocket. They just beat the shit out of me.' They were driving back across the rim of the cauldron, all windows open.

'And you say you've spoken to the police.'

'One of them came to get a statement. The doctor translated for me, though God knows what he said when I came to the bit about the metal shoes. The policeman listened politely, offered me a cigarette and told me he was a fan of Manchester United. He showed me some kind of Greek supporters' club card.'

'Were they Greek, these three men?'

'I suppose so. Though I only saw the one face.'

'The saint.'

'Kim, I know what you're thinking. But I'd swear I wasn't concussed when I got out of the car. I remember inspecting the damage. I was shaken, but the accident had made me hyper-aware.' Mike stroked his cast, as though he could still feel the blows that had broken his arm. 'Then there was the . . . Oh, I don't know.'

'Go on.'

'I've just remembered this stupid old man at the taverna before it happened. He was angry because I'd been mocking the saint. He walked off cursing me. Somehow it must have all got mixed up in my mind.'

Mike fell silent until they reached the junction of two roads, one leading back to Kamari, the other to the monastery of St Michael. He asked Kim to stop the car. They both got out.

The white dust road wound up into the hills above the cauldron before starting to drop on the other side. 'Do you want me to drive up there, Mike? Take a look?'

Mike didn't answer. He gazed along the track. The place was heavy with the baking heat. The ecstatic chant of cicadas sawed against the enfolding silence.

'Mike . . . ?'

Kim put her hand on his shoulder. He was shaking with fear.

'Come on. Let's get you home.'

They stopped in the village for some shopping. Mike

was fêted and had his plaster admired by the tomato lady's husband. While he faced a barrage of questions, Maria hissed at Kim from her dress shop, semaphoring frantically.

'Reuters,' said Kim.

'Don't get caught up,' begged Mike.

Maria almost dragged Kim inside the shop, kicking at the wooden wedge which held the door open. It flew into a rack of Lurex frocks. Maria slammed the door so hard Kim distinctly saw its glass wobble. 'The egg!' cackled Maria in Greek, nodding and smiling. 'The egg!'

'What are you talking, Maria? What egg!'

'The beautiful egg! It was from you? Yes?' Maria was stamping the floor with her foot and clapping her hands. She was laughing hysterically. Kim looked appalled. Her face only seemed to make Maria cackle louder. Maria fell to her knees, drumming the floor rapidly with her fists. 'What a beautiful egg!'

Kim looked at the door as if hoping someone might come in. 'Maria –'

Maria scrambled to her feet. 'It was you, yes? Say it was you! Say it! Say it!'

'What are you talking about, Maria?'

The Greek woman suddenly stopped laughing. Her jaw sagged. 'The egg! He has a beautiful egg! Here!' She pointed to her eyebrow. 'Lakis! It must be you! Say it was you!'

'Yes. It was me.'

Maria shrieked and slapped her hands together. Then she patted Kim's face and kissed her on the cheek. 'I knew! I said it was you! That bastard, he deserves it. Ha!' Maria's mood changed abruptly as she curled her lip and let fly a torrent of Greek invective, some of which Kim understood, most of which she didn't. Lakis' name was snarled somewhere amongst it. Then Maria laughed again, and kissed her once more.

'I have to go,' Kim said, extricating herself from Maria's embraces. 'Mike's outside.'

'I knew it! I said it!'

As she walked down the cobbled street she could still hear Maria's celebrations from inside the store.

'She's in a good mood,' said Mike.

'Yes.'

They passed the Church of the Virgin and stopped in at Kati's shop. She was on the telephone as they walked in. Kati fired a few more words into the mouthpiece before saying '*Yia soo, Maria,*' and looking pointedly at Kim. Then she replaced the receiver with a delicate click. She kissed Mike and sat him down in her chair before making fresh coffee.

'So what's been happening in the village while I was away?' Mike wanted to know.

'Nothing.' Kati didn't even blink. 'We are very dull. Life goes on.'

'What, nothing at all? No gossip? No scandal? I'm disappointed.'

'You,' said Kati. 'You are the talk. Your accident. And telling everyone of your fight with *Agios Mikalis*. You are the talk.'

'So that got back, did it? Should have kept my mouth shut.'

'Don't worry, Mike! You have to be a little crazy sometimes to be ... not crazy the other times.' Kati kept her lips straight but smiled with her huge brown eyes. Mike only looked baffled, as if there was no bottom to her remark.

'Oh, I almost forgot,' said Kim. 'I met someone new yesterday.'

'Who?'

'The shepherd. You know, Mike, the one who passes our garden every day.'

Kati suddenly looked uncomfortable.

'Manoussos. You must know him, Kati.'

'Yes. I know of him.' She was staring out of the window with a preoccupied air. The mention of Manoussos had clearly disturbed her.

'I must say, he seemed very nice.' Kim decided not to mention the Turkish bath. She didn't want to suggest she'd spent any time with the man.

Kati got up and began to rearrange pieces of pottery on a display shelf. She moved each of the objects a fraction of an inch. 'Did he speak to you? Manoussos?'

'Oh yes.'

'That's unusual. He's a strange one. He doesn't speak with people.'

'Oh?'

'Not often. Only for essential things, when he comes to the village.'

'But he seemed very kind.'

'Yes. But be careful. I heard something. I heard that this shepherd spies on your house.'

'Who told you that?'

'Lakis.'

'And of the two, which one would you trust? Lakis?'

Kati turned from rearranging her pottery. 'No.'

Mike suspected there might be some conversation going on beyond the words used. He was about to open his mouth when Kati asked him how he was going to swim with his arm in a cast.

97

'With difficulty. But I'm going to try.'

On the way back to the house the butcher's wife yelled her greetings, and the tomato lady looked up from her garden and waved as they passed in the car.

'You're a local celebrity,' said Kim.

'Really? I thought they were waving at *you*.'

When Manoussos drove his flock by the house that afternoon, at first it seemed he wasn't going to stop, but Kim called to him. He turned shyly, flicking at his animals with a switch cut from the slope. Bare-chested, Mike shook his hand.

'Kim has been telling me about the Turkish bath. I would like to go and see it.'

'Perhaps even tonight?' Kim suggested.

'I have much work. Much work. Go together. Take your husband. Now you know. And for you,' the shepherd gestured at Mike's bruises, 'it is very good. Now is the time.'

'Perhaps another time you'll come with us?'

'I would like that.'

He refused an invitation to drink coffee and went on his way.

'A frightening-looking man,' said Mike, after the shepherd had gone.

'But he's painfully shy. And although he looks a bit fierce, there's something warm about him.'

'Yes. I don't know. I'm not sure. Yet.'

Kim made Mike wait until dusk before taking him to the Turkish bath, so that he could have the full candlelight experience. She'd bought a dozen candles in Palioskala, and Manoussos had left his church candles behind. She lit them all. It was a magic grotto. Orange light rippled on the black mirror of the water and flickered in the welcome draughts from the doorway. The light illuminated helixes of steam climbing and thinning at the apertures.

'It's magnificent!' Mike's words rounded under the dome, hung suspended in the air for an excited moment.

Kim undressed. The light ran like oil on her supple body. She hesitated before getting in, letting Mike admire her. She cocked her head to one side in a gesture that was part shyness, part venery. His eyes swept over the ripe bulge of her mons pubis where a bead of moisture nested in the rich tangle of brown curls. She was an apparition; a goddess. It was as if he'd never seen his wife naked before. He shivered.

She eased herself into the water, keeping her eyes on him. He followed her example, careful to keep his cast on the concrete lip of the bath. The heat enveloped him totally. Kim's earlier analogy of gentle sexual penetration wasn't lost on him.

'Christ! Ahhhh!'

'Ummmmmm.'

'Ah! Ah! Ah!'

'Uhhuuuhu!'

'Ow!'

'Don't splash!'

They lay in the water, arms and legs spread, like a pair of pink starfish. Time enfolded them.

'We're cooking,' said Mike.

'Time to get out.'

Kim led the way and plunged into the sea. Mike followed gingerly, swimming in circles on his back with his cast in the air. He staggered out and collapsed on his back on the beach. The rocks swung around his head, the waves hissed at the shingle.

'The planet. The planet! Hey! Do you feel like . . .'

'Like we've been smoking something? Yes.'

'Earth's natural highs. I could get to like this.'

Kim straddled him, her skin smelling of brine and fresh weed. Her wet hair hung in his eyes as she planted a kiss on his lips, her mouth tasting of salt. The kiss made his teeth tingle. 'I've missed you,' she said. She seemed strangely energised.

'Wait,' she said, climbing off him.

'Where are you going?'

She ducked back inside the bathhouse. 'Two minutes.'

He lay back looking up at the night sky. The stars were brilliant, like an astronomer's map. He was so light-headed with the effects of the bath that his imagination easily superimposed geometric figures linking up the points of light like astrological drawings in white chalk. The Gemini twins. The Sagittarian centaur. Hey! he wanted to say. Look at that!

She came out of the bath, vapours rising from her body like the steam from Creation, her skin shell pink, perspiration plastering her hair to her head. She smelled of fresh sweat, a whiff of sulphur on her as she straddled him again. She was hot; she made burning contact against the sea-cold of his own skin. Even her mouth was hot. She lowered her head to slip his cock between her lips, delicately trailing her teeth along its engorged length. Then she licked him along the furry line of his chest; planting slow sucking kisses up to his neck, gently squeezing his balls with her hot hands.

He wet his own fingers with his mouth and probed inside her, but she was already wet. She shifted her hips and steered him into her, plunging down on him with a weight that made him gasp. She was scalding inside and out. Fire chased through him, igniting on the scorched nerves of his cock, flaring in his brain. He almost fainted with pleasure. He glanced up at the sky and saw the god-like figures of the astrologer's chart turned to watch, with cold, distant interest.

Afterwards they lay gasping in each other's arms, barely conscious. She was sprawled over him, her wet hair on his chest. Then, as heartbeats subsided, he heard the words, a woman's voice, like Kim imitating another's voice. He heard the words very clearly, but as if from a great way off: *The angel-militant beats and oppresses men, but I give you this.*

He raised his head. 'What?'

'Uh?'

'What did you just say?'

'I didn't say anything.'

'You sure?'

She lifted her head. 'Sure,' she said, stroking his cheek.

Mike settled back again. Voices. The island was full of voices. 'This place,' he said. 'This place!'

13

Live without a water supply within a few yards' reach and it
is possible to know the true value of a length of pipe and a
simple faucet. Mike and Kim had to relearn every few days
what they had all their lives taken for granted. Water is the
essence of the essential.

They eked it out; cooked with it sparingly; drank it
carefully; and used only a mouthful to clean their teeth.
The parched landscape of midsummer approved of this
frugality. The water from the Church of the Virgin sparkled
clear at the lip of Mike's container. He still had one good
arm, and was determined not to fall short of the chore of
water-carrying. Kim had told him about her approach to
the soldiers; but she discouraged him by suggesting that
their water was stale and came from storage containers.
This may have been true; but Kim was determined not to
encourage truck with the boys from the lookout post.

The water outside the Church of the Virgin, meanwhile,
was crystal and cold, piped directly from the hills. It tasted,
at any time of the day, of morning dew. It could have been
bottled and shipped and sold in Sainsbury's, Kim asserted.

'I'll go,' Mike had said that morning, snatching up the
plastic container.

Kim was rinsing breakfast plates in the saline water from
the pump. 'OK. See you later.' He was already twenty

yards from the house when she shouted, as an afterthought, 'And if you see the saint on the path to Kamari, kill him.'

He turned. Why had she said that? But she had already gone back up to the house.

If you see the saint on the path to Kamari, kill him. Mike was still turning the words over in his head as his container overfilled, and the water splashed at his feet. After replacing the filler cap, he took a deep slurp of the water, then cupped his hands in the flow to wipe his sunburned neck. He looked up and saw the door to the church was open. An Orthodox priest came out carrying some withered flowers.

Mike had previously taken only a cursory glance round the church. He left his water container by the tap and went in.

The Church of the Virgin was of standard Byzantine construction, half of it scooped out of sheer rock. Its interior was dark, reeking of mastic incense and candle wax. The stone floor was meticulously swept, and silver icons hung from the spotless whitewashed walls. Three lamps burned dimly on the altar, where, typically, someone had left a box of matches and an old Lucozade bottle containing oil for the lamps. It was barely distinguishable from the chapel at the monastery on the hill, which he and Kim had visited, or from a thousand other small Greek Orthodox churches dating from the Middle Ages.

It had two particular features. The first was its part-preserved Byzantine fresco on one wall. The fresco had survived the island's four-hundred-year occupation by Ottoman Turks only because it had been plastered over at some point in history. The ancient plaster had peeled back earlier in the present century, to reveal the art treasure behind it. The gold and silver paint was still faintly luminous; the spectral figures strong and impressive.

The second feature, a much more recent embellishment, was the painting above the altar, at the point where the back wall met the ceiling, of a huge, single, unblinking eye. Presumably commissioned at some time to distract and offset the evil eye for worshippers, the painted eye gazed back with disconcerting severity. Dizzying lines of turquoise, sable and black radiated from the eye, and these lines commanded the upper space of the back wall. Whatever intention lay behind its commission, its presence was not at all comforting.

Mike found himself examining the fresco, if only to look away from the oppressive, all-seeing eye. He was able to trace in it some kind of obscure narrative until a figure in the mural pulled him up short. The burning eyes were unmistakable, as was the shaven head. If he needed any further confirmation, it was there in the two sinister hooded figures drawn either side of him, and in the metal shoes. St Michael, the angel-militant, bearing a heavy staff, looked directly out from the painting.

It was impossible! The fresco was over six hundred years old, but here was an accurate representation of the man who had thrashed him on the mountain road. Mike couldn't tear his eyes away from the figure. True, he had ducked into the church earlier in the season, but not for more than half a minute: he had never inspected the mural closely enough for the picture to lodge even in his unconscious memory.

He felt dizzy. His vision swam.

If you see the saint on the path to Kamari, kill him. The words echoed within him, as from hidden chambers. He wiped a bead of sweat from his brow. The church became dank and oppressive; the eye burned into him from the ceiling. He felt a wave of nausea; then anger and confusion.

His thoughts were muddled as he made to leave the place. At the door he made the mistake of looking back. The eye seemed to summon him, to command him to return. A taste of bile rose in his throat. There was a terrible throbbing tension in his head. He turned in dizzy confusion back to the mural. The image of the saint loomed large in front of him. The space around him receded. A hot shiver chased across his skin like a livid rash and a feeling of hatred burned in him. He recalled the humiliation and pain of his beating, and thought of the piles of metal shoes; of Greek incense and Tuscan knives, and the horrors of this outrageous religion. His trembling hand fumbled in his pocket, guided by the spirit of his anger. Rage possessed him as he pulled a penknife from his pocket. He opened it and scratched a deep X across the face of the angel-militant.

He mouthed an obscenity. The knife scored into the white plaster behind the painting, stabbing at the fresco until the head of the figure was thoroughly defaced. The tension drained out of him. The act of vandalism was a moment of instantaneous catharsis.

Then he was instantly mortified by what he had done. His hand flew to his head. He looked to the door. There was no one there, but it occurred to him how easily he might have been caught. He put away the knife. *Jesus! I've just vandalised a fucking thirteenth-century fucking priceless fucking Byzantine mural!* He knew that if he'd been caught he would have been horsewhipped.

He got out quickly, his hair clenched tightly in his hand. He picked up the water container and walked swiftly towards his car, muttering to himself, 'Noooo, no, no.'

'Mike, how are you? How is the arm?'

It was Kati, carrying some post, coming towards him. 'Here. I saw your car and I picked up this letter for you from the post office. Mike, are you not well?'

He felt dizzy with shame. 'No. I'm sick. Excuse me, Kati, I have to go home.'

'Yes, go home. Here, take this letter.'

He reached the car and hoisted the water container on to the back seat. Then he got in and doubled up, clutching his stomach and groaning, repeating over and over, 'Thirteenth fucking century fucking Byzantine fucking irreplaceable . . .' Finally he pulled himself together enough to drive home.

He parked the car and carried the water along the beach path, muttering to himself. A rowing boat had been upturned on the beach for repainting. Its underside had been partially daubed blood red. Someone had abandoned the task halfway, and the paint looked viscous and sticky in the heat. The careless painter had managed to splash paint all over the stones around the vessel. A large pot of red paint had been abandoned next to the boat, its lid only loosely replaced. Along the path, swallowtail brimstone butterflies were out in profusion, but Mike didn't see them.

'What's wrong?' said Kim when he got back.

'Nothing. Here's a letter for you. I've got a splitting headache. I've got to go and lie down.'

'It says Nikkie's coming.'

Mike's heart sank. 'When?'

'Tomorrow, according to this letter. We'll have to go to the airport to collect her.'

'We? I don't fancy the drive. She's your friend. You go.'

'She says she's left Chris.'

'Again.'

'You've never liked her, have you?'

'No.'

'Because she's a feminist.'

'Not because of that. Put it like this, she's the kind of feminist who wears her cunt on her sleeve.'

'Be kind, Mike.'

But Mike was having difficulty being kind even to himself. He'd recovered from the shock of what he'd done, but not sufficiently to be able to confess it to Kim. He would, eventually, but it was too soon. Might it not have seemed so mindless an act of vandalism had he not himself been a lover of history, art and the museum object? He felt like the anonymous British tourist who had desecrated a visitors' book at a nearby German war memorial with the words: 'FIRST WAR SECOND WAR TWO-NIL FUCK YOU'.

They sat on the patio under the vine canopy. He was sipping a glass of ouzo, she was reading a fat paperback that had at some time been dropped in the water.

'Kim, before I went into the village, what made you say that thing about the saint?'

'Uh?'

'The saint. When you shouted to me.'

'What thing?' She carried on reading.

'You said: *If you see the saint on the path to Kamari, kill him.*'

She looked up. 'Did I?'

'Yes.'

'I don't remember. I might have said it.'

'It had the sound of a classical quotation. Or Biblical. I wondered where it came from.'

'There was a TV programme in the sixties called *The Saint*. Maybe I got it from that.'

'Don't fuck!'

'Hey! What are you getting angry about? I don't even remember saying anything!'

'Sorry.'

'You're getting too hot. Go and have a swim.'

It was a good idea. Mike drained his glass and strapped on his plastic sandals to protect his feet from the spines of sea urchins. Then he ran down to the water with a roar, causing a splashing and a commotion that was an affront to the sleepy afternoon. Kim shook her head and went back to her book.

Mike dunked his head and opened his eyes under the milky-green sea. His ears plugged with water. Time was suspended in a green jelly: fronds drifted by; urchins anchored themselves to the sea bed; he could see two miraculously tiny sea horses, like question marks, drifting around a waving anemone, disproportionately large eyes in translucent skeletal frames; the entire life of the ocean muted into a distant, dull rumble. Then he surfaced again, coming up like a whale, water rolling from his head, the light dazzling, the heat of the afternoon almost a roar in his ears. But the memory of his vandalism in the church hadn't disappeared, as he'd hoped it might.

He cleared his nostrils and his ears of water, looking back at the house. The sky suddenly creased, as if buckling under weight, and his mouth opened in an involuntary enunciation of words. He heard a voice not unlike his own say: *But you were right to do it.*

What? What was that he had said? And where had the thought come from? As if there was a part of his mind with a life of its own, a green-jelly world with miraculous creatures moving on a different timescale, obeying alternative laws of nature, attending on other values. The crease in the sky had gone: it was regular impenetrable cloudless blue.

His skin prickled with the salt. The oracle.

After failing to win Eurydice back from the under-world, Orpheus was hacked to pieces on the mainland by the women of Thrace. His head was cast into the sea where, alone with his lyre, it washed up on the rocks of the island. Here it continued to speak oracles.

The talking head. What if it wasn't a particular place? What if the island itself was the oracle?

That was it! He staggered out of the water and ran up the beach.

'Kim! Kim, listen! I've just understood something! Kim, listen!'

Kim was dozing. She blinked at him.

'Yes yes yes. You see it's here. We're sitting on it.'

'What are you talking about, Mike?'

'It explains everything! This place. Why these strange things keep happening. Things I haven't even told you about.'

'Calm down, Mike. You're not making any sense!'

'It doesn't speak *to* us.'

'It doesn't?'

'No!' Mike swatted the air. 'It speaks *through* us.'

He was trembling with the force of this idea. His face was flushed and his pupils blazed huge in his eyes. He was manic. Kim regarded him with some concern. She got up. 'I'll make us a drink.'

Mike followed her under the vine canopy, sat down, stood up again and marched over to the water pump; here he cranked the handle a few times to no apparent purpose, spilling water across his feet. He turned to find Manoussos watching him from the gate. They stared at each other for longer than was comfortable.

'I came at a bad time,' said Manoussos.

'It's all right.'

'No, I come again another time.'

'Manoussos!' Kim came up behind Mike. 'We're just having coffee.'

The shepherd looked slightly bewildered as he was towed up the garden path by his arm. He was pressed into a seat under the vine. Kim laid out olives and sliced tomatoes and sticks of cucumber, and white bread still fragrant from the baker's. Mike sat drumming his fingers on his knee.

'Mike loves the Turkish bath!'

'The bath!' said Mike too loudly.

'It's good?'

'My bruises. One hundred per cent better already.'

Manoussos nodded thoughtfully. 'Per cent,' he repeated.

'I want to go again today.'

The shepherd held up a hand in admonition. 'Please. Not too much.'

'Sugar?' said Kim.

'Do you know any stories of this coastline?' asked Mike.

'*Gliko*. Very sweet. Stories?'

'Legends. History. Folk tales.'

Manoussos slurped his coffee. 'I don't understand.'

'Something to eat?' offered Kim.

'What do people say about this strange place?'

'Just a little. Yes, it is strange.'

'So there are stories?'

'I don't know any stories.'

They all became quiet. The shepherd sucked at his enormous grey moustache. His clothes carried a faint, milky odour of goat or sheep.

'Were you born here, Manoussos?' asked Kim.

'Yes.' He pointed beyond Kamari. 'My father was an old man when I was a boy. That land over there he fought for with a pistol, after they threw all the Greeks out of Turkey. He lost everything. So he became a shepherd. Here.'

Mike pointed in the opposite direction. 'Do you know anything about the man who stands watching?'

Manoussos looked away, but not in the direction Mike pointed.

Mike was insistent. 'You must see him every day. He stands on the edge of the rock, looking across the water.'

Manoussos shuffled uncomfortably.

'Mike,' said Kim.

'No, over there,' Mike persisted. 'I'd like to talk to him. I've a feeling he could tell me something about the island.'

'Mike!'

He suddenly became aware that Kim was telling him to shut up. He hadn't until that moment realised the depth of the shepherd's discomfort at his questions. Now he felt foolish, and a little dizzy, and it left him wringing his hands. Kim filled the air with smoothing talk about life in Britain. Manoussos had seen sheep dogs on Greek television. He was interested in the idea of such dogs, who worked in the fields, and of their owners, who spoke to them through a sequence of whistles. It seemed incredible to him. A kind of magic.

When Manoussos got up to leave, they both followed him to the gate. Here he turned and said to Mike, 'The man you speak of, looking out to sea from the hill: he is crazy. But if you want to speak with him, I will take you to him.'

'I'm sorry,' Mike stammered, 'I didn't want to cause any problems . . .'

'It's not a problem.'

'I shouldn't have asked.'

'Tomorrow. In the morning, when I pass by this way, you will come with me. We will go across the hills. We will walk with the gods.' He flung his arm in the air, and turned his back. '*Yia!*'

Leaving Mike and Kim to gaze after him.

'Walk with the gods?' said Mike.

Kim was frowning. 'That's neatly got you out of meeting Nikkie at the airport.'

14

The watcher on the ridge was up early and looking out to sea. Mike had checked. The grey, immobile figure was as reliable as a weather vane.

Mike was ready in the morning when Manoussos came by with his flock. The shepherd had a canvas bag over his shoulder. He looked somewhat sullen, as if he'd had a bad night's sleep; though Mike would come to recognise this as his normal aspect. His gruff, stoical appearance and huge bristling moustache hid an occasionally jaunty spirit and a surprising gymnasticism of the mouth. Manoussos had a habit of pursing or reshaping his lips before delivering his verdict on any given subject. He did so now as he looked out to sea.

'Storm later,' he pronounced. Mike looked for signs, mackerel clouds, distant haze, movements on the water, anything, but saw none. The shepherd nodded fiercely and set off along the beach behind his flock. Mike followed at his elbow. By making sucking noises with his cheeks the shepherd steered the animals up into the hills behind the house. They seemed to know where to go, and though he occasionally tapped them lightly with his traditional shepherd's crook, he hardly needed to use it.

Up in the hills he drove the sheep one by one through a

hole in a rough hedge. He dragged a desiccated bush of bleached twigs into the gap and seemed content to leave his flock to graze.

'Now,' he said, gesturing up the hill, 'we walk with the gods.'

They followed a sheep track through the thin scrub and the grey-green cushions of saxifrage and clumps of sage. Brilliant pink clusters of aubretia leaked like ichor from the clefts in the bone rock. A pair of goshawks wheeled above them, and Mike trod the single-hoof-width path carefully, puzzling over Manoussos' words.

Manoussos stopped and made a silent gesture with his hands, of wafting scents into his nostrils. Mike pantomimed deep breaths, filling his lungs with the rich, snuff-like compound of spice, rock flowers and warm dust. The shepherd nodded his approval before proceeding.

They dropped through a diagonal path and reached a further outcrop of rock where another flock of animals was grazing. They were perhaps sheep of another species, or more precisely goats; it was difficult to tell exactly, since they resembled neither Manoussos' flock of sheep nor the English variety of goats. Mike learned the use of a shepherd's crook when in a sudden movement it was hooked around the neck of one of the creatures and dragged in by the shepherd. He had spotted a wound on the flank of the goat, and he painted the wound with something like iodine from a bottle.

'Are these also your animals?'

Manoussos nodded gruffly, scanning the flock with keen eyes. At last he seemed satisfied, and waved Mike on. Mike plunged across the hill, but Manoussos summoned him back.

'No!' he called. He was pointing at the animal track which rolled on down the diagonal. 'With the gods.'

Mike looked at him and realised he'd misunderstood the Greek's accent. He was being invited to walk the path of the goats, *the gots*, not with the gods at all. He laughed out loud. Manoussos wanted to know what was funny. Mike tried, but the irony didn't communicate.

Manoussos simply looked puzzled and said again, 'Yes, we walk the way of the gots.'

The incline began to flatten out and they came to a field, knee-high with thin, parched yellow grass. Manoussos stopped him. 'Please. Be careful. Walk exactly behind me, because this field, it calls to the snakes.'

'Snakes?'

'Many snakes. Only be careful.'

Manoussos went ahead, using his crook before him like a minesweeper. After a few yards Mike heard a rustle in the grass, and another, but saw nothing. Then he saw the grass wave in serpent motion as another snake sped from the outstretched crook. Suddenly snakes were zipping all around, detectable only by the frantic swish and sudden lash of grass stalks.

'Jesus!'

'Many today,' Manoussos said quietly, making slow progress through the grass.

The field was alive. Mike felt his skin prickle and was seized by a momentary paralysis, in which for an instant he had a clear impression of looking down on himself and the shepherd from a height of about twelve feet. He could see his frozen self, and Manoussos moving forward slowly, sweeping his crook through the grass. The departing snakes left tracks through the grass, tracks which seemed to inscribe clearly identifiable shapes and symbols before

117

fading. The symbols were letters of the Greek alphabet: here a Greek omega, here a sigma, there a lambda, mu, nu, pi, rho, here an omicron.

The snakes were spelling out words in the Greek alphabet, words of arcane order, language beyond Mike's literacy and comprehension. Mike felt a wave of panic as the alphabetical shapes multiplied in the grass and faded. Then he heard the shepherd's voice, as if from a distance.

'Don't fear.'

Mike was called back into his body, and the shepherd's words were enough to move him on. The number of creatures darting from the crook was diminishing, until they ceased entirely. Manoussos straightened his back and moved forward with more confidence. At last they reached the edge of the grassy field. Mike sighed with relief.

'We came through the centre of them,' said Manoussos.

'I was afraid.'

Manoussos stopped and turned. 'Yes. I felt the grip of your fear. You let it take you . . .' Here his words trailed off and he waved a hand skywards.

'Why were there so many?'

'I told you. This place, it calls to the snakes.'

'What do you mean by it calls them?'

'It calls them. They like to come.'

'Why?'

Manoussos hacked at a blade of grass with his crook. He made sucking noises with his mouth and pushed out his lips. Then, impatiently, he said, 'Not everything in this world has a why.' He turned away and began to make a path up another rocky slope of loose rust- and red-coloured chippings. 'Mikalis,' it was the first time he had used Mike's name in the Greek form, 'Mikalis, you are like a lovely child. Always why why why. Ha! Ha ha ha!'

Mike didn't mind. It was the first time he had heard the Greek laugh out loud. In any event, there was a fatherly tenderness in his manner. They made slow progress up the slope, and every few minutes Manoussos would pause to turn his head, making his moustache dance on his lip before repeating softly, 'Why why why.' Then he would laugh before proceeding further up the hill.

They reached the brow of the hill and Mike was surprised when the abandoned monastery hove into view, like a ship appearing from behind a rock. They crossed the apron of land between the courtyard and the descent to the sea, and Mike sat under the fig tree outside the tiny, locked church. He was sweating heavily. The clapperless bell resonated with dry heat. He took a swig of bottled water. Manoussos also took a mouthful but declined to sit.

'The man isn't here,' said Mike.

'He will come.'

Manoussos stepped over to one of the dusty cells. He reached up and took something from a ledge behind the lintel stone. It was the key to the church. He unlocked the church and pushed open the door without going inside, as if the entire purpose of their journey had been to give the place some air and a little light. Then he walked out of the courtyard, and when he returned Mike noticed that the canvas shoulder bag had been emptied.

Mike went inside the church just to appreciate the cool. The light from the open door fell on the framed painting on the wall. There was the wretched thief stealing from the garden, shot by the monk's arrows. It was strange subject matter. He remembered the old lady present on their first visit who had tried to explain something about the painting. Manoussos saw Mike studying the painting. He seemed not to want to come inside, and he spoke from the doorway.

'It is the hermit, Agios Ionnou. He lived in the cave below. Have you seen it? He steal from the garden and those monks – they kill him.'

'He lived in that cave? So it was a real event?'

'Real? Of course it was real.'

'When?'

'When when when. I don't know when.'

The painting itself was perhaps a hundred years old, or less. But the event it depicted could have happened a thousand years ago, if indeed it had happened at all. Why would the Christian monks slay a Christian hermit who was living in the cave not far from the monastery? Not for a handful of olives.

'I want to take a look at the cave.'

When Kim and Mike had visited the monastery before, Kim had been in too much of a hurry to swim to want to explore the cave. The path from the monastery wound down perhaps two hundred feet before it passed the gaping jaws of the cave. Scooped out of black rock glistening with damp, the cave went back a considerable distance. Even from the outside it was possible to discern within its gloomy interior the broken-tooth shapes of fat stalactites. One side of the cave was dry, the other half dripping with the still-forming, already man-sized structures. They were numerous, a crowd of brutish subhuman figures steadily evolving. The unceasing drip from the hanging formations created the only sound.

One of the clump formations had been converted into a primitive shrine. The usual little compendium of matches, brown wax candles, oil and empty retsina bottles stood on a dry table of rock, itself once formed by the dripping limestone. A single eye had been crudely painted on the wall with distemper.

'Do people come here, Manoussos?'

'Sometimes. It's very old. One time a professor comes here from Frankfurt and he speaks to me. He says this was a cave of Artemisa. Old religion.'

'Artemis? It's probably true. She was worshipped in caves. Then early Christians liked to colonise the old sites of worship for their own religion.'

'Shall we go? I don't like this place.'

'Why's that?'

Manoussos flicked back his head. 'I just don't like it.'

They returned to the monastery. As they were approaching the courtyard, Mike heard a low murmuring, a rhythmic, steady chanting. It was coming from somewhere behind the yellow decaying walls of the church.

'He is here,' said Manoussos.

They went behind the church, where a man was sitting cross-legged on the grass. His eyes were closed, and his head beat gently back and forth in time to the soft wailing issuing from his lips. It was indiscernible as Greek or anything else. Perhaps it was a prayer, or a hymn or a chanted mantra; Mike thought so because the man was dressed in the rags of an Orthodox priest's robes. Faded to grey and hanging in strips from his legs, the robes had been patched and sewn many times. He wore no priest's stovepipe hat: his hair fell halfway down his back and his iron-grey beard completely obscured the lower half of his face. A large nose protruded from under the fringe of his wild, unkempt hair.

He seemed to be aware of the presence of the two of them, but he continued to rock gently as he chanted, occasionally lapsing almost into silence but always returning to his chant. Beside him lay a small pile of provisions: a large piece of goat's cheese wrapped in greaseproof paper;

two loaves of bread; dry biscuits; olives; pieces of fruit; a jar of oil. Mike guessed these things had been the contents of Manoussos' canvas bag.

Manoussos sat on the floor near to the hermit, and Mike followed his lead. At last the man stopped chanting and opened his eyes. He pointed a finger at Mike and said some words in Greek. His eyes were brilliant. They were like the sunlight on the sea, sparkling from within his dirty, weather-ravaged, crumpled-leather face. He smiled, and resumed chanting softly.

'What does he say?'

'He says God is coming,' said Manoussos. 'He asks if you know that God is coming.'

The chanting continued, then the hermit abruptly switched his rhythm. Now he seemed to be almost whimpering. He moved his head back and forth, as if conducting an argument with unseen spirits.

'He lives here all the time?'

'In the monastery. In the cave. He is crazy.'

'And you and other people from Kamari bring him food?'

Manoussos made an almost imperceptible shrug. It signalled yes, but it also meant he thought nothing of it. Without warning, the hermit scrambled forward and pressed a greasy hand on Mike's forehead. Mike was alarmed, but Manoussos only laughed. The hermit spoke rapidly.

'He says you have been touched by the saint.'

'What?'

'He says the saint came to you.'

'My car accident! He's talking about my car accident!'

'He wants to know if when the saint came, he came as an angel or as a demon.'

'What? I mean, he beat the shit out of me. He must have been a demon.'

'*Daimon*,' Manoussos said to the hermit.

The hermit took his hand from Mike's head and nodded sagely before speaking.

'He said he too saw the saint. But he was a demon who wanted to beat him, so he ran away and hid in the cave below.'

Mike looked at the hermit, who was nodding vigorously at a translation he couldn't possibly understand. Then the man closed his eyes again, and resumed his whimpering, monotonous chanting.

'I told you; he is crazy.'

Mike looked at the demented figure rocking gently back and forth. Certainly this was not going to be the man who would help him with his search for the mysteries of the Orphic oracle. Mike got up to leave. Manoussos followed, but before he did so, the hermit grabbed his hand and kissed the back of his wrist. Then he shouted something at Mike.

'God is coming,' said Manoussos. 'He said to tell you that God is coming.'

15

Kim reached the airport before dusk, in time to see the jet aircraft land. The plane bounced. There was a crescendo of squealing brakes. The air around the terminal was sullied with a smell of fuel and melted tyre rubber. Watching from the fence beside the runway, she spotted Nikkie in the line of white-skinned British tourists breaking rank across the hot tarmac towards the arrivals shed.

The cool of evening failed to penetrate the airport buildings. The shed purporting to be an arrivals hall was steamy with perspiring pink-skinned British tourists waiting to step on to the return flight. The single giant fan bolted to the ceiling and rotating sluggishly did nothing to relieve the claustrophobic atmosphere or spur on the ministrations of the lethargic, blue-shirted Greek officials. Kim chose to wait outside, sitting on a stone until Nikkie came out.

Nikkie had left Chris, the letter had explained, *for good*. Kim doubted it. Nikkie had on two previous occasions left her husband for good before returning to him, presumably for bad. Kim's loyalties were divided. They had all known each other from around the same time. Kim had been a student nurse when Nikkie had tried to recruit her into a group with the impressive title of Radical Midwives. Chris was a trainee medic. They had met at a party. Kim had witnessed Chris go – literally – weak at the knees at the sight of Nikkie. He'd interrupted their talk, aggressively, to ask for a definition of a Radical Midwife. Twelve years on – and this was part of his problem, according to Nikkie – he still didn't understand what she was talking about.

Neither did Kim ever really understand what a Radical Midwife might aspire to be, but it seemed to Nikkie less important for Kim to understand than for Chris.

Thinking she was being patronised, Kim had once challenged this. 'Why?'

'Because he's a fucking doctor,' Nikkie had snarled.

The letter hadn't specified why Nikkie had left Chris this time, though it hardly needed to. Kim had heard it before. Chris didn't beat her; he wasn't a compulsive skirt-chaser; he rarely drank anything stronger than mineral water; he wasn't a drug addict or a compulsive gambler. Indeed, his weak knees had never hardened since the original encounter at the party. According to Nikkie, however, his faults were much more insidious – and fundamentally dishonest – than any of those things.

'He oppresses me with his intelligence.'

'It's as bad as that, is it?' Kim had said drily.

Kim saw Nikkie emerge from the shed, casting around anxiously. She was clutching a battered leather suitcase. On spotting Kim she dropped the case and grabbed her friend as if the airport was the open sea and Kim was a passing piece of driftwood.

'My God, I thought you hadn't come! I was about to turn around and go home! Thank God you're here, Kim!'

'Of course I'm here! How are you, Nikkie?'

Nikkie was trembling. 'Relaxed! For the first time in years I feel really relaxed. I've found the courage to leave him and now I can feel truly relaxed.'

Kim's heart sank. 'You look great.'

'That's because I'm . . . It's because I'm *focused*. I am. I feel focused, for the first time in ages.'

Kim picked up her suitcase and carried it to the car. Nikkie was still talking. 'I'm vibrating from the flight. Is it me or is this whole island vibrating? It's the aircraft, isn't it? It's just that I'm so sensitive to vibration, it leaves me shaking for hours afterwards . . .'

She was like a lighted firework. To damp it a little, Kim suggested they call in at a taverna on the way back. Before they reached the taverna Nikkie made her stop the car so that she could get out and be sick by the side of the road.

'Oh God,' she said as she climbed back into the passenger seat. Kim proffered a tissue and Nikkie wiped her mouth. 'I think I was sick on a frog.'

The roadside taverna was empty apart from them. The waiter called them beautiful ladies and made a great fuss. Nikkie saw off half a bottle of wine in under five minutes.

She was a tired beauty; a tall ash-blonde with hungry lioness eyes set inside a delicately crumpled package of smile lines. On good days her figure was seductively reed-like, on others, dangerously thin. She paraded the shape of a catwalk model – to the envy of thousands of women – but in her own eyes her virtues were always diminished.

Breasts. She had no breasts to speak of. Along with most other adolescent girls she had developed the self-conscious habit of folding her arms and rounding her shoulders to disguise the burgeoning – or late development – of female glands. Unlike most women, Nikkie had never outgrown the habit. She usually sat with arms folded, walked with arms folded and could even – by supple exercise of the wrist or by pinning the spine to a table with a little finger extended before her – read a book with arms folded. In the odd moments when she fell into silence, her eyes might inadvertently fall on Kim's exemplary chest: not in envy or admiration, or even desire, but in a spirit of genuinely horrified bafflement at the arbitrary dispensations of nature.

'What will you do?' said Kim.

The taverna was surrounded by an olive grove. Electrical wire snaked between the branches to light red and blue and yellow bulbs. A violet light under the taverna window was part of a machine to attract and electrocute insects.

'I might not go home,' said Nikkie as a large moth crackled and fried in the violet-light machine. 'I might just stay on here after the week is up. How's Mike?'

'He's fine; though he had an accident and broke his arm. Today he's gone off with a shepherd.'

'He must have been disappointed he couldn't come and meet me.'

'He likes you, Nikkie; even though you don't get along, he does like you.'

'Where do you find the *time* to be so *kind* to people?'

Kim was accustomed to Nikkie's habit of lacing flattery with criticism. She assessed her friend in the unflattering light of the coloured bulbs. The woman had such voracious needs. She hoped they would be able to give her a holiday from herself. 'Shall we go?'

'One more glass. Where's that handsome waiter?'

The young waiter came over. Nikkie folded her hands under her chin and ordered another drink. She smiled at him. She had a trick with her eyes: like a motorcar's powerful headlamps, she could set her eyes on dipped or beam. She gave him full beam.

Encouraged, the waiter pulled up a chair and sat down.

His English was execrable, but he tried. 'Where from? *Deutsch? Ingliz?*'

Nikkie switched to dipped. She leaned forward fractionally. 'My friend and I have much to talk about. We don't want your company. Go AWAY!'

The waiter grinned stupidly. He glanced at Kim, who was looking away. When he looked back at Nikkie, he got the message. He stood, picked up his tray and spun on his heels.

'Who the hell do they think they are?' demanded Nikkie.

'He's just a boy,' said Kim.

Another insect crackled as it was electrocuted on the violet light.

16

Kim had made arrangements for Nikkie to stay in a comfortable but modest hotel in Kamari village. Nikkie had acted wounded.

'But I thought I'd be staying with you!'

'There's no room; and believe me, you wouldn't like to share the floor with the scorpions.'

The little fat woman at the family Hotel Apollo made a great fuss of Nikkie, patting her cheeks, bustling round her, showing her to an irreproachable room overlooking the illuminated Church of the Virgin. She was magnificently indifferent to Nikkie's sulky pout and tight-folded arms.

'It's not expensive, Nikkie!'

'It's not the money. I don't want to be on my own.'

'You're not going to be on your own. You'll be with us every minute. This is just for sleeping. You can unpack later. We've arranged to have dinner in the village.'

When Kim parked the Renault in the village *platia*, Mike was already at a table with Kati and Vassillis. It had been Kim's idea to invite others along: she thought it might take some of the stiffness out of the reunion. Mike and Nikkie always behaved like two people who had given each other offence, in a way mysterious to all concerned. Nikkie showed no eagerness to get out of the passenger seat.

I'm not having this all week, thought Kim. She leaned over and grabbed Nikkie by the chin. 'The Greeks don't like people to be miserable.' Nikkie's eyes welled; she looked like a child about to cry. Then she reset her features on brilliant and got out of the car.

'Right. Let's go.'

'That's better,' said Kim, leading her over to the table.

And Nikkie was charming. She blazed goodwill. When Mike stood up to greet her she hugged him in a way that surprised even the Greeks; she took Kati's hand in both of hers and remarked on how healthy everyone looked; she allowed Vassillis to kiss her own hand in a gallant gesture. She showed great interest in Kati and Vassillis, encouraging them with clever questions and listening to their replies as if they were the last Greeks on earth. When the waiter came she quietly ordered a bottle of champagne and five glasses, and showed no bad grace at all at what came instead. She poured the sparkling wine herself and offered a toast to old friends and new.

When Vassillis ordered an array of shared dishes for everyone, Mike noted, she encouraged this manly formality. When Kati spoke of her work with the village women's co-operative, Kim observed, her admiration was as sincere as spring water.

'Your friend is wonderful,' Kati whispered to Kim, when Nikkie was turned to Vassillis, headlamps on full, '*sympathitikos*.'

'Yes. She is.'

'Hey!' said Mike. 'I saw Lakis on my way here. He's got a huge piece of sticking plaster on his head. He seemed to be avoiding me!'

'Try some *spanokopita*,' Kati said to Mike, forking a piece of the pie into his mouth.

'Drink!' said Vassillis, tapping Mike's glass with his own.

'Who's Lakis?' Nikkie wanted to know.

'Our landlord. Wonder what he's been up to?'

'Order another bottle of wine, Mike,' suggested Kim.

'He sounds a rogue,' said Nikkie.

'What is rogue?' said Vassillis, and when Kati flashed him a look he got out of his chair and shouted, 'Here's to everyone! *Yia mas!*'

'*Yia mas!*' they all said, clinking glasses.

'Can anyone stand up and shout *Yia mas*?' Nikkie wanted to know.

More food arrived. 'At any time,' said Kati.

'So tell us what you did today, Mike,' said Kim.

'I heard you ran off with a shepherd,' said Nikkie.

'A shepherd?' said Vassillis.

'I didn't *run off* with a shepherd. I went to look at the monastery with a shepherd.'

'What shepherd?'

'Manoussos the shepherd,' Kim said to Vassillis.

'You went with Manoussos the shepherd?'

Kati had a piece of meat caught between her teeth; she made a great fuss of finding a toothpick.

'Yes,' said Mike. 'It was an interesting day.'

'What did he say, this Manoussos?'

Kim thought Kati looked a little pale.

'Not much; he doesn't say much.'

'These prawns are beautiful,' shrieked Kim. She speared one and held it out for Vassillis to bite. 'Try one of these, Vassillis! Where is the lemon? Give Vassillis the lemon!'

'Who wants more wine?' shouted Mike. 'Where's the waiter?'

'He's crazy,' Vassillis said through a mouthful of prawn.

'Not so crazy as the hermit on the hill.'

'Who's the hermit on the hill?' slurred Nikkie.

'Eat! Eat!' implored Kati. 'Don't talk! Eat!'

'Someone fill Nikkie's glass,' ordered Kim, seeing Vassillis with the bottle in his hand.

'Here's to the smell of Greece!' Nikkie waved her glass in the air.

'How do we smell?' Vassillis, wiping a few drops of Nikkie's spilled wine from his arm, wanted to know.

'Yes,' said Kati, 'how do we smell?'

Nikkie thought for a moment. A few heads turned from other tables, momentarily alarmed by the group's sudden lapse into calm.

'A Greek island,' said Nikkie, 'smells of salt water; and of sage and wild oregano; and of hot olive oil from the tavernas; and pine leaves from the hills; and goat—'

'Definitely goat,' Vassillis put in.

'—and dead seaweed; and wine; and naphthalene—'

Kati blinked. 'Mothballs,' said Kim.

'—and charcoal; and sulphur. I like it all.'

'Sulphur,' said Mike. 'Yes, sulphur.'

'Sulphur?'

'Yes. Leaking from the ground. Maybe something to do with the volcanic activity. Like at the hot bath.'

'You found the hot bath?' said Vassillis.

'Manoussos showed us.'

'What does he say? What does Manoussos say?'

Kati looked agitated again. Kim, at least, noticed.

'He says it's good for you.'

'Maybe two or three times a year it's good. But it's radioactive.'

'Radioactive?' Mike and Kim chimed together.

'Yes. And it makes you crazy, that place.' Vassillis let his head loll forward, like someone intoxicated.

'Manoussos told me he goes there once every two weeks.'

'That's what I say. Manoussos is crazy. A crazy shepherd.'

'Has everybody stopped eating?' said Kati.

Vassillis tugged Mike by the sleeve and spoke in his ear in a low voice. 'Nikkie's list of smells. It was very good. But she missed one thing. Excuse me.'

'What's that?'

'A woman's hole.'

Kati turned and stared at him, and then said something in Greek.

'I don't believe what I just heard,' said Nikkie.

'What did you hear?' said Kim.

Vassillis ignored everyone else and addressed only Mike. 'But don't you agree, Mike? Down at that place, the hot bath. This is the smell of that place.'

'Well—'

'What's he talking about?' Kim wanted to know.

'Don't ask,' said Nikkie.

'Well, he's right. I was trying to place it the other day, and I have to admit . . .'

'Watch him. He's become thoroughly Greek,' said Nikkie. 'Scratch a Sensitive New Age Guy and you'll find a SNAG.'

'What?' said Vassillis.

'Chauvinist bacon.'

'Here we go,' said Mike.

'Don't get into it,' said Kim.

'I'm surprised we lasted this long.'

'We need your consent to speak, do we, Mike?' said Nikkie.

Vassillis, bewildered but aware he'd unwittingly tripped

a switch, raised his glass aloft. 'Anyway. For all the good smells of the island. *Yia mas!*'

'*Yia mas!*' everyone said in hollow unison.

'Look,' said Kati. 'When we organise the women's co-operative, we have problems with some of the men. One man wouldn't let his wife attend our meetings. She couldn't fight him. She couldn't defy him. So we organised our meeting in the square, just outside her door while she was scrubbing her doorstep. That way she never left her house but was with us at the meeting.'

'Lovely!' said Nikkie.

'But Vassillis is not what you call "chauvinist"; and Mike also, I think not. There is always a way we woman can get around a problem.'

'Which woman was this?' Kim asked.

'Soula, who lives by the Church of the Virgin.'

'That reminds me,' said Vassillis, 'did you hear what happened in the church?'

Mike blanched. 'No. What?'

'Someone did something to the painting in the church. Very bad. The priest, everyone in the village, they are all angry now, trying to find out who did it.'

'What did they do?' asked Kim.

'They spoiled the painting. They took red paint and threw it all over a painting.'

'Red paint?' Mike shifted uneasily in his chair.

'Yes. A can of paint. Thrown all over the eye above the altar.'

'The eye?'

'Yes, the eye.'

'But who would do such a thing?' Kim exclaimed.

'Tourists maybe. Football hooligans. Or sometimes if a man in another village has an argument with the church, he wants to do something but he will be afraid to do it in his own village. So he comes to another village. Who knows?'

'Who knows?' Mike agreed.

Kim and Mike accompanied Nikkie back to her hotel. Kim went inside; Mike hung back, saying he was going to look at the church.

The door was open, admitting to a soft orange radiance within. Mike stepped inside. Numerous candles had been lit, their light attenuated by a dense cloud of incense. Mike sensed some ritual or blessing only moments old. Two stepladders and a wooden plank had been erected as scaffolding above the altar. A plastic bucket stood on the plank.

The vandalism had not completely obscured the eye. An ugly puddle of rust-coloured paint had splattered the image with obvious impact, draining towards the altar wall in a narrowing stream. A small figure in widow's black was kneeling on the plank, oblivious to Mike's presence, working ineffectually on the stain with a weak, circular application of a scrubbing brush. It seemed to Mike they must have asked the oldest woman in the village to clean up the mess.

Mike stepped back and his eyes fell on the evidence of his own private act of vandalism. Somehow he'd hoped it wouldn't be there, but the scored plaster was still fresh, like an open wound. Obviously it hadn't been noticed in the outrage over the paint attack.

An Orthodox priest came in. He wasn't the local priest, to whom Mike had spoken once or twice before. With a beard reaching halfway down his chest, this one was a huge and portly figure, intimidating in his black robes and stovepipe hat. The priest stopped abruptly in the doorway and regarded Mike with what could have been either surprise or suspicion. Mike felt himself colouring and was grateful for the cover of shadow and incense smoke. He pointed to the eye.

'Very bad. *Poly kako.*'

The priest offered no acknowledgement. The frail old woman kneeling on the plank stopped scrubbing and turned to look at Mike. Her gaze was more searching and baleful than that of the eye she'd been commissioned to clean. Mike repeated his words before squeezing through the door past the priest.

Outside he lit a cigarette and waited for Kim to come from the hotel. She was some time.

'She didn't want me to leave her. She's been sobbing and trying to get me to stay at the hotel with her.'

'It's only for a week,' Mike said glumly.

'Just be kind, Mike. Just be kind.'

17

Manoussos woke from the old nightmare with a faint cry on his lips. The sun had slipped from the zenith. A nearby goat ceased ruminating to stare at him in some surprise. The shepherd's eyes were pasted almost shut. His headscarf had slipped and he felt vaguely foolish before the animal's gaze. He sat up to toss a stone at the goat and it moved on.

He uncapped his flask and sipped warm water. He had slept too long. The old nightmare had taken hold of him, and when it had him, it would never spit him out until it was done with him.

Nightmares, Manoussos knew, sucked something vital out of you. They clung like the pads of the eight-legged fish, and they fed. What did they take? Not blood; not seed; not marrow. It was difficult to say. People thought nightmares were like ordinary dreams, bad dreams, evil dreams, but they were mistaken. A nightmare was a spirit. You couldn't see it, but it must feed, and what it needed to feed was hard to say, but when you had lost it you knew that it had gone. Something like your water content was gone after a nightmare, he knew that for certain, because he never wanted to urinate after waking from a nightmare. But it was much more than the mere draining of water; it was essence, it was spirit, *kefi*, that was stolen. He would have to dance to reclaim *kefi*. Dancing kept the nightmare away; he had not danced for some time, and that was why the old nightmare had returned.

But today he did not feel like dancing.

Not since the day the earth had trembled, and he had seen Mike the Englishman come out of the house and make an English dance in the garden. It was a curious dance, to be sure. It was a dance without balance, without focus. It was a reckless dance, expressing no suffering; but somehow, Manoussos had concluded, it had *kefi*. Yes, an Englishman's twisted kind of *kefi* – and why shouldn't the spirit of men from a cold climate be different – but *kefi* it was. This was why he liked Mike.

Mike was like a package waiting in the post office, unopened, unexamined. He had seen his spirit fly briefly, in the field of snakes, but without control. He could be taught to dance. Manoussos wondered how the Englishman kept his nightmares away.

Once, when he was in the merchant navy, Manoussos had seen a film in which an Englishman had arrived in Greece and was taught to dance by a Greek played by Anthony Quinn. It was a good film but the dancing had irritated Manoussos. It was not a proper Greek dance, this butcher's dance. It had no fire, no blood. It was a footling, childish piece of dancing.

It was his father who had taught Manoussos to dance; his father who had fought for this piece of the island with a brace of pistols. And his father had learned the dance from many generations, passing it on to their sons like a flaming torch. It could be traced back to a great-great-grandfather who was a sorcerer, his father had told him.

What a dancer his father had been! A man vicious and violent, a brute of a man, but what soul! What suffering!

What joy! What *kefi*! When he danced he was beautiful, always. His father had told him that a dancer was a flag on a pole, able to summon its own wind.

Not like that, Manoussos! The dance must not be soft, not limp! Call up your own wind, Manoussos! Let the wind run through you and guide you in the dance!

It grieved Manoussos that he would have no son to whom he could pass on the dance. It was a hurtful thing. But he hoped that Mike might one day ask him to teach him to dance. Then the English at least would know a proper Greek dance; and he would have corrected the error of this popular film.

'Hey!' Manoussos called to the goat. It stopped chewing and looked up at him. 'Fuck Zorba! You hear what I say? Fuck Zorba!' The animal, unimpressed, went back to chewing the cud.

Then the old nightmare came back to him.

If those English knew what had happened in that house they would not want to stay there.

He took from his pocket a small bottle, tightly stoppered. It was an object he carried with him every-where. His father had shown him how to prepare it. The bottle was filled with discoloured olive oil, and immersed in the oil was a dead scorpion. Manoussos held it to the light. The scorpion turned inside the yellow-black liquid like an astronaut in a gravity-free environment. Should he ever be stung by a scorpion while in the hills, Manoussos would drink the oil. His father had sworn this was the only truly effective antidote to the scorpion's venom.

He had never been stung. He had come to see the bottle, which he had carried with him for years, as a protective talisman. It was not the drinking of the concoction which defeated the scorpions, but the magic it radiated to keep the creatures away. Magic. Did the English know about magic?

He returned the bottle to his pocket. What was it about this place? Was it the house itself? Or was it just this piece of coast? Or the entire island? Or was it the same everywhere, the whole world over?

One time there came to the island a Hindu holy man, living in the village. It was the strangest thing. An Indian holy man, with his followers all from Germany and Holland and England but no supporters from India, living for a while in Greece. The islanders learned a new word when all his young followers went around telling the villagers that the island was a *chakra*. No one was too impressed, since these people had a habit of leaving debts unpaid; and after a while, when the holy man went to live in Switzerland, the young people went home.

Whatever a *chakra* was, and Manoussos never properly understood the term, he perceived the island in a different way. His father had told him there were spirits beneath the earth, constantly wrestling for supremacy.

'Do they ever stop?' Manoussos had asked him.

'Only to copulate.' His father had roared with laughter.

'What happens then?'

'The volcano blows. The earth quakes. The sea falls on us.'

'What happens to us?'

'To us? Hmmm. Well, we die; and if we don't die, well then, each time we are taught a new dance. Come on, my little Manoussos, let us see you dance!'

Manoussos had got to be seven years old before realising what an impressive and spectacular liar his father was. He was a magnificent spontaneous liar. He'd once lied his way out of jail and into a convent of eager nuns, he claimed. He was fiercely proud of his ability to distort the truth. What a dancer and what a liar!

Manoussos came to believe that nothing was true, and that all of life's descriptions, measurements, markers, boundaries and tramlines were provisional. And though a universe of stormy disorder attended on this perception, it was a chaos in which he was able to find a quiet centre. Unlike his father, however, this fostered in him a firmness about his actions and a need for certainty in his speech. It could only resolve in a taciturn nature, whereby the ordinary commerce of human exchange was severely limited.

If he had repeated his father's stories of spirit-demons wrestling beneath the earth's crust, and the priest had roared, he never reiterated them again. Though he never gave any more or less weight to the Christian fantasies of the priests. Their stories of loaves and fishes and virgin births and the powers of the angel-militant, the island's patron saint, were no more nor less true than his father's speculations.

Manoussos' younger brother had been different. For him the intervention of the Christian gospel had stemmed their father's manias, had restored perspective and had vanquished unbearable uncertainty. He became devout, scholarly, a favourite of the priests and a closed book. Meanwhile Manoussos had remained open and unresolved, an inscrutable text wherein all things both were, and were not.

Dance and Nightmare. These were the two forces that ruled Manoussos' island, and indeed his world, his private world. They manifested themselves as spirit demons, eternally opposed, an elaboration of his father's 'earth spirits' configuration. Nightmare was the world in which the ground slipped away and anything could happen; Dance was the movement which kept the earth spinning and the glue which held the world together, focused it, bonded it, resolved it.

Manoussos knew that Nightmare didn't only come with sleep; that much he'd witnessed himself. It crept up on you in the moments when you lost awareness. Nightmare might come in bouts of drunkenness; with sunstroke; or summoned by the priests' religion. Because there *was* something there, throbbing under the skin of this damned and beautiful island, aching for relief under its hot skirts, just beneath the surface. It was a vibration. It was a drumming.

Manoussos hauled himself to his feet and readjusted his cotton headscarf. Steadying himself, he blinked into the furnace of the sun, raising one arm slowly until it was horizontal to the ground. Then he let his arm drop slightly. Guided by the vibration under his feet he began to rock gently in an unsteady gait, until he lifted his left leg and hopped to the right. Then he spun around, slapping the heel of his boot hard as he spun; stopping dead, slowing his heartbeat; and then resuming his swaying motion, he lifted an arm to point at the sun before stooping to flick the earth with his fingers.

Manoussos was dancing away Nightmare.

18

On the second night of Nikkie's visit, in the early hours of the morning, Mike woke from a bad dream. Beside him Kim turned in her sleep and slumbered on. Outside, corrosive moonlight flooded down, leaking through the slats of the battered wooden shutters like ectoplasm, moist, viscous and gem-bright. He was wide awake.

He turned on to his side, trying to slip back to the furry kingdom. Then he heard a shuffle outside.

He raised his head.

Now there was nothing audible, but there could have been no mistake. He had heard a scuffling. It was the sound of something, perhaps an animal, moving about in the hedgerow or the long grass at the side of the house.

There it was again. A shuffling and a swishing of long grasses, and a low, asthmatic wheezing. It was followed by a stifled sob.

Mike swung his legs out of bed, but hesitated before setting his bare feet on the cold, dark floor. Reaching for matches, he lit an oil lamp and replaced the glass. He made a sweep of the floor with the light before getting out of bed, pulling on his jeans and checking his shoes before slipping them on. He was careful to avoid waking Kim.

The garden was awash with chromium light. The moon

was full, a lactic gland swollen and hanging low in the clear sky, trailing a thin trickle of milky light across the calmed sea. The water was like oil.

Mike waited on the concrete patio under the vine. Everything was in place, but shining with supernatural radiance: the formica-covered dining table with its irregular chairs; the kitchen area with utensils and pans hanging above the camping stove; the cushioned bench set against the whitewashed wall; the vast painted flower pots; the queer-shaped gourds hanging from the canopy. The moon had spilled its milk everywhere; nothing was permitted to languish in the realm of the ordinary. Everything had been granted filmic intensity. Objects stood in musical proportion to each other.

It was the painting he had been looking for. It was what he had come to this country to find. Tomorrow he would begin work, set about capturing this moment.

He was still trying to internalise the spectral world of this moonlit scene when he heard another stifled sob. He turned to see what at first he took to be a bundle of clothes at the corner of the concrete patio.

'Nikkie!'

She was lying on the ground, her head slumped on the grass and one arm hooked over the corner of the raised patio. Only the upper half of her body was visible – the reason he'd initially mistaken her for a bundle of rags.

'Nikkie, what are you doing there?'

Mike hadn't seen much of Nikkie that day. Kim had taken her for a drive to the neighbouring town of Limanaki and to a picturesque sandy beach where they'd spent the entire day. Mike had been more than happy to be left alone. He'd actually set up his easel and unpacked his paints for the first time since arriving on the island.

Interesting, Kim had remarked, how a sudden urgency to work had coincided with Nikkie's arrival. Mike had had to ignore the jibe. He'd made a daub of the boat moored at the garden gate, and a couple of efforts at representing the face of his assailant in the hills. His work lacked enthusiasm, but it was a start.

In the evening they'd gone together to a taverna, where they were joined by a Dutch couple Kim and Nikkie had met on the beach. Mike talked with the Dutch, and had little interaction with Nikkie, though he'd noticed how enthusiastic a convert she was to the local grape. She'd been unsteady on her feet when they'd escorted her back to her hotel.

'She's on holiday,' Kim had said, a little sharply, when he'd commented on the fact.

She certainly was on holiday, Mike thought, crossing the patio to help her up. He assumed she was blind drunk as she lay sprawled and sobbing.

'Nikkie,' he said softly. 'Come on, Nikkie.'

She lifted her head and squinted at him. Traces of vomit were on her lips. 'You never told me,' she gulped.

'I'm sorry, Nikkie.'

'You never said anything.'

'I'm sorry.' He kneeled down to help her to her feet. But when he reached out to lift her, his movement was sharply arrested by an appalling smell which hit him like a draught.

It was an odour of rot and putrefaction, a miasma. He recoiled, his stomach quivering. She saw, and she smiled at him, her jaw hanging open. Something was terribly wrong. Now he realised why he couldn't see the lower half of her body. She was actually *buried* up to her waist in the dry soil.

'Wha . . .?'

'Help me up, Mike. Help me up.'

Mike stepped back. Nikkie let her head fall to one side, then, using her arms as levers, she pushed herself out of the soil, wheezing as she did so, hoisting herself with awkward, difficult movements. When her waist had cleared the soil Mike gagged. From her torso down Nikkie was inhuman. She was arachnid. Four pale-brown wavering limbs dragged behind her, beneath the long segmented length of a flicking scorpion's tail. The stench of her was overpowering. Her crustaceous lower half glimmered with dirty translucence in the moon's light. She was half scorpion.

She shook herself free of the soil and climbed on to the patio.

'Kim!' It came out from Mike as a strangled whisper. 'Kim!'

Kim answered from the room, 'Let me sleep.'

'God, Kim!'

But as the scorpion woman approached, Mike looked again and saw it no longer had Nikkie's face. The upper body was naked and it had the face of a woman he'd never seen before, and it spoke in German.

'I have come back,' it said. 'I have come back.'

Mike retreated. The creature moved forward, pinning him to the door by the chest. He couldn't breathe. The quivering sting coiled over her back, targeting in on him.

'KIM! KIM!'

Suddenly Kim was there, holding his face, standing naked on the patio beside him. The creature was gone. Kim's body was still warm from the bed, smelling of sleep. Mike looked around him. The moon was as hard and as glittering as a diamond. The garden was still awash with its incandescent white light.

'You've been sleepwalking, Mike.'

'Sleepwalking?'

'Sleepwalking and dreaming. It was a nightmare. A bad dream.'

'A dream.' Mike looked at the objects on the patio, the tables, the chairs, the kitchen utensils, the gourd. If it was a dream it was an exact replication of the present scenario.

'Tell me what it was.' Mike didn't want to. 'Come on. Let's go back to bed.'

Mike didn't want to do that either.

Kim suddenly became aware of the beauty of the moonlight. 'Hey! It's incredible! Look at it, Mike!'

'I've been looking at it. While I was asleep.'

Kim lit the gas stove. 'I'll make us a drink. We can go and sit in the boat. It's so beautiful!'

She pulled on some clothes and they took mugs of instant hot chocolate down to the rowing boat. She put a blanket around Mike's shoulders, and coaxed the dream out of him. He treated her to an edited version.

Kim thought for a moment, and then kissed him lightly. 'Fear of feminists,' she pronounced.

He groaned. 'I knew you'd say that.'

'Bit of misogyny coming out. You've gorra problem with women.'

Mike shook his head and smiled. 'If you say so.' He drained his mug.

They climbed out of the boat and walked slowly back up to the house. Mike got a whiff of something from his dream. He stopped on the edge of the patio.

'Smell that?'

Kim looked down the side of the house, between the hedgerow and the whitewashed wall. 'Smells like a knacker's. Something must have died down there. You'll have to check it out in the morning.'

'I will?'

'Yes, you will.'

Kim went inside and Mike looked back at the moon. It seemed to fill the sky. He went over to the spot where he'd found Nikkie in the dream. The earth was undisturbed. He shook his head again and went back to bed.

Sleep was a long time coming.

19

Mike rowed. Nikkie squatted in the rear of the boat, facing Mike. Kim sat on the prow gazing ahead, her bare legs dangling over the edge and not quite touching the water. The rowlocks on the Greek boat were set to make rowing easier from a standing position. Even with his arm in plaster Mike had insisted on taking a spell with the oars. He was stripped to his shorts, the effort causing him to break sweat. It glistened on his flexing muscles.

Nikkie appraised him coolly from the back of the boat. Mike tried to avoid her eyes, which was difficult. 'Fit,' she said. 'This man is fighting fit.'

'Ummm,' Kim said dreamily from the prow. 'It's all the swimming and the rowing. He never looked so good back home.'

'Now it's hurting,' said Mike. 'Someone take over.'

Nikkie wanted to take the oars, so they swapped positions. The vessel tilted precariously as they stepped around each other.

'It's easier if you stand up,' said Mike.

'I know how to row a fucking boat.' It was true, she did; but after a dozen strokes she conceded without a word and stood to row, tight-lipped with determination. All of the time she kept her lioness eyes on Mike, who fixed his own

151

gaze on the castle ring of Limanaki and the Turkish coastline beyond.

They were making for the rock opposite the house. The boat was loaded with barbecue equipment, snorkelling gear, wine and ready-assembled *souvlaki*. Mike had made some weak protest about wanting to paint but Kim had threatened to squeeze the paint over his head. Thus he found himself in the boat avoiding Nikkie's searching looks.

When Mike did glance back at her, he found Nikkie an inspiring figure as she stood erect in the boat stroking the oars through the water. Her skin was the colour of honey even before the Greek sun had licked at it. Her hair was tied in a Scandinavian plait, and renegade pubic hairs of the same golden colour broke ranks at the groin of her black swimsuit. Unlike Kim, Nikkie never shaved under her armpits. Beads of perspiration glistened on her armpit hair as she leaned to take the backstroke. Mike looked away again.

He was still disturbed by his dream of Nikkie as a scorpion-woman. The crooked sting was entirely visible over her shoulder as she rowed, an after-image burned into his brain. It wouldn't go away.

The mystery of the noxious smell behind the house had been solved that morning, and couldn't be blamed on Nikkie. Mike had taken a scythe and hacked his way to the rear of the house, where he found the decomposing carcass of a young fox. The fox had somehow got itself entangled in a roll of rusting wire mesh buried in the weeds. He had no idea how long it had been there, but he shovelled up the carcass, doused it with kerosene and burned it in the bin at the back of the garden which they used for incinerating rubbish.

The boat bumped and scraped against submerged boulders a few yards from the rock. Slippery velvet green weeds streamed from the rock, waving in the water.

'Easy! Easy!' Mike leapt out of the boat, guiding it between the rocks until it beached on shingle. 'Out! Out!'

Nikkie shipped her oars. 'You're so masterful.'

They unloaded the boat and set all the gear under the shadow of a rock, and spread their towels. The beach of fine yellow sand was just wide enough for three people to stretch out comfortably. Kim steeped the wine bottles in a cold rock pool, and together the three of them dragged the boat on to the shingle.

'Now we can relax,' said Mike.

'Relax if you want to,' said Nikkie. 'I'm already relaxed.'

'You're already relaxed? That's good news for all of us.'

'You two can just STOP IT NOW,' said Kim. 'And if you don't, I'm going to take the boat and leave you here together. Marooned.'

Mike held his tongue. Nikkie bit her lip.

So they installed themselves for serious sun-worshipping. Kim and Nikkie sprawled out immediately on their backs. Mike sat up, leaning on his elbow, twisting a straw of grass in his mouth and gazing back at the house, a splash of whitewash on the distant shoreline. The rocks behind the house were slightly misted, golden and mauve where the stone was visible, the humped spine of the sleeping dinosaur only a vague outline in the mist. The yellow sun pulsed.

'What's the matter?' Kim murmured to him.

'Nothing.' He lay back on his towel.

Kim stretched out between Nikkie and Mike. After a few minutes the two women took off their swimsuits. Mike kept his shorts on.

He was amazed at how differently formed were the two women. Kim's breasts were heavy, with burgundy-coloured aureoles like dark plums; Nikkie's nipples were like small amber beads. His wife's skin was moist and luscious where Nikkie's was dry like soft kid-leather, and caramel to her friend's honey gold. The variance in their bone structures might have suggested they were of different races; and where Kim's cunt seemed generously offered, like a burst fig, Nikkie's seemed buried and hidden deep in a dense jungle of hair.

'He's looking at our bodies,' said Nikkie.

'Only as a painter might,' said Mike.

'Why has your husband still got his shorts on while we're naked? It doesn't seem fair.'

'Take them off him.'

'No, you.'

'No, you.'

'You take them off him.'

'No, you take them off him.'

'All right,' said Nikkie, getting up. 'I'll hold him down, you take his shorts.' She kneeled on Mike's chest, pinning his arms before he had a chance to move. There was a murderous gleam in her eye. Kim tugged off his shorts.

The two women stepped back, giggling at him because he had a monstrous erection.

'Satisfied?' He was embarrassed, but made no attempt to cover himself.

'No,' said Nikkie, 'but we could be.'

'Go for a swim or something,' said Kim.

Mike turned over and lay on his belly, moulding his engorged cock into the hot sand under the towel. But he was painfully erect, so he took Kim's advice, wading into the sparkling aquamarine water up to his groin until the beast was subdued.

'You're starting to burn,' Kim said when he came out of the water. He lay down on his belly and she sat on his bottom to massage sun lotion into his dry skin. Then she rubbed oil into Nikkie's back, and Nikkie in turn oiled her. They lay under the baking sun, each like a culinary dish prepared for a banquet of gods.

Mike fell asleep, and when he woke the two women were talking about him in hushed tones.

'What are you saying?'

'Wouldn't you like to know?'

He felt moody and irritable. He made some snapping remark and growled about the heat. Then he staggered into the water, plunging his head into what he'd come to think of as the big green jelly. After swimming round for a few moments he came back singing and chattering and preparing the barbecue for lunch. Who was hungry? he wanted to know. Who would like wine?

'Is this the same man who went into the water two minutes ago?'

'Can't be. That one was a miserable old grouch with a sore head.'

Mike laughed and poured wine for everyone. He built a fire from driftwood and fuel they'd brought over with them, and laid out everything for the barbecue.

There were no matches to light the fire.

'I'm sure I put them in the boat,' said Kim.

'I'll go,' said Mike.

'You can't row the boat there and back,' said Kim. 'I'll go.'

Nikkie lay back on her towel and closed her eyes. 'Do you need me to come back with you?'

'I'll manage. Try to stay friends while I'm gone.'

They dragged the boat back into the sea. Kim expertly plied the oars in the water. She was gone.

'You're burning again,' said Nikkie, moments later. She came behind Mike, unstoppered a plastic bottle of sun cream and massaged some into his shoulders. Then she rubbed some into his bottom. 'Why didn't you say anything?'

'I'm sorry.'

'Sorry, huh? Where's that? There was just that bloody party, and no chance for anyone to say anything. Is that fair?'

'No.'

She got up and looked across the water. The boat was already a diminishing dot. She squatted beside him, and rolled him on to his back so she could massage oil into his chest. The oil smeared in his chest hairs. She smoothed it clear with her long, elegant fingers. Then she swung a leg across him so that she sat astride him, her bottom pressing into his groin. 'Who was that erection for?'

'Nikkie . . .'

'Who was it for? Be honest. Was it for Kim? Or for me?'

'It was for both of you.'

She squeezed herself against him and ran her fingernails along his shoulder blades. Then she leaned across and licked his lips with her tongue. She smelled of warm skin and sun lotion. These smells, and the smells of sea and sand, were strong, but the perfume of her sex overpowered all of it. He felt the tension transmitting to him through the focus of her tight little cunt; like the damp sucking pads of an octopus limb. 'How long does it take to row across?'

Mike didn't answer. At last she climbed off him and he was unable to disguise his sigh of relief.

'Bastard.' She went and stood by the water.

'What were you talking to Kim about? While I was asleep?'

'Don't worry, I didn't tell her anything. And I'm not going to; what do you take me for? She was telling me about your dream.'

'She thinks it represents a fear of people like you.'

'It was obvious what it was. You're afraid I might tell her something. Telling tales, see? The sting in the tail? While Kim wants to sleep on? Don't worry, I'll let her sleep.'

'Why did you leave Chris?'

'Not because of you.'

'Are you going back to him?'

'No. Not now. He knows about you and me for one thing.'

'For Christ's sake, Nikkie! You told him!'

'What do you expect? These things come out at unexpected moments.'

'Chris is a friend.'

'As is Kim.'

'But she doesn't know, Nikkie. She doesn't *know*.'

Nikkie came back and kneeled on the towel beside him. She put her hand on his arm. 'So you're having an adventure on a Greek island, and you and Kim can play together like children. I understand that. Have your new honeymoon. But you insult me if you think I don't understand all that. You don't have to behave as if I didn't exist for you. It happened. It's still happening, even if you pretend it's not.'

'Would you know if it stopped happening? For one of us, I mean.'

'Yes. It's a vibration. There's a sexual tension. I'd feel it if the rope went slack. I've told you; I'm sensitive to vibrations.'

There was a sound of oars labouring through the water. 'Kim,' said Mike.

'This whole island,' Nikkie said, almost to herself, 'never stops vibrating.' She went over to the bag of supplies, taking out a knife and a cucumber. She sliced two cucumber rings and lay back on her towel. Mike waded out and helped Kim with the boat. When they came back Nikkie seemed almost asleep, with two cucumber rings covering her eyes.

'Have you two been getting along?'

'Famously,' Nikkie murmured. 'I offered Mike my body while you were away, but he rather politely declined.'

Kim smiled. 'You didn't miss anything.'

Mike took the matches and lit the barbecue. He climbed the rock, looking for wild oregano to season the skewered beef. Nikkie didn't take the cucumbers from her eyes until the meal was ready. They ate a lunch of kebabs, salad, fresh bread, olives and red wine. It tasted like a meal must have tasted on the first day of Creation, if God was also a vintner.

After lunch they fell into deep lassitude. Heat hazed on the far shore. The whitewashed House of Lost Dreams rippled and distorted in the light, like a mirage. They might have fallen asleep.

'Teach Nikkie how to snorkel,' Kim said lazily.

'I know how to snorkel,' said Nikkie.

'Show her anyway, Mike.'

So Mike took Nikkie snorkelling, to show her the green-jelly world of urchins and anemones and sea horses and angel fish. Occasionally underwater they brushed hands to draw the other's attention to this or that aquatic miracle.

Kim watched them happily from the shore.

She was glad that her husband and her old friend could swim together.

20

Mike tried to explain his understanding of the myth of Orpheus to Nikkie.

'Orpheus descends to the underworld. Having charmed the lords of death with his singing, they grant him the right to return to the surface with his wife Eurydice. But he is warned not to look back at her. He almost makes it, but looks back at the fatal moment. Too late: she's turned into a pillar of salt.'

'And?'

'It's clear, isn't it? He's searching for his lost self. The conscious side descends into the unconscious, looking for the "better half" of himself.'

'His feminine side.'

'If you like. And at the last moment, as they are about to emerge into daylight, he panics and loses the object of his quest.'

'It's the sun and the moon,' said Kim. 'He's the sun, she's the moon.'

'Eh?' said Mike and Nikkie together.

The three of them were carefully treading the broken cobbled streets of a deserted village in the hills beyond Limanaki. The reclaiming speed of Nature was alarming. Kati had told them the village had only been evacuated some twenty years ago, but already the roofs had tumbled and the walls were toppled and broken with climbing weeds and the branches of fig trees. Grass had broken through the cobblestones and thick, velvet pads of moss grew on the exposed ruined walls.

In every sense, Nature seemed to have enfolded the tiny village to its bosom, reaching out with limbs of vines to pluck down stones one by one, sliding roots through cracks to undermine walls, gently drawing the best efforts of a civilisation back into the belly of the earth. Its effects were not startling; the profusion of wild flowers, the green cushions of moss, and the ochre of broken stones made nature's reclamation seem a loving gesture, a restoring act rather than a destructive one. The village had stood on a fault line, and its inhabitants were considered to be living under particular threat of earthquake; they had been moved to a new village, visible further down the valley and laid out in the lazy geometric grid of modernity.

The collapsed village seemed a monument to a momentary arrogance, only temporarily suffered to endure. The affront seemed not to the ruin of the buildings, but in the idea that they ever even existed. Now, still bearing a few mouldering possessions and rotting clothes of their former occupants, the broken buildings spoke eloquently of the transience of this fleeting life. One house had a spilled suitcase tossed in a corner of a room; another, a few plastic kitchen utensils and a broken bowl. The baker's ovens were easily discernible in one building, bricks still dusty with flour.

Kim wandered ahead, shielded from the sun by a straw hat and dark glasses. The other two followed behind, Nikkie arguing every step of the way.

'But why would Orpheus look back? Why would he? The

stupid bastard has gone into the underworld looking to recover his dead wife, right?'

'Right.'

'And he's been warned on no account to look back, or he'll lose Eurydice, right?'

'Right.' Mike was exasperated.

'So he's almost made it, and what does he do? He goes and looks back. Therefore he must have wanted to look back!'

'It's a metaphor, Nikkie! What it's saying is, you can't bring the past back to life. What's dead is dead, what's lost is lost. Eurydice is turned into a pillar of salt, which is to say the salt tears that come with crying and grieving over the past. If you want to turn it into a love story, that's what it's saying!'

'Sorry. It won't wash. It seems to me he ditched her.'

Mike laughed out loud. 'What do you mean "ditched" her?'

'He wanted to be rid of her.'

'How can you say that? It broke his heart.'

'Orpheus was a poet, right? Poets need tragedy in their work and in their lives. If he'd got Eurydice out he wouldn't have been able to be miserable. Eurydice was sacrificed on the altar of poetic tragedy.'

'Aw! Surprise, surprise. It's a feminist fable.'

'That's right.'

'You're mad.'

'You're both mad,' said Kim. They had come upon her crouched over a well. A fat stone-coloured lizard cooled itself in the cleft of a nearby wall, hoping to go unnoticed. She was looking down the smooth masonry of the shaft to the black pool at the bottom.

'What's down there?' asked Mike.

'Just your own reflection. But perfect. Like a black mirror.'

'Let's go,' said Nikkie. 'This place makes me feel sad.'

They drove the Renault along a dirt track snaking inland. Kim told Mike to stop when she spotted something through the trees. They all got out and followed her through an olive grove.

'The amazing thing about this island,' she was saying, 'is the stuff you can stumble across.'

The grove of grotesque, twisted olives gave way to a clearing. Two temple columns stood slightly higher than the trees. A number of broken columns lay on the ground, but a third erect pillar stood off at an angle to the ruined temple. It was a tiny and unspectacular Greek temple, but remarkable for its neglected condition.

'Doesn't anyone care about these things?' Nikkie said.

'There are lots of them. And no one comes out here.'

The pillars were made from rough local stone, and they bore little decoration. To label them Doric was to overstate, though they were embellished with scrollwork at their heads. Charred earth nearby betrayed a recent fire. A rusting metal shrine, of the roadside type placed by Greeks who have survived car accidents, stood in rickety defiance at the base of the pillars. There was a candle and a wine bottle inside the metal box.

'Looks like someone has tried to Christianise this site,' Mike said.

'Do you think there's still a struggle going on?' said Nikkie.

'For the soul of this island? Of course there is,' said Kim. The two looked at her. She shrugged.

Mike crossed to the lone-standing pillar and stood beneath it. The sky was on fire with pink clouds chased into spiral formations. He reached out a hand to trace the texture of the stone, but as soon as his fingertips touched the pillar, it toppled backwards. It hit the earth with a dull thud. Something went skittering from the yellow grass, heading for the cover of the trees.

The two women looked at him with astonishment.

'I hardly touched it!' Mike protested.

'It's all right,' said Kim. 'That column's been standing there two thousand years. It was due for a change.'

'I swear I hardly breathed on it.'

'Your husband,' Nikkie said, taking off her sunglasses to look at Mike, 'is a vandal.'

'A barbarian,' Kim agreed. 'An enemy to art and beauty.'

On the drive home, Mike tried to rationalise that the toppled pillar must have been casually stood on end quite recently, by some visitor to the site. But Kim and Nikkie weren't having any of it. They teased him without mercy. He was a wrecker. A philistine. A monster and a desecrator of holy places.

That night Mike dreamt he was walking through a vast temple of numberless white fluted columns. As he passed by them, the columns toppled behind him, one by one, landing silently, each in a cloud of raised dust. Painted on each of the white pillars, but not appearing until they fell, was the sign of the eye from the village church. At the end of the procession of columns, but retreating away from him with each step, was the rickety rusting metal-box shrine he'd seen earlier that day, its gate door hanging open.

When he woke from the dream he was sitting naked in the rowing boat at the bottom of the garden. Kim was wading in the water, bent over him, her hand cupping his cheek.

'What am I doing here?'

'You've been sleepwalking again. Come on back inside.'

He looked around him with amazement. There was no moon. Black waters lapped and knocked against the boat. The moorings stretched and slackened with the swell. He shook his head in disbelief before climbing out of the boat and letting Kim lead him, by the hand, back to bed.

Within moments he was asleep again. Kim lay propped on an arm, observing him by the light of a single candle. The sleepwalking episodes were becoming more frequent, almost regular. On some occasions she could lead him quietly back to bed without waking him; or sometimes he would wake, like tonight, sitting in the boat or wandering vaguely on the beach. More disturbing were the occasions when he would wake her by returning after a nocturnal prowl, climbing back into bed still deep in the thrall of sleep. Sometimes she would speak to him and he would answer strangely from a dream, and often in words she couldn't understand.

It had alarmed her at first, and now it was beginning to frighten her. This had never happened to him in England. She felt certain it had something to do with the house, the place. Her instincts crackled with the certainty of it, but her rationality failed to explain it. It was as if something took hold of him, inhabited him: some parasite spirit agitating when he was at his most vulnerable. She declined to tell him the frequency of these excursions. She didn't want to add to the sum of his anxieties. Mike, she decided, already had enough demons chasing him.

21

'I want us to leave this place,' said Mike.

They were taking their customary morning dip, chasing sleep away in the nerve-tingling sea. The sun was a pallid yellow disc, fattening with each second. Kim surfaced, water sluicing from her hair and glistening over her breasts. She wiped water from her eyes, blinking at him with astonishment.

'Leave? We can't leave! Why do you want to leave?'

'We've had no luck here. The place isn't good for us.' He turned his bronzed back on her and waded out of the water, his plaster cast hanging grimly at his side.

Mike walked up the garden. Under the vine canopy he poured himself a coffee and slumped in a chair, resting his cast on the table. He couldn't tell Kim the things that were distressing him: they were all either trivial or unspeakable.

For the trivial, his cast itched and sweated in the Aegean heat; sometimes he wanted to tear at it with his teeth to get at the crawling skin underneath. He found it difficult to paint properly with one arm because of the weight of the cast. And when he did make time and space enough to paint at all, he felt overwhelmed by lethargy and disinterest.

For the unspeakable, that initial sense of unease, the brooding, almost prophetic quality of the place, had never gone away. He wondered if Kim too had been equally aware of it, consigning it like him to a dark corner of her consciousness without being able to forget it. An ominous background music. Then there was his accident. No one had taken him seriously and Kim too had dismissed it as the delirium of a concussion. But every time Mike thought about his assailants, he felt a sick wave, a tiny flip somewhere in the pit of his stomach. Hallucinations and dreams faded with time, became overlaid, superseded by new dreams. But the encounter on the mountain was branded on his mind's eye. The integrity of the vision was intact; it was stamped in fire and ice. As for his vandalism in the church, he still shuddered at the notion that some spirit had momentary possession of him; yet stronger than this was the recollection of the priest and the crone working late in the church that night to remove the red paint from the mural. They were somehow unreal; phantom figures accusing him with their stares. As if they had known.

And somehow Mike had come to blame his ill luck and his inexplicable behaviour on the house. He couldn't say why it was the house; his feelings were utterly illogical, and yet in his bones, in his *marrow*, he felt the presence of the house everywhere, even when he was miles away from it. It was all-pervading, like a leak of dangerous gas.

Now Nikkie had arrived, and he couldn't get it out of his head that the house had delivered her up with a malicious sense of nemesis. He felt certain Nikkie was going to spill the beans to Kim; that he would have to face the consequences; and that some inexplicable spirit of the house had engineered it all. He couldn't get it out of his head that he'd been thinking of her in the days before the letter arrived to telegraph her visit.

Mike was an intelligent man. He knew this thinking was

rampantly egocentric, dangerously solipsistic; that other events and people moved in their own private universes, and that not everything in this world had him at its centre. But that was the rational part of his mind, and he was beginning to give up on rationality. Rationality was like a fisherman's net: it managed to trap some of the more obvious and bigger things floating around out there; but reality was also made up of everything else which managed to slip or wash through the sizeable interstices of the net.

And while he waited patiently for bone to knit, his plaster cast was itching like crazy.

Kim came up behind Mike, placing her cool fingers on the back of his neck.

'What is it?'

'It's this place,' Mike repeated, 'it's getting me down. Nothing has gone right for us since we moved in here.'

'Like what?'

Mike looked around desperately for an illustration. 'Like my accident.'

'This place made you drive while you were drunk?'

'I wasn't drunk. I don't feel good here. And the place is crawling with scorpions –'

'I don't notice them any more.'

'And there's no electricity –'

'I like it like that.'

'And now Nikkie's turned up.'

'Ah! Now we're getting somewhere. This is all because Nikkie is here.'

'Not because Nikkie is here. It's this place. There's something about it I don't like.'

Something he didn't like. Kim could hardly pretend not to know what he was talking about. Bizarre things had indeed happened around the house; and though she hadn't forgotten the occasional feelings of depression which on certain mornings had weighed her down, they hadn't returned. The incident with Lakis had been ugly and upsetting, but her feelings about the house itself had remained uniquely positive.

She remained enchanted by the beauty of the location, overwhelmed by the never-ending nature movie. How could she consider walking away from skies of cinematic intensity, or leaving seas and landscapes like galleries of unfolding art. Unfolding, yes, as if to a purpose which would one day be revealed. It was extraordinary, to be forever poised on the brink of some strange revelation. It didn't matter that she took this revelation to be permanently deferred, a given condition. But it was like a tension forever opening up new possibilities. Life seemed larger. Life seemed to come closer. Why couldn't Mike see it like that?

And she often felt stronger here. It was curious, but she drew strength from the place. She'd never been so physically fit in her life, and she felt an aching prime deep inside herself. It reflected in the suppleness of her muscles and the tones of her skin. Her breasts felt larger and yet more buoyant, her nipples almost permanently erect. She also knew that her vaginal scent had changed mysteriously, and in bed she was more demanding, more inventive. She wanted Mike more often, and while he gave himself freely, she luxuriated in the sense of power and fulfilment this brought her. These moods, these strengths, they were not entirely unlike those conferred and withdrawn by menstrual cycles, but this was something different. Something which seemed to ebb and flow, and not from the house, but from the earth beneath and about the house.

Yes, the place was strange but if anything she felt

revivified. If there was a cost somewhere in the unpredict-ability of life, she was prepared to pay it. Nikkie was correct: there was a vibration, a tremulous movement beneath the surface of things. It wasn't the movement in the earth's crust: it was the sense in which the sky could split at any moment, showering them with the very meaning of life; and yet that expectancy was balanced by a restraining confidence that it never actually would.

That tension between those two things was what made the place so remarkable. She didn't want to give that up. She would not give that up.

She turned to speak to Mike, but before any word had escaped her lips an extraordinary picture flashed into her mind. The scene before her eyes was lit with countless tiny white lights flickering like votive candles in a darkness. She blinked, and the momentary vision was gone. Shaking the after-image from her eyes, she dismissed the vision as an overdose of sunlight.

Nikkie was waiting at the gate. She remembered they'd planned to take her to the hot bath.

'Nikkie's here. Are you coming, Mike?'

'I'm going to stay and do some painting.'

'That's right. You stay here and paint your little pictures.'

Kim carried her irritation all the way to the hot bath, but it dissolved when she and Nikkie eased themselves into the steaming trough. Not knowing who might appear in the daytime, Kim advised Nikkie to keep her swimsuit on. Her advice was ignored. Nikkie was an enthusiast for the bath. Her skin erupted in a pink semblance of post-coital flush, and she offered up a corresponding chorus of sighs.

'This is better than sex.'

'Almost,' said Kim.

The heat, with its array of minerals and salts, radiated to the bone. It flushed along the spine and nestled at the base of the cortex before discharging with infinite tenderness, through the back of the brain.

'If I close my eyes,' murmured Nikkie, 'I can see pictures. Bits of cinema dissolving into swirling abstracts. Then moving murals. Then cartoons. Then fragments of film again.'

'Yes. Amazing, isn't it?'

'You know, that Greek man was right.'

'What Greek man?'

'Kati's husband. Vassillis? He said this place smelled like a woman's cunt. I thought he was just being wicked, but he's right.'

Now that Kim came to think of it, she too could see that Vassillis had a point. There was that obvious marine odour, plus a sensuous, streaming perfume, at once heady and an incitement. Could it be the gases leaking from the ground along with the smells of sulphur? And as she reflected, she recalled that the stone entrance to the trough was indeed a narrow cervix, giving way as if to a womb.

I'm sorry.

'Pardon?' said Kim.

'I didn't say anything,' breathed Nikkie. Her eyes were closed. She was drifting in a state of semi-consciousness.

'I thought you said something. Never mind. Mike has been so moody since his car accident. I don't know why. Why do you suppose he's so antagonistic towards you?'

'Uh.'

'No, I don't know either. Sometimes I think it's the antagonism which disguises attraction.'

'Hu . . . uh.'

'There's more things in heaven and earth . . .'
I'm sorry. Don't blame Mike. Can you forgive me?
Kim lifted her head from the stone lip of the trough. Voices. She'd heard voices in this place before. There was no mistake. She had heard the words clearly, somewhere inside her own head, in Nikkie's voice and as if Nikkie had spoken them. But Nikkie floated in semi-slumber in the steaming water, her eyes closed. 'Forgive? Forgive what?'
'Uh?'
Then again. *It shouldn't have happened. You don't fuck your friend's husband. But I wanted him. And you know, it was a way in which I could get closer to you. Because you close off from me, Kim. You close off.*
Kim drew herself out of the water, too swiftly. The disturbed water burned her. She hoisted herself out of the trough and shivered.
Nikkie opened an eye and saw Kim's face. She lifted her head. 'What is it, Kim? What's wrong?'
'Nothing. I come often and it's not good to stay too long.' She climbed out through the narrow opening.
'I'll get out too.'
'No. Stay a while longer. You won't get another chance.'
The sea breeze hit Kim with a blast of icy air. She ran out on to the shingle beach, shivering, a towel around her shoulders. Above her head was the mauve and yellow rock with the broken pathway hanging over her. The rock loomed massive and obstinate, unable to help her. What had she heard?
She threw off the towel and charged into the sea, swimming underwater until her lungs were straining, but when she surfaced the words continued to echo in her head. Nikkie came out of the bath, approaching her nervously, looking at her strangely, but patently unaware herself of

173

the message Kim had received with perfect clarity.

'Are you all right?'

'Yes. I just got a bit hot in there. Now you should swim.'

Nikkie sensed something had happened, but had no idea what it might have been. She swam, as instructed. When she emerged from the water, Kim had composed herself, and the incident was soon forgotten.

By Nikkie.

22

The heat of the afternoon lay like a heavy blanket on the still sea. Lodged deep in the water, apathetic and unstirred, the rowing boat was glued to its own bright reflection; its mooring ropes slacking against all lack of resistance. The air was stale and warm, like a sleeper's breath.

Mike, Kim and Nikkie lay stretched on towels on the dry ribbon of beach between the garden and the dead water, in the unsatisfactory shade of the single, spindly tree. A bottle of red wine was uncorked but, because too warm, had been only half consumed. Their quiescence had distilled them into a semi-conscious silence. The heat had enfolded them, but each into a little languid parcel where although no words bubbled to the surface, thoughts still cooked.

Mike was thinking about his morning's painting session, while the women were away at the hot bath. Short of ideas for subject matter, he'd tried to reinterpret the painting from the deserted monastery in which the hermit-thief was shot by an arrow. He'd chosen a plasticity of form, where certain figures assumed large proportion and others were relegated to a swirling background. After working for over an hour cursing the limited usefulness of his broken arm, he surprised himself with the results. By the time Kim and Nikkie returned, he had something impressive to show them.

They had stood under the vine canopy, nodding at his work.

'It's strong,' said Nikkie. Then she turned to him and said again, 'Strong.'

'Sweat's gone into that. Literally. I was dripping all over it and I just painted it in.'

Kim found herself making minute observation of these small exchanges between the other two. 'It's what you came here to do,' she said.

Mike found himself wanting to explain his thoughts on the subject. 'That cave. It was the cave of Artemis. Then it was Christianised, and John the anchorite lived in the cave. But Artemis turned her victims into deer before hunting them down with her bow and arrow; John the anchorite was shot with an arrow when the monks mistook him for an animal. In the original painting there is a sun and moon in the sky at the same time. Christ is the sun god, Artemis is the moon goddess. That's her sign, see?'

'So what are you saying?'

'The painting represents a struggle between Christianity and the old religion for possession of the sacred cave, and for the soul of the anchorite.'

'Maybe,' said Nikkie, 'maybe the struggle still goes on. Maybe the goddess hasn't surrendered this little island.'

Mike lay on the beach thinking about Nikkie's words. The skin under his plaster itched. The memory of the beating he took from the angel-militant also itched. The ferocious visage of the saint would flash into his mind from time to time, challenging, threatening, and he would push the thought aside, almost with an effort like physical labour. But the recollection would never quite go away. It itched. It sweated. It burned, but always at the periphery of consciousness. Like the eye in the church, once you had been fixed by its stare, you might turn your back on it but you could never dismiss its baleful presence.

'What are you thinking about?' said Kim. Mike, stirred from his reverie, groped for some placatory response before realising she was talking to Nikkie.

'Guess what?' she murmured into the sand.

'Chris?'

'Right. I was just thinking, I wouldn't be at all surprised if he followed me here.'

'Don't think it if you don't want it. Thoughts have an uncanny way of making themselves happen around here.'

Mike sat up suddenly. 'Hi, Chris!' he said.

The two women looked up in horror. Then they relaxed. There was no one there. Kim snatched a handful of dry weed and flung it at Mike. It stuck in the oiled hairs of his chest. They all sank into the sand again.

Something small broke the surface of the still sea. The water glooped, and all was calm again. 'Does he know where you are?' Kim asked.

'No.'

'You didn't tell anyone?'

'I told my mother.'

'Isn't that the first person he'll ask?'

'I suppose so.'

'So you did want him to know where you are,' said Mike.

'No. Yes. Shut up, Mike.'

'Yes, shut up, Mike,' said Kim.

Mike shut up, as instructed, and they fell into silence. No one passed by, nothing stirred. The day was becalmed and time itself seemed to falter. But time must have passed, because the sun sank a little in the sky, its reflection lancing across the water. The earth exhaled steadily. Mike felt a shift in the shadow of the tree. He looked behind him and blinked. *Oh my prophetic soul.*

'Chris! You're about half an hour late.'

'Shut up, Mike.'

'Yes, shut up, Mike.'

'I went to the wrong village,' said Chris.

Kim and Nikkie turned their heads in a synchronous movement. 'I don't believe it,' said Kim.

'What?' said Nikkie. 'What?'

Chris stood on the path, gripping his leather suitcase, glaring down at the company. He was wearing city shoes, black jeans and a black shirt, all of which exaggerated the waxen appearance of his pale skin. His white face glistened with perspiration. His brow was creased with horizontal anxiety folds, rubberised troughs which plunged suddenly, like the contours of a valley on a relief map, on to the bridge of his nose. Runnels of sweat trickled from his dark hairline and across the blue shadow of his heavy jaw. The dark shirt didn't disguise the huge sweat rings under his arms. He was melting in the heat.

'The wrong village?' said Mike.

'How dare you!' screamed Nikkie, scrambling to her feet.

Chris finally put his heavy suitcase down on the beach, and looked at her.

'What do you mean, the wrong village?' Mike laughed easily. Now they were all on their feet.

'You look all in,' said Kim.

'How dare you follow me here!' shouted Nikkie. 'How dare you!'

'Could I have a glass of water?' said Chris.

'I can do better than that,' said Mike.

'You have no right! No right whatsoever.'

'Water will be fine. I walked from Limanaki.'

'Don't give him any water! Don't you dare give him a glass of water! Don't give him anything!'

Kim picked up Chris's suitcase and carried it up the garden. 'You walked from Limanaki! Mike, he's *walked* here from Limanaki!'

'Put that case down! He's not staying here. You're not staying here.' Nikkie conducted her protestations while walking backwards towards the patio, one step ahead of Chris and Kim, her snarling features inches from his nose. 'Don't you dare sit down! Don't you dare!'

Mike handed Chris a glass of beer and Chris sat down at the table. 'Thanks, Mike,' he said pointedly.

'Jesus Christ!' Nikkie exploded. She ran into the house and slammed the door behind her.

'Walked from Limanaki, eh?' said Mike.

'Not all of the way. I got a lift in the back of a three-wheel truck, sharing with a goat. Do you actually live here?' He looked around him like a man who suspected he'd been lured into a trap.

'Yes,' Kim admitted. 'How did you find us?'

'There was a man in the village with a big piece of plaster over his eye. He didn't seem to want to tell me at first.'

Mike and Kim looked at each other. 'Lakis,' they said together.

Nikkie came out again. 'Would you tell me what you think you're up to, following me here?'

Chris thought for a moment. 'That's right, I'm following you here.'

Nikkie became suddenly calm. 'What do you expect to happen? What do you think will result from coming here like this? Is this part of some bizarre scheme you've got in your head?'

Chris sniffed before answering. 'I've come to take you home.'

'Shit!' screamed Nikkie. 'Shit shit shit!' She leapt off the patio block and bounded down the garden to disappear along the beach path.

Mike allowed a decent interval to lapse before raising his beer glass and saying 'Cheers!'

'Cheers, *Mike*,' said Chris, again a little pointedly.

Mike and Kim joined Chris at the table. Kim asked what the weather was like back home. Chris asked how they coped with the heat. Mike enquired as to political developments in the UK. Chris recounted a funny story about a television journalist and an egg. Kim sighed and said she didn't miss any of it; Mike sighed and said he did, sometimes. They'd been away for three months, yet they spoke as if it were as many years. Meanwhile Chris's relationship with Nikkie wasn't mentioned.

'You'd better take Chris into the village and fix him up with some accommodation,' Kim said.

'Is Nikkie staying here?' Chris wanted to know.

'No room,' Mike said, reluctantly lifting Chris's case. He didn't particularly want to go with Chris, but he didn't want Kim to take him into the village either.

When they were halfway down the path, Kim called Mike back. 'Take him for a drink or something,' she whispered. 'Keep him away for a while.'

Mike found Chris a room as far from Nikkie's hotel as he could manage, which was a distance of about five hundred yards. It was a battered old villa with marble floors and a pungent odour of naphthalene. Grey paint flaked from the antique window shutters, and a cock crowed in the yard. Chris was equipped with a gigantic brass key about seven inches long with which to come and go.

Chris stepped out of his sweat-caked clothes and took a shower. He put on a pair of knee-length shorts and a purple T-shirt so garish it made Mike wince. As they walked down the cobbled street back to the centre of the village, Chris found his pockets too small to take the key, so he was forced to carry it around in his hand. Clutching the key in his fist, he appeared like a man about to solve some mystery or other.

They passed by the Church of the Virgin, and Mike took him inside. The red paint splashed across the eye had faded slightly, but was still highly evident.

'Is that the evil eye?' said Chris.

'Yes,' said Mike abstractedly. His handiwork was also still evident on the mural.

'Why would they have the evil eye on a church?'

'You've misunderstood it. The eye on the wall is meant to draw the evil eye. That is, if one of the congregation was trying to put the evil eye on another person, it would be distracted and drawn by the eye on the wall, sparing the rest of the congregation from its malevolent intentions.'

'So who has the evil eye?'

'Could be you, could be me. Anyone who wants to cause mischief for other people.'

'Right,' said Chris. 'Glad we've got that straight.'

Mike looked at him. *Does he know?* Nikkie claimed she'd told Chris about the affair, but Mike didn't know whether to believe her. Nikkie was capable of it, for sure, but she was not above saying such a thing just to elicit a reaction from him. The way Chris was playing things, it was impossible to tell. His eyes darted from side to side, as if he couldn't quite figure how life had delivered him to a place like this at such short notice. He also avoided eye contact.

Chris was in a twitchy mood, but given the difficulties between him and Nikkie, that would be understandable. 'Let's go for a drink.'

Chris followed him out of the church and surprised Mike by saying, 'Yes. Let's get drunk.'

They found a seat at a seafront taverna. A breeze had picked up off the water and waves were foaming on the sandy beach. Chris laid his key on the table and the waiter brought them beers. It was early, and few other tourists were about. Mike did most of the talking, describing the drive down from England. When the waiter came again Mike was able to impress Chris with a bit of Greek, but the furrows in Chris's brow showed no signs of smoothing.

Some beers later the street began to fill with tourists looking for a place to eat and with locals making their summer evening *volta*, strolling up and down the seafront to see and be seen. Chris burped his beer and blinked at the tanned, soaring legs of a couple of passing Scandinavian girls.

'Yes,' said Mike, 'time to eat.'

They adjourned to Riga's rooftop restaurant, where Mike was known and welcomed. Riga the proprietor sat at a corner table, nursing a bottle of seven-star Metaxa and greeting everyone with a low growl, followed by a sharp rap of his glass on the tabletop. Riga was a fierce and impressive example of ageing Greek masculinity, with a head of iron-grey hair matched by a sprawling moustache the texture and colour of steel wire. This unusual greeting, which had discouraged many a faint-hearted tourist in its time, was actually a salutation, and if it was received by some as a warning shot, Riga would have been the last to deny its intention as such.

Once past the ferocious guardian of the rooftop

restaurant, however, the adventurer could be expected to find the best food on the entire island, with not a *souvlaki* or a grilled chicken or other tourist dish in sight. Mike and Chris ate heartily, washing down their dinner with two bottles of red wine to supplement the beers they had drunk while waiting. They finished up with brandy and cigarettes. Riga strolled over with his Metaxa and gave them each another quarter-pint of brandy on the house.

'Where your wife?' he growled at Mike.

'At the house.'

'With my wife,' Chris added, a little tipsy.

You married?' Riga looked disgusted.

'Yes. You?'

Riga looked even more disgusted. 'Of course. Or why am I here, washing dishes.'

'I've come to get my wife,' Chris announced loudly, looking at Mike. 'She ran away from me.'

'You run after her?' Riga shook his head bitterly. 'Take your chance. Go.'

'What chance?'

'Yes, go! Because when a man is marry, he die.'

'No,' said Chris. 'Matrimony is an honourable and life-enhancing institution.' He just about got the words out.

'What?' roared Riga.

'He said he likes marriage,' Mike translated.

Riga squinted at Chris and then surveyed the other diners as if he couldn't believe how many fools could turn up at his restaurant in a single evening. 'Give me back my brandy.' He scooped up Mike and Chris's complimentary drinks and took them away.

Moments later he returned with the glasses of brandy and set them down again. 'My wife pull my ear and say I must give you the brandy.' He topped up the glasses. '*Yia sas!* he cried, and retired to his own lonely table like a whipped dog.

'It's all an act,' said Mike, supping his brandy.

'I know that,' said Chris, looking across the terracotta rooftops. 'I too have a keen sense of theatre. As do you, Mike.'

Mike said nothing. On the way out Chris missed his footing slightly on the steps, and almost crashed into a table of Germans. 'I'm sorry,' said Chris, 'but my wife has left me.'

Mike rescued him, or them, and gently propelled Chris down the winding, dimly lit cobbled street.

'It's the fresh air, Mike. It hits you when you come out.'

Mike shook his head. 'It's an open-air restaurant, Chris.'

'My key! I've left my key!'

Chris hastened back to the restaurant, leaving Mike to wait for him under a dull-yellow streetlamp. A clump of goblet-shaped white magnolia streamed perfume from behind a parched wall; huge moths orbited the lamp in dizzying spirals. Mike hated this. He had the feeling Chris was going to spring it on him at any moment. In some ways he hoped he would, at least while Kim wasn't there. He prayed they might be able to reach some sort of position which kept the truth from Kim.

Chris returned, bearing the giant key. He stopped Mike. 'Where to next?'

'To the Black Orchid rock bar.'

'You're trying to keep me away from Nikkie.'

'That's the idea. Just for tonight. Then we'll see how things look in the morning.'

Mike took him into a bar with violet light and loud music, where they drank imported beers. Chris fell in love with the girl serving behind the bar; he told her his wife had run away, but that she would be an acceptable substitute. Then he got chatting to the two Scandinavian women who had passed by their table earlier in the evening.

'My wife ran off with another man,' Mike heard him say. He seemed to want everyone to know. At one o'clock in the morning Mike extricated him from a knot of drunken German football supporters who seemed happy to count Chris amongst their company. When they emerged from the bar, Chris heard the sounds of a disco from across the bay.

'One more bottle,' said Chris.

Mike groaned.

'Just one more bottle.'

The open-air disco was almost empty. There were enough coloured light bulbs to illuminate the entire village, and all of the tables were deserted. It was a phantom disco. Music thumped with dispiriting obstinacy. Two or three waiters stood by the bar smoking cigarettes. Two more beers were produced. Mike's stood untouched on the table, Chris took an aggressive swig at his own bottle, white foam frothing down his face. Chris suddenly took a notion to wander on to the empty dance floor. There he shuffled his legs apart, as if to more evenly distribute his fluctuating centre of gravity, and began swaying joylessly from side to side in barely approximate time to the music. The last remaining customers left. A waiter came across and spoke to Mike.

'We're about to close.'

'I think we all are,' said Mike.

The music ended and the coloured lights flickered off in relays. Chris didn't seem to want to come off the empty dance floor. He stood in the dark with his head hung forward, as if his neck had been broken. The waiters shrugged, locked up the equipment and went, leaving a gate open for them. Mike walked across the dance floor. Chris was swaying slightly.

'Piss off, Mike.'

'Come on, Chris. I'll walk you back.'

'Piss off. I'll find my own way back.'

'Let me take you.'

'I'll go when I'm ready. I mean it. You fuck off home.'

Mike knew when to quit. He told Chris he would come to his room in the morning, and followed the waiters out.

Chris came round about an hour later, with his head on the table. His skin had stuck to the plastic tabletop and it tugged slightly as he lifted his head. A shiver went through him. His own bottle stood empty alongside Mike's untouched beer. He took a mouthful but felt nauseous. He looked up and the few dim speckled stars swam in the night sky.

Then he remembered Nikkie, and why he was there. He snorted. It came out half-growl, half-sob.

A second gate admitted on to the beach. Chris got up and went out of the disco compound, stepping down on to the sand and shingle. The tide broke in a low muffled restraint. There was a boy sleeping on the beach, maybe spilled from the disco. He looked like something deposited by the tide.

'A young Odysseus,' said Chris. The boy slept on, oblivious.

Chris looked up the beach in the direction of Kim and Mike's house. He had a confused idea Nikkie would be there. He resolved to go up to the house to confront her. He had no idea of the time.

His progress along the beach was slow. The shingle rolled under his feet and he fell on his knees. The globe turned suddenly and the sea rushed him from behind. His feet got wet. He had to stop twice to check his feelings of rising nausea. Then he noticed a fire burning on the beach somewhere near his friends' house.

The fire got larger as he approached it. Bright tongues of yellow and orange flame licked at the sky. A figure passed across the fire, and he assumed the Hansons had organised a barbecue. He felt vaguely annoyed that they'd failed to invite him to their beach party, but he was too drunk for the sentiment to register deeply. He staggered on in the direction of the glowing flame. Nikkie would be there. He had something to say to them all. He made rapid progress towards the fire. Indeed it suddenly appeared to be no more than a few yards away. He stopped and blinked, and the flames seemed to grow. There was a moment of clarity amidst the stupor: the fire was actually moving towards him. The flames were six or seven feet high, illuminating a circle of the beach with eerie light. The flames, and their unnatural and phosphorescent projection, were still moving towards him.

Dumb horror suddenly penetrated senses retarded by alcohol. Chris realised he was looking at a man in flames. The man was on fire from head to foot. Yellow streamer-flames reached up into the night sky, orange pendant-flames dripped from his burning form as he made his way along the beach. Chris could see the man's hair and beard clearly on fire, as were his legs and torso, yet he made steady progress, seemingly undaunted by his plight. The man carried a staff, also aflame. His shoes glinted, reflecting white firelight. He passed deliberately close to Chris, so desperately close that Chris had to put out an arm to shield himself from the passing fire. Chris felt the slick wave of heat wash over him and got a whiff of scorched hair from his own arm. The burning man passed by and proceeded up the beach. Chris staggered back and fell to his knees, vomiting across the stones.

When he looked up, the burning man was wading out to sea, the flames slowly extinguishing in the black water.

23

Now what had happened? The other woman had arrived and there was trouble in store for everyone. As if there wasn't already a whore of a confusion built into the foundations of the house.

Sometimes Manoussos gazed down from the hill, at the house and its apron of patchy garden, and at the irregular movements of its animals: the feral cats stalking the bushes; the scratching of the chickens; the grazing of the ass; the flights, settling and realignment of the ornamental pigeons ... all of these things left vibrant trails in the garden, whorls, curlicues, helixes, crisscrossing trails for Manoussos to read. The garden before him was like a card of fortune.

Today a goshawk wheeled from the air and alighted near the water pump, while the young couple slept. Had it circled from the east, the proud hawk would have spoken with a different voice. But it came from the hills behind the shepherd's left shoulder.

Bonds will be broken. Friendships will cool.

These were strange times. Manoussos had looked from his own position to the one who stood on the cliff edge watching out to sea. Every day he was spending more and more time, waiting, waiting. God is coming. Will he wait until his death? And in that moment of death will he think himself confirmed in his vision? Madness and death. A whore of a confusion.

This other woman had taken him by surprise. Manoussos had always seen the link between Kim and Mike, the husband and wife link, a silver-blue thread invisible to the ordinary eye, shining like fish scales, pulsating, thickening as they came together, spinning out into airy thinness as they left each other's side, strong as steel cable but supple as a whiplash, and seemingly unbreakable. Unbreakable and inviolable. Manoussos understood these threads as *fibres of affection*; he had been seeing them all his life. Indeed it was years before he realised that these fibres were not available for everyone to see, that not all eyes could see them spin and play and vanish and reappear, as they did now. They had been the source of much suffering to him in times past; and occasionally of advantage; and once they had saved his life.

But then this other English woman had come and things had changed: he had identified another fluid line connecting her to Mike. Even from this distance, from this vantage spot on the hill he could tell that they either were or had been lovers. Though their fibres of affection were contracted and flimsy, perhaps even already dying, they were unmistakable.

And so there they were, and he was afraid that these threads might cross, and then there would be sparks. Because if such fibres were to cross, the one woman's with the other's, then, well, they would be like live conduits of electricity coming into contact.

And already something had happened, between Kim and Mike. Some unspoken thing which had dulled their own fibres of affection since the arrival of this woman. And then this new man had arrived, and he clearly was the husband of this second woman, with his own complications. Po po po!

Manoussos had hoped to be of help to Kim and Mike in this business with the house. But this, this was all human complication. Affairs of the heart. He had never understood people and their behaviour and he had never pretended to. He didn't see what he had to offer.

Manoussos felt sad because he had an inexplicable love for the two English children. It was not simply the *philia* of the normal fibres of affection and friendship which he felt; nor yet the *erotas*, the attachments of passionate and sexual love; nor even the *storge* of tender parental and familial care, those fibres of a different colour. It was in the sphere of the true *agape* in which he loved them; in that he could see the best and the worst in them, the highest and the lowest degrees. The love he had for them was the love he had for life itself. There was no reason for it. It was beyond being known; but there it was.

This was why he felt sad, because he couldn't help them in these ordinary and impossible matters. It was a damnable whore of a confusion, and he could only watch.

24

A guillotine of sunlight sliced through the darkness when Mike kicked open the shutters to Chris's room. The room reeked of sleep, sweat and the sweet rot of alcohol. The giant key and a dirty wad of drachmae lay on the bedside table under a still-burning electric lamp. Chris blinked at the intruder and shut his eyes against a wave of nausea.

'It's late,' said Mike.

Chris got up without a word and went out to the bathroom in the hall. Mike heard him retching.

'Good boy. Get it all up.'

Mike sat on a plastic chair outside the room under a great arch of mauve bougainvillea while Chris tried to recover his humanity. It was noon, and the cock was still crowing. Chris was a long time about it. Finally he appeared, very pale behind an expensive pair of sunglasses. He looked like a boxer who had gone the full distance in a losing bout. They had to walk quite slowly to a seafront taverna, where Mike prescribed a caffeine breakfast. The sun was strong and bazouki music tinkled from speakers wired in the trees.

'At least you found your way home.'

'Only the first time. When I reached the door I remembered I'd left the key at the disco.'

'That awful disco?' said Mike. 'I'd almost forgotten about that.'

'Then I found it on the table where we were sitting, next to your full bottle of beer. Then I couldn't find my way back again. But since you found me safe and sound this morning, I must have made it, eventually.'

'Yes. You must have. Try a yoghurt with honey.'

Chris winced, and readjusted his sunglasses on the bridge of his nose. 'Mike, something happened last night.'

'Yep. You got blind drunk and you were abusive to me.' Mike was pouring dark honey from a plastic sachet into an earthenware pot of full-fat yoghurt.

'I mean something abnormal.'

Mike set down his spoon.

'There was a man. On the beach. Mike, he was on fire, from head to foot. And he wasn't running or screaming. He just walked on up the beach.'

Mike said nothing.

'Well?' said Chris.

'Well what?'

'Tell me I was drunk.'

'I've just told you that.'

'I mean tell me I was shit-faced. Tell me I was too drunk to know what I saw. Tell me I was hallucinating.'

'All right. You were hallucinating.'

Chris carefully rolled up both of his sleeves. There was a dark mass of hair on his left forearm, but almost none on his right. 'Behold, Esau my brother is a hairy man, and I am a smooth man.' He shoved his right forearm under Mike's nose so that the smell of burned hair could be appreciated. 'The burning man came so close to me that all the hair on my arm was singed.'

'Yes. Complicated, isn't it?'

'Yes? Yes? Don't say *yes*. Say, "Come off it, Chris, you

must have had an accident with your cigarette lighter when you were drunk."'

'If you insist.'

'No no no, Mike. You're not going about this the right way. Please tell me that I was out of my head. End of story.'

'Right. You were out of your head.'

'What? Are you saying you believe me? Is that what you're saying? Because if you are I'm going to punch you in the mouth.'

'You're getting angry because I believe you?'

'I don't want you to believe me! I want you to fucking well talk me down out of it!'

'Calm down.'

'Calm down? Calm fucking down? How can I calm down when you're DELIBERATELY SITTING THERE BELIEVING EVERY WORD I SAY? Jesus!'

Mike offered him a cigarette, which he refused. 'In any event, Chris, you don't smoke; you never smoke even when you're drunk; so you are unlikely to have had an accident with a cigarette lighter. What did this man look like?'

'What? The burning man? I don't want to talk about it.'

'OK.'

'He . . . he was tall. He carried a stick, a staff, also on fire. I think he had a beard. And his shoes . . . they were . . . I don't know . . .'

'Steel shoes?'

Chris took off his sunglasses and peered across the table.

'Yes,' said Mike. 'I do believe you.'

'You've seen it too?'

'Not exactly the same. But something like it.'

Chris rubbed his singed arm and looked ill. 'Hair of the dog?' he suggested.

Mike ordered two glasses of Metaxa. Chris held the amber liquor up to the light. Then he took a good swallow.

'This is a strange place,' said Mike. 'I can't explain these things.'

'Have the local people seen it?'

Mike shook his head. 'It's different for different people. That's another thing: I don't even like discussing it. Talking about it makes it seem more real. I'm starting to formulate a theory. These visions: I think they come from inside us. Where are you going?'

'I'm going to be ill. I shouldn't have had that brandy.'

Nikkie's job was to pump water into a plastic bucket before swinging the bucket up to Kim. She had to climb three steps of the ladder before she could reach Kim, who waited on the outhouse roof, arm outstretched. They were filling the oil drum supplying the cold-water shower. Nikkie had already broken a fingernail.

'How many buckets does it take?'

'About sixty. Keep pumping.'

'Do we have to do this now?'

'You're the one who keeps taking a shower every time you have a dip in the sea. You can help me fill it up.'

Nikkie was too busy sucking her bleeding finger to catch any resentment in Kim's voice. Kim was in a mood to make her do something around the place, make some contribution. Squatting on the roof amid the fishing nets and boathooks, she looked down on Nikkie's feeble one-handed pump action with uncharitable thoughts. *Yes, you'd have others up and down like a monkey on a stick running after you, wouldn't you?* She watched Nikkie climb two rungs up the ladder, her trembling arm holding aloft the spilling bucket; and reaching down, she deliberately let the bucket slip. Water cascaded over Nikkie.

Nikkie shrieked. She was wearing an expensive pair of khaki shorts and now they stuck to her thighs. Her pretty pink pumps were soaked.

'You've got to come up the ladder, Nikkie! Come up the ladder! I can't reach the bloody thing down there! Don't be so bloody lazy! Go and get changed.'

Nikkie went up to the house and Kim sat back on the pile of fishing nets. Her feelings were moving at a depth difficult to sound. The uncanny experience at the hot bath had not resolved in her; she was not entirely persuaded that what she'd heard was an echo of the truth; and yet she was prepared to convince herself it was. Something freakish had spoken inside her, with Nikkie's voice, alluding to a betrayal, and whatever inexplicable energies were gathered around this place, she had come to respect them, and to listen for them. It was not the accuracy of these hallucinations she trusted, not the fine detail, nor the outer shape; it was some rough-hewn veracity, a pointing from the heart. Familiar but forgotten chords were sounded by these incidents. They rang long-silent bells.

So with the idea planted in her mind that Mike and Nikkie had been unfaithful to her, vast nets were left to trawl in dark waters; and when they were hauled up it was true that certain memories, moments, glimpses, coincidences, causes and effects that might link one with the other suddenly lay glinting and writhing and gasping for breath in the bottom of that very slimy selfsame net.

The colours of the Aegean change from the shallows to the depths; from turquoise to peacock to impenetrable cobalt blue. So shifted Kim's thoughts into darker waters, looking for confirmation. It can't be. It could be. It is so.

Was there a hierarchy in the language of betrayal? she

wondered. Was the betrayal of friendship a greater offence than her husband's infidelity? Had Mike violated her twice, once by doing it at all, and again by choosing her friend with whom to do it? Close ties of friendship could never after all draw abreast of the intimacies between husband and wife. Or was the double-edged hurt Nikkie's responsibility? Nikkie who was so quick to castigate the male, to invoke the protective circle of sisterhood. Kim was unable to blame them both in equal measure. And was it not women, she recalled in conclusion, who ultimately controlled the gate?

Would Nikkie accept that line of reasoning? Never in her worst feminist nightmares would her friend subscribe to a line of religious blame running back to Eve. But that was because she didn't understand or recognise her own sexuality. Unlike Kim, who knew both the best and the worst in herself, and who therefore was a more competent controller of the gate.

Artemis, whispered the voice inside her head. And then, *I would never do that. It is I who am the feminist, Nikkie, not you.*

'What did you say?' Nikkie, changed into a brilliant tangerine swimsuit, was looking up the ladder.

'Pardon?'

'I thought I heard you say something.'

'No. I didn't say anything.' Nikkie was looking at her oddly. 'Get pumping.'

Nikkie returned to the pump. She cranked the handle two or three times, but the pump had run dry. She tried again, but the pump made a sucking noise, like a dyspeptic squid. Staring up helplessly, she fingered the seam of her swimsuit at the crotch.

Kim came clattering down the ladder, snatched the

bucket and took it to the water's edge. She returned to pour sea water into the pump head before cranking the handle, whereupon the flow of water from the pump was resumed.

'Priming,' she said, scrambling back on to the roof. 'Get pumping.'

Nikkie filled her bucket. This time she didn't make the mistake of failing to climb the ladder before handing it on. Kim emptied the water into the huge, black-painted oil drum, where it swelled to a depth of about two inches. At this rate the task was going to keep them busy all morning.

Nikkie pumped. 'I was hoping just you and I could row over to the island this morning.'

'Why?' said Kim. 'What are you up to?'

'Up to? I just thought you and I could have a nice day over there together.'

Kim looked at the rusting boathook lashed to a six-foot wooden pole. It lay across the roof alongside the fishing net next to a broken anchor. Kim could have quite happily picked up the boathook and used it like a javelin on Nikkie. 'No, you don't think that.' Kim emptied another bucket and handed it back.

'What?'

'You don't think that at all. You're just playing games with Chris.'

'He needs shocking out of his complacency.'

'So you think it's all right to use us? To come here and use us as your marital gymnasium? Don't pretend to be surprised – you think if you and I jump in the boat and go off to the island, then Chris won't have any way of talking to you today.'

'Look, I admit that that's partly—'

'No. Don't admit anything. Never admit anything.'

'What are you talking about?'

'Give me the bucket. Does it never occur to you that what might suit your schemes might be a disruption of someone else's plans?'

'What schemes?'

'Can't you see that while you want to escape from Chris I might not want to get away from Mike? Or even that Mike and I might want to be together irrespective of whatever games you want to play?'

'Kim! Why are you being so hostile?'

'Think, Nikkie. Just think. Why might I want to be hostile? Try to imagine what might be going on in another person's head for once. Just for once.'

Nikkie turned around in astonishment, as if she might find the answer somewhere behind her. She turned back to face Kim. 'All right. I apologise. I was only thinking of myself. It just seemed like a good idea to go over to the island to get away from Chris and to be together with you.'

'Why bother?'

'Why bother! You know I don't want to see him!'

'Bullshit, Nikkie! You knew he'd come here after you! You even told your mother to tell him where you were! You knew he'd come racing out here after you, and you knew you could use me and Mike as a safe place to play out your little opera. And when you're good and ready and you've strung Chris out for long enough you'll go back home with him. I've seen it all before and it's boring, Nikkie, it's boring!'

Nikkie ran out of the garden and stood on the edge of the water, her eyes fixed on the further shores of Asia Minor.

'Take the boat and go!'

'Don't worry, I will!' Nikkie released the moorings and climbed into the boat. It tilted dangerously. She clattered the oars and drew away from the shore in unsteady motion.

Kim watched her go before continuing with the chore of filling the water tank. She hoped she hadn't made a mistake. Her ambiguities had been completely lost on Nikkie – or at least so Nikkie had pretended. But how could she confront anyone? What evidence was she proceeding on, beyond a mysterious whispering inside her own head, in the dizziness induced by a hot spa?

She discarded the plastic bucket, abandoning the job before the shower tank was half filled. A swim, she decided, might discharge some of her agitation. She waded out into the water and could see that Nikkie had already reached the rock and was climbing out of the boat.

After swimming for twenty minutes, Kim felt better. The water effervesced around her, the tang of salt made her smack her lips. She waded out and crossed the beach to the garden. A white pigeon sat on the water pump and didn't move as she drew under the shower, as if the birds were coming to recognise and trust her. She stripped off her swimsuit and stood aggressively naked under the shower, turning it on and letting her morning's labours sluice the salt from her back.

Her instincts were to shower quickly, to conserve the water for others, but she ignored the impulse and enjoyed the deliciously selfish sense of the oil drum draining. She closed her eyes and let it run.

She became aware of a delicate perfume scenting the air around her, subtle and natural, perhaps like magnolia streaming from a garden a long way off. Kim opened her eyes. With the shower running into her eyes, the garden seemed overlaid by that milky film she had seen before. The light dissolved around her, settling strangely on the whitewashed wall of the outhouse and the brilliant blue sea. It was the lacquer of dreams. The white pigeon perched unmoving on the ornate handle of the water pump. It looked oddly waxen. Its head was cocked, its eye was fixed on her. She felt a tight gripping in her bowels, a small fist of fear inside her.

For a moment everything was out of joint. Far off she could hear the weird, clunking xylophone of sheep bells in the hills. They filled the air with eerie music; like strings plucked on primitive or ancient instruments. Then the water from the shower stopped suddenly, finished. It dripped on her. She looked up, and through one of the holes crudely punctured in the home-made metal shower head she saw something.

It was something fine and slender and a bright emerald colour, but even as she watched she saw what seemed to be a brilliant crimson tail emerging from the hole behind the green reed. The thing expanded to fill the hole but continued to be drawn down through the hole towards her, pushed by the weight of the water above it, its flag of red now outdazzling the green stem. The red seemed to fatten as she watched it, like a creature emerging from a chrysalis, almost sprouting red wings as it slipped, with painful slowness, through the hole above her head. At the last moment she reached up, but before she grasped it, the thing exploded into crimson form, dropping through the air until she caught it between her breasts.

It was a flower, the head of a mountain lily, five petals drawn back, red as painted lips, bush of stamens hanging untouched. She held it in her hand, standing under the still-dripping shower, and a voice whispered in her head.

Artemis, said the voice. *Consider her ways.*

25

'She took the boat over to the rock,' Kim told Chris when he arrived at the house with Mike.

Chris looked across at the rock, assessing the distance.

Mike caught something in Kim's voice, so he said, 'Chris has been seeing men on fire.'

'Has he?' said Kim, 'Well, ask him if he wants coffee or tea.'

Mike followed her under the vine canopy, where she lit the gas under the kettle. 'What's the matter with you?'

'Nothing's the matter with *me*.' Then Chris joined them, so Mike left it.

The three of them sat under the vine sipping coffee in silence until Kim suddenly said, 'Relationships.'

Chris looked up. 'What about them?' Mike swept a hand through his hair.

'They're too complicated.'

'I'll go along with that,' said Chris, warming to the subject.

Mike got up and started fiddling with a reel of tangled fishing line.

'Between any four people,' said Kim, 'did you realise that there are six relationships going on, not four? For example, there is my relationship with Mike, Nikkie and you, Chris. Then there are your relationships with Nikkie and Mike. Then Mike's with Nikkie. Six relationships.'

'All going on,' said Chris.

'That's right. All going on.'

'But that's assuming each relationship to be integral,' said Chris. 'I mean, you count the relationship between me and you to be one single relationship. You're assuming there's an objective way of looking at it. What if my perception of that relationship is completely different to your perception of it? Doesn't that make it two relationships? Mine with you and yours with me?'

'So you're saying Mike's relationship with Nikkie is not the same as Nikkie's relationship with Mike.'

'Exactly. It's a matter of perception. What is reality?'

'So we have to double the score.'

'Twelve. Twelve relationships. All going on.'

'All going on.'

'Ow!' Mike held up a thumb. A small fish-hook had embedded itself in the soft flesh and had drawn a tiny trickle of blood.

Kim ignored him. 'Then there's the coupling to think about.'

'The coupling?'

'Yes, the pairing. Mike and I have a specific relationship, as a couple, with you and Nikkie as a couple.'

'Inter-marital, you mean.'

'And you with us. So that makes fourteen relationships.'

'All going on,' said Mike. 'I just thought I'd say it before anyone else does.'

'Then there's the gender issue,' Chris insisted.

'Gender?'

'Come on, Kim! You and Nikkie as girls together, versus me and Mike as boys together. That makes a total of—'

'Sixteen. It's all too complicated.'

'You could take it further. You could look at triads—'

'Stop!' said Mike, setting down his fishing line. His eyes were slightly moist and his voice was louder than should have been necessary. 'Stop! It's other people who complicate relationships, that's all! *Other* people. When Kim and I are on our own we hardly ever have a disagreement. But when other people come into the frame, that's when the trouble starts!'

Chris thought about this hard for a moment. Then he stood up. 'Right. I'll just uncomplicate this situation for you by leaving. I'm going to join Nikkie on the rock.'

Mike also stood up. 'I didn't mean it literally! I mean, not this minute!'

But Chris was already halfway down the garden, with Mike following. When he reached the edge of the water, he stripped off his shirt and shorts down to a pair of day-glo orange swimming trunks. 'Can you swim out to the rock?'

'Before I had this plaster on—'

Kim joined them. 'Only if you're a strong swimmer, Chris.'

Chris waded into the water. 'We'll find out.'

Then he was breaststroking through the water.

'What's he up to?'

'God knows,' said Mike. 'God knows.'

Kim and Mike, as if mesmerised, watched Chris swim out to the rock. He seemed to make good progress until about halfway, and then slowed in the current between rock and shore. It seemed to pull him off course, and then he recovered to put in a sudden spurt. The last two hundred yards seemed to be taking him forever. They could see that Nikkie was standing on the edge of the tiny beach, hands on hips, waiting for him.

'How dare you follow me here! How dare you!' said Mike, filling in the caption for Nikkie. True to form they could see Nikkie waving her arms and stomping around the beach. They could hear the shrill cry of her voice but not the exact words. Then they could make out Chris dragging himself up the beach on his hands and knees before collapsing on the sand.

'He's all in,' said Kim.

Nikkie was not to be discouraged. She stood over him, waving her arms in remonstration and stamping the sand, her voice carrying across to them like the cries of a distant seagull. Then they saw Chris get to his feet. Nikkie ran away and Chris stepped out of his day-glo orange swimming trunks before sitting down on the sand. When Nikkie returned, he reached out an arm and was repaid for the gesture by an unmistakable blow to the side of the face.

'I don't know if I heard it, but I *felt* it,' said Mike.

Chris was rubbing his face. There was more incoherent shouting from the two naked figures.

'I wish I could hear what was being said!'

'You don't have to,' said Mike.

Then Chris cupped his hands to his mouth and tried to bellow something across the stretch of water at Kim and Mike. It was lost to the deep. They saw Nikkie take another swipe at Chris, which he managed to avoid before promptly wrestling her to the ground with a rugby tackle. The couple writhed on the sand.

'What's happening?' said Kim.

'I don't know. I can't tell.'

It was impossible to see what was going on. The distance was too great. All they could make out were the two lithe bodies locked together and squirming on the sand. They seemed to stay like that for a long time without resolving the matter. Then they became perfectly still for a while before the wrestling resumed.

'Are they fighting?' Kim wanted to know.

'I think they might be . . . I think that what they're actually doing is . . .'

'I think you're right. I think they're fucking.'

'No,' said Mike. ' I think they're still fighting.'

'Are you certain?'

'No. I'm not.'

'Funny,' said Kim.

'What?'

'Well, it seems all right to watch if they're practically killing each other. But not if they're in the middle of a loving act.'

'Sod it,' said Mike, turning back up to the house. 'You can't see anything either way.'

Some hours later they returned from the island, with Chris rowing and Nikkie sitting on the prow of the boat. Together they moored it neatly and each carried an oar up the path. The heat of the afternoon had passed and the best of the day was distilling out. Nikkie made tea for everyone. Nothing was said about the struggle on the rock. Kim knew better than to ask, but Mike didn't.

'Well?' he said.

'Well,' said Nikkie sweetly, pouring tea.

Nikkie looked sleepy and relaxed. Chris looked subdued, but content. Whatever had happened, they had reached some kind of harmonious truce, even if they weren't prepared to explain – and it was only Mike who seemed to be fretting for an explication of events – who had surrendered what, how, and under what conditions. Nikkie was surprisingly solicitous. Chris had sunburned his legs, and she asked Kim for something she could apply; and when Kim gave her the local remedy, Greek yoghurt, Nikkie made jokes about licking it off later anyway. So there was no further doubt in anyone's mind, even Mike's.

'What do you want to do tonight?' Kim wanted to know.

'Look, Kim,' said Nikkie. 'I'm really sorry about this morning. You are right, I have been using you both. Selfishly. Chris and I thought we'd go out alone tonight. To give you and Mike a bit of space.'

Kim was too taken aback to answer.

Mike got a few moments alone on the beach with Nikkie before they left. She'd gone down to sit and watch the pyrotechnic sunset. The flaring red balloon of the sun seemed huge, an alien engine throbbing in the sky, discharging energy moment by moment.

'Does she know anything?' asked Mike.

'Hope not. Why?'

'I'd die if she knew.'

'Why do you ask?'

'She's behaving strangely. Saying weird things.'

'Yes. I noticed. Anyway, I haven't told her anything.'

'Would Chris say anything?'

'I don't think so. I couldn't swear on it.'

'Is everything all right between you two now?'

She nodded. 'As all right as it ever might be.'

'That's all right then,' said Mike. 'Isn't it?'

There was a movement behind them. It was Chris.

'Look at that sun,' said Nikkie. 'Mike's going to paint that.'

'No,' said Mike. 'It can't be done.'

Chris squinted into the source of the fireworks shooting across the water. Pink and lavender clouds were shifting hue by the second. The water rippled like the scaly back of a mythical beast. 'No,' he agreed. 'It can't ever be done.'

After they had gone, Kim and Mike spent an evening under the vine canopy watching the stars come out. They sat quietly in the ripening dark. Mike left it until Kim was no more than a silhouette before lighting the oil lamps. The sea was silent. The only sound was of cicadas, or the occasional ping of moths and other insects battering themselves against the smoky glass of the hanging lamps. That and the sound of Kim's mind working away on some troublesome subject, a sound like ants stripping a vine, which only Mike could hear.

He was relieved to have some time with Kim away from Nikkie and Chris. He feared Nikkie's volatility and the unpredictable nature of Chris's behaviour kept him on edge. They were like children playing a secret game of tossing back and forth a grenade they had found in the garden. Now, however, he had realised that he was equally afraid of being alone with Kim; for his wife had somehow spotted the grenade, and was waking to a realisation of who had left it in the garden for the children to find.

He loved Kim; loved her as she sat there, working away on her private thoughts, the dull yellow light forming a soft halo around her as she gazed through the phantoms of the darkened garden to the black, whispering sea beyond. It was her vulnerability to hurt which terrified him. He hated Nikkie and Chris for bringing this explosive danger within her proximity. He hated Nikkie for being as weak as he himself was.

He stood up and moved behind her. She seemed almost asleep; but she was not asleep: she was wide awake, but a long way distant. He leaned forward and kissed her on the top of her head. Sliding his arm around her to cup her breast, he felt her stiffen.

'Let's go to bed,' he whispered.

'You go,' she murmured. 'I'll come later.'

He hesitated to leave her there, but reluctantly went inside. He lay awake in the dark, aware of her sitting on the patio just the other side of the wall, the other side of the shutters. It was two hours before she came inside. He pretended to be asleep, but he could hardly fail to notice how, in slipping between the sheets, she avoided letting her body touch his.

26

Nikkie's package holiday had come to an end. She was to take an early flight the following morning. Chris, having succeeded in his mission, had arranged to leave at the same time through a domestic airline to Athens, where he could connect with a scheduled flight home.

A farewell meal was arranged at Riga's rooftop taverna at 8.30 the night before the departure. They all met in the *platia* for an aperitif before proceeding to Riga's. Nikkie was dressed to kill. She was looking sunkissed and relaxed, and causing havoc with the waiters, her short dress advertising the uncrossable sandy deserts of her long, tanned legs. Kim looked slightly prim and bohemian by comparison; Mike looked at her and knew she felt it too. Unlike Nikkie, Chris had shed his bright plumage and had returned to the all-black outfit in which, anxious and perspiring, he'd arrived a few days earlier. He seemed to be declaring his holiday already over. Although equilibrium was restored between him and Nikkie since their imprecise struggle on the rock, Mike felt that Chris looked strained, twitchy.

'Cheers,' he said, gulping a large gin and tonic.

'*Yia mas!*'

'Stuff that *yia mas* crap. It gets on my nerves.'

'All right, Chris,' said Mike. 'Cheers. Does that make you feel better?'

'Yes, but don't clink my glass next time.'

When someone suggested they move on to Riga's, Chris insisted on ordering a further round of aperitifs. 'It's our last night,' he kept saying. He was taking his drinking at a clip. Mike felt slightly nervous.

They were lucky to find a table on the small flat roof at Riga's, but somehow Sofia squeezed them in. Chris sat with his chair precariously near the edge of the roof; deliberately so, thought Mike.

They ordered *dolmades* and *tsatsiki* as starters, washed down with huge glasses of yellow wine. Chris decided he didn't like *dolmades*, so he tossed one over his shoulder into the cobbled street below.

'Muck.'

'Don't,' said Kim, 'because you'll offend them.'

'What do I care about that? I'm going home tomorrow.'

'You might be; but we're not. Leave it on the plate if you don't like it.'

'Anyway,' Mike told him, 'you've been eating it all week without complaining.'

'That's right,' said Chris. 'I've been eating shit all week. Isn't that so, Nikkie?'

'Chris,' said Nikkie, and everybody heard it as a warning shot.

'All right,' said Chris. 'Let's have some more wine. I'm only joking.'

They were generously served with lamb *stifado* and *spanokopita*, and with Greek salad and specialities of the house. Both Mike and Kim were proud that they could bring visitors to a taverna like this, something with character and ambience and traditional Greek food, not something tacked up for the tourist business. They were halfway through the meal when live music started up from the yard below, which was busy with drinkers rather than diners. The music was not bazouki playing, but a traditional duo with *lira* and *lauto*; the former a violin-shaped descendant of the lyre, but played across the lap and over which a bow is drawn to produce an eerie and hypnotic wail; the latter belonging to the lute family, counterpointing rhythmic chord changes against the compelling beat of the *lira*.

'Oh no,' said Chris when they started up, 'do we have to have this with our dinner?'

'I love it,' said Kim, 'I love it!'

'You don't have to pretend to like everything Greek simply because you're living here.'

Kim was quite stung. 'I'm not pretending anything. I actually do like it.'

'Give it a chance,' said Mike. 'It's hypnotic. It gets into your blood.'

Chris slapped a mosquito on his arm. 'So does malaria. That doesn't mean I'm going to pretend to have a taste for all things Greek, just to contract it.'

'This isn't a malarial zone,' said Nikkie. 'Stop talking rubbish.'

'It's our last night,' said Chris, pouring wine for everyone, 'and I can say anything I want. And why has everyone stopped drinking?'

The music played on. The diners ate. They drank. The exotic wailing instruments of the duo climbed to a mesmerising beat, hit a faultless, rhythmic groove, and stayed there. When the musicians stopped for a mouthful of wine, it was to a burst of enthusiastic applause.

Chris returned to his theme. 'I mean, I can't see the fascination with this country anyway. What is it exactly that makes you want to stay here?'

Kim felt a sudden thrill of protectiveness, as if the island was a small child around which she wanted to throw her arms. 'That's just it: if you don't feel it, you can't see it.'

He ignored her. 'I mean, it's like some Third World country, isn't it? The trouble is, these people are peasants who all think they're going to get rich by ripping off tourists.'

The music started up again, soaring strings effortlessly reclaiming the insistent hypnotic groove, nerve-tingling, inciting, provocative.

'So what? I'm a peasant,' said Mike.

'Me too, at heart,' put in Nikkie.

'We know about you two and your weaknesses,' Chris said quickly, 'but the thing is, have you seen how they dispose of rubbish in this country? Follow any track off the beach road and you'll see, if you don't smell it first.'

The conversation was already turning sour before Kim said, 'You'd be better off back in England.' Chris was leaning back on two legs of his chair, waving a wine glass. How easy, Kim observed, it would be to push him down into the street.

'Yes,' said Nikkie. 'Why don't you shut up?'

Dancing had started in the yard down below. People were clapping or loudly toasting the dancers, observing the custom of offering a glass to them in a salute to their style.

'I'm just interested,' Chris persisted, 'no, fascinated, to find out what makes two people want to run off to a place like this.'

'We're suckers for punishment,' said Mike.

'Well you must be, because all you get here is lazy

service, unhygienic conditions, shit food—'

'For God's sake,' said Nikkie.

'But what I really want to know, what I *really* want to know more than anything, I mean what I *really really* want to know above all other things—'

'Yes,' said Mike, angry now, 'what do you really want to know?'

'What I want to know is: did you like fucking Nikkie from behind?'

For a moment time hit a fault line and the world dislocated; the table became a vacuum, and the music flattened around it like a hard shell holding back external events.

Mike stared at his empty plate. Nikkie looked away. Kim looked at Mike.

Chris carefully put his glass down, the music filled out and the world poured in again. 'I mean,' Chris was trembling, 'she won't let me do it that way. It oppresses her. I wondered if you were allowed to oppress her. With a fuck from behind.'

Nikkie glowered.

'Satisfied?' said Mike. 'Are you satisfied now?'

'I already knew,' said Kim.

'What?' Chris was astonished.

'Mike, answer his question,' said Kim.

'Kim—' Nikkie tried lamely.

'Just answer his question.'

'I don't remember—' Mike lied.

'Don't remember?' said Kim. 'But look at her, this is the woman we're talking about. How can you not remember? Perhaps you can remember, Nikkie? Help your husband out, why don't you? He wants to know. No, Chris, it now appears that everyone is suffering from amnesia. Perhaps they went in for sodomy, what do you say, Chris? And I'm sure he put it in her mouth, aren't you?'

Chris clearly wished he hadn't started it, but Kim hadn't finished. 'What was that word you taught me, Mike? Oh yes, perhaps they liked felching. Do you know what that is, Chris? Mike fucks her arse then sucks the semen back out again. Or perhaps—'

'Please, Kim,' said Mike. Chris was hanging his head.

'But isn't this what you wanted, Chris? And who were you trying to make feel the most uncomfortable? I thought about that. Was it Nikkie you were trying to embarrass most? Or did you want to hurt Mike by telling me? Or was it me you really wanted to humiliate because you've been humiliated? Which was it?'

Now no one would look at her.

'Let me tell you something, Chris. Yes, I already knew. But when it was unspoken, even though I knew it to be true, I could somehow live with it. But you see what you did? You spoke about it, and the words are out. You made it real. You gave it substance. So now it's a real thing, and I can't live with it.'

Kim got up and grabbed her handbag. Mike stood to go after her but she put out a hand. 'No, Mike. Don't chase after me. Don't follow me. This is not one of the games played by these two sad creatures.'

Mike saw what was in her eyes, and he knew not to try to follow. She turned and skipped down the steps, and went out into the street. One of the dancers smashed a plate, and then another one, to cheers.

Chris, hopelessly drunk, was weeping into his hands. Nikkie got up and put a hand on Mike's arm. 'I'll go after her,' she said.

The rest of the diners had become interested in what was

happening at their table. Mike challenged them with a glower. They all turned away and pretended to resume their conversations. He too thought about tipping Chris from the roof; but he guessed that that, after all, was probably what Chris wanted.

Nikkie squeezed her way through the dancers in the courtyard and ran out into the street in pursuit of Kim. She asked some tourists if they'd seen her; but she couldn't make them understand. Her heel twisted in the cobblestones and she had to limp back towards the village *platia*. She paused at the tap beside the Church of the Virgin. It was dripping, so she tried to turn it off, but the faucet was loose and the tap continued to drip. She wanted to take a look inside the church; she had a feeling Kim might have gone there, simply because she would have had nowhere else to go. But she hesitated. She'd already been upbraided by a priest for stepping inside a Greek Orthodox church while wearing shorts: the best parts of a woman's body were an abomination, it seemed. And now her shoulders and her arms were as bare as her legs.

She hovered at the door, and stepped inside.

The church was illumined by the soft radiance of a single candle flame at the altar. Kim was sitting on a bench against the wall, gazing at the burning candle. She was aware of Nikkie, but didn't look up.

Nikkie stood in the centre of the church and her attention was drawn upwards by the eye painted above the altar. For a moment it pinned her. A flicker from the candle made it flex briefly. She hugged herself. She felt naked before it, and ashamed. The eye swept across her exposed flanks. It looked up her skirt. It froze her, and it seemed to penetrate to her vital organs. Her bones chilled, and she shivered.

She tore herself away from the eye and stepped across to

Kim, meekly settling down next to her without a word. After a while, Kim said, '*The weak go to the wall*. Do you know where that expression comes from? It's from the days when our churches were like this, and the only seats were these benches along the wall. Old and frail people couldn't stand through a long service, and even though they were squeezed away from the light, they had to go to the wall.'

Nikkie said nothing.

'I sometimes wonder what is weak and what is strong,' Kim continued. 'Are they strong who take what they want? Or are they strong who deny themselves? You see, it's never as simple as the priest tells it. I mean, how do I know what temptations you are up against? We can't be all the same. My will might be stronger than yours; but then again it might just be that my desires are so much weaker. Which is it? We'll never know. Do you believe in God?'

'No,' said Nikkie.

'Me neither. Mike does: he's a believer down to his fingernails. But then I believe in something else. The Goddess, perhaps. I don't mean some theoretical feminist answer to God either. I don't know what it is. But it's much more frightening than God. Churning out miracles without a purpose. A slut goddess. One that smiles on adultery. Yes, she would approve of the adultery, but not of the betrayal of friendship. That's *too* sacred, Nikkie.'

'Mike loves you. He doesn't love me.'

'I know that. Of the four of us, I feel saddest for Mike. He wouldn't know why you did it. I've stood next to men in completely innocent situations, and a wave or a leading scent passes over you, and it's like an angel – not a demon – whispering in your ear to do it and you think *yes*, and yet they've never known. Again, is that because I'm stronger, or because my desires are weaker? Anyway, I've stood off;

I've let it pass. But Mike doesn't understand that you let it happen not because of any unstoppable desire for him, but because of your envy of me.'

Nikkie looked up at the all-seeing eye.

'That's right,' said Kim. 'You see, I'm wiser than you are.'

Nikkie was crying. 'It's just sex, Kim. Mike loves you. It's just sex. It makes fools of all of us.'

She tried to take hold of Kim's hand, but Kim withdrew it icily. She stood up. 'When you did that you let something out of the bottle, Nikkie, and now it doesn't want to go back in again. Go home. Go back to England.'

Kim's footfalls echoed on the stone floor as she left the church. Nikkie sat for a long time after she had gone. She knew she had lost Kim's friendship forever, that there was no going back. She felt a knot in her intestines, a nausea that denied her even the comfort of being able to apportion blame elsewhere. She did not feel sorry for herself; she felt sick with self-loathing. She felt herself being folded into darkness.

She sat there for a long time. Kim's words hurt her more than anything Chris might say; more even than Mike's rejection. She despaired. Then a sudden draught broke her trance. Nikkie shivered, stiffened. She stood up suddenly. *Something just came into the church*, she thought.

She glanced nervously around her. The candle had burned down to a stump and was casting shadows under the benches.

What is that smell? Is it something I know?

There was indeed a sharp, unpleasant odour displacing the tang of stale incense. It seemed to be filling the place, but from no particular direction. It leaked in at the door and at the ceiling and from behind the altar. It was an animal smell; rancid; the smell of the knacker's. It was strong: it stung her sinuses. Nikkie backed towards the wall, holding a hand to her mouth, the backs of her knees butting against the old wood of the bench on which she'd been sitting. She felt a slippery, greasy motion in her intestines.

'Who's there? You're frightening me.'

Nikkie reached an arm along the back of the bench to steady herself. She tried to draw herself to her full height, to look strong, but she didn't feel it. On the floor at the foot of the altar was a noose of light thrown by the candle. A circle of red light, the darkness seeming to gather around it, concentrating it. The candle burned dim and the disc of light flipped slowly twice, like a spinning coin. Then another nauseating wave of the foul odour was released, fiercely, like a blast from a furnace. Her scalp was crawling. An animal scuffled in the weak red light.

An ape. It's an ape.

Two red eyes blinked at her, and the ape bared its yellow teeth. It was a full-sized baboon, crouched and shivering below the altar. It looked at her with almost questioning eyes. Then it began to chatter aggressively.

Baboons? There are no apes in Greece. No baboons. How did it get in here? Where did it come from?

The stench of the animal had become overpowering. Nikkie gagged and held her hand across her mouth. She backed away towards the entrance to the church, but as she did so the animal became more excited, chattering at her, making short leaps towards her before retreating to the altar. She was afraid it might claw her. She came within a yard of the open doorway. As she turned to run outside, the baboon made a leap at her, narrowly missing.

Wild-eyed with fear, she stopped at the dripping tap. The

thing didn't seem to have followed her from the church. Keeping a watch on the church door she backed down the street, and returned to Riga's restaurant.

27

After Kim abandoned Nikkie in the church she walked to the *platia*. Live music was playing at one of the busy tavernas. Garish light stung her eyes. A breeze lifted from the sea and the waves lashed at the beach. The wind flapped the tablecloths in the tavernas and cleared some of the seafront restaurants of their customers. Kim sat down at an otherwise deserted taverna and ordered a glass of Metaxa.

Within minutes she was being pestered by two Greek boys making *kamaki* with the tourist women. By now she knew enough Greek abuse to turn their ear-to-ear smiles into sneers. But as soon as she had rid herself of them, two more threatened to take their place. She left her brandy unfinished and walked along the seafront, past the last taverna and up the steady incline of the road. Beyond the last streetlamp, cars tooted as they passed.

She had little idea of what she was doing or where she was going. She was approaching the house, but she had already decided not to go back there. Instead of taking the track down to the beach, she followed the red shale path up into the hills behind the house. The moonlight was bright enough to pick out the path ahead of her and although there was a breeze from the south, it was warm.

She climbed to the top of the hill and found, in an

outcropping slab of red rock, a cleft where she could lean her back. From there she could not quite see her own house, but she could see the waves beating into the shore, and the distant lights of Limanaki crested by the illuminated fort.

In the other direction she could see the promontory, where the mad hermit stood in the daytime looking out to sea. The promontory was a black finger of rock scratching at the beach, and though she could barely make out the knuckle on which the hermit liked to stand, she knew he wasn't there now. He always went in when the sun went down. Like her, he was a sunset watcher, but he'd never appeared after that, even on the brilliant moonwashed nights when visibility was high.

But now she felt as though she had picked up the baton from him, the baton of his chaos. She was his moon sister, taking over to watch the night as he did the day. What did he see? And would she see it?

It became a seductive possibility, to sit there, watching, every night, moon or no moon, wax or wane. This night the moon was horned, the north star suspended from its nether tip, streaking the water. Light angled towards her like a silver arrow from a bow.

A nightingale sang from a bush behind her.

It *had* made a difference that Chris had spoken of the affair between Nikkie and Mike. Before that moment, she had been able to preserve the knowledge of it in another part of her mind where it could do no harm, a bird's tongue in aspic. She had known it, internalised it, accommodated it within herself; but this external confirmation set it free, and the bird's tongue was shrill, persistent, maddening.

Before that evening, it was just an unresolved thought, half-formed words. *Affair. Mike and Nikkie. Together.* But now the words had become real things, crystallised, a hard currency of betrayal, coins falling on plates at a dinner table paying for an endless sequence of images she couldn't get out of her head. Nikkie with her legs wrapped around Mike's back, Mike sucking at her skinny breast, Nikkie closing her lips around his stiff cock, and on. Chris had infected her with his obsession, the sickening carnality that had obviously been playing on the back of his retina every time he saw the two of them. He had forced her to share it with him, and it made no difference whether your eyes were open or closed, the wounding pornography of it played on and on and on.

She shook her head to free herself from these images. Actually tried to turn her head away – from what? From herself? It was ridiculous, it wasn't the physicality which hurt her, but the intimacies that had been invaded and looted. So why did she persist in tormenting herself with these endless visions of her husband copulating with her friend?

But Kim knew she was lying to herself. There was no greater intimacy than what lay betokened in the physical. Whatever anyone said about the spheres of spiritual or platonic or cerebral union, there was no absolute consummation other than plain hard fucking. It was about penetration and reception; about surrender, each to the other. It was about the fire that consumes and cleans and remakes, the fire of the gods.

And it had been stolen from her.

The nightingale behind her sang with a prickling urgency, as if neurotic about the brevity of the night and the burden of a story which would take much longer to tell. It paused only to signature its song with a distinctive punctuation of four even notes. Whoever said the nightingale sang sweetly? Kim wanted to know. Sweetly? This is the song of emotional crisis, the bearer of a tragedy who cannot find a listener who will believe in the depth of her distress. Something so personal and profoundly heartaching that she has to go out at night looking for an audience just so that she can try to understand the thing herself.

With the moon hovering over the water and with the nightingale singing at her back, Kim fell into a doze. She dreamed a feverish dream of wild women, their naked bodies smeared with juice of berries. There was firelight, there was drumming, there was excitement and an acrid smell in the air. One woman fell to the floor in a fit. Leave her, the others said. Kim was given a terracotta jar in which ivy leaves and berries swam in a greasy substance, and she was exhorted to drink. It stung her throat. She coughed in her dream, and coughed herself awake.

The nightingale was gone. The moon had moved across the face of the water. A scorpion, silvered in the moonlight, scuttled beneath a rock several yards away. She closed her eyes and fell asleep again.

The women again. The ground swung to and fro deliriously before her. Some women were drumming. Then the drums refashioned themselves into bizarre xylophones constructed of leather strips stretched across the open cavities of men's skulls. The rhythm changed as the women played these macabre instruments. She was awoken again by the sound of sheep bells close by. She opened her eyes to see one of the nearby sheep look up at her from its grazing, evidently as surprised as she was.

They were Manoussos' sheep. He would be somewhere behind them. She got up quickly, brushing dust from her clothes. It was a beautiful fresh morning, the sky still a ceramic white-blue. The sun was up and the moon hadn't yet disappeared from the sky.

Manoussos was slowly making his way up the sheep track towards her, moving his flock along. He hadn't yet seen her. She considered hiding, but it was useless. He looked up and stopped in his tracks. He had seen her. He hastened towards her.

The shepherd was so surprised to encounter her on the hillside, he spoke to her in rapid Greek, and in the paternal mode. '*Pou pas? Pou pas, pedia mou?*' Where are you going, my child? He shook his head quizzically from side to side, demanding an answer to this mystery. They conversed in Greek for the first time, but Manoussos seemed not to notice.

'But what are you doing here?'

'It's all right. I'm just walking.'

'Just walking, is it? At this hour?' He grasped her wrist with his rough leathery fingers, rubbing the back of her hand to feel the cold of night on her skin. She knew the shepherd could tell she'd been out all night. He was wearing a headscarf knotted above his brow. His eyes looked black and severe, but his face was creased with anxiety and concern for her. His iron-grey moustache bristled with a life of its own, independent of mood. 'This is not good. No, child. What are you doing on the hill all night? Where is Mike?'

'He's at the house.'

Manoussos had let go of her hand and was wringing his own together. He was in a terrible state of agitation. 'Where is your husband? Where is Mike? He should not leave you on the hill at night, like this. What is he thinking? What is going on?'

This time Kim put her hand on his arm, to calm him. 'We

had a fight. An argument. But it's all right. Really it is.'

'A fight?'

'Yes, a fight. Husband and wife. Sit down with me a minute. Talk with me.'

But Manoussos didn't want to sit down. 'I don't like it!' he shouted. 'On the hill at night, I don't like it!'

He looked away from her and banged his crook on the ground. Then he fumbled in his pocket, producing a packet of dirty-looking goat's cheese and a few olives. He handed them to her and gave her his water bottle. 'Now you must eat some breakfast,' he said illogically. 'You shouldn't be going around without breakfast. No.'

She ate some of the cheese gladly, but Manoussos had no patience. 'Come on. We must go back to the house. We must speak to Mike.'

'No, Manoussos—'

'Together we must go. Together.' And he beckoned her forward, setting off down the hill at speed. Kim knew it was utterly useless to resist. Manoussos would prevail until things were resolved in the way he thought appropriate. She followed him down the hill, at a distance of several paces, but near enough to hear his steady drone of complaints and dark mutterings.

When they arrived at the shuttered house, Manoussos stepped up and rapped sharply on the door with his shepherd's crook. After a pause Mike came to the door, bare-chested and blinking at the sunlight.

'Here she is,' Manoussos declared. He had reverted to English. 'Here she is.'

'I looked all over for you.'

'I'm all right.'

'I tried everywhere.'

'Manoussos insisted on bringing me here.'

The shepherd nodded at Mike severely, as if to confirm the correctness of his course of action. He sniffed. 'I'm going,' he said, wagging a brown finger at Mike. 'Don't leave this woman on the hill again.'

Manoussos left the garden and began to ascend the hill, complaining loudly in Greek, returning to his sheep.

'Are you going to have some breakfast?'

'No.'

'Are you sure?'

'Yes, I'm sure. Have the other two gone home?'

Mike looked at his watch. 'I think so. I hope so. Nikkie was in a strange state when she came back to the taverna.'

'Should I care about Nikkie?'

'No. Do you want to talk?'

'Talk? Mike, that's the last thing I want. I don't want to hear a word. There's been too much talk. If we talk now, I'm afraid bad things will happen.'

'Kim—'

'Did you hear me? I said I don't want to talk. Now I'm going inside to sleep. Don't follow me.'

Mike stood back. He knew Kim never said these things lightly. He knew that to follow her inside would inflict more damage than he'd already done. He watched her close the door after her. In a tree above his head a white pigeon fidgeted on a branch, cooing quietly and uneasily.

28

It was after midnight at the House of Lost Dreams, the third night following Kim's vigil, when Manoussos had brought her down from the hills. There was no moon. Mike sat under the vine in the weak circle of yellow light cast by the hurricane lamp. The light was dim because the lamp-glass was blackened with carbon, and Mike had neglected to clean it. A gecko on the whitewashed wall behind him seized a large moth, tearing the wings in its jaws.

Mike sat in silence, nursing a glass of ouzo. A little water added to the ouzo flared like vapour trails across a sky before turning the liquid milky and cloudy. Out on the sea the bright prow lamp of a night fisherman glided by, incredibly close in, it seemed, almost as if about to row up the garden. He could hear the gentle passage of the oars drawn slowly through the water. That night two or three of them plied the waters.

Almost no words had been exchanged. Mike had tried, only to be met by a freezing silence. Then in anger Mike had challenged her to leave.

'So why don't you go? Why don't you? If you can't stand to speak to me, why not get out? Go back up on the mountain – why don't you?'

She answered that. 'Because this is my place. Because I've always wanted to be here. You're the one who wanted to get away from here. So why don't you? Don't ask me to go for what you've done. This is my place.'

He didn't entirely understand her. He recognised all the words, but failed to accommodate the passion with which she staked her claim on the place, the house, the surroundings; as if all of that had become more important than their relationship, as if their marriage was a mere adjunct to those things, and not the other way around.

Mike's response was to booze. Total immersion. He sat in ouzo-soaked silence. Kim was inside, sleeping, or pretending to sleep. Of all the freakish things that had happened around that place, this for him was the strangest, the most disturbing: that she should be there, in close proximity, and yet living at an emotional distance of light years; that they should eat from the same table, share the same dishes, and not speak; that they should lie together at night in the same bed and not touch. These were the things that made him sit up late at night, drinking.

The booze had done its job, deadened nerves, numbed him, closed him down. His mind was on a loose trawl in the dark, a net washing through cold black waters. No moon. His mind was not sleeping, but neither was it awake, exactly. There were *thoughts* down there, in the deep, resting on mud and occasionally releasing a bubble to pop at the surface of Mike's consciousness. They were down there sure enough. The thoughts he was trying to chase off with alcohol. But it didn't matter how long he sat in the dark, eventually the net would drag, make weight, and he would be forced to haul net by his prow lamp and look at the thought-thing writhing, snapping, stinking and dredged up in his net, the thing he least wanted to see: *I've lost her. My God, I've lost her. I just know it. There is this terrible certainty in me that terms between us have changed horribly.*

*Some awful shift and I won't get her back. My God, I just
know it's so.*

He knew this to be true in the way that the body knows
before the mind has had time to recognise what is
happening. He felt a tightening in his chest, a fist squeezing
his innards. Of all the inadmissible events that had
happened in this place, this was the most unthinkable, the
least tolerable.

He got up and staggered to the edge of the concrete
patio, resting a hand on the wall where the gecko,
unmoving, watched him with bulging, scared eyes. He
vomited loudly, retching up the thought-thing trapped in
his night's trawl of freezing, shadowy waters.

29

Three weeks passed by with Kim maintaining the integrity of her careful distance. The preposterous silence had been strained before being broken, but a new economy of communication had sprung into being to take its place. It was communication with a chilling practicality, primitive, utilitarian. All talk was stripped of abstract relations. Verbal exchange was a debased currency in which all their language was concrete, formal and simple. There was no play, richness, metaphor, irony or affection in anything they had to say to each other.

The normal emotions and sensitivities began to freeze. Ice formed, almost visible between blocks of words.

'Where are you going today?'

'To the village.'

'I want to take the car.'

'Take it. I don't need it.'

Kim found reasons to take her away from the house in the daytime. She did some work for Kati, cleaning and preparing rooms for tourists; she undertook some administration for the women's co-operative, communicating with the tour companies; she offered favours in minding Maria's or Kati's stores if they needed a break. For most of these things she was paid modest wages. This saved her from having to ask Mike to advance money from their joint savings. More importantly, she didn't have to hang around the house while he drank.

There was an entire set of complicated rules by which they lived in this way, remarkable in that none of these rules had been agreed as such, yet they were observed as if mounted on a brass plate screwed to the wall above the bed. Amongst these, Mike was not allowed to mention or discuss the difficulties existing between them, nor the affair with Nikkie. Neither was he allowed to question Kim about what the future might hold. She in turn was not permitted to pass comment on his appalling drinking, or the neglect of any domestic chores around the house. She meant to punish him by withdrawing all intimacy and affectionate relations; he responded by drinking himself beyond a point where this could hurt him. In each case the greater damage was done to themselves by their own actions.

The final rule related to physicality. They were not allowed to touch each other. Even though they shared the same bed, and a hand or a foot might accidentally brush the other, it would be withdrawn, until it was impossible to even attempt reconciliation. The opportunity for rejection would give the other partner too severe an advantage. So the stroke or caress which might just possibly end this hopeless situation was never offered.

Of the two of them it was Kim who was the most rigorous overseer of these conditions. She managed to imply, mysteriously and without ever alluding to them, that violation of these rules might lead to even further sanctions, and to the ultimate withdrawal of what little proximity remained. In this regard, Mike's suffering might have appeared to be the greater. But this was not necessarily the case; she had an extra capacity to inflict these wounds on herself.

And because all hurt is like any wound, scabbing over with some unpleasant crust, it easily became transformed into a kind of loathing of the object of the hurt. It is not possible to bear hurt indefinitely. A vile process of rationalising away the hurt takes over, for survival's sake. And love being suspended, all kinds of negative emotions crouch at the ready, waiting to storm the ensuing vacuum.

Then the question is asked: why are we here together at all? Why at all? When it was such a mistake? But this, the most dangerous question, was never asked openly. Only some freezing charity between them kept it away.

Meanwhile Mike had returned to the hospital to have the plaster cast removed. He drove himself to the hospital and back again. On his return he showed his arm to Kim: a matter of practical interest, and therefore permitted. The hairs on his arm had grown thicker and darker under the plaster.

'How is it?'

'A bit weak. But let me show you this.'

Mike held his arm up for her to see an unusual disfiguration. On his forearm was a distinctive purple scar in the shape of a Greek omega: Ω.

Kim held his arm to look. 'Can you remember doing it?'

He didn't want her to know how it felt to have her cool fingers touching his arm again. 'I remember having the shit beaten out of me by those three monks or whatever they were. I remember it just as clearly as if it was yesterday, and nothing else.'

'Weird.' She let his arm drop.

Kim started to go out in the evening with her new friends amongst the women of the village. Mike ventured out only rarely. Occasionally they went out together, to keep up appearances, or perhaps out of habit, if some other couple invited them. On one such evening they were waiting, wordlessly, at a taverna for Kati and Vassillis to appear. A waiter came by and said something to Kim in Greek, which Mike missed. She laughed sweetly and sexily, and answered him at length. He saw a vivacity in her eyes he hadn't seen for some time, a flirtation, light on water. It cut to the raw. He was surprised at the fluency of her Greek. The smiling waiter stood with his tray hanging at his thigh, and Mike was unable to follow half of what was being said between them. He commented on it when the waiter had gone.

'I'm speaking a lot of Greek with the Greek women,' Kim said. 'It develops if you don't talk English all the time.'

'I don't seem to be talking much to anyone in any language lately.'

'You should get out a bit more.'

'Where?'

'Meet some tourists.'

'I don't want to meet tourists. All they want to do is eat *souvlaki* and get pissed in the rock café.'

'Better in company than to sit home doing it.'

'Thanks,' Mike snapped, 'but I prefer to sit home.'

'Please yourself.' Kim looked at her wristwatch. 'Here come Kati and Vassillis. Don't let them pay again. Will you pay?'

'I'm paying all the time.'

Kim looked at him. He couldn't detect what was in that look. Her eyes were like a mosaic of pity and contempt, sympathy and boredom. It was all there.

'How long will this go on?' said Mike.

But the others had arrived. Kim stood up to greet them. It was time to be pleasant, in company.

30

He drinks, and that will do him no good. That is the direct path to loss of soul. There are spirits which come from the mountain and spirits which come from inside a bottle, and if he goes too far with his drinking he will not be a friend to himself.

He will not be able to fight when the day comes.

Why? thought Manoussos. Why? Why did you let her go on the day when I brought her down from the hills and delivered her safely into your hands. When I did all that, still you let her go. I found her there on the hill, the moon's chill on her lovely skin, the stars on her shoulders like a shawl. She frightened me. There was inspiration in her eyes. Some spirit from the hills or from the moon was in her. She made me quake with her looks; I had to turn away so that she wouldn't see the trembling of my hand. But I brought her down to you. And still you let her go! Were you afraid too, Mikalis? Were you afraid like me?

Manoussos sat against a rock, his arms cradling his crook as he watched the house. He had seen Mike sleeping on the patio, his head on the table. He had been there all night. Now the moon had him too.

Does the moon have you too, Mike-Mikalis? Has her sweet agony won you over, that you sit out here at night waiting for her withered gifts? Fool. You let that woman go and walked straight into the arms of the moon.

Manoussos spat. The ball of white spittle rolled in the dust. If he had such a woman he would not let her go. He would have slapped her, taken her by force, locked her indoors for some days until she had cooled off. Why, Mike, are you such a fool? Don't you see what you have there in that woman?

The shepherd shook his head. What did he know about women? Nothing. Less than nothing. What right had he to advise the man how to use his wife? When women made him so afraid?

This was something he did not like to admit. Never never admit. But it was true. Women were open to the universe, open. That's why they had holes, of course, to be filled with spirits, angels, demons, energies, powers, babies, life. Against all these, a horn was a small thing to fill a woman's hole. Ha! Ha ha!

Manoussos heard his own laughter echo back at him from the arid rock. He was afraid for a moment that his mirthless cackling might have woken Mike, or given away his position. He pushed his headscarf back an inch on his head and told himself it was no laughing matter. Then he couldn't remember why he was laughing anyway. What he did remember was that he must be a help to Mike.

He recalled the morning when he had seen Mike perform what he thought was an earthquake dance – a poor effort to be certain, little more than a jig. Now, he had never seen Mike dance another step since that day. Perhaps that was the secret. Perhaps he had lost his spirit somewhere, misplaced his *kefi*. Could that be a way in which Manoussos might help? Could he help him to rediscover it through the dance?

He must be careful. Very careful.

He must teach the Englishman without arousing his self-consciousness or exciting either suspicion or scepticism. The English, he mused, were a race who were *capable* of flying, but who fell back to earth very easily. It was a delicate matter. Dance magic was as frail and as light as the dust on a moth's wings.

Manoussos knew the five dances of the left hand. His father had taught him the five dances, and he had taught him well. When he was a boy, when other boys were learning their *syrtaki* dances, their butcher's dances, Manoussos was in the hills with his brother and his father, being schooled in the dances of power.

Manoussos did not hate the *syrtaki* dances so popular with tourists and film-makers. They were fun, sure. They were festival dances. In fact these dances were less ridiculous than the discotheque dances made by tourists. Once he had looked inside a discotheque to see how they did things. It had made him fall over with surprise! How he had laughed! Someone had bought him a beer and he stayed, laughing and imitating this preposterous movement of the hips. Then they grew tired of him laughing, he knew, but it had given him insight into their culture. In the discotheque dance he had seen their lives. It had made him feel giddy and unfixed like a jellyfish on a wave. Childish and sexual at the same time. To dance in this way, it was like having your bare bottom tickled with a feather, a man could do nothing but laugh and laugh and laugh until they asked you to leave their preposterous discotheque, which he had done, still laughing.

The *syrtaki* dances, the Zorba dances, were fun for festivals and for dancing with children and tourists. But they were not dances of power.

They were not like the five dances of the left hand.

241

The first dance, the dance of the thumb, was the dance of *kefi*. This was the dance of spirit, of joy, in which a man converted his joy and suffering into dance, and was purified by the hot river of fire summoned in the steps of the dance. This dance was suitable for public places and public expression. It was celebrated at the festivities of Easter or of name-day festivals. In order to learn any other dance, Mike must first be taught this dance.

Could Mike be taught these dances? Only if he wanted to learn them, truly wanted to learn them. And for that he must show willingness. And he must suffer humiliations.

The second dance, the dance of the index and martial finger, was the dance of war with spirits. It was a dance suitable before battle of any kind. If he learned no other dance – other than the dance of *kefi* – Mike was going to have to learn this one. This was the pointing finger, and therefore the dance of the path of resolution. This was the dance which would take him to the grave and out again.

'I have looked into the heart of this man,' Manoussos said suddenly, aloud to the flawless sky, 'and I believe he may learn some things.' Then he nodded to himself, as if he had silenced the protests of some unseen dissenter.

The third dance, the middle finger, was the dance of sexual arousal. This was appropriate, the middle digit living like a phallus between the two legs of the adjacent fingers. He had seen tourists offer this finger as an insult of sexual connotation; and the English conjoined two fingers, the phallic and the martial finger for a similar gesture of offence. This dance, the dance of sexual arousal, he would not be teaching Mike. Manoussos himself had used this dance only once before, and with terrifying consequences. He had paid the price.

Over and over.

The fourth dance, for the finger which – free of all the others – will not stand erect, was the dance of animals, fishes and birds. Manoussos was able to make his fourth finger stand on end independently of the others. It had taken practice. He had not forgotten how difficult it was – without bunching those other four digits – to make the fourth finger stand up while the others cowered. Only mankind, of all the earth's creatures, walks erect. It was also the finger with a mysterious connection to the heart, a nerve traffic conducting the secret essences of life and the spirit of all living things. Different cultures adopted the fourth finger on right or left hand for the bearing of the marriage ring, for this magical matter of heart and the spirit which goes to the source and procreation of all life. This was a dance for which Mike had propensity. Manoussos had witnessed it that day in the field of snakes. With an instinct for safety Mike had tried to fly. Perhaps he could master this dance.

The fifth dance, the final and most terrifying, was the dance to stop time. This was the dance of the little finger. Existing as it did on the edge of the map of the hand, it lived at the end of the world. Manoussos had experienced it once only, in its teaching, when it was handed over. It had destroyed his father. This dance would never be taught, to Mike or to anyone. It would die with him.

Five dances of the left hand. The dance of life itself; of conflict; of sex; of transformation; and of death.

He was sure he could teach Mike the first, the dance of *kefi*. It was likely the Englishman could also learn the dance of animals, birds and fishes. It was even possible – just possible – he could master the dance of war with spirits.

But before he could do any of these things he must stop poisoning himself with alcohol. Already his life was changing. By this time of the morning, the shepherd mused, he should be up with Kim and swimming in the sea. Now the sea swam in him. And Kim slept on, inside the house and far away. And the more Mike was possessed by the spirit of alcohol, the more Kim was open to the dangerous influence of the house.

We must stir Mike out of this, he thought, and place him on the path of resolution. If he will not be a friend to himself, I, Manoussos, must be a friend to him.

31

Two hours after Kim had drifted off to sleep she was awoken by a crashing and a clattering out on the patio. It was Mike, returning drunk and incoherent from the Black Orchid rock bar. He'd taken to spending his evenings drinking expensive imported beers under ultraviolet light, boring any tourist who could be bothered to pretend to listen to his mumblings above the high-decibel soundtrack. When he woke her up like this she found it almost impossible, with anger rising in her throat, to get back to sleep.

The door swung open and slapped against the wall. She lay in the dark, choking back her desire to scream at him, pretending to be asleep. He lurched towards her and within moments he was stretched out on the bed, perspiring heavily, snoring loudly.

Disgusted, she got out of bed, pulling the covers with her. She dragged some chair cushions outside and assembled a bed on the patio before closing the door on the tooth-saw rasp of Mike's snoring. She climbed into her makeshift bed and lay propped on an elbow, gazing up at the stars.

It was a clear night. Billions of stars seemed visible, spilled across the sky like sugar crystals. The thin, cloudy band of the Milky Way made a stream across the heavens;

she tried to understand it as a disc, herself positioned on its rim and peering into the centre. She looked up into the night sky for a long time before falling asleep again.

She was awoken by the sound of the door opening. She knew some hours had passed, because the sky had changed colour from sable to mauve, and the stars were less visible. Mike was naked, shuffling across the patio with strange, automated movements. He negotiated the step and set off down the garden path. He was sleepwalking again.

She thought about leaving him to it. But even though at that moment she hated him, she couldn't bear the thought of him coming to harm while he was asleep. It was a puzzling impulse which drove her almost to distraction. She didn't care to what grief he might come while he was drunk; but when by sleeping he imperilled himself in this way, she was driven to protect him. It was as if she considered him, in these circumstances, to be grappling with forces, spirits, demons which were beyond his resources to defeat. Drunk, he might step off a cliff or into the sea, and she would see him as entirely responsible for his own actions. But when he prowled in his sleep, she felt frightened. Here he was in a different element, hopelessly out of his depth, and drowning.

Kim got up and followed him noiselessly down to the beach. His naked skin was silver in the moonlight. He stopped by the moored boat and began scratching amongst the stones on the beach. She preferred not to wake him. To do so would mean that she would have to sit with him for a while, because whenever she woke him in this condition, he always came to in a state of some shock. On most occasions she had simply been able to watch him safely back to bed. She waited until the moment would come when he could be guided back up to the house.

At last he seemed to find what he was looking for: a smooth white stone. He held it up to the moon's bright light before taking up position, like an athlete, to throw it far out into the water. It plopped at a distance from the shore. Then he waited, as if for some kind of answer. After a while he shook his head and, muttering, recommenced scrabbling amongst the stones until he found a similar but larger missile to throw.

He did this three times, on each occasion seeming to wait for a response, shaking his head and muttering. Kim watched in dismay. Finally he turned, and not looking at Kim but seemingly across her shoulder, he said clearly, 'But you see they must come back, eventually.'

After that Mike seemed to have lost his purpose and Kim recognised the moment to gently steer him by the elbow. She managed to get him back up the garden path without waking him. He stumbled on the step, but then found his own way back to bed. Kim covered him with a blanket and went back outside, closing the door on him. She returned to her own makeshift bed.

She tossed and turned, unable to drift back to sleep. Within half an hour the garden began to whiten hazily with the light of false dawn. Kim tried to cover her head with her blankets, but something stopped her from dozing. She lay with her eyes closed, but with thoughts spinning in her head. The sense of the day stirring was too difficult to resist.

She turned at last and blinked from under her blankets. The phantom grey-white of dawn was already turning yellow; colour was seeping into the garden and flickering on the surface of the sea, like something trying to ignite. She knew from experience that the sun would at any moment squeeze over the mountains to spill golden light across the bay.

She chilled. Someone was in the garden watching her. Not more than fifteen feet away, studying her intently. Kim sat up with a start.

It was a woman. She stood under a tree. Her hand was reaching up to grasp one of the branches. Kim let out a stifled cry.

The woman showed no sign of moving, and no alarm. She was about the same age as Kim. She was a large-boned woman, with honey-coloured hair falling across her eyes. She was trying to smile, but bitterly. Kim felt a great wave of sadness emanating from the woman; a terrible depression akin to that she herself had experienced in inexplicable moments while in that house.

Instinctively, Kim knew exactly who the woman was.

'Eva,' she said.

Kim got up and stepped down from the patio on to the grass. At that same moment, the great yellow disc of the sun flooded across the crack between the hills to the east. Yellow light lanced across the blue sky, inflaming the trees. The woman's face was eclipsed by the brilliant rays. Kim was dazzled. She blinked and shielded her eyes with her hand.

When she looked again, the woman had gone. There was no one there. But out of the incandescent light something came fluttering towards her. It circled in the air before her. It was a large butterfly, a stunning blue and red and grey swallowtailed butterfly. Miraculously, it alighted on the side of Kim's face, where she felt its presence like a kiss of infinite tenderness. A shiver passed through her. Kim's skin flushed white-cold, and then hot.

And within a moment the butterfly had gone.

32

Mike woke with a pile-driver hangover that morning. In the outhouse he found a scorpion on the toilet seat, and he crushed it with his shoe. When he pumped water into a bucket to flush the toilet, the pump mechanism seemed to grind dryly inside his own head. He went back up to the patio and had another glass of ouzo under the vine canopy. It made him feel better. It deferred the ravages of the hangover.

Kim had already got up and left the house while he slept.

After drinking half a bottle of ouzo he made a somewhat foggy decision to take a walk into the village. He took the short cut across the rocky track, where the bored soldiers eyed him warily. In the village the tomato lady waved him a cheery hello and he struggled to return the smile. The butcher's wife wished him good afternoon and he offered a brave *Kali Mera*. Maria at the dress shop called to him and he waved back at her.

He loitered by the Church of the Virgin before approaching Kati's shop. Kim was inside, chatting with Kati. He passed by the window, but they didn't see him. He hoped Kati would catch sight of him and call him inside. He loitered as a customer went in, and when the same customer came out he walked by the window again, affecting a look of bored distraction, turning only at the last moment. He thought he saw Kim look away; but he was uncertain whether or not she'd seen him.

He walked around the corner and leaned his back against a wall. *Let me in*, he prayed. *Please let me in*.

It was a full twenty minutes before he admitted she wasn't going to come out of the shop. He fretted. He knew he should go but he couldn't tear himself away. If he returned to the house, he knew that within ten minutes he would find himself wandering back towards the village, to wherever Kim was. He felt hollow, feverish. He was running a temperature. At last, in a condition of misery, he headed towards the *platia*.

For the extraordinary nature of his obsession was that, even though when together at the house with nothing to say to each other – or prevented from speaking by the burden of what should have been said – he couldn't stand to be out of her presence. If being with her was an appalling kind of torture, being apart from her was something worse.

He sat at one of the tavernas in the square and ordered a glass of Metaxa. Most of the tourists were settled down on the beach, stretched on the afternoon griddle. It occurred to him how dirty and tired he must look. He was unshaven, he'd slept in his clothes for the past two nights. The bloom of sweat on his brow had the sugary, sticky saturation of alcohol. His face flushed hot at the thought.

He changed his seat, to get an uninterrupted view of the street through to the back of the village, in case Kim should come by that way. Then he ordered another drink. He twitched. He stroked his hand through his hair several times. He shuffled in his seat. He stood up with the intention of going back to the house, then changed his mind and sat down again.

He was burning up inside. If only Kim would speak to

him – properly speak to him – for two or three minutes, he would feel better. He only needed a small dose of acknowledgement to get him through the day. Some tiny nod of recognition of what they really meant to each other; some humanity in it all. He was convinced they were playing a game, based on denial of true feelings; and he needed occasionally to break the rules of the game by blowing a whistle so they could take time out to cry and hug each other for a moment, even if they then had to proceed with the game. But Kim was playing as if there was no game, as if this was all the real thing . . .

He suddenly felt violently disposed towards her. There was a knock of blood in his brain as he thought what he might do to her with his bare hands. Then the moment passed, and he felt weepy.

I'm sick, he muttered to himself. *I feel sick.*

What was the use of all this hanging around? Where did it get him? More than once he'd caught himself waiting around on corners of different streets, at odd hours of the day, like an addict waiting for the delivery of an illegal package. When all he wanted was a moment or two with her in which she would demonstrate some emotion. But she had become so cold. Like someone dead. She was an emotional wraith. Why couldn't she understand he didn't want to say anything to her, at least nothing explicit? But if she would just cradle his feverish head for a moment in her cool hands, just to show she still cared, just enough to give him a sliver of hope.

His veins itched. His skin prickled. He tossed back another glass of brandy, winced at its strength and felt momentarily better. *Kim, you can't just take it away from me. You can't just withdraw it like that.*

He loved her. He was in hell.

Mike got up and left the taverna without paying. The waiter shrugged and collected his glass, watching Mike shamble down to the beach: he would be back. When Mike got on to the beach he kicked off his shoes. He fell heavily on the sand. A woman called her children away from him. He glared at her, pulling his socks off. The sun was yellow, waxy. The sand was hot. Mike popped open the buttons on his shirt and lay back on the sand. Within a few moments he had fallen asleep.

When he came to, the beach was deserted, the sun had set. Lilac water was lapping quietly a few yards from his feet. He sat up. He had a headache. Scrambling to his feet, he dusted sand from his shirt and trousers. It was stuck to his face where he'd been sweating. He felt in his pocket for his house key, but couldn't find it.

He climbed off the beach and stood in the road, dithering. Kati and Vassillis came by. They stopped. Kati approached Mike, almost nervously, and cupped a hand under his cheek. She flicked away some of the sand sticking to his face.

'Mike, you don't look too good.'

'I've lost my key.'

'When did you eat last? We're just going to eat now. Come with us. We want some company.'

'Yes,' said Vassillis. 'Come with us.'

'No. I've lost my key.' He took a step away from them, but Vassillis followed.

'Today is my name-day. There is a festival. Join us.'

Mike held up his hands. He didn't want them. He didn't want their sympathy. He didn't want to be with them. He jumped back and set off up the road, breaking into a little trot. They stared, astonished. 'No,' he said again. 'I've lost my key.'

'Kim will be there,' Vassillis called.

Mike pretended not to have heard. He ducked into the Black Orchid bar. The ultraviolet tube lighting inside was no brighter than the exterior dusk. It suited his mood. He sat on a high stool at the bar and ordered an imported beer from Panayota, the pert young barmaid in a baseball cap. She uncapped a bottle and tipped him a wink. Eventually the bar began to fill up with young couples nursing sunburns and digesting oily moussaka dinners. They were all dressed beautifully in holiday clothes new from the wrappers. The women bared their legs, the men their muscular arms. Mike became momentarily self-conscious about his unkempt appearance. Then he burped loudly and the feeling went away.

But in the deep violet light of the bar, these visitors looked like angels, deeply tanned, healthy, the whites of their eyes dazzling like the figures on a Byzantine church painting. They spoke in many different languages. Mike tuned into the general din of their conversations and it was like listening to the host speaking in tongues.

'Fuck the saints. Fuck the angels,' Mike said to the bar population in general. People pretended not to have heard. Panayota placed another beer in front of him.

'From the saint,' she said.

'Is this from you?' Mike slurred.

'Say nothing,' said Panayota.

'Come to the festival. St Vassillis' name-day. Say yes.'

Panayota served two people before making up her mind. 'OK. Wait until ten o'clock.'

So Mike drank four or five more beers, waiting until Panayota was relieved from behind the bar. Vassillis had said that Kim would be at the name-day festivities, so he wanted to be there, even though the best he could hope for was a table from where he could watch her. This he could do, but not alone.

He studied the young Greek girl stylishly mixing Tequila Sunrises and Blue Ladies. Panayota was a student in Athens, working the summer in her cousin's bar. Diminutive and pretty, she had sand-coloured skin and a perfect row of pearl-bright teeth. She was as untouched as a mountain violet in the dew. Her eyes were bright with virginity and a vague sense of her own desirability.

Look at you, Mike thought cruelly, you stunningly beautiful virgin. You will save yourself for your husband and he will stick it in you on your wedding night and you will conceive immediately. Then you'll pump up like a pigskin and you'll never bother to come down again. Then like all the other fat Greek women you'll grow a soft, downy moustache on your upper lip and no one will ever know you once laughed like a bell and mixed cocktails in a bar lit with soft lights.

She saw him looking at her, and wanted to know what he was thinking.

'Evil thoughts,' he said.

'What kind?'

'Come here.' He beckoned and made her lean across the bar so he could whisper in her ear. 'Are you a virgin?'

'Are you a fool?' she said, dancing away.

'Why d'you say that?'

'We have a saying. I don't know if it can translate. A fool and a virgin, they lie together.'

Mike puzzled on it for a moment. 'Do you mean they tell lies together? Or they lie down together?'

She waved him away. She thought he was teasing her. He wasn't.

It was nearer eleven o'clock before Panayota could get away. The festival of St Vassillis was taking place at the Church of the Apostle, situated at the edge of the village. Tables had been laid out in the courtyard. Amplified bazouki music announced the festivities a quarter of a mile away from the event. When they got there the party was already hitting its peak, with a crowded dance floor and a litter of broken crockery to show the tradition of plate-smashing had been honoured. Mike and Panayota found a table at the rear of the courtyard.

A few heads turned and registered the two of them together before turning away. Panayota, Mike knew, was there to practise her English. He didn't flatter himself. She chattered away happily as he looked around to see whether he could catch sight of Kim. In the crowd he saw Kati and Vassillis sitting with Maria. He saw the tomato lady, red-faced from drinking, sitting with someone who was presumably the tomato man. The butcher and the butcher's wife sat with Lakis and his wife. The entire village had turned out. But no Kim.

Then he saw her on the dance floor. She was laughing and performing a version of the *tsifteteli*, a kind of belly dance, while two handsome young Greek men shouted encouragement, kneeling before her and clapping in time with the music. Then another man dragged up a chair and exhorted Kim to climb on it to continue her dance. The men roared their approval as Kim gyrated her hips. Mike brushed a hand through his hair.

'Come on,' said Panayota. 'Let's dance.'

He resisted, but she prevailed, tactfully leading him to another part of the dance floor, where she tried to show him how to execute a Greek dance. He deliberately made a hash of it, to the tolerant amusement of his fellow dancers.

It was a grisly parody of Greek dancing, holding his arms out and creeping back and forth like a man on a tightrope, which somehow seemed appropriate. For a moment he really was up there on a rope, surrounded by a sea of upturned faces. Then he heard a drum roll and he felt himself toppling. There was no safety net and he hit the floor heavily, vaguely aware of the flashing heels of the dancers stepping around him.

He looked up and Kim was standing over him, shaking her head. Then she was helping him up. There were gaps in his sequence of vision, brief blackouts staggering the sequence of events. When he got to his feet it was not Kim who had helped him up but Panayota. He realised how drunk he was and shouldered his way through the dancers to his table, with Panayota following.

'I think you cut your head,' said Panayota, brushing his hair back.

'Are you going to lick my wounds?'

'No.'

'Let me put my tongue in your mouth.'

'Fool.'

'Virgin.'

He closed his eyes and when he opened them again, the girl had gone. I don't blame you, thought Mike. I don't blame anyone.

He sat alone for a long time. People were going home. The band had stopped playing, waiters with their sleeves rolled up were clearing away empty bottles. Someone touched his shoulder from behind. It was Kim. He made to speak, but she leaned across him and stopped his mouth with a kiss.

His head swam. Before he'd recovered, she had disappeared into the shadows.

Panayota had returned. She was standing beneath a tree, looking at him from under the peak of her baseball cap. Draped over her shoulders was a man's denim jacket.

'Where did you get the coat?'

'I'm a little cold. My cousin gave it to me.' She gestured over to a table where a few stragglers remained. Mike realised his actions and his behaviour with the girl would have been closely observed. No one in this village missed a trick. Mothers watched daughters, brothers spied on their sisters, and cousins were protective about what they themselves were denied. 'Shall we walk back into the village?'

They made slow progress. When they reached the *platia* Mike said, 'Why am I trailing around with a virgin on my arm?'

'Fool.'

'Don't you say anything else?'

She looked at him coquettishly, her eyes liquid, like dark wine. Mike blinked. Could these beautiful virgins guess at the depth and rage of men's desires? He wanted to do something to shock her. The demon in him wanted to tie her to his bed. The decent man in him spoke up and found another way. He would make a confession to her in the church of her name.

He grabbed her arm. 'Come on. I'm going to show you something.'

'Where are we going?'

'To the Church of the Virgin. I'm going to show you something I did there.'

It was a potentially fatal admission. Mike knew that, but had a deep need to exorcise himself. Yet it was too late. When they reached the church, something had got there first.

The illumination had been switched off. Mike stood on the threshold of the church, some instinct telling him not to go in. Panayota waited nervously behind him. From the doorway he could see a candle flickering at the altar. The huge eye above it stared at him from the half-light, but it was not that which arrested his progress. Some vile smell warned him not to take another step inside. It was sharp as ammonia, but it was putrid and warm and alive, the smell of a wild animal. His mind flashed back to the time he had entered the church to see the old crone scrubbing at the wall and the giant, unknown priest observing him from the doorway. For the first time he thought that they might not have been people at all, but spirits.

But this was something else. There was a red light flickering at the base of the altar, perhaps some trick of the light reflecting from an icon. The red light resolved into a disc, and a sound, like the screech of an ape, lashed out at him from within the church. The hairs on his neck flushed erect.

'Get out,' he said.

'What is it?'

'Get out!'

He ran out of the churchyard, to the tap. He wrenched it on and put his head under the water. *There's nothing there*, he said. *Nothing there. It's all in your head.*

'I changed my mind,' he said to Panayota when she caught up with him. He squeezed water from his hair. It dripped along his face and neck. 'There was nothing there.'

'No,' she said. 'I could smell it. There was something.'

'Don't tell me that. I don't want to hear that.'

'This is a strange village. Things happen here. I know.'

He swung away up the street but at the corner he stopped in his tracks. At a distance of a few houses, Kim stood in a

doorway saying goodnight to a Greek man Mike recognised as one of the taverna's waiters. They were half in
shadow, the yellow light of a streetlamp falling from behind
them. There was a smell of jasmine in the air. The waiter
was trying to persuade Kim to go inside with him. He was
holding her hand, and his free arm rested lightly on her
shoulder. Mike heard Panayota draw up behind him. He
ignored her, and watched.

Kim was laughing softly. Mike could tell she was teasing
the man. But he could see the moves, the posture, the
disguised urgency with which the man was trying to steer
her indoors.

Don't go in there, Kim. Don't go in there with him.

Kim pulled away, and Mike thought she was going to
move off. But then the man touched her hair, and it
tumbled in his hand like a dark wave. Kim turned and
kissed him, and the kiss went on. Mike felt constriction
rising in his chest. He began hyperventilating.

Not in there, Kim. Please not in there.

The man whispered something to Kim. Mike was about
to make his presence known when she said something and
stepped inside. The waiter followed her and the door
clicked softly behind them.

Still hyperventilating Mike turned and collided with
Panayota, and the impact caused him to double over and
vomit against a whitewashed wall. Three days of ouzo,
brandy, raki, red wine, white wine, beer, anger, fear, hurt,
pain, guilt, self-loathing and nothing substantial but a
handful of olives, followed by a string of black bile retching
from deep inside his bowels. He was down on his hands and
knees still vomiting.

Panayota gently rested a hand on his back and he puked
once more. She left him a few moments before daring to

touch him again. He seemed to be staring in horror into his own vomit. She tried to pull him away. He didn't resist.

He stood up, wiping flecks of vomit from his mouth with his sleeve. 'It doesn't matter where I go,' he said, recovering his breath. 'It doesn't matter where I go or what I do. Everywhere. In the grass. In the stones on the sand. In the snake trails in the fields. In the stars or in that pile of puke. I keep seeing letters. Alphabets. Signs and sigils, and runes. Writings. Things I can't read. Messages I can't decipher. Do you know what I'm talking about?'

She said nothing.

'How can you know? You're a virgin. How can you know? Kim's gone in there. How can you know what that means?'

Three men were approaching from the other direction. One of them was Panayota's cousin. He called to her, and paused to wait. Mike heard a protective and proprietorial tone in the call. 'I have to go now. Will you be all right?'

'Yes. I'm all right.'

'Good night,' she said, joining the men. All three of them shouted, '*Kali Nikta*' to Mike.

'Good night,' he replied, leaning his back against the wall. 'Good night.'

33

Mike was woken by a hammering on the shutters. He opened his sticky eyes. Sunlight filtered by leaves oozed between the wooden slats, fresh and sharp as lime juice. Someone shouted, 'Arise!'; Mike sat up in bed and his head detonated. Kim was not there. The events of the previous evening came back to him. Recalling it was like opening a cupboard from which the contents come clattering on your head.

After seeing Kim go indoors with the Greek waiter, he had wandered the streets in a daze. Then he'd returned home, and having lost his key, he'd had to break a pane of glass in the door to get in.

Again the call from outside: 'Arise!' There was something oddly penetrating about the archaic form of this cry. The old-fashioned command had Biblical weight. Mike pulled on some trousers and flung open the door.

Manoussos stood outside. The light fell on him in a curious way, making him seem softly luminous. A blue headscarf was tightly knotted over his forehead, and his dark, liquid brown eyes rested on Mike with malevolent intensity. His eyes were narrowed, multiplying the crease lines in the soft tanned leather of his face, readable crease lines which dived and took refuge under the tangle of his iron-grey moustache.

'I have come,' said Manoussos.

He was carrying his canvas bag across a shoulder. It seemed stuffed with misshapen objects. Mike didn't know what to say.

'I have come,' the shepherd repeated.

'This is apparent,' said Mike.

Manoussos nodded, evidently missing Mike's irony. Mike shook his head and pushed past him, padding barefoot across the patio and down the garden to the water pump. Manoussos followed. Mike stuck his head under the pump and cranked the handle, but nothing happened. He cranked at the handle in growing irritation.

'The pump is dry,' Manoussos observed.

Mike ignored him and grabbed a bucket to dunk in the sea. He came back to prime the pump, but his efforts failed to produce water. The shepherd shook his head and clicked his teeth.

'Why did you come?' Mike said.

'Swim first.'

'What?'

'First you must swim.'

'Why?'

'Because when Kim is here, you swim. Now I see Kim is not here, and you no longer swim. Me, I don't swim.' He pressed a hand to his chest and threw his other hand in the air. 'Never. I don't like it. But you have an affinity for fishes. I see this. And yet now you never swim.'

'What are you gibbering about?'

'Believe me; it's better if you swim, if you want Kim to come back.'

'I don't feel like it.'

'No. The only swimming you do now is in a great big pot

of alcohol. And you look like shit. Swim! Swim! You are better when you swim.'

Mike was still slightly fuddled with sleep. He didn't exactly understand why he was having this conversation. He looked out across the water to the rock. His head was pounding. Morning sunlight skittered on the water in fine, lace-like lines. The rock looked moist and purple, an apparition in the water. The sea between would be cold.

'And if I swim, then what?'

'Then I will tell you.'

'Tell me? Tell me what?'

'I will tell you of this house. Why it is not a house of good fortune. Why it is not a good house in which to live.'

Mike was startled. He gazed back into the shepherd's unblinking eyes, and saw there extraordinary reserves: pinnacles of wisdom and deep valleys of experience hitherto unnoticed. He also saw in that gaze a critical faculty, as if his own responses at this moment were being carefully monitored. Manoussos' status had subtly shifted, and Mike felt unnerved, and slightly afraid.

'All right.' Mike broke the deadlock. He stripped off his trousers and stepped naked on to the beach. He waded out a few yards before flinging himself into the water.

The cold turned his skin inside out. The water fizzed and effervesced around him. He plunged his head under the water and opened his eyes to the green jelly. Mike stayed under, wondering why Manoussos had suddenly arrived at his door. The world of waving anemones and black scrotal urchins seemed today to bear a great melancholy, an absence; there were no striped fish, no sea horses at play in the weeds. It was a shadowy world of loss and disappointment. As his lungs began to hammer, the previous night's events haunted him again: Kim stepping into another man's house, the ape-like stench inside the Church of the Virgin. He opened his mouth in protest, and his lungs filled with sea water.

He surfaced, coughing and spluttering salt water. He was able to stand with his head above water, his sinuses ringing and his head pounding. He shivered. An uncomfortable pulse ran through his body beneath the gentle waves. He turned and began to breaststroke slowly back to the house.

Manoussos was sitting under the tree on the beach, patiently awaiting him. He followed Mike up to the patio and stood around while Mike dried off. Mike offered him a coffee. Manoussos considered this invitation long and hard, as if to accept might somehow deflect his purpose. 'Yes,' he pronounced at last. 'Yes. I will take a coffee with you.'

Manoussos sat on the bench against the wall, still clinging to his canvas bag. Mike set the kettle to boil and uncorked a bottle of ouzo. A glass offered was dismissed with a wave. Mike shrugged and poured one for himself.

'The fat worm gets fatter,' said the shepherd.

'Meaning what?'

'The fat worm lays its eggs in alcohol.'

Mike shook his head and took a drink. There was silence while they waited for the kettle to boil. After a while Manoussos continued. 'Then the eggs hatch inside a man. They hatch another fat worm. Then the worm can abide nothing but alcohol to make it grow. It calls to its brothers: "More! Still more!" And so the man feeds the fat worm until the fat worm takes over the man. If you look through the outward appearance of such a man you will see his true self represented. He has become the fat worm.'

'A charming story.' Mike drained his glass of ouzo,

though Manoussos' words had managed to sour it somewhat. 'Here's your coffee. That won't cause too many
problems for you, will it?'

'Coffee is more acceptable.'

'Good. I'd hate it to be unacceptable.'

Manoussos grunted and slurped at his cup. After each
slurp he sucked noisily at his moustache to clean it of coffee
residue. He never took his eyes off Mike, who was twisting
in his seat, growing increasingly nervous.

'What was this thing you were going to tell me about the
house?'

'Yes. About the house. I was going to tell you something
about the house.'

'Well?'

'Not here. We should walk together in the hills. I don't
like this place. I prefer to talk about it in the hills.'

'I'm sorry, Manoussos. I'm not up to a walk in the hills
today.'

'No?'

'No.'

Manoussos looked crestfallen. He put down his coffee
cup and considered for a moment. Then he stood up. 'I
must go.'

'What? I thought you'd come here to tell me something
of importance! Now you say you want to go!'

'It is a delicate matter.'

'Look, Manoussos, I don't know what is going on in that
Greek head of yours, but you could at least do me the
kindness of telling me what you came here to say!'

The shepherd hovered for a moment, seeming to reflect
on Mike's words before sitting down again. He was clearly
agitated. He opened his canvas bag, seemed to make a
decision, and from it withdrew a cloth-covered object.

He unwrapped the object as if removing swaddling from a newborn baby. It was an antique *lira*, complete with bow. Mike was familiar with the musical instrument. He'd seen many examples, but this specimen was rather smaller and certainly much older than any he had seen hitherto. It was a museum piece, and Mike guessed it to be perhaps two hundred years old. Manoussos pored over the instrument as if searching it for tiny imperfections, lightly stroking the polished wood of its hollow body.

'It was given into my father's father's keeping by a Turk. In those days we Greeks lived in Asia Minor. Even when it came into my family it was already very old.'

'It's a beautiful piece.'

Manoussos looked up, as if the remark was redundant and foolish. 'No one can make such an instrument today,' he declared. 'Impossible. You cannot make this on a machine. It has within it the soul of its maker. Was he not a man who made this? All his joy and his imperfections of character, they are inside this. If you make this with a machine it has no human flaw. If it has no human flaw it cannot make music, but is merely another machine for making sounds. It has no *kefi*, and no suffering.' By way of peroration, he looked fiercely at Mike and barked, 'You don't get better *lira* than this.'

'I'm sure.'

Now that the matter had been settled, Manoussos nodded. He fixed the fish head of the instrument deep under his ribcage, holding its tail on his thigh. With a showman's sense of precision, he angled the bow across the instrument and drew it slowly across the strings.

The thing emitted an eerie, high-pitched wail. It was not a sweet sound. It set Mike's teeth on edge. The hangover throbbing inside his head was revived by the sound.

Manoussos repeated the note. It hung in the air, unchallenged, not wanting to fade.

'Is that not beautiful?' the shepherd said proudly.

'Yes. Very.'

Manoussos smiled. 'You are a liar, Mike. This is the note for dispelling unwelcome spirits. Does it make you feel uncomfortable? It should. It is the fat worm in you which feels uncomfortable. Ha ha! The fat worm! Should I play it again?'

'Please, no.'

He carefully laid the instrument down on the bench beside him, and looked up into the vine canopy. 'How much do you know? Of this house, I mean. How much do you know?'

'I know a German woman tried to kill herself here, because she had an unhappy affair with Lakis.'

Manoussos shook his head. 'Who told you this?'

'Kati from the village. At least, she told it to Kim, and Kim told me. Isn't that the truth?'

'The truth? English people! English people! Sometimes you are like children. What do you know of the truth! English people!'

'I know that Greeks can be impressive liars.'

Mike meant this remark as a return insult, but it met with a roar of approval from the shepherd, who repeated it over and over, as if to savour the phrase. 'Impressive liars. Yes. Yes. Impressive liars.' Then he became suddenly serious again. 'I will tell you what my father told me concerning the Holy Trinity of the truth. He told me when I was too young to appreciate the joke. First, he said, no one tells the whole story. Second, he assured me I should never try to tell the whole story. Thirdly, he said to me if anyone ever tries to tell you the whole story, don't believe them.

'Anyway, Kati told Kim only part of the story, or not even part. Actually it was a lot of nonsense.'

'So there was no German woman called Eva?'

'Oh yes, there was a German woman called Eva, and she was Lakis' lover, and she lived here in this house. That much is true. Everyone knew. It was an open secret. For a Greek man to take a lover is no great news; only if he does not does it become news. But the village was scandalised because Lakis, who is a donkey of a man, was doing it under everyone's nose.

'Anyway, finally Lakis' wife drew a line and said no more. She ordered him not to see Eva any more and told him to throw Eva out of the house. He didn't love this Eva, she was something to flatter his manhood. Lakis did stop seeing her, but he was unable to get her to leave this place. She simply dug in. What could he do? He just stopped coming down here.

'But Eva was no fool. She knew how to get her revenge on Lakis. Whether she wanted to punish him, or to make him jealous, who knows? But she made a kind of open house of this place. It was said she seduced half of the men of this village. Life at this house was like a continuous party. There were comings and goings. It was even said that prostitutes came here from Palioskala.

'How much to believe? You know how women and priests talk in a village like this. Make up your own mind. But it was true that many of the men would come here from the taverna and stay late. I can attest that there was dancing and singing and card-playing, and boozing, all hosted by the fun-loving Eva. As a young man I more than once passed by the gate there and tried to steal a glance at the woman. She was beautiful. But they spoke about her as if she was the Whore Of Babylon.

'It was the talk of the island, what was going on at this house. Finally the women of the village became outraged enough to want to do something about it. They were forever talking about what they were going to do. This and that, or this other thing. But it was almost as if they were afraid, either of Eva or of this place.'

Manoussos paused for a moment, and stroked his throat. 'Have you been here when the sirocco blows, Mike? No? Even this far north we can sometimes be tortured by these winds from Africa. There is nothing like it. It is said of some islands that if a man kills his wife during the time of the sirocco, the judge and jury will take a lenient view of his behaviour. I can believe it. A hot wind. It blows in your mouth like the breath of an unwelcome lover. It hangs on you like a burning blanket. You carry it on your back from place to place like a corpse.

'I have spent sirocco nights sleeping with my legs in the water, just to try to get some peace. Your skin itches and sweats. Your blood crawls in your veins, you want to break something. Yes, for no reason you see another man and you want to break his face.

'So the sirocco was blowing this time, and no one could sleep, and so the parties at this house went on later and later. The men would steal away from their houses and come down here.

'It was at the time of the Festival of the Horse. In the village of Ipassus on the black-rock side of the island there is a three-day madness of galloping horses up and down the streets of the village – you should go to see it. There is a tradition from this village of entering a team in the races. All the men go to race or to cheer or just to get drunk. So it was then. All of Eva's men friends deserted her to go the Festival of the Horse. She was left alone.'

'When was all this?' Mike asked.

Manoussos thought for a moment. 'Twenty-five years ago. When all this tourist thing had just started. When no one knew how it was going to change us Greeks.

'And then it was that the women of the village saw their chance. Nine of them banded together and they came down here to chase Eva from the house. I could name each one of them. And they had had drink, in order to be able to do this thing.'

'How do you know all this?'

'Because, Mike, I was crouched behind that hedge over there watching it all. Yes. I knew all the men were away at the festival. I came down myself to see this woman, to get what I could. Eva was sitting here on the patio, quietly reading a book under an oil lamp. But I was too cowardly, dithering at the gate when I saw the procession of the village women coming along the path with burning torches. I hid myself in the bushes. Then they came in and their eyes were terrible. I think even then I knew what was going to happen. Their eyes were like the eyes of frightened horses. They were terrifying.

'They went up to her, up to this very patio where we now sit. She stood up. I couldn't hear what was said, but I saw one of the women slap her. I was astonished when she fought back. She returned the slap, and for a moment I thought it could go either way. Then in the next moment they were all upon her, beating her, slapping, kicking. She managed to crawl into the garden, but they followed behind, raining blows. They stripped her and then they did it.'

'Did what?'

'They hung the poor woman from that tree.'

Mike followed Manoussos' gnarled, pointing finger to

the tree standing against the outhouse, by the pump.

'But—'

'You know every one of these women.' And Manoussos named them. Amongst them was the butcher's wife. Maria from the clothes shop. The woman he knew as the tomato lady. And Kati.

'I don't believe it!'

Manoussos shrugged. 'Everyone knows. And now I have chosen to tell you.'

'But was there no trial? Weren't they put in prison for this? It was murder!'

'This is a small village, on a small island. Eva was an outsider.'

'What are you saying?'

'The policeman who cut her down was Lakis' brother-in-law. The doctor who performed a postmortem was Maria's cousin. The coroner was the uncle of one of the women.'

Mike looked at the tree, and the garden, and the white doves settled on the fence. It all seemed changed, reshaped, indelibly stained. He let out a deep sigh of astonishment and incredulity mixed.

'This,' Manoussos announced, 'is the secret shame of our village. It is shame on all the women who did this thing. It is shame on all the men. It is shame on me who cowered in the bushes and allowed it to happen.'

'Manoussos, why did you choose to tell me this?'

'Because this house still bears the shame. And it has come between you and your wife.'

'You mean the ghost of Eva is in this place?'

'Not just the ghost of Eva. Not only the dead leave spirits behind them. Here is the ghost of all of us. Those of us who did this thing, and those of us who failed to stop it.'

They sat quietly for a while as Mike tried to take all this

in. 'Do you remember the field of snakes?' Manoussos asked him. 'Just as that field calls to snakes, this place calls to spirits.'

'But I never thought this place was all bad!'

'Are snakes all bad? No. They are what they are. And I believe this place was as such even before Eva came here. It was a dangerous place for her. As it is a dangerous place for you and Kim. See how the trouble comes to you?'

'What trouble?'

'Where is Kim now?'

'That's my fault. I did something which has driven her to hate me.'

'But it happened because this place called trouble to you. I saw this when I saw your friends come here.'

The two men sat in silence for a while. Mike was still trying to grasp the implications of Manoussos' revelation. Half of the village women were murderers. From now on he would always be looking deep into their eyes.

'I can help you,' Manoussos said suddenly.

'What?'

'I can help you find a path back to Kim.'

'How?'

'First you must come with me, up into the mountains. Together we must spend some days.'

'And how will that help me?'

Manoussos looked tired and irritated. 'What must I say? What must I say? Here, I offer you my hand. Take it. But don't ask me always to explain.'

Mike thought about it for a moment. Three or four days up in the mountains with a mad teetotal shepherd, who stank of sheepshit, for who knew what purpose? 'I'll pass.'

'Pass? What is pass?'

'I mean I don't want to go up into the mountains.'

Manoussos' face flushed red under his crinkly tan. He got to his feet and snatched up his musical instrument, carefully rewrapping it before placing it back in his canvas bag. Without saying a word of farewell he marched down the garden to the beach, and with his head up strode briskly along the beach path and out of sight.

Mike watched him go and wondered briefly whether he had passed up some momentous experience.

34

Later that afternoon Kim appeared. Mike was stretched out on the patio bench, in a fitful sleep, or perhaps inhabiting some dimension between sleeping and waking. Her shadow fell across his face. When he opened his eyes, she was lounging back in a chair. She was watching him.

'Hi,' she said softly.

He sat up too quickly. His head swam. 'Hi.'

She looked good. She was dressed simply, in laundered blue jeans and a white blouse. A pair of dark leather sandals advertised the rich tan of her legs, and Mike noticed a leather band on her left ankle. She was also wearing a gold chain on her wrist. Kim had never previously gone in for gold.

'Do you want a drink?' he asked, standing up.

'No. I just dropped by.'

'Dropped by? Does that mean you're leaving again in a moment?'

'I thought you might want me to.'

'Since when did my wishes start counting again? Stay . . . Go . . . Do what you want.' She brushed a hand through her dark auburn waves and the fine gold bracelet glimmered at her wrist. It could have been linked to his heart, it snagged and tore so.

'It's just that I didn't know,' Mike went on, 'that you would unilaterally vary the contract.'

'*Unilaterally vary the contract?*' she repeated. 'What sort of language is that? You sound like a lawyer.'

'Do I? Well, we are a kind of divorced couple, aren't we?'

'Are we?'

'That's how it seems to me. Seems to me we're a divorced couple but we've got no other place to go, so we stay in this house, chummy as a pair of scorpions.'

'Perhaps I should go. You've woken up in a bad mood.'

Please don't go! his mind screamed. *Please!* But he couldn't bring himself to say it. He couldn't bear to appear weak. It was more important to try to find a way to hurt her. 'Stay if you want. It's just that I'm meeting someone later.'

'Someone?'

'A friend. A tourist.'

He searched her for some flicker, some twitch of jealousy. He felt she knew it was a lie. 'That's good, Mike! I worry about you drinking every day. Some company would be good for you!'

He'd rather feel her loathsome pity than her sympathetic support for another relationship. 'Where did you get the gold chain?'

Kim looked sleepily at the chain on her wrist. She paused before answering. 'Kati bought it for me.'

'Kim, you don't have to lie to me.'

'What?'

'You don't have to tell me obvious lies. I'm not going to drown myself in the sea because a salad-boy bought you a gold chain.'

'I don't believe I'm hearing this.'

'Kim, it makes no odds to me if you want to wear his fucking bracelet!'

'I wouldn't take any payment from Kati for spending some time in her shop; so she bought me this as a gift.'

'Whatever you say.'

'Look, I think I should go. You're in a sour mood.'

Please stay! I can't stand it when you go! 'Maybe you should. We're not able to communicate any more. The only thing we have to say to each other is lies and pass the salt. Stay at Kati's last night?'

'I did, as a matter of fact.'

'Really. Kati's, eh?'

'Mike, I came here to—'

'Some things can't be mended, can they? Lies drive people apart, don't they? I've been doing some thinking about our marriage. It was built on lies, wasn't it? There never was any honesty in it. I'm not putting all this on you. We built our nest out of deceit. Deceit and deception. Perhaps the idea of us separating is our one chance for the truth. Perhaps we're being presented with a chance.'

She was dumbstruck. Her lips clamped tight. He could see she was choking back tears. *Don't let her go*, panicked the tiny voice inside him, *don't let her go!* But he was excited by the degree of hurt he could return to the source of his own hurt. 'We probably had to come out here to find that out, didn't we? To uncover the truth? That's right, isn't it, Kim?'

'Mike, I came here to tell you that I was ready to start talking again.'

'Oh! *You're* ready now! *You* are ready to talk now. You've had your revenge, have you? Do you know what they call you in the village? *Kali Orexi. Bon appétit*. Good eating. Because you're known to all the waiters in the village. Well, there's something unappetising about you now.'

Kim was at sea. 'Mike, it's not about revenge—'

He couldn't resist putting the boot in again. 'What was it then? My humiliation? You won, Kim. You won, fair and square. You succeeded. Now go back to your waiter. Be happy.' He sat down with his back to her and poured himself a glass of ouzo.

She waited for a moment before getting to her feet. She wandered down the garden path in a daze.

Call her back! Get her back here! For God's sake, you can't do this!

When she was out of sight, Mike went indoors and lay down on the bed. He could hardly breathe. Tears never came easily, and when they did they welled like hot blisters. He shook in a paroxysm of rage and self-loathing. Now he hated Kim more than ever. He blamed her for not seeing through to the true Mike, the one that wanted to hold her and confess everything and forgive and be forgiven. He railed at her through his tears for not seeing that he didn't want to hurt her, and that every thrust of the knife was inwardly directed. Wasn't she the one who should know? Wasn't it her responsibility to separate the true self from the angry, false self? Wasn't that why she had married him? To know him better than he knew himself?

He hated her now for making him love her, for the loss of control of himself, for the appalling weakness of loving. Above all he could not forgive her for failing to see beyond what he had just done; and for the crime of failing to stop him from disembowelling himself on his own vicious pride.

35

From his own house on the hill between the village of Kamari and the fortress-topped town of Limanaki, Manoussos could see the bay – if not the house – where Mike and Kim lived, and he could see the abandoned monastery on the finger-shaped promontory beyond the house. Thus every evening at sunset when he pulled off his boots and socks and sat barefoot in an old armchair in the sloping field outside his door, he looked directly across at the tiny figure who gazed out to sea.

'Any minute, old friend.'

The shepherd lit a cigarette and bit on the sharp smoke. He knew the movements of the eternal watcher, just as he knew the movements of the sun across the sky. Indeed, there was an uncanny relationship between the watcher at the monastery and the setting of the sun. Manoussos had previously timed him on the gold watch bequeathed by his father. Every evening, precisely three minutes before the sun touched the horizon, the hermit would turn and retire from his sentry post. He had no timepiece himself, Manoussos knew for a fact. Some accurate clockwork of the body guided him with unfailing precision, some deft instinct, every day, and had done for several years.

'There.'

The figure on the edge of the cliff turned and vanished.

Manoussos had stopped timing. He knew that in exactly one hundred and eighty seconds the copper disc would spill across the waves. He waited for the minutes to pass, and when the sun did kiss the water, he exhaled a plume of smoke and got to his feet, as if now granted permission to move.

It had not been a good day. The business with the Englishman had ended badly, and he had felt a loss of face. He could not return there again. Then in the hills one of his animals had fallen from a rock and had to be destroyed and carried home. Not a good day.

His dog, tethered by the chicken pen, whined and fretted to be stroked. He patted the dog and pressed back its ears. Then he went indoors to fetch his *lira*.

Manoussos' house consisted of one room, most of which was taken up by a large brass bed. There were numerous framed pictures cluttering the walls, pictures of his father and mother, of his grandparents, of family members he could no longer identify. There was a picture of his brother preparing to enter the priesthood through the seminary in Thessaloniki. Otherwise the walls were hung with oil lamps and dusty embroideries. The shepherd hated the indoors, and stayed out as long as possible. He regarded a man within doors as somehow reduced, less than the aggregate of himself. The hills and the skies and the rocks were lungs and organs essential to life, whereas the house was a place only for sleeping, just as a church was a place only for praying. No, a man indoors was like a musical instrument without strings, stripped of all potential. The *lira* was lying on the bed in its cover. He picked it up and carried it outside.

He sat down in his armchair and unwrapped the instrument. Settling its head under his ribcage he held the bow poised above the strings and looked over at his dog. He made the bow produce a high, pulsating screech. The dog whimpered and pressed its belly to the floor.

Manoussos laughed and muted the note by pressing his hand across the strings. 'Forgive me, little dog! I'm a bad man to tease you. A bad, bad man.' He played another note, deeper, with a lower frequency. The dog leapt to his feet and barked at him. 'I agree! I agree! It's more acceptable!'

If only it were so easy with people, he thought.

He muted the note with his hand again, readjusted his seating and planted both feet firmly on the dry earth, feeling the dust between his toes. When making music it was essential to have direct contact with the soil; for all music was the earth singing. Sad songs, or tunes of joy and gaiety, airs of melancholia, songs of regret or anticipation or of thanks, they were all the earth crying out in its loneliness to be heard.

Manoussos' music was roots music, *rizitika*, sometimes the pure and unaccompanied vocalisation of 'deep singing', sometimes the hot-blooded airs of the *lira*. It mattered not. What did matter was the soul in which they were offered, the spirit in which the lamentations of the earth were interpreted. It required right posture, right breathing, precise instrumentation and the proper centring of the musician. Nothing less was demanded than total commitment to the song.

He waited for his moment, and drew the bow slowly across the strings to produce a skirling note which dropped and climbed, dropped and climbed again before he launched himself into a stirring, racing piece. Spiralling notes were reclaimed and repeated, stamped out in rapid four-four time marked by clicks of his bow. He gripped the earth with his toes as he played. His eyes closed; he was utterly possessed by his music.

He repeated the theme seven times before lifting his head and singing a deep-throated but emotional accompaniment. It was a song of unrequited love, of wells drying, of tears burning. It was a very old song. With only the dog for audience he gave the performance everything. The verses came and went, but the vibrant, scorching music of the *lira* never abated. The dog lifted his head, watching his master throughout the entire piece.

When he had finished, Manoussos' eyes opened, and the dog lowered his head again. The shepherd smiled, because he knew the dog had been listening. He was a worthy audience, listening in approval as the dusk fell.

The shepherd rested a moment, preparing to play another song. Suddenly the dog's ears pricked. The animal scrambled to its feet and barked, once. Manoussos squinted into the dusk in the direction of the dog's interest. Something was out there. The dog tugged on its chain and began to bark wildly. Manoussos stood up, laying his instrument on the chair behind him as the dog scrambled to be free of its tether.

Someone crossed the path from behind a rock and began climbing the slope towards them. Manoussos felt his fists tighten instinctively. He was unnerved: he was unaccustomed to receiving visitors.

It is him. He has found his way here.

Manoussos silenced the dog as Mike stepped up to him. 'I was wrong,' said Mike. 'I'm a fool. I don't know my own mind.'

'Tomorrow,' said the shepherd. 'Be ready in the

morning. Carry some water. We will go up into the hills for some days.'

'And food?'

'No. You will not be eating.'

36

Mike was already awake and waiting on the patio when the spear-fisherman waded silently abreast of the house the following morning. He had not slept at all well. His dreams had been filled with monstrous visions of the shepherd, and when he awoke the door to his room was standing ajar. Kim was sleeping. She had returned some time in the night without waking him.

The lean, bronzed spear-fisher made tiny rippling pools around his ankles, anklets of yellow and pink from the rising sun. He instinctively looked up, catching Mike's gaze. He nodded briefly before passing on. Mike thought about leaving a note for Kim, and decided against it.

Manoussos' arrival a few moments later was heralded by the trespass of sheep on to Mike's garden. Then the shepherd himself was standing at the gate, bearing his crook and his canvas bag.

'You have water?' he called softly. Mike indicated the plastic container he'd filled from the tap outside the Church of the Virgin. 'Good. And a blanket. You will need a blanket.'

Mike fetched a sleeping bag from inside, loading both it and the water container on to his rucksack. He silently closed the door behind him. Manoussos stopped him at the gate, fixing him with burning eyes. 'You are ready?'

'Yes.'

The shepherd nodded, turned, and with a step almost military in its execution barked the Greek command, '*Embross!*', meaning *Forward!*

Together they climbed the paths through the hills behind the house in silence. The sheep regulated the pace at which they moved, grazing ahead and on either flank. The sun climbing in the sky behind their backs was shifting from rose-pink to yellow, a giant engine charging up in readiness for a power surge. The ground was still fresh with the night's coolness, the path still springy underfoot.

When they passed through the stegosaurus outcrop, Manoussos turned to gaze across at the promontory at his right hand. The hermit watcher was up and about his business.

'Poor sod,' said Mike.

The shepherd turned. 'You pity him?'

'Yes.'

'And I. I pity him also. *Embross!*'

They crossed scrubby fields and paths through quince and fig trees, and dusty tracks winding in and out of shady olive groves. It was almost two hours before Manoussos would stop for a mouthful of water. They paused under an olive grove where Mike rested his back against a twisted and tortured trunk. He was panting, the shepherd was not.

Manoussos handed Mike his water bottle, watching him carefully as he drank. They sat quietly for some minutes. The shade was delicious. The leaves of the olive, reflecting silver in the sun and green on the underside, hung on the branches in a frozen shower of shimmering light. There was no breeze to stir the trees, and yet they seemed to contain their own movement, another world of life. The knotholed, twisted trees crouched in perverse shapes, like agonised spirits.

'Olive groves are ghostly places,' said Mike.

'Ghostly? What mean you by ghostly?'

'The trees. They're like living things.'

Manoussos looked puzzled. He peered intensely at Mike, as if trying to see to the murky bottom of this statement. 'Of course they are living things.'

'I don't mean living things—'

'So what do you mean?'

'I mean . . . I don't know what I mean. Perhaps I meant *sentient* things.'

But Manoussos had stopped listening. 'See those holes in the tree? My father told me if you put your eye to one of those holes you can see another world.'

'Really?'

'He was a liar.'

'Did your father lie to you about lots of things?'

'Yes.'

'And mine,' said Mike. He took his cigarettes from his rucksack.

'No!' said the shepherd. 'No cigarettes. While we are in the mountains together, we survive without.' Mike sighed putting them away.

They fell into silence again. A lizard flicked its tail across a tree root. Mike spotted a scorpion lurking under a stone. He kicked at it.

'What is it?'

'Scorpion.'

'He will not hurt you in the daytime.'

'Not if he's dead he won't.'

Manoussos shook his head. 'I am not afraid of the scorpion. He will not sting Manoussos.'

'Why?'

'Why? He will not sting me because I do not fear him. He will sting you because you fear him. Do you want to know why I do not fear him?' He fumbled in his coat pocket and withdrew the bottled insect. He passed it for Mike's inspection. 'If he sting me, I drink this. No problem.'

Mike examined the dirty liquid with the dead scorpion in suspension. 'What is it – some kind of antidote?'

'This was given to me by my father; and his father gave it to him. Very old.'

'So how do you know it still works? Come to that, how do you know if it ever worked?'

'No. You don't understand. Nobody ever did drink it, because they were never stung.'

'Yes, so how does anyone know if it's effective? You don't know for sure, because no one has ever tried it.'

Manoussos twisted his moustache and contorted his face into a model of exaggerated patience. 'Again, you don't understand. If you have this – the antidote as you call it – you don't need to take it because he will not sting you. Now you understand me?'

'Not really. I mean, you still don't know whether the stuff will do any good. It might be completely fucking useless. It might make you worse!'

The shepherd snatched the bottle from Mike and shoved it back in his pocket. 'Sometimes,' he said angrily, scrambling to his feet, 'I think you are completely stupid. Come on. We go.'

Manoussos spat short, unintelligible commands at his grazing flock, rounding them up for movement. He used his crook to deal one of the sheep a sharp slap on the hindquarters. Mike felt that the blow was somehow aimed at him.

They climbed still higher, and the successive groves of olives began to give way to forests of conifer trees. They were higher into the hills than Mike had ever been on foot. The air there was fresher and scented with pine. Manoussos was following a path Mike would never have recognised. With the sun still climbing in the sky they made their way through the pine trees, and then down a steep valley to cross a dry river bed; thence back up the other side of the valley and among more dense pine forests.

Manoussos was saying little, calling occasionally to his sheep to marshal progress. The flock slowed the journey but gave it an odd sense of purpose, as if the animals knew something Mike didn't. The sun was already past its zenith when the shepherd called a halt and declared that they could now rest in the shade. Apart from the one brief halt, they had been moving steadily for over six hours. He'd chosen a spot at a clearing in a pine forest where the flock could graze on scrubby, boulder-strewn grass.

He took out his water flask. Mike noted how he would always hand the water on before drinking, always putting his own needs second. While Mike was swigging desperately from the flask, Manoussos rummaged in his canvas bag, producing a small paper sack of wizened black olives. He withdrew a fistful and dropped them into Mike's hand.

Mike counted them. Fifteen olives. Fourteen if the very tiny one was discounted. He anticipated that this handful of bitter fruit was likely to constitute breakfast, lunch and supper.

But they tasted so good! Mike, who had become an aficionado of the Greek olive, and who now understood the rivalry between olive-producing islands, found them quite unlike any other he had tasted. Though the skin of the fruit was wrinkled and unappetising, they were fleshy, wholesome and deeply savoury. Perhaps they had been marinated by some special process. He complimented the shepherd and asked about them.

Manoussos looked thoroughly disinterested in the subject. He ate his own handful of olives quickly, spitting the stones into his hand. Then he curled up with his back against a tree, making a pillow of his hands.

'Now sleep,' he said, and seemed himself to drop off to sleep almost immediately.

Mike looked around him and decided there was little else to do but join the siesta. He took his sleeping bag from his rucksack, laid it on the ground and stretched out.

When he awoke, it was with a start, and with a faint cry on his lips. He sat upright. Manoussos was sitting a few yards away, cross-legged, nursing his crook and watching him intently. Mike looked around him. The sun had slipped in the sky, the heat of the day had distilled out. There was a strong smell of pine in the air, and the tree trunks had a peculiar blue look. Manoussos was still regarding him, the soft leather of his face crinkling around his narrowed eyes. Mike got to his feet.

'Yes,' said Manoussos. 'It is as I thought. Now we go on.'

'What is as you thought?' said Mike, brushing pine needles from his sleeping bag, trying to blink himself awake.

The question was ignored. 'For two hours more, we walk. Higher. Then we will have arrived.'

'Arrived where?'

'At the place we are going. There is water there.'

It was a Greek two hours, and a journey which seemed almost as long as the morning's trek. The terrain became more difficult as they drove the sheep up a mountain slope strewn with red and black volcanic rock. They had passed above the tree line. Here the plants growing on the hill became more alien-looking. The scarcity of water had forced nature to arm the plants with spikes and structural defences resembling wire mesh. Heat and dryness had drained colour from the herbage, leaving the landscape of rocks and loose boulders dotted with spiny cushions of frost-blue and mustard-yellow vegetation. Here and there strange black-leafed flowers thrust from the stony ground, trumpet-shaped and poisonous-looking. Still the sheep managed to find something to nibble as they were herded higher.

It was not until the sun had disappeared over the mountain that Manoussos called a halt. They had arrived at a spot of level ground, where two gigantic clumps of volcanic rock leaned together, as if fused on the day they touched whilst still molten-hot. The rocks were black and red and streaked with yellow and white minerals. Manoussos set down his crook and his canvas bag at the foot of the fused rock, and told Mike to look for firewood.

'Soon it will be dark. We must have wood.'

'Give me a minute,' said Mike. He was still breathing hard from the climb.

Manoussos moved away, grumbling. Mike recovered his breath and went looking for fuel. It wasn't easy; they were beyond the tree line, but it was possible to find dried, withered bushes and the brittle branches of shrubs bleached by the sun. When he thought he had collected enough he sat down by the rock. Manoussos came back towing a tangle of dead brush and scoffed at his efforts.

'How long will this last you in England? Five minutes? Don't you know nothing? Go and get more. We need more. You don't have time to sit on your English arse. Go!'

It was dark before Manoussos was satisfied with their store of fuel, and before he would let Mike unpack his sleeping bag. Mike was sweating heavily, his hands black and scratched and bleeding. He was hungry, yet he hardly dared ask if there was anything to eat.

The fire flickered into life, quickly consuming the small, tinder-dry bushes in a delirious crackling. Manoussos banked up the fire until it had settled a bed of embers, and then loaded it more slowly. The air was filled with aromatic smoke. Mike's nose twitched at a smell like incense from the church.

'Mastica,' said Manoussos, reading his thoughts. 'It grows up here. This is the resin you can smell.'

'It's magical,' said Mike, moving closer to the fire.

The shepherd thought about this for a moment. 'Yes. Yes, you are right.' Then he sat next to Mike and took some olives out of his pocket.

'Do I get any more of those?'

'No.'

Mike said nothing for a while. 'I'm to survive on smoke from the mastic, am I?'

'That's a good idea.' Manoussos spat a stone into the fire.

'You won't object if I get myself some water?'

'Yes. Drink water. It's very good for you.'

Manoussos was unperturbed by Mike's bad grace, or was pretending not to notice. He was content to gaze into the flames as he chewed his olives, occasionally tossing new sticks of brushwood on to the fire.

He was contemplating how he might get the Englishman to ask to be taught how to dance. Manoussos could not direct the question nor even suggest it. It must come from Mike himself, motivated by his own spirit of enquiry. Yet

Mike was not an obvious candidate for dancing, so how was it going to be done?

The shepherd got up and went over to his canvas bag, from where he took out his *lira*. He set the instrument against his ribcage, levelled the bow and drew it across the strings. It released a rising note, reverberating strongly, mournful and insistent. It hung in the air. Manoussos repeated it.

'Mike, can you make the music live with the smoke from the fire?'

'How do you mean?'

'Watch the smoke. And listen.' Manoussos slowly drew the bow across the strings, releasing a new mournful wail, twisting and spiralling and dying in the air. He did it again.

'I see what you mean. The music seems to echo the shape of the smoke; or the smoke seems to imitate the music, one or the other.'

'Watch again.'

Manoussos released more notes into the night air, and they did indeed seem to ride on the swirling of the smoke, springing into life and then dying away in eerie relationship. Mike shook his head and laughed. 'Yes. A good trick.'

'Trick?'

'Yes. It's a good illusion. But it's all in the head.'

Manoussos stopped sawing on the strings. He shook his head quizzically. 'I don't understand what you mean, "in the head".'

'I mean it's all in the mind. It's, er . . . subjective.' Mike looked at the shepherd as if this might all be a little beyond a Greek peasant. He felt his cheeks flushing. 'I mean that *in your mind*, that is, in our minds, it seems as if the smoke and the music are somehow tied together. That is, it's only us that string the two things together. This is philosophical, I suppose.'

'Philosophical.'

'Yes.'

'Mike, I don't know. Maybe my English is bad. Maybe you are just a stupid person.'

Mike laughed, but Manoussos was looking at him in all earnestness. 'Probably the latter. Yes. It's best to proceed on that basis.'

The shepherd looked slightly crestfallen. 'If not in our minds, where else could it be? Did I not make the fire? Did I not make the music?'

'I will admit,' Mike put in hurriedly, 'that the smoke and the music do somehow seem to dance together.'

The shepherd looked at him suddenly, his dark eyes gleaming. 'Dance! Yes, they dance! So they do! Watch again!'

And Manoussos played. He played notes of mournful intensity, a kind of lamentation. Again the music seemed to blend with the smoke in the night air.

'It reminds me,' said Mike, 'this music reminds me of Irish pipe music. What they call a "slow air".'

Manoussos glared at him. *Shut up, you fool. Shut up and ask me. Ask me.* He improvised his way from the eerie wailing of the lamentation to a sprightly dance in four-four time, offering a count by clicking his fingers on the body of the instrument. Mike's head was nodding in time with the music, and the shepherd smiled at him. *That's it. Now ask me. Ask me to teach you to dance.*

But Mike didn't shift. He only let his head nod along with the astonishing, brisk, complex figurations of the music. Manoussos by now was nodding encouragement. He smiled and twitched his moustache at Mike; he jiggled his eyebrows suggestively; all with the intention of urging Mike to his feet, something that would have been second nature to a Greek. But Mike stayed with his buttocks deep in the dust.

Manoussos' elbow swayed back and forth with impressive energy. Mike looked a little unnerved at the changing expressions on the shepherd's face. The smile had gone, to be replaced by a sudden scowl; then the smile returned, momentarily. Then Manoussos looked up into the black sky and mouthed something inaudible, though he never ceased playing or missed a beat.

When Mike's feet started tapping, albeit self-consciously, Manoussos redoubled his efforts. He mounted a wild riff, releasing it squealing into the night air, all the while exhorting Mike to dance through facial expressions of gymnastic invention. He nodded purposefully at Mike's pathetically tapping feet, and then flicked his head at the night sky; he pursed his lips and smiled shyly and suggestively and shook his shoulders, until Mike began to feel somewhat alarmed.

Suddenly Manoussos stopped the music dead. He slumped over his instrument, as if he had been shot.

'Why did you stop?' said Mike.

'Why indeed.' He got up and piled more wood on the fire. It flared and crackled angrily, releasing billows of mastic perfume on to the air. He walked around the fire, kicked a few stones away to clear a yard of earth and then sat down to pull off his boots and socks. He stood up, grasped his instrument and set his feet in the dust.

'Now,' he said.

And he began to play again. This time he struck up a much simpler air, playing in the same time as before but with fewer rippling notes. And as he played he began to dance. It was the kind of dance Mike had seen on festive occasions and name-day parties, a dance he'd tried to imitate when drunk. Manoussos crept forward slowly, as if treading an invisible line in the dirt. He dropped on one knee, swayed to right and left and hauled himself upright again. He stepped backwards, again down the same invisible line, and then jumped forward with extraordinary lightness. The music was hot-blooded, it scalded the nerves, and the shepherd nodded with vigorous approval when Mike started clapping his hands in time.

Manoussos broke off again in the middle of his number. A wind got in amongst the fire and blew smoke across his face. He stared at the baffled Mike in disgust, his arms hanging lifelessly at his sides, holding his bow and his *lira* by the neck like a strangled bird. 'What is the matter with you, stupid Englishman?' he roared. 'Any Greek worthy of the name would have been on his feet hours ago! Get up, you man of clay! Are you made of stone? Where are your legs? Where are your wings? Get up and dance!'

Mike shuffled under his gaze. 'Look, Manoussos,' he said, 'if you want me to dance you're going to have to teach me.'

'YES!' roared the Greek. 'YES!' His arms shot up in a V formation, waving instrument and bow at the stars. The red firelight lit up the joy on the old man's face. His eyes were like stars. '*Etsai enai, morei! Ekies o horos tora! Ne Mikalis, ne!* You have the dance! Come! I thought you were never going to ask me!'

He raced over and dragged Mike to his feet. Then he kissed him repeatedly, with passionate, slobbering intensity, on the side of his face.

'What do you mean?' said Mike, wiping saliva from his cheek. 'Why was I supposed to ask you?'

'Come here! Stand here, behind me. You know nothing. Nothing. Don't worry; I love you, little Mikalis. Not all stupidity is a bad thing. Now, this dance I am going to teach you is called the dance of *kefi*.'

37

Mike woke in his sleeping bag, feeling exhausted, hunger gnawing his stomach. After they had finished dancing – a session which had endured for three or four hours – Manoussos had made Mike sit up to watch over the flock of sheep. He wouldn't tell Mike what he was supposed to be watching for. Mike knew there were wolves on the mainland, but was unaware of any on the island. Perhaps a fox could take one of the smaller animals.

'Foxes? Is that what we're looking for?'

'Look for anything,' Manoussos had said. 'Look for all things.'

Then, after himself sleeping, the shepherd relieved him of this duty in the middle of the night. Mike had collapsed in his sleeping bag, and had fallen asleep instantly. Now as he blinked around him, the day had whitened and the sun was nudging over the hill to the east. He looked around; the shepherd was sitting on a stone, watching him.

'Breakfast,' said Mike. 'I must have breakfast.'

The shepherd raised his eyebrows. Mike groaned; he knew too well this Greek gesture for 'no'.

Mike got out of his sleeping bag and went to fetch some water. His face was puffed with sleep and his eyes were still glued. He had woken in a foul, irritable mood only to be greeted by the tyranny of the shepherd's unexplained regime. He wasn't even sure if there was a regime; he suddenly felt Manoussos was proceeding by whim, and for that reason he was unhappy about having handed over control of his diet.

'Look, I can't be expected to dance and stay up counting sheep all night on an empty stomach. I've got to eat something, even if it's only a few rancid olives.'

Again the shepherd raised his eyebrows, reinforcing the gesture by a slight raising of the chin. Mike fell back on his sleeping bag in disgust. 'I didn't sleep well.'

'I saw.'

'You saw?'

'Your spirit. It departs from you while you sleep. I have seen it before.'

Mike looked up. 'When? How? What do you mean?'

'Yesterday as you slept. Your spirit gets up and walks. Sometimes it even takes you. Last night you were dancing.'

Mike's legs ached. 'I know all about that.'

'No. I mean while you slept. In the night you got up and you danced again.'

Mike felt a thrill of fear. He recalled Kim telling him about his nocturnal wanderings. He'd always suspected her of playing down the frequency of these episodes. 'Sleep-walking? Was I sleepwalking?'

'I told you: you were dancing. I had to stop you and return you to your sleeping bag.'

'Was it the dance of *kefi*? Was it the dance I learned last night?'

'No, it was an awful dance. Some dance I have not seen before. A dance of nightmare.'

'Why do you say that?'

'Mike, this is why you are here. This is why you must not eat. A spirit worm has taken hold of you, and we must clean him out. By fasting, and by dancing we will have him out. The fasting will make him hungry and the dancing will make him dizzy.'

Mike scratched his head and looked across at the yellow sun hoisting itself free of the mountain range. Whatever the spirit worm was feeling, he shared the experience. Hungry, yes, he was, and he was still faintly dizzy from the previous night's exhausting round of dancing. Manoussos had instructed him in the dance of *kefi*, and as a teacher he'd proved to be something of a martinet. He had made Mike dance behind him, to imitate his moves exactly. Mike had been sedulous in copying the steps, but not accurate enough to prevent the shepherd from bawling and cursing and making him repeat tiny moves. It astonished Mike that Manoussos could even see him from in front, but when challenged he claimed to be watching Mike's shadow, which he said betrayed errors more clearly.

The dance of *kefi*, Mike was told, was a dance which could be exhibited at all public festivals and tavernas; one which would not be out of place at any presentation of traditional Greek dancing. He knew the word to correspond roughly with the English word 'gaiety' or 'mood of joy', but its application for the dance was more complicated. Indeed, the dancer was expected to express his spirit of gaiety but, Manoussos assured him, in the context of his *suffering*.

'You must show your suffering, and how you overcome suffering, to achieve *kefi* in the dance,' Manoussos had shouted, clapping out time with his leathery hands.

Mike had practised the dance moves around the campfire until his thighs burned with the strain. His arms ached from holding them out at his sides. Manoussos had been obsessive about correct posture, down to the detail of how the fingers should be held. In particular for *kefi* he insisted that the thumbs be crooked and held rigidly in a certain position. Mike understood he had to somehow transform his suffering – whatever that meant – into gaiety – whatever that might be – in order to demonstrate what Manoussos called his manliness – whatever that might be worth. He didn't see how he could do it merely by the slavish imitation of the moves imparted.

When he complained Manoussos said, as if it had been obvious all along, 'Yes; not like a robot. Around these moves you must make your own. To express *kefi*, you must create.'

'You mean I can improvise?'

'But you must know these steps first.'

Manoussos accompanied Mike's dancing by leading him, or by playing the *lira*, or simply by falling to one knee and clapping time. Often he would stop the whole business, crying insults and dismissing Mike's best efforts, making him go over a step again.

'*Droubas! Malaka! Poutane!* Why don't you watch me! Why make a whore of a confusion out of the whole thing? Are your feet too big? Not like that! Like this! Come on!'

Manoussos insisted he do everything with minute accuracy. It was essential he said, because the dance of *kefi* was the doorway to all other dances.

'What happened to the Zorba dance?' Mike protested. 'Can't we do the Zorba dance instead?' Manoussos had responded with an evil glare.

'Now let me see you create,' he said when he was reasonably happy that Mike had mastered the basic steps. 'Let me see you dance your suffering.'

'I'm suffering. I'm suffering all right.'

'Good. Let me see it in your steps.'

Mike had been dancing his 'gaiety' for three hours, and he was shit-sick of it. 'Look,' he said angrily. 'I've had enough. I'm going to bed.'

Manoussos ignored this protest, stuck the *lira* under his ribcage and struck up a passionate and exotic piece which took Mike by surprise. It was a whirling dervish. Even though he was exhausted by the evening's efforts, his feet wanted to go with it. They wanted to move in the dust contrary to his anger.

And he was angry. As he stepped out the moves taught to him over the past two or three hours he began to realise how angry. He was angry at the shepherd's bullying. He began to think of the things that had brought him to this place, and to this pass. He thought of Kim, and their arguments, and the hurt he had felt over her; then he remembered with self-disgust his meaningless affair with Nikkie. He stamped out his anger in the dust, almost toppling, recovering, correcting his stagger in a step, a leap. The wild music drove him on, picked up his anguish like a wind and carried it. He saw Kim's face before him. He spun around and slapped the heel of his boot, hard. He stopped, rocked, dropped to one knee and stroked a fist through the dust. The music fizzed in his veins.

The next thing he knew was that the music had stopped and Manoussos was holding him by the arms. 'Mike! Mike!' He was calling as if from a great distance.

'What is it? Why did you stop?'

'How long have you been dancing? This last dance? How long?'

'Two or three minutes. Why do you ask?'

'Over half an hour. More. You were gone, Mike. You summoned your *kefi*. It was available to you. You did very well, Mike. Only you must not let it control you.'

'Half an hour?'

'More, I say. And I saw your worm spirit. He was so dazed by your dancing he came to take a look. But he saw me and then he went back inside. Mike, you achieved something. I have been hard with you, but something came of it. That is enough for tonight. Tomorrow I will teach you how to control the wind of the *kefi*. You must know how to saddle the wind.'

'Can I sleep now?'

'No. First you must guard the sheep.'

That had been his first evening on the mountain with Manoussos. After dancing, he had watched the sheep until the fire had died down and the stars came out like fruit on a tree, close enough to be picked. He had sat on a rock with his sleeping bag drawn around his shoulders to ward off the chilly night air; and though he had seen nothing his senses were alerted to some presence in the night.

Something was out there.

There was no particular sound to be heard. He could see nothing unusual. But he sensed it.

Everything had seemed strange to him from the moment he had embarked on this expedition. He didn't know now whether his senses had been teased or overstimulated by the behaviour of the shepherd; or whether too much pure oxygen breathed down by the mountain had inflamed his imagination. The stars seemed to crowd in to observe, like an auditorium in the sky. And something, whether it was animal, man or spirit, was circling the camp.

Circling. Very slowly. His scalp flushed.

When Manoussos had relieved him, he told this to the shepherd. The man had merely nodded and told him to get some sleep.

Now here was Manoussos telling him he'd spent his resting time sleepwalking. Or rather sleepdancing. Small wonder he was exhausted.

Mike took a deep breath, filling his lungs and savouring the freshness of the morning air. His head thumped. His belly groaned.

'We must begin again,' said Manoussos. 'We don't have much time.'

'Time? It seems to me time is the only thing we've got.'

'You know nothing. Look at the sun. Look at the moon.'
Mike looked up: it was true that the moon was still hanging low in the sky behind his back, fading with every moment the sun climbed higher.

'Have you had your breakfast of olives?'

'I have.'

'And were they good?'

'They were very good.'

'Good. I'm glad someone enjoyed their breakfast.'

Manoussos nodded in agreement, though he looked slightly puzzled at Mike's remarks. Mike sniffed; being ironic with a Greek was an entirely useless enterprise. 'Now dance.'

Mike took up position by the ashes of last night's fire. 'More damned *kefi*?'

'No. *Kefi* is not a dance for morning. Morning is a time for birds, so this we use. Now. In my style.'

Manoussos demonstrated a completely different dance. Indeed it was less of a dance than a rapid stepping movement, with the feet close together, one crossed slightly behind the other, with the dancer balanced on the balls of his feet and springing lightly from one foot to the other. The arms were held out and at the sides, the hands held limply, the middle fingers pointing downwards.

'This is much easier,' said Mike, stepping out the beat in the dust.

'Good. Continue for one hour.'

Mike stopped. 'You're crazy.'

'With music you can do it.' Manoussos sat down with his *lira* and began to play a light stepping piece. He didn't seem to consider for a moment that Mike might not co-operate. 'Hup hup hup hup!'

Mike began to dance. Within two minutes he was feeling bored and stupid. He was less self-conscious when dancing around the campfire.

'NO!' screamed the shepherd. 'NO! Not with this face!'

'What?'

'Not with this face can you dance! No! Change your face!'

Mike sighed and tried to change his expression of exasperation. He persisted with the dance. After ten minutes his calf muscles were screaming. Manoussos barked encouragement, occasionally laying down his instrument and clapping his hands sharply, urging on the stepping dance. Then he would return to his music with augmented vigour.

Mike closed his eyes and began to think of Kim; thoughts of anger and sadness that could override the pain in his legs.

'Good!' roared the shepherd. 'Good! Don't lose the step!'

The feeling went out of Mike's legs, though he found the music propelled him through a pain barrier. He was sweating heavily. The stepping dance was more taxing than anything from the previous night. He pushed himself to the limit, and when after an hour Manoussos told him he could stop, he collapsed. Manoussos gave him permission to drink some water, and a break of about fifteen minutes.

Then he said he was ready to teach Mike another dance.

'Look,' said Mike. 'I'm not an athlete. You seem to want me to behave like an athlete.'

The shepherd considered this for a moment, and then agreed. 'Yes. You must be like an athlete.'

When the sun reached its highest point, Manoussos called a halt. The afternoon, he declared, was for talking and sleeping. Mike staggered to the shade afforded by the huge, volcanically fused boulders, and pulled off his canvas shoes. But he found that when he took refuge from the agony of his legs, his hunger pains returned. Manoussos tried to talk with him, but all Mike wanted to do was to stretch out on his sleeping bag.

He dozed, and fell asleep. When he woke, Manoussos had gone. The sheep had strayed across the apron of the hillside. The yellow sun seemed sluggish in the heavens, like a huge lizard's eye.

Mike sensed something watching him. He got to his feet and walked to the black ring of the dead campfire. He had a commanding view; before him the hill grazed by the sheep fell away into a valley, with conifer trees beyond. To the right lay the raggedy mountain range sweeping around behind him. To the left he could glimpse the sea. There was nothing, and no one, save the alien plants and cacti, turned sullenly in on themselves in the heat of the afternoon.

Perhaps Manoussos was spying on him. He suspected so. He could see nothing, but he was certain something was out there. Circling.

Mike thought about leaving. He guessed he could find his way back down to Kamari; in any event, he only had to follow the direction of the sea, and he knew where the sun set each day in relation to the village. He suspected that the shepherd was mad. Whatever he was trying to achieve by bringing Mike up into the mountains, it was too elusive a goal for Mike's comprehension. It was always possible there was no aim to it all; that Mike had been recruited into a lunatic's jaunt in the hills. His reason told him all this was so, and rationalised that his best – and safest – course of action would be to take up his water and leave immediately.

But another side of himself, a deeper and more intuitive sense, had to stay. He felt he had begun something, and must see it through, no matter how unproductive or wasteful the experience. He'd persuaded himself he was watching the entire scenario as a detached observer, but a maggot of doubt gnawed at his own scepticism. There was a feeling that some revelation was at hand, that something was emerging out of all of this. A chain-wheel had been set in motion. And even though he liked to think he could leave at any moment, the plain fact was he couldn't tear himself away.

Besides all of this he had now genuinely spooked himself with ideas that someone or something was watching the proceedings. Something *was* there. He would now have been afraid to take the trail back alone.

'What are you looking for?'

Mike was startled. The shepherd had come up behind him, as if from nowhere. 'Where have you been?'

'To make sure the sheep didn't stray too far. Are you ready to begin again?'

'Yes.'

38

Kim, Kati and Maria were collecting up fallen or broken pieces of ceramics in Kati's shop. Moments earlier a minor earth tremor lasting no more than four seconds had rippled through the shop. Though the tremor was hardly experienced by the three women, it had been strong enough to shake loose shelving and send a few items of pottery clattering to the floor.

Maria had walked in at the moment of the tremor; Kati and Kim had looked at her as if she'd caused the damage.

'Someone has been telling big lies,' Maria said, replacing an unbroken conical vase on the shelf. 'We say that, Kim. Every time the earth moves like that we say someone has been telling big lies.'

'And we know who was telling them,' said Kati.

'Hey! Don't look at me. I don't have any lies to tell. No one tells me any lies to pass on these days, so I have to tell the truth, and that's much less interesting.'

Kim knew all this was addressed to her. Maria expected to be updated on Kim's personal situation every day, and pretended to be offended if she wasn't.

'Speaking of liars,' said Maria confidentially, 'you should look out for Lakis. He is saying things about you in the village.'

'What things?'

'Ignore it. It means nothing.'

'What things, Maria?'

Maria got down on her knees pretending to look for other fallen objects. 'Oh nothing; in the taverna he says you are sleeping with all the men of the village.'

'That's nothing? Thanks a lot.'

'Look,' soothed Kati, 'Lakis is a well-known liar. He's trying to get his revenge for that egg you gave him. The women of this village know him. None will believe Lakis.'

'And the men? What will they believe?'

'The men,' said Maria, 'will believe what they want.' She got off her knees and looked Kim in the eye. Then she reached across and wound her finger in Kim's hair. 'What the hell. Let them talk. They talk of me, and I always know if they are talking of me; it's because they want to have me.'

'Shameless,' said Kati. 'She's shameless.'

Maria smoothed her dress to her buttocks before sitting down and putting her feet up on a stool. 'I would like to be shameless. But now all the men look at Kim because they think she might be available. Why? Because she is so beautiful. Kim, I hate you for being so beautiful.'

'Kim is still married to Mike,' said Kati.

'Is Mike good in bed?'

'Don't answer her,' said Kati.

'I haven't got much experience to compare him with,' said Kim. 'But yes, I suppose he is, yes.'

'I knew it. I said to Kati when we first saw the two of you: I bet he is good in bed.' Kim saw Kati blush. 'Well if you don't want him, Kati and I can have him.'

'Kim wants him,' said Kati sharply. 'Who said Kim doesn't want him?'

'But Kim has plenty of admirers. What about Giorgos the waiter?'

'Giorgos? I had a flirtation with him. But nothing came of it. He's nice, but it's not what I want.'

'Do you want Mike back?' Kati asked softly.

'I don't know. I don't know! Sometimes I think yes, I want him back. Then at the house the other day you can't imagine how hateful he was to me. Like a child. And I thought: no, I don't want this at all. Now he's disappeared without a word.'

'I have something to tell you about him.'

'Oh?'

'It seems he has gone into the hills.' Maria looked at Kati. 'With Manoussos.'

Kati looked alarmed. 'When? Who told you? When was this?'

What was it, Kim wondered, about the mere mention of the shepherd that could make women like Kati and Maria behave so strangely? She'd noticed it too with some of the other village women – the tomato lady, the butcher's wife. There was a distinct frisson whenever his name came up. It was not fear exactly, and not contempt. It was a tension, always poorly hidden, and it would come over them like a storm cloud.

Maria looked back at Kim. 'Do you know Apostolis, the man who goes by your house every day fishing with a spear? He saw them go off together two days ago.'

'Oh,' said Kati. 'That's not good. Not good.'

'Well, at least he won't come to any harm with Manoussos. Kati, why look so worried? Where have they gone?'

'Into the hills,' Maria repeated.

'Manoussos,' Kati said, 'is crazy.'

'But he won't let Mike come to any harm. Will he?' Kim felt a sudden thrill of concern for her husband's safety. 'What is it, you two? What aren't you telling me?'

'We are only concerned that he doesn't fill Mike's head with rubbish,' said Kati.

'But he's not dangerous, is he? You wouldn't describe him as dangerous?'

The two Greek women returned a hard stare.

'Tell her,' said Maria. Kati glared at her. 'Tell her.'

'Tell her what?'

'Tell her what happened.'

Kati lit a cigarette. Kim noticed her fingers were trembling. Some tourists came by, peering through the window. Maria got up and locked the door. She closed the blind on the tourists outside.

'The German woman at your house,' Kati said. 'The House of Lost Dreams. Most people think she didn't hang herself. Most people think she was murdered. Manoussos was there that night. He was involved.'

'Involved? In what way involved?'

'He may have been fighting with Lakis. He was a rival for her affections. The German woman. Look, Kim, this is all speculation. No one knows for sure what happened.'

Kim noticed Maria looking disgusted with Kati's account; but also that she'd decided not to contribute any further information herself. 'Are you saying Mike's up in the hills with a murderer?'

'There are stories about Manoussos' father. People in this village feared him. When he died in the hills, none of the men would go up to his house to bring down the body. All refused. In the end they had to pay some gypsies to bring his body down to the church.'

'Why were they so afraid?'

'Because he was some kind of a sorcerer.'

Kim blinked in an effort to make sense of what was being said.

'I only tell you this,' said Kati, 'because he may want to fill Mike's head with nonsense and stories of what happened at the house that night. If he does, don't believe anything.'

'But what can I do? Mike is up there in the hills with him.'

'Nothing. You can do nothing. Only wait for him to come down, and then tell him what we have said. Tell him to have nothing more to do with Manoussos. Tell him Manoussos is crazy. Crazy and dangerous.'

Kim thought about Mike alone in the hills with the shepherd. She remembered the first time Manoussos had taken her to the hot bath, how kind he had been, how formal and correct. She couldn't believe that Mike might be in any danger. And yet she'd always been aware that beneath the millpond gentleness of Manoussos there had been a brooding and potentially violent undertow. She had identified it that very first day, in the dark glitter of his eyes.

The two women studied her reaction to their revelations. She looked at them and then saw their faces suddenly turn to surprise. In an instant all three of them were up and steadying ceramic ornaments on the shelves as a second tremor vibrated through the shop; but it was even smaller than the first, and it passed even more quickly.

Kati looked at Maria in exasperation.

'Don't look at me,' cackled Maria. '*I* didn't lie!'

39

On Mike's second night in the hills he became thoroughly convinced someone was out there besides him and Manoussos. Though his hunger pains had gone away, the lack of nourishment had left him feeling weak, and the almost constant dancing had drained him.

As on the first night they had built an aromatic fire, and again as on the first occasion, Manoussos had set him to watch over the flock. Mike huddled in his sleeping bag watching the campfire die down. A brilliant searchlight moon was up, flooding the slope before him. Nothing could go unseen in that light. More than once Mike had the strange impression that the bizarre plants and cacti were swelling and feeding on the night air, urging themselves towards the moon's light. These momentary hallucinations he dismissed as the effects of exhaustion and fasting.

Then he was shaken out of his complacency by a brief flare to the left of his vision. The sleeping bag slipped from his shoulders as he scrambled to his feet. Whatever it was, the flare had died down; but it had been accompanied by an unmistakable hiss, like a sudden ignition of gas. Now it had gone, and as he surveyed the moonlit slope there was nothing in his field of vision to suggest its cause. Then he saw it again, this time to the right about thirty or forty yards away. An instantaneous burst of mercurial blue light and a fleeting hiss, like the sound of a small Guy Fawkes rocket.

Mike instinctively looked round for a weapon. There was nothing, only dried brush piled high for their fire. He remembered that Manoussos carried a knife for practical purposes. It was in his canvas bag. He stepped over to the sleeping shepherd. Manoussos snored on undisturbed under his thin woollen blanket. His canvas bag lay on the dirt next to him. Then there was a crack, like the sound of a branch snapping underfoot. Mike looked all round. The moon lit every available spot, there was no possible hiding place, yet there was nothing to be seen, not even the smallest animal which might have been drawn by the sheep.

Mike bent over and drew the bag to him, careful not to waken the shepherd. He rummaged inside the bag, trying to feel for the knife. He put his hand on the cloth-wrapped *lira*, and on what felt like the bag of olives. He felt the weight of the large clasp knife when a powerful hand grabbed at his wrist.

'What are you doing?' It was the shepherd. He had awoken.

'Something is out there. I'm looking for the knife.'

Manoussos sat up immediately. He let go of Mike's wrist. Mike had the knife in his hand. 'What did you see?'

Mike pointed out the places where he thought he'd seen the flares. The shepherd got up and walked round the rock, sniffing, nodding. 'Yes,' he said. 'He has come.'

'Who?' Mike hissed. 'Who has come?'

'It is your enemy.'

'My what? What fucking enemy?'

'He is here. Can you smell him? What were you going to do with the knife?'

'Do? I don't know. Defend myself, I suppose.'

'Give me the knife.' Mike handed the clasp knife to the

shepherd. He felt relieved that Manoussos was taking charge. The shepherd opened the knife and asked, 'Again, where did you see this thing?'

Mike once more pointed out the spot where he thought the last disturbance had occurred. Manoussos nodded, and then flung the knife as far as he could towards the place Mike had indicated.

'What are you doing? Are you giving him the knife?'

'The knife is no good to you. You cannot fight him with this knife. Now go to sleep. I will watch.'

'Sleep? You must be joking! I can't go to sleep! There's something out there! What's all this talk about an enemy? I haven't got an enemy!'

'Lie down, Mike. Nothing will happen while I am here. I will watch for you. In the morning I will explain to you. But not now.'

Despite Mike's furious protests, Manoussos would not be drawn. He took up position on a rock, holding his crook and wrapping himself in his woollen blanket. He would answer no further questions. Eventually Mike calmed himself and climbed inside his sleeping bag, though it was some time before he managed to sleep.

Just before dawn he woke in a fit of sobbing. He knew he had been dreaming, but couldn't remember what the dream was about. Manoussos was still sitting on his stone, eerie in the grey light, crook cradled in his arm. The shepherd nodded and said softly, 'Good. It's good. Now go back to sleep.'

In the morning he woke feeling light-headed and disoriented, but strangely refreshed. He was surprised to have awoken with no hunger pangs. Indeed if a hearty breakfast had been placed before him, he might not have been able to touch it.

As he helped himself to water, it seemed that the morning was drawn with peculiarly deep shadows. The rock cast its purple shadow at a curious angle; the lines in the shepherd's face seemed deeper furrowed, as if enhanced by mauve crayon.

'Ready to dance?'

'No. Not until you tell me what we're doing and what's happening here.'

'Later. First, dance.'

'You gave me your word.'

Manoussos took off his headscarf and used it to wipe his face and neck. His silver hair was surprisingly long, falling well below his collar. He brushed it back with a large, leathery paw. 'Sit.'

They sat down in the dust. Mike waited a long time for Manoussos to begin. The shepherd looked into the sun as if for inspiration, and then he stared hard at the red dust. 'To speak is very difficult.'

'Try,' said Mike.

'I am not one for speaking. To speak of a thing makes it not the thing. But I will try. Here, I teach you to dance. I must not ask you to dance. You must ask me to teach you to dance.'

'Why?'

'The will must come from you. Or you will never learn the dancing. There are five dances.' He counted them for Mike on his hand. '*Kefi*, which you learn well, and which is the doorway to all others. Of these there are two I will not teach you. Never. The first of these is the dance of sexual arousal.'

'Sounds fun.'

'You know nothing. Once I made this dance. Once. I almost lost my mind. And it almost destroyed the village, as it almost destroyed me. Never again will I dance this dance.

'The other is the dance to stop time. This dance is too terrible, even more than the other one. So terrible, the dancer must die. If I dance it for you, I must die. My father gave me this dance when he was dying, and it hurried on his death. His heart gave way. I will not pass this dance. It will die with me.

'Of the other dances I can teach you, the first is the dance of animals, fishes and birds. I started to teach you yesterday morning. You have good feel for this dance. Of the five dances it is your natural dance. But you do not have it yet. This dance will give you power to change into any animal, fish or bird in your sight. Believe me, Mikalis, this is a terrifying thing.'

Mike said nothing.

The shepherd cleared his throat. 'The other dance, which I will teach you today, is the dance of war with spirits. This is not your natural dance, but it is the one you most need.'

'Why do you say that?'

'Because you are clawed by spirits, inside and out. Last night you saw them.'

'What you called my enemy?'

'Yes. He was there. But you have seen him already. He has wounded you before.'

'The angel? *Agios Mikalis?*'

'If this is how you see him, yes. To you he may be an angel; to others an ape; to others again a voice in the grass. But he is the one who has worked his way between you and your wife.'

'Is there only one spirit?'

'No. Many. But he is your chosen enemy. This is why I

must teach you this sacred dance. Because you must make battle with your enemy. You must meet your enemy in the road.'

The thought of another encounter with the angel-militant was enough to freeze Mike. Part of his mind was trying to sort Manoussos' words into some coherent psychological framework, whereby spirits could be read as weaknesses of the will, bad habits, slovenly character traits; things that might have come between Kim and himself. That was how he had understood the journey so far; but this evocation of the warring saint was too close to real, physical experience for his own liking. He'd encountered the angel once already and paid with a broken limb. For him the angel had never been a delusion or a metaphor. The angel had been a flesh-and-blood, violent adversary.

'These spirits,' said Mike, grappling to understand. 'How long have they been with me?'

'This I cannot answer. Maybe you brought them from your country. Maybe they attached to you when you had your motor accident in the mountains. But I can say this. There is one thing that has given them all flesh.'

'What is that?'

'It is that house. The House of Lost Dreams.'

Yes. I have always known. It is the oracle.

The words reverberated inside him. The oracle. He suddenly reached an understanding about the nature of the oracle, the house, the island. It was as if he had come to a plateau in his thinking, from where he could see clearly.

There was the sacred and the profane. And the sacred lived just below the surface of life, hidden, but eternally present. It drummed, it throbbed beneath the skin of things, but it was lost to the profanity of life. The need to survive, to exist on a mundane basis, to eat daily bread: all this laid a topsoil, a shell between man and the sacred.

And here on this island, revelation of the sacred was always imminent. For some reason the sacred was closer to the surface here than at any other place. The soil thinned. The shell cracked. The sacred shone through. Scratch away the soil and it was revealed in burning energy and radiant colours. But the sacred needed to speak, and it would fasten upon anything it could find, abstract or concrete, to give voice to itself. Fragments of dreams. Butterflies. Ghosts. Fields of snakes. Unspoken thoughts. Old religions. New religions. Pagan gods. Christian saints. It didn't matter: it was all tongue to the oracle.

Here the sacred had found a way to speak through the profane, for those who could listen. It had used Mike's violent opposition to the church to return to him. It might use Artemis to hunt him down or let him pass. It could enact in him the legend of Orpheus if it chose. It was indiscriminate; frightening; magical. This was the island mystery.

And this was the meaning of the legend. Orpheus was everywhere, journeying beneath the surface, to the place where the sacred would be revealed. But it was impossible to remain in permanent view of the sacred, and the sacred was covered over again by stone. Eurydice was lost. But the oracle still found voice through the poetic soul of Orpheus. And it was here, at this place, where the sacred broke though, where the eyes could be stripped of scale, and the ears unstoppered. This island was the talking head. The House of Lost Dreams its tongue. The oracle.

'That place,' Manoussos continued, waking Mike from his reverie, 'it is a kind of volcano. Spirits pour from that place. Good spirits, bad spirits. But spirits are like ashes in the wind. They need places and people to give them flesh.

It is a place of prophecy and dreams; of fulfilment; of lust; of murder.

'It is a place where the earth does her dance. You have been there when it trembles. Let me say, Mike, when I saw you and Kim come there I was afraid for you. I know the power of that place. Why? My family owned that land. My father used to go there. He had his reasons. There was no house in those days.

'Then my father lost that piece of land to Lakis' grandfather in a card game. But I think my father pretended to lose. He wanted to get rid of it. He was afraid of the place. Perhaps he was right. Lakis' family never had any luck. Then there was the killing of the German woman. Wrong. All wrong.'

Manoussos shook his head sadly. Then he got to his feet. 'Enough talk. Now dance.'

Mike also scrambled to his feet. 'Wait. Wait. I want some time to think about this.' He was busy trying to unscramble his own revelation from Manoussos' talk of spirits. Was he admitting to the real existence of the magical and the spiritual?

Manoussos guessed, or read, his thoughts. 'So you still have doubts? Fine. Go back down. Go and live your life in the House of Lost Dreams. What is it to me?'

Mike looked at the Greek shepherd and he was met with a steady and inscrutable gaze from eyes as dark as black olives. It was a good question. What was it to him if he didn't give up his time to help Mike? The question, not put, but utterly implicit in that disconcerting, unblinking gaze was: do you want to find a way back to Kim or don't you?

'All right,' said Mike. 'We dance.'

40

Astonishing! It really was astonishing. The *sensation* was of the earth rotating under his feet. He could speed it up or slow it down by making the step faster or slower. There was also an uncomfortable itching in his index fingers, which were held pointing at the ground and in a crooked position. Manoussos had taken pains to demonstrate this finger posture, physically manipulating them into the right position. Mike had been performing this dance now for over twenty minutes. His leg muscles ached and his fingers burned with a hot itch, but the effect of the dance was too exhilarating to want to stop.

This was the dance of war with spirits.

It was another dance of stepping action. Manoussos had Mike using his right foot to scrape at the ground lightly and with the barest of contact between foot and earth, like an animal pawing at the dust or a child playing on a scooter. The monotony was relieved by steps to either side and a swaying action of the body, as if the earth was moving and the dancer sought to balance himself.

Manoussos had Mike stripped to the waist to perform this dance. The shepherd played a single note before setting the instrument aside and urging Mike on with rhythmic handclapping. The first thing Mike had experienced – after he had passed over the threshold of pain – was a strange muffling of sound in his ears. This in turn produced a dizziness which almost had him toppling, but he heard Manoussos' voice, as from a distance, exhorting him not to lose his step. He closed his eyes to concentrate, and when he opened them again the light seemed dazzling. Then the curious sensation began.

At first there was a low rumbling, and the ground actually slipped a yard under his feet. He felt a click as it happened again, and this time the earth rolled steadily beneath him. The sensation was of the globe moving under him, as if it had been loosened by the action of his dancing, and was now gliding more freely like a lubricated ball bearing; except that the giant ball, on which he danced like a circus performer, was the planet itself.

The globe ran freely under his feet. For one terrifying, dizzy moment he felt he could spin the earth and that mountains, continents and oceans would pass beneath him. His heart knocked wildly in his chest. He stopped.

'No!' Manoussos roared. 'Don't stop! You don't stop!'

But it was too late. The illusion had been broken. Mike pressed the palms of his hands to his chest and put his head between his knees. He was panting, and perspiring heavily.

'No! Now it's too late! Too late! Why you stop? Now we must begin all over again!'

Manoussos was furious. He kicked a stone in disgust. Mike could hardly collect his breath to speak. 'I'll try again. When I've recovered.'

The shepherd jabbed a finger at the sun. 'After noon you cannot do this dance. Never. We have wasted half of the morning in idle talk, and now this.'

'Tomorrow then.'

'Tomorrow we are not here.' Manoussos sat down and took a swig of water. 'We cannot stay.'

Mike joined him. 'Why can't we stay? Not that I'm complaining, but why?'

'Your enemy is getting nearer all the time. And after tonight the moon will not protect us.'

'Where will we go?'

'It is not decided. Now, stop speaking.'

'But I need to—'

'Stop speaking! Please.'

So they sat in silence for some minutes as the sun climbed higher in the sky. Manoussos' sourness was deeply oppressive. He sat in surly stillness, his hands resting limply on his thighs. Mike felt uncomfortable. He tried to meet his eyes, but the shepherd wouldn't look at him.

'I'm ready to dance again,' Mike said finally. It was the last thing he wanted, but he felt it was the only way to appease the man's appalling mood.

Manoussos nodded and fetched his *lira*. 'This time I will give you a sound.'

Mike took up position, his arms outstretched, index fingers curved and pointing downwards. Manoussos bounced his bow across a string, offering a deep reverberating note to beat time in place of the hand-clapping. Mike stepped out the dance in the red dust. He worked hard to overcome the desperate ennui and hardly dared to let the tedium he was experiencing show in his face. The steps by now were repetitive and mechanical, and by dint of imagination he was able to lift himself from the physical effort involved. Eventually the same sensations took over him: a burning in his fingers; a muting of sound; intensification of light; and a frightening misfiring of the heart. This time he danced through it, attuning himself to the repetitive throbbing of the distant *lira*. The illusion of the ground rotating beneath him reoccurred. He allowed it to happen. The speed of the ground moving underfoot was astounding and breathtaking. It filled him with a new strength, like a second wind inside him. The earth spun faster and faster, until he lost sense of time. He danced on, until exhaustion overtook him and he felt himself falling. He fell a long way, and for a long time. Then the earth came up to meet him with bruising impact.

He was lying on the floor, utterly out of breath. His sweat was caked with dust. Then he felt a cold sensation on his head. He looked up and Manoussos was splashing water on his face.

'What happened?' said Mike.

'What happened? You fell.' Mike looked dismayed. 'Don't worry. It was good. You summoned a martial wind. It's enough. It will help you.' He pulled Mike to his feet and told him to sit in the shade of the rock. Mike had to huddle into the rock to find any shade; the sun was like a furnace almost directly above them. Mike's head was throbbing.

The shepherd gargled some water and spat it out. 'You did well. This worm spirit in you became dizzy and came out. I had to wrestle with it, but now it is finished. *Telos.*'

'Wrestle with it?'

'Yes. It wanted to go back inside you but I took it in my hands and killed it for you. I threw its corpse behind this rock.'

'Its *corpse*? What are you talking about? Is it there now?'

'Yes. Behind this rock.' Mike stood up but Manoussos put a restraining hand on his wrist. 'Don't look.'

'Why?'

'It is very ugly.'

'I want to see it.'

'I advise against it.'

Mike shrugged off Manoussos' hand and rushed behind the rock to take a look. He stared down at the dust and the flakes of stone. There was nothing there. Nothing at all. Mike walked back round the rock. Manoussos was massaging his sleepy eyes with his fingers.

'There's nothing there.'

'No? Well it must have gone.'

'What do you mean, gone?' Mike spat. 'There never was anything there.'

'Look, it was a spirit. Do you think it lies like a dog's corpse rotting in the sun for days? After some minutes it will . . .' Here Manoussos waved a hand in the air, gesturing at the sky. Mike muttered something under his breath. 'What, you don't believe me? Then I ask you this question: if now I offer you one brandy, do you want it?'

It was true that the very thought of a brandy, or of alcohol, made Mike feel distinctly nauseous. But when he summoned the idea of food of any kind to mind, he found the same sensation. He looked at Manoussos with deep scepticism.

The shepherd looked at the dust at his feet and shook his head sadly. He smiled wistfully. 'I do this for him and he calls me a liar. What gratitude. I do this for him . . .'

Mike looked at the muttering old man, with his crumpled leather face and silver hair, and his sly half-closed eyes, and it occurred to him that this was all *theatre*. The shepherd was being distinctly theatrical, pretending to be saddened by Mike's failure to display gratitude. Mike wondered what he'd expected to see behind the rock. A rotting sea snake? A bloated maggot? More than that, he wondered what the hell he was doing up there on the mountain at all.

And yet there was the dance! Hadn't that been remarkable?

He looked up at the sun, stuck in its current position overhead. It was like the unblinking yellow eye of a predatory reptile.

'Time to sleep,' said Manoussos. 'And I must prepare.'

Mike resisted the temptation to make some withering remark. 'Prepare for what?'

'Wait and see.'

Manoussos settled himself for a siesta. Mike sat down a little way off, too furious to consider sleeping. The sun rippled outwards, as from a stone tossed in a golden pond. Shadows crept from the skirt of the huge rock. The drone of insects at noon was like the steady pulsating of an engine centimetres beneath the earth's surface. Inevitably Mike was lulled to sleep.

He woke two hours later feeling groggy and irritable. Manoussos was awake and watching him. The hunger pangs, having retreated for some time, were back with a vengeance. Mike snatched up the water container and drank. His bowels were in a state of disorder, so he went some way off into the scrub out of the shepherd's sight.

When he returned, he noticed that Manoussos had a sizeable scratch on the side of his cheek. A smear of blood was still damp behind the silver stubble of his chin. There was also a cut on the back of his hand.

'What have you been doing?'

Manoussos gestured with his head, signifying nothing. Mike persisted.

'While you slept. Your spirit got up and walked. We struggled.'

'I was fighting you in my sleep?'

'Your spirit was trying to make contact with your enemy. I had to prevent it.'

'Wait, wait, wait—'

'Mikalis, we don't have time to talk. We have much work to do before it gets dark.'

Mike looked at the sly old shepherd. There was the whiff of fox about him. It was entirely possible he had inflicted those small wounds on himself.

Manoussos was determined not to let Mike think about it too long. 'You must begin now. Collect mastic bushes. As much mastic as you can find. We will need everything you can bring. Come, you must be ready before the sun goes behind the mountain.'

Mike sighed and looked around him. It was no small order. Much of the available mastic brush had already been burned. He would have to cover some ground to gather any quantity.

'And if you see anyone,' Manoussos added, 'don't talk with them.' With that he marched away in the direction of his flock.

Mike spent the rest of the afternoon doing as instructed. Manoussos' admonishment not to talk to anyone seemed wholly redundant. There was no one else around; and who would have any reason to come up to this inhospitable place? Shadows lengthened, lizards flicked their tails under volcanic stones, the temperature dropped suddenly. He had assembled a pile of tangled mastic bushes, both green and dried, against the rock.

Manoussos nodded. 'Now rest, and wait.' Mike was about to speak, when he was silenced. 'Rest quietly.'

After a quarter of an hour had passed, the shepherd took a swig of water. Then he began to climb the fifteen-foot-high rock. Mike was impressed by the old man's agility and the ease with which he found invisible toeholds on the stratified rock. When he had hauled himself to the top, he took off his boots and socks. Then he took off his headscarf, stuffing it in his pocket. Drawing himself to his full height, he planted his feet decisively on the rock, and waited. The sun was descending over his shoulder, crimson, flaring and vast in the sky behind him. Manoussos tilted back his head and began to sing.

It was a Greek root-song of unguessable antiquity, a traditional folk-song reverberating across the pastures of time. The depth of Manoussos' vocalisation and the power of his 'deep singing' was a revelation to Mike. The soaring melodies were complex and alien; unlike songs in the Western tradition, this seemed sourced in the depths of Asia rather than Europe. Mike was unable to understand the song; it strained his Greek to recognise more than one or two of the words. But beyond words, the song was one of sadness and tender supplication. Mike was touched by the sustained notes and the shifting vibrato, resonating as it did across the entire valley.

It was a long song. The exotic melodies were offered to the air like gifts. Mike looked up and saw a goshawk hovering high overhead. A shiver chased through him. Then he looked back at the shepherd singing on the rock. There was something heart-rending about the strength and frailty conjoined in the man, in the thought of his lungs straining in his chest, tiny and defiant, standing on his rock and singing into the vastness of the valley and into space itself. Inexplicably, it produced in Mike a deep sob. In the next moment he found himself racked by a profound fit of uncontrollable weeping. The song echoed through him as he wept. His sense of time and place dissolved.

When he began to recover, Manoussos was kneeling in the dust with him. He felt the shepherd's large hands lightly stroking his hair.

'Good. Good, all is good.'

Mike felt ashamed. 'I'm sorry. I don't know what hit me. I'm sorry.'

'Sorry? Why sorry?'

'I feel completely foolish. I was sitting listening to your song. Then I started bawling like a baby. I'm sorry.'

Manoussos looked puzzled. 'But this was the song of tears. It is natural for you to weep, and it was my intention that you should. Why be sorry?'

Mike wiped his eyes and looked at him. 'We don't cry easily where I am from.'

Manoussos studied him for a moment. Then he said, 'Now I understand why it is. You are from a cold climate, where the tears can freeze on a man's face. I think this is why.'

Mike looked at him. With this preposterous suggestion, he realised the shepherd was being both earnest and kind. He laughed. 'No. No, it's not that. We made a taboo of weeping. That's why.'

Manoussos got to his feet. The sun had disappeared behind the mountain, but its rays still glittered coldly on the visible stretch of water in the distance. He lit the fire. 'Then,' he said, 'your situation is even worse than I thought.'

'Tell me about the song, Manoussos.'

'I sang of a man who spent three years digging a well in the hard earth. He dug the well so that his loved one would come and live with him in that arid place. But he lost her, and his tears filled the well. Now only eagles and hawks drink from the well. Then I thanked the sun for his protection for these last days, and I asked the moon to protect us one more night. It was the song of the sun and the moon.'

That evening Manoussos seemed less disciplined about the dancing than before. He seemed edgy and uncertain. He had Mike practising the three dances he had taught him, but on two or three occasions he broke off playing to go and check behind the rock or to examine his flock. He would answer none of Mike's questions about what he was looking for, and every time the fire showed signs of dying he jumped up and piled it high with mastic brushwood, until the air was heavy with the rich, sweet incense of the resin from its branches. When he resumed playing, Mike noticed he did so with a distracted air, looking about him from time to time as if constantly expecting something to happen.

The moon was full, a sharp, bright bead in the sky. When Manoussos let the fire die down, the moon seemed to fatten and to move closer. Once again it illuminated the entire slope. Manoussos pulled his blanket around him and lay down to sleep, instructing Mike to guard the flock, with his life if necessary. As the shepherd slept, Mike mused on his nights in the mountains. He was ambivalent about the entire experience. Though he felt weak and fatigued from the fasting and the strenuous dancing, he felt he had made some kind of psychological breakthrough in self-knowledge. He had been pushed to his physical limits; his body and his emotions had been tested; and his mental state had been altered through the dancing and fasting. Though he now felt weak and light-headed, he knew he could enjoy his last night under God's canopy before returning to the village tomorrow.

He couldn't resent Manoussos' trickery any more. He saw it for what it was – a theatrical means of pushing experience to its limit. He did wonder about how the wily shepherd had staged one or two effects; but he was rather pleased with the way he'd stood up to the rigours of the last few days. It certainly hadn't done him any harm, and at the very least he could return to Kamari in the morning having mastered a dance or two for the village festivities on the next name-day. For that reason alone he offered a few words of thanks to the brilliant and ponderous moon flooding the mountain slope in silver light.

A light breeze picked up from the distant sea and Mike shivered, huddling his sleeping bag tighter round his shoulders. Cicadas chittered ecstatically on the moonlit slope. He looked at the shepherd snoring obliviously a few yards away and considered what a remarkable creature he was. Anti-social, taciturn, he had come to them out of the hills like some kind of faun, equipped with a *lira* instead of panpipes.

It was while he was looking at the snoring shepherd that something light hit him on the back of the neck. He put a hand to his head and looked round. There was nothing. He looked up in the sky, unable to guess where the object might have come from.

A few moments later another object hit him again on the back of the head. This time he saw that it was a small white stone. He picked it up. The stone was wet, and had a brackish smell about it.

It occurred to him that Manoussos was playing games. His hands were out of sight and he could easily have been flicking stones in the air. Mike made a play of going and looking behind the rock, and up and down the moonlit mountain slope. Then he settled again, with the shepherd at the periphery of his vision, waiting for another flake of stone to come flying from the sleeping figure. He watched for some time, but it seemed that the shepherd had outsmarted Mike, and made no movement.

A third missile, this time no small object, struck him on the side of the head. Mike gasped and stood up. He put his hand to his head and found a small trickle of blood.

'Manoussos!' Mike hissed. The shepherd didn't stir.

Mike stood over him. Perhaps he was sleeping after all. But it was impossible. No one else was out there. He scanned the slope carefully, to where it disappeared in a dark line of conifers about a quarter of a mile away. He walked over to the rock and stepped around it.

As he came round the rock, he stopped to listen. The cicadas seemed to have grown excited. Their rhythmic chitter was faster, speculative. He looked up at the moon. Already it was waning, just past pregnant fullness. He looked back down the slope and this time he saw a large white stone hurtling towards him.

He put up a hand and ducked. The stone grazed his wrist and cracked like a rifle shot against the upright wall of the rock behind him, leaving a wet mark where it impacted. This was no game. If that boulder had connected with his head, it would have dashed his brains out. Someone out there was trying to hurt him.

'Jesus Christ!' Mike peered along the illuminated ground, looking for shapes in the cactus humps and amongst the dwarf bushes. Inconceivable that someone could be out there, lying full length to hurl stones at him. Then another boulder came seemingly from out of a split in the night itself, again cracking with a sharp report against the wall of the rock.

'Manoussos! Manoussos!' Mike ran over and shook the shepherd angrily.

'What is it?'

'If you've got any of your cronies out there you'd better tell them the joke is over!'

'Mike, what is it? Are you awake?'

'Awake? Of course I'm awake!'

Manoussos scrambled to his feet. 'Be calm. Be calm. Tell me what happened.' Mike described the stone-throwing. 'It's your enemy. Now he is getting very near.'

'Bullshit, Manoussos! We've come past all of that!'

Manoussos stared at him, and asked him a second time, 'Are you awake?'

'Why do you keep asking me that?'

'I want to make sure it is not your sleeping spirit, trying to trick me. Your sleeping spirit is aggressive, always trying to fight me.'

Mike was exasperated. 'We're under attack! Someone is lobbing boulders at me!'

'Relax! He will not attack while I am awake.'

'Are you going to persist with this?'

'What? You think I am tricking you? Look around for yourself! Who do you think hurls the stones? Tell me!'

'I think you've got someone out there!'

'I? I have someone out there?' Manoussos laughed a loud, mirthless laugh. He ran out into the scrub, his arms wide. 'Hear me, my soldiers!' Manoussos cried at the top of his voice. 'It is I, Manoussos the shepherd! Your commander! Your captain! Lay down your arms! Come in out of the night! The Englishman is my prisoner! Come, comrades! Manoussos the shepherd commands his private army to desist! Peace is declared. Come and receive your medals! Manoussos will pin medals to your chests!'

He stood for a moment, bare-headed in the moonlight, as if waiting for someone to appear. Then he turned and walked stiffly back up to Mike. He put a hand to his mouth and whispered confidentially to Mike, 'It seems they refuse to give themselves up.' Then he dropped the pose. 'Yes, Mikalis. The Greek can also be *ironic*, ha?'

Mike picked up the sleeping bag that had fallen from his shoulders. His hands trembled.

'Don't worry,' said the shepherd. 'He will not attack you while I am awake. He cannot. Try to sleep now. I will watch.'

But Mike was in no mood to sleep. He stayed close to the shepherd. After an hour he had calmed himself, and persuaded Manoussos to play something soothing for him. Manoussos obliged with a plaintive piece that again reminded Mike of the traditional slow airs of Gaelic music. It was a comfort in the cold night as Mike huddled in his sleeping bag.

Manoussos stopped playing. 'Your animal helper arrived today. Did you see him?'

'No,' said Mike. Then he remembered the goshawk in the sky. 'Unless you mean—'

But the shepherd hushed him and put a finger to his lips, as if to mention names was forbidden. 'You called him in the dance. It is good.'

'I want to ask you about this enemy you speak of. My enemy. Who is he?'

'You know who he is, Mike.'

'I'm sure I've no idea.'

'Yes, you know him. You know who he is.'

'Why is he my enemy? Who is he?'

'You know. For sure you know who he is.'

Manoussos started to play again, softly. The waning moon moved in the sky, and it seemed to pull the music towards it, upwards and away, as if music were a precious metal drawn to its magnet; or a gift offered by way of appeasement; and as the softly wailing notes of the *lira* tore and broke free skywards, so Mike too felt something of himself drawn by the moon, until at last sleep overtook him.

41

It was the third night of Mike's absence and Kim was becoming seriously worried. Her anxieties had transmuted through several forms. Her initial reaction after Mike had disappeared was to be disgusted by his infantile behaviour. She knew he regarded her dalliance with the waiter Giorgos as an act of revenge over the affair with Nikkie, even though he'd no idea what had or hadn't happened that night. And in turn he had stayed away at night as a counterattack.

It angered her. He was keeping score. It almost tempted her to play him at that game. She knew she could win; she knew she could easily confirm the rumours Lakis was trying to put about the village, if that was what she wanted.

But it was not what she wanted. The business with Giorgos was not what she wanted. She had used him for a few moments to console herself, and now the waiter was disappointed. He could not let her go easily. She had hurt his pride, and that had brought with it a new set of problems. So on the first night of Mike's flight into the hills – for that was how she saw it – she hadn't been worried. Let him, she'd thought. Let him play his games.

Then the women in the shop had frightened her with this story about Manoussos. They said he was crazy. They said he was dangerous. They'd even suggested he was an

339

unpunished murderer. She began to have wild notions about what purpose the shepherd might have in taking Mike up into the mountain. Had all his actions hitherto been designed to lull them into a false sense of security?

What troubled her more was knowing that Kati and Maria had left some essential information out of the story. Some vital part, at which she could only guess. She knew Maria had wanted to tell her; but Kati had held back. Her speculations invariably led to an uncomfortable foreboding about the shepherd; something the people of a small village would not want to be made public knowledge. Some secret they were prepared to live with, even at their own risk.

It was then that the dream had returned. Or rather at first it was not a dream, but a momentary hallucination as Kim waited on the patio, angry at Mike for putting her through this, anxious for his return. She had been sitting reading under the oil lamps and had looked along the beach. Then she had felt it: the sense of oozing in the night air. That same sticky, milky lacquer which had overtaken her, and the place, on other occasions. It was becoming familiar to her. The unpleasant metallic taste in her mouth was becoming identifiable. She had looked up.

There was a swarm of tiny lights, a cluster, flickering in the darkness, like butterflies. They were like live things, superimposed over her vision. As she stared at them, they moved, realigned, and finally resolved into a single procession, the lights growing larger, like burning torches, moving towards the house.

In an instant the vision had gone. The milky haze had retreated. There was only the moon's light and the darkness of the cold sea, but it had scared her. It had frightened her enough to wish that Mike was there with her.

She had gone inside and had locked the door, not against Mike but against things she couldn't define. That night the dream returned. Her vision of the flickering lights recurred in the dream. But this time it was linked to a dream she had had some time ago: the dream of the wild women dancing and drumming in the hills.

The lights in her dream resolved into the amber-illuminated naked bodies of the women, drumming their skull drums, drinking their ritual libations, falling to the floor in epileptic frenzy. Then the women took up flaming brands, and she, Kim, was one of the women. And as they proceeded down the hill, naked, and with torches held high, they had murder in their minds, murder and unspeakable lust. But in the dream something changed. The women passed into the contemporary world, and the place was the village, and the path they walked was the path to the house. And this was the point at which Kim had woken from her dream with an exclamation on her lips.

She had felt for Mike next to her. So distressed was she by the dream that she had to get up and walk about. Outside on the patio she relit the oil lamps, though the moon was strong enough to see everything. She had gone down to sit in the boat, which had always been strangely comforting. It was here she had sat the night the scorpions had driven them out of the house. That evening Mike had held her, and had poured her a glass of wine.

Scorpions and bad dreams. Both had driven her out.

On the third day she had waited in all afternoon to see if Mike would turn up. At dusk, Giorgos, the love-sick waiter, had come creeping along the path, almost hiding in the hedgerow. He called to her softly from the gate.

'I told you not to come here,' she said sourly. 'Why did you come? I don't want you here.'

It was true. She didn't want Mike to see Giorgos hanging around the house.

'I had to come,' said Giorgos.

'Don't tell me that.'

'It's true. I had to see you. Anyway, I know Mike is not here.'

'I don't care if he's here or not. Don't come here. What do you want?'

'Please tonight. Let me take you to dinner. Just tonight.'

'It's not possible, Giorgos.'

'I have borrowed a friend's car. We can go to a village where you are not known. Only to eat together. I ask nothing more. Nothing.'

Kim had refused. Giorgos had persisted. He had threatened to make a scene. He almost began to weep. Kim was afraid that Mike might return at any moment to misinterpret the scene. She considered the alternative, of waiting in for Mike, counting the moments, fretting over his safety. Finally she conceded. She agreed to go with Giorgos, but only to a restaurant, to eat, and for nothing beyond.

'It's all I ask,' Giorgos had said, with pathetic gratitude.

Giorgos had irritated her by driving through the village, against her wishes. They had passed by a taverna at which sat Lakis and a couple of his cronies. They were enjoying a quiet beer in the early evening. Kim saw Lakis look up as they drove past, and noticed how he registered their passing with a tiny twitch of a smile.

'Stop the car!' Kim had screamed. She forced Giorgos to reverse to the taverna and made him wait in the car as she got out. She approached the men's table. They looked up.

'Good evening to you,' she addressed them in impeccable Greek.

'Good evening.'

She stood close to Lakis, looking down at him. He had to angle his neck to meet her eyes. He was smiling broadly. 'How are you, Lakis?'

'Let's call it good,' he smiled. 'How about you?'

'And you, Kristos? And you, Theo?'

'Good, good,' the men said.

'You know something,' said Kristos, a man with whom Kim had always got on well. 'Your Greek is really very good these days.'

'Good,' said Kim. 'Because I have something to say to Lakis which I'd like you all to hear.'

'What?' said Lakis, smiling, showing his gold fillings. 'What have you to say to me?'

'Look at this eye of mine. This one, the left eye. It's an evil eye. And I want you to understand that it's on you, Lakis. It's fixed on you. Why? Because you have an evil tongue. You are a dirty piece of work. And if you say any more lies about me to anyone in the village, I'm going to bring harm on your head. Understand? Harm. And tell people in the village what I have just said, if you dare.'

Lakis was too stunned to speak. The other two men were looking away, at the glowing tips of their cigarettes.

'I apologise to you, Kristos, and to you, Theo. This curse is only for Lakis.'

'Yes,' said Kristos quickly. 'Yes.'

'That's fair,' said Theo. 'It's only fair.'

'Good night.' Kim turned on her heel and got back in the car. The three men stared after her in astonishment.

'What did you do to them?' Giorgos wanted to know.

'Shut up and drive.'

Giorgos had taken her up in the mountains to a village called Paliohora, where a beautiful taverna enjoyed a cantilevered terrace view to the sea. The food was excellent, the wine was good. Giorgos was charming and kept the conversation light. Then when Kim asked to be taken home, he had spoiled the evening by declaring undying love for her.

'I'm not one of your tourists,' Kim had said contemptuously.

'This thing I feel. It's not for tourists.' He was close to tears again.

'Look, you don't love me. You only want to fuck me. And just as I told you the other night in your house, it's not what I want.'

'I know you didn't go home to Mike that night,' he said sulkily.

'You mean you followed me, you swine? Anyway, if you followed me, you know I stayed at Kati's house that night. And don't bring Mike into this.'

'You humiliate me,' he tried.

'By not sleeping with you? You're easily humiliated.'

'I love you, Kim. I love you.'

'Yes yes yes.'

Then Giorgos had astonished her by bursting into tears. A taverna full of diners notwithstanding, he laid his head on the table and roared. When she tried to stop him by placing a hand on his arm, he shrugged her off and roared even louder. When after a full five minutes his extraordinary full-lunged fit of sobbing showed no sign of abating, she had to get up and walk out of the taverna.

With no idea of where she was going, she needed to get away. She walked through the small village and along the darkened road leading out. A hundred yards from the taverna she stopped to breathe in the night. The scent of magnolia was on the air. She turned to find the magnolia tree, which was behind her, and as she looked over the hedgerow she saw a hundred tiny flickering lights.

They were like the lights in her dream.

Tiny orange lights danced before her eyes, like moths or butterflies. She moved closer. The scent of magnolia was overwhelming. It was some moments before she realised that what she was looking at was the village graveyard. At the foot of each headstone a small candle had been lit and placed inside a glass jar. The light danced in each glass and glinted on the black marble stones, illuminating the faces of the markers and softening the harsh angles of the marble. The headstones seemed like black portals. The effect was one of silhouette, of light and shadow, of souls remembered, and the black shadow of death spinning out in another plane just beyond the lights. Each tiny flame was like a whispered thought, a memory intact, trapped in time against the encroachment of the dark.

This was how Giorgos found her, watching over the unearthly beauty of the graveyard. Perhaps the scene had a sobering effect on him too; he had recovered himself, and was ready to take her home. She hardly seemed to notice him behind her.

The effect on Kim was one of extraordinary peace. This is how it ends, she thought. We don't have time, Mike. We don't have time. Where are you? What are you doing?

42

Mike was eager to get back down the mountain. He was anticipating food, beer, cigarettes, everything which had been forbidden. Manoussos had allowed him to break his fast with a few black olives produced from the same packet as those he'd tasted on the first day with the shepherd. They exploded on his palate like citrus. Within a few minutes of swallowing them he had serious stomach pains.

The shepherd reproached him gruffly. 'I told you to chew them slowly and for a long time. But you went at them like a wolf.'

'Yes,' Mike groaned, tying his sleeping bag to his rucksack. 'I *wolfed* five olives. Five.'

'Irony? Is this the irony? Yes, I see it. Come on, we go.'

'But you're going in the wrong direction. Surely Kamari is that way.'

Manoussos had rounded up his flock and was herding them across the crest of the hill towards the far valley, deeper inland. 'Kamari? Did I say we go to Kamari?'

'No, but—'

'No. We do not go to Kamari. Come. *Embross!*' He slapped one of the sheep with his crook. Mike found himself falling in behind, adjusting the straps on his rucksack. He had no confidence now in either finding his own way back down, or in having the strength to make the journey. His head was light and he felt vaguely disembodied, but for the raging pains in his gut. He'd hitched his wagon to the shepherd, and now he found himself unable to cut loose.

'But where to, Manoussos? Where are we going now? I don't have any more strength left in me. I have to know where we're going.'

'Come!'

Mike exploded in a fit. He threw his rucksack on the floor. A volcanic surge of anger rose in his chest. 'Listen, you sheep-fucking shit-stained ewe-breath greasy little arsewipe of a Greek peasant, either you tell me where we're fucking well going—'

'Arsewipe? What is arsewipe?'

Mike suddenly saw himself from above, as with the time in the field of snakes. He was able to look down on the ridiculous red-faced figure bellowing at the shepherd.

'It is good you have this anger. You will be able to use it.'

Mike's normal perspective returned, but now he was lost for words.

'We go,' Manoussos relented, 'to find the *mageesa*.'

'The what?'

'Everything I have done is merely to prepare you. But only the *mageesa* can set you on your path.'

Mageesa? Mageesa. Mike was unfamiliar with the Greek word. Yet he felt he should know it. 'Who or what is the *mageesa*?'

'Of course,' said Manoussos as they moved steadily down the steep side of the valley, 'we don't talk lightly of the *mageesa*.'

'Of course. How foolish of me.'

'And please, Mikalis, Mike; when we find the *mageesa*,

please do not use this word. It is not appreciated.'

Manoussos would say no more on the subject, though he tried to lighten Mike's spirits with information about the locality in which they found themselves. It seemed they had crossed some district border where, Manoussos confessed, the people were sometimes a little strange in their customs.

'You don't say.'

'Yes, it's true, Mike. Believe me.'

After walking for an hour they came to a whitewashed house nestling almost halfway down the valley. It was curiously remote, and certainly approachable only by donkey or on foot. Mike could see a dusty yard in front of the house. There was a chicken coop and a pile of firewood stacked against the wall of the house. A large black dog was tethered to the chicken coop; it appeared to be sleeping in a dry vegetable plot, some of which was being cultivated under irregular bits of glass. A figure clad entirely in black stood in the courtyard, holding something in both hands and watching them approach. The door to the house stood open.

'The *mageesa*,' Manoussos whispered. Then he cleared his throat and spat.

If this was the *mageesa*, then the *mageesa* was a widow. She wore the traditional Mediterranean widow's black: shoes, stockings, black dress and cardigan and a full black headscarf which covered not only her forehead, but also her neck and the lower part of her chin. The object she was holding was a tray, on which stood two glasses.

'Where is your Greek?' Manoussos said. 'She knows no English. You will need your Greek.'

As they drew near, the dog leapt to its feet and began barking furiously, straining on its leash so hard it dragged the chicken coop an inch or two towards them. It flung itself in somersaults trying to break free, all for the pleasure of sinking its huge jaws into their soft limbs.

Manoussos offered the widow a greeting. Mike mimicked him weakly. She remained impassive, regarding Mike steadily and with, he thought, a rather disapproving expression. Her face was dry and wrinkled like an old shoe. Her mouth seemed turned down in a permanent sense. There was something dehydrated and brittle about her; something as dry as the dust in her yard. Even her eyes lacked sheen, as if time had sucked them of all moisture, and as if toil spared her nothing of this tiny vitality.

Manoussos reached for one of the glasses from her tray. Though she made no further gesture to indicate as much, Mike felt the other glass was for him, and lifted it from the tray. '*Yia sas!*' They both toasted her health. It was raki. Mike felt the fire of the drink scorch the lining of his empty stomach. The rush of alcohol made his scalp itch. Still she regarded him steadily.

Manoussos introduced him as Mikalis. Having been briefed to remain formal, Mike said in impeccable Greek, 'I have found you well.'

Throughout this exchange the dog had been barking constantly and loudly. When they replaced the empty glasses on the tray, she silenced the animal with a word. It lay on the floor with its head between its paws and looked wistfully up at the men.

The old woman made to go inside. Manoussos followed behind her.

'She seemed to be expecting us,' said Mike.

The woman turned and wagged a finger at him. '*Milate Ellenica,*' she said severely. Her voice was surprisingly vigorous. '*Mono Ellenica.*'

'*Ne,*' Manoussos said, with equal but affected severity.

'Speak only Greek.' Then he nodded at the old woman, as if some disputed matter had now been settled, and followed her indoors.

The house was swept and rather bare. She led them into a kitchen cum living room. Its main feature was a large pot-bellied stove, out of commission for the summer but essential for winter in these hills. The woman indicated they should sit at a table covered with a plastic tablecloth. The tablecloth had been sliced in many places, where a knife had passed through bread, perhaps, and had forgotten to stop. When Mike sat down, he was faced with a wall containing a large drawing of an eye similar to the one in the Church of the Virgin.

The woman chopped a few tomatoes and cucumbers, which, along with a chunk of white bread, she placed before them. Refilling the glasses with raki she addressed Manoussos. 'He is drawn by the eye.'

'It's like the one at the church,' Mike said in good Greek. She looked at him coldly. 'Yes. Yes.'

But Mike was more taken by the small salad placed before him. 'Thank you for your hospitality,' he said. The woman nodded briefly.

She then called Manoussos aside, and the two went to a corner of the room where they turned their backs on Mike and spoke in rapid, hushed tones. When they had finished, the woman sat down beside Mike while the shepherd remained standing.

'She has agreed,' Manoussos said, 'to set you on the path. But first she must take a look at you.'

The crone held out her hands to Mike. For the first time he saw the marks on her palms. Whether they were inked or tattooed he could not tell. Letters of a mysterious alphabet, in faded black, were drawn in the sections of her hands between the knuckle joints of her fingers. Whatever alphabet they represented, it was not Greek. She indicated that he should place his hands in hers. She looked hard at the front and back of Mike's hands, made a *moue* and then looked from his hands to his face.

Her dry eyes pinned him like an insect to a board. She looked deep into his eyes for a long time. Then she searched his face slowly, as if she was looking for something in particular, hidden in the shallow wrinkles around his eyes and mouth. Mike felt paralysed. He was not sure if he could have moved if he'd wanted to.

He found himself resisting her. He didn't know what was going on, but he didn't like it. He was getting tired of submitting to Manoussos' schemes. He decided it was time he took more control of the situation. The old woman didn't smell too good and he didn't appreciate the close proximity of her face as she looked hard again into his eyes.

Suddenly she dropped his hand and dealt him a fierce, stinging slap to the face. Mike was shocked. He put a hand to his cheek. The woman was jabbering loudly at Manoussos.

'She apologises, but she saw a spirit climbing on you,' said the shepherd. 'She had no choice but to shock it out of you. She says spirits don't like to be slapped. She hoped it didn't hurt too much.'

Mike was speechless. His face was still stinging. She'd caught him sharply. The woman took his hand again and looked back into his eyes. It took Mike a few moments to recover. He'd been too shocked to feel anything other than surprise from the blow. Now he began to feel angry. He felt like returning the violence.

Then the woman dealt him a second, equally vicious slap to the face. Now she was shouting at Manoussos, who translated. 'She apologises again, but she says you are crawling with spirits. These spirits stop her from seeing what she must see. She has to slap them out of you. She says don't take it personally.'

'Don't take it personally?' said Mike. He was nursing his jaw, now aching from the second slap.

The woman, still uttering unintelligible Greek, got up from her chair and moved across the room. Here she picked up a plastic beaker and drank something before sitting down again and taking up Mike's hands.

'She's not going to hit me again!' shouted Mike.

The woman put her hands on his cheeks and made as if to kiss him. Mike pressed back in his chair.

'Open your mouth!' shouted Manoussos.

'What?'

'Open your mouth! Do it!'

Mike opened his mouth and the crone spat something into the back of his throat. It burned.

'Swallow it, Mike! Swallow!'

He gagged, jumped from his chair, coughed and swallowed the substance inadvertently. He bent double in a coughing fit. The woman patted him tenderly on his back. She gave him a glass of raki. Mike drained it to wash the bitter taste from his mouth.

'That's it!' Mike cried when he'd recovered. 'That's enough!'

The old woman said something to Manoussos. 'She says she knows what you did in the church.'

Mike was stunned. 'What? What does she know?'

'Some desecration in the church. What have you been doing, Mike?' The shepherd was laughing

'I made a scratch on the wall.' Mike sat down again. He was feeling dizzy. His mouth had become numb. The raki had gone to his head. His own words felt unmanageable and bulbous in his mouth.

'Look at the eye,' said the woman. Mike understood her and directed his attention at the eye on the wall. He was having difficulty focusing. He felt his own eyes flickering closed, against his will. 'Stay awake!' she shouted. 'This is you!' Then Mike felt another slap to his face, but this time, though he felt the blow, it didn't sting. It made him laugh. Another blow to the face, and he heard her words from a great distance, 'Stay awake.'

He smiled and refocused on the eye on the wall. But now the room was bathed in flickering white light, and he appeared to be alone. He wasn't in the crone's house any more, but had somehow been taken to the Church of the Virgin in the village, and was looking at the eye above the altar. He was relieved. He could go home. He was tired and confused, but at last he could go home. He looked again at the eye, and saw that it was covered with red paint. The paint was still glistening, still running along the wall. But something was wrong.

The paint was not running *down* the wall, it was running back *up* the wall, rushing into a central spot as if gathering itself together. The paint was drawn magnetically inwards to a specific spot. Here it bubbled before lifting from the wall in a fountain, projecting out from the wall in a long arch to land accurately in a tin. Mike felt himself snigger at the trick. Everything was running backwards. Then he noticed that the tin of paint was held by an unidentified pair of hands. The hands carried the tin out of the church. Mike followed. It was dead of night. The entire village was deserted.

Mike followed the hands carrying the tin down to the beach. The hands stopped by an upturned boat, half coated with the same red paint. A tin lid leapt from the floor into the hands and the lid was fixed back on the tin. The paint was replaced under the boat. The hands went further up the beach to Mike's house. Mike followed the hands as they went into the house and got into the bed there. Not until he was in the bed and looking at the hands did Mike realise they were his own hands. In bed next to him, his wife slept on.

'Kim!' he screamed. 'Kim!'

The old woman was slapping his face. Mike was back in her house again. He put a hand up to stop her striking him once more. His head was cloudy but he could see clearly again. 'Did I do that?' he said in Greek. 'Was it me?'

The old woman didn't answer. She got up and fetched something from a drawer. Manoussos was looking at him oddly.

'It must have been in my sleep. When I was doing all that sleepwalking, back at the house.'

'She said a spirit had taken you.'

'Manoussos, what's happening?'

'Be calm. Do as she says.'

The woman returned with a large sheet of paper and a pencil. She gave them to Mike. 'Name,' she said. 'Write.'

Mike felt slightly nauseous. He had to steady himself before he could focus to write. When he'd written his name the woman snatched up the paper, squinted at it then screwed it up in disgust. She got up to get more.

'Expensive!' she shouted. 'This paper is expensive!' It was perfectly ordinary cartridge paper. 'Don't waste it like a fool! Write in Greek! In Greek! I can't read this other nonsense! In Greek!'

Mike had a struggle to recall his alphabet. His mind was still fogged. He wrote:

ΜΙΚΑΛΙΣ ΗΑΝΣΟΝ

She looked again, twitched her nostrils and seemed happy with what he had written. 'Now where you were born.' Mike wrote:

ΚΟΒΕΝΤΡΙ

She pronounced it slowly, almost painfully. 'Coventry.' Then she said, 'Now place of death.'

Mike had heard the word clearly, *thanatos*, death. But it didn't make sense. He looked to Manoussos for help. The woman protested at his hesitation. The shepherd said, 'She says you know it. She says everyone knows it, and that you should think for a moment.'

Mike considered. He had no idea what she was talking about. He shook his head. The woman let out a sigh of exasperation, and for no apparent reason the word Manchester popped into Mike's head. So he wrote:

ΜΑΝΖΕΣΤΕΡ

'Father's name,' she said.

ΖΟΣΕΦ

'Mother's name.'

ΔΕΒΟΡΑ

When Mike had finished she snatched up the paper and drew a circle around all of the words. She got up and fetched a large dish, in which she placed the paper. She lit candles and incense. Mike recognised the familiar scent of mastic. Then she set light to the paper. It ignited in a melodramatic burst, flames a foot high. The paper burned quickly, leaving a pile of withered black ash in the dish.

The woman placed the dish on the table. She sat and peered into it. Mike shuffled uncomfortably and she rebuked him with a stare before returning to study the dish.

She did not spend long peering into the ashes. It was a matter of seconds. 'Difficulty,' she pronounced. 'Difficulty.'

She stood up and spoke rapidly to Manoussos, gesturing at Mike as she did so. 'She says it is possible you may be reunited with your wife, but spirits prevent you from doing so. She says you have too many contrary spirits inside you. Chief among these is your spirit enemy. It is he who excites these other spirits. She says you must confront your enemy spirit and defeat him. There is no other way.

'To confront your enemy spirit, you must be set on the Path of Souls. She is prepared to set you on the path. This is dangerous and you must do exactly what she says.'

'What is the Path of Souls?'

'She says the Path of Souls begins in the sea, passes by her front door and continues to the graveyard in the village of Paliohora. Paliohora is just beyond the valley; do you know it?'

'I've driven through it once.'

'Once you set foot on the Path of Souls you must not deviate an inch. Not one inch. You must let nothing distract you or lead you from the path. On the path you will meet your enemy spirit.'

The woman waddled outside, and Manoussos beckoned Mike to follow. She pointed out a path leading further down the valley, which she said was the Path of Souls. Indeed Mike could see something of a path, perhaps nothing more than a goat track, but unusually for goats, proceeding in a miraculously straight line. It went up the other side of the valley, she assured him, and ended in the graveyard of Paliohora. Then, in Greek which Mike understood perfectly, she asked who was to pay the twenty-five thousand drachmae.

Mike looked at the path plunging down the hill and then back at the expectant face of the old woman. She was still waiting for an answer. The raki was bubbling in his head. Their faces looked distorted, out of joint. Mike saw the gloriously funny side of things, and fell down on his knees, howling with laughter and thumping the dust. Even the dog stood up to look at him. Mike saw this and laughed even more. 'Fifty quid! You did all this so that you could each pocket fifty quid!'

Then Manoussos was lifting him by the arm, trying to calm him. The old shepherd looked terribly anxious. 'Mike, now is not a time to laugh,' he whispered urgently. 'This is not a good thing.'

Mike looked at Manoussos' bulging eyes and began laughing again. The old woman hovered in the background. Mike saw Manoussos beckon to the woman, saying, 'I. I will pay.' Then, with terrible earnestness, he turned to Mike. 'I hope you will give me the twenty-five thousand drachmae; because I don't have it; and if I don't bring it, we are both in trouble with this old woman, eh, Mike?'

Mike recovered to say, 'Don't worry. You'll get it.'

'You must go now,' said the woman. 'Go now. Time is short. Take the path.'

'Yes, go, Mike. Go. Remember, let nothing tempt you

from this path. Here, take my crook. My father gave it to me. I will wait here for your return. Now go.'

The crone approached him. 'If you see the saint on the path,' she said fiercely, 'kill him!'

Mike sobered for a moment. The words, even in Greek, came back at him like a recurring nightmare. Manoussos was loading his rucksack on his back, but he needed no encouragement. He wanted to put distance between himself and these lunatics as fast as possible. He hurried along the straight path. He turned only once to see man, woman and dog watching him go. Then the path dropped, and they were out of his line of sight.

43

When he felt there was absolutely no chance the shepherd and the old crone might follow, Mike took off his rucksack and sat down on a stone. Rummaging in the bottom of the rucksack he found the cigarettes proscribed by Manoussos. He lit one with trembling fingers, inhaling deeply and appreciating the rush of nicotine to his system. He regretted not having had the forethought to stuff a couple of bottles of beer in his pack.

Perhaps it was the sting of the nicotine, but he felt oddly light-headed. The day had curious visual intensity. From the position of the sun he figured it must be around noon. The sun was so bright it almost bleached everything in his field of vision, and he found himself having to squint around as he smoked his cigarette. Shadows cast at odd angles. Boulders sweated.

He'd decided his best course of action would be to press on down the valley and make for the village of Paliohora. It would be much closer than Kamari, and from there he would be able to get a ride back down to his house, or at least into Kamari. In any event, the last course of action was to backtrack and risk encountering Manoussos and the old woman at the house. Even should he try to sneak round it, he was sure to be given away by the barking of the rabid dog.

Mike had had his fill of Manoussos. He'd also had enough of the crone.

He finished his cigarette and proceeded down the path. His mouth was still rather numb from the vile substance the old woman had spat into his throat, and the unpleasant flavour of something like herb bitters stayed as an aftertaste, occasionally fetching up into his mouth. His face flushed hot at the thought of the events in the house, and he was perspiring heavily as he bounced down the track towards where the valley floor levelled out.

He had been walking for half an hour when his heart began to hammer alarmingly. He had to stop to recover his breath. It was then, while surveying the track ahead of him, that it seemed the path had about it a faint luminosity. While the straight, dusty way ahead was bleached and drained of colour in the noonday sun, it was enlivened – or so he thought – by a light lime-coloured mist hovering a few inches above it. Though the rest of the arid land around was also whitened by the intense sunlight, it seemed that the lime mist never strayed from the path. The Path of Souls. And now, as he looked, he saw the faint mist stretch for a mile in front of him, across the floor of the valley and directly up the other side.

I must be hallucinating, he thought. *Something in that vile stuff she spat in my mouth.*

He was glad to be carrying Manoussos' crook, for it helped put a spring in his stride and it gave him a confidence to step out the distance. At last he reached the valley floor. It was strewn with boulders, between which yellow stalks of dry grass struggled to grow, along with pretty violet clumps of campanula. At the other side of the valley floor he saw a man sitting astride a large boulder a few yards from where the track passed.

'*Yia sas*,' Mike greeted him.

'*Yia! Yia!*' The man slipped down from the boulder and leaned against it lazily as Mike approached. He was a peasant, perhaps a shepherd like Manoussos, wearing filthy work clothes and a grubby headscarf. He had a heavy growth of stubble on his chin and, Mike noticed, a vicious outbreak of cold sores around his lower lip. He surveyed Mike slyly, with dark, half-closed eyes. '*Pou Pas?*' Where are you going?

Mike was accustomed to the unashamed inquisitiveness of Greeks; it was not uncommon for a rural Greek to detain someone half an hour to ply them with questions about their business, family and deeds. 'To Paliohora. I go to Paliohora.'

'*Mipos ehete cigaro?*'

'Yes, you can have a cigarette.' Mike fumbled in his pocket to produce his packet. He was about to walk over and offer one, when the man stiffened, and then looked away, almost too casually. Mike looked down at his own feet. It occurred to him that to step across to the man, he would have to leave the designated path for the first time since quitting the house.

He held out the box instead. 'Here.'

The peasant smiled at him shyly. Leaning with exaggerated laziness against the rock, he gave a seductive little flick of the head, suggesting that Mike should bring the cigarette to him. 'Take one,' Mike repeated.

The peasant was still smiling. 'Bring it here.'

'Please. Come and take one.'

Mike felt a dirty wave of fear creep along his spine to raise the hairs at the nape of his neck. The expression on the peasant's face changed. Suddenly he was alert and sneering. 'What's the matter with you! It's only a few metres. Can't you manage a few metres? All I want is a cigarette! What kind of person are you?'

'Here it is. Come and take it!'

'Christ in heaven! Are you some kind of crazy person? Look! It's just a couple of steps! Jesus! You must be a crazy man! What's the matter with you?'

Mike took a cigarette from the packet and tossed one over to the man. It landed in the dirt at his feet. At this the peasant flew into a fit of rage. He walked towards Mike and then stepped back, pacing round the boulder he'd been sitting on. 'What? Do you think I'm a dog? Do you think I'm an animal that you can throw cigarettes at me? Am I not a man? Bastard! Am I not a man?'

The peasant stamped his feet and then without warning charged at Mike with a clenched fist. Mike made to dodge him, but the man drew up within a yard or two of connecting with Mike and scurried back to the rock. He ran at Mike a second time, but again scampered back before getting in close. Every few moments he released a volley of abuse. 'Bastard! Queer! What kind of piece of shit are you!'

It was the path. The man was afraid to step into the line of the path. Mike was almost hypnotised by him. Then he recovered, picked up his rucksack and hurried on. He heard the man run up behind him again, but turned to see him back off. The peasant quickly fell behind, still shouting abuse, but seemingly unwilling to follow.

After Mike had started to climb the slope on the other side of the valley, he looked back. Now there was no sign of the fellow. Mike could see the rock, but his would-be assailant was no longer there.

Mike was out of breath, and still trembling slightly from the encounter. He sat down and thought about it for a moment. It occurred to him that the peasant might have been genuinely insulted by the tossing of the cigarette; but it did seem that the man was trying to lure him from the path. And unless Mike was imagining things, the man seemed frightened by, or unwilling to intrude on the misted path himself. Spirits. All this talk of spirits had him spooked. But the man had behaved like a crazed dog. Mike shook his head. He would never know.

He pressed on. The gradient of the slope was gentle, and the land was slightly less arid than that he had left behind. Bushes of columbine and clumps of rock violets made the track seem less hostile, though the earth was still a powdery white dust underfoot, dotted with grey volcanic boulders. He stopped to take a drink of water, and heard the yammer of dogs higher up. The sound quickly died away.

The path levelled out, and it was here he heard the dogs a second time. Now he could see them: a pack of hounds apparently tethered to a bush perhaps a hundred yards away. They saw him coming and began to bark and howl again. Then they were suddenly silenced, and he had to laugh. For what he had seen was pure hallucination. The 'hounds' were not dogs at all, but a collection of grey- and yellow-coloured rocks ringing a bush. The sound had somehow suggested the dogs to him, and he had made himself visualise what wasn't there.

Illusions. He was fighting against illusions. But as he drew closer, he saw that he was mistaken. They were dogs after all; and what he had taken to be a bush was a woman standing in the midst of them. One arm was outstretched towards him and she was holding something close to her face in the other hand. She appeared to be pointing at him.

He approached more slowly, then let out a cry as again he realised that what he'd seen was nothing more than the bush and circle of rocks he'd taken them to be. He'd hallucinated an entire tableau. The illusion was vacillating in and out of focus. *This is crazy. You're losing your mind.*

He was now within thirty yards of his hallucination, for so he took it to be. But this time there could be no mistake. It *was* a woman and she was indeed surrounded by dogs, all watching him, ears pricked as if waiting for her command. Mike now saw why he had hallucinated her as a bush. The complication of branches was actually a bow and arrow in her hands, and it was clearly aimed at him. He was afraid. He had lost all confidence in what was real, and what was not.

The woman was dark, Asiatic, with a hooked nose. She wore a tunic and her bow and arrow were silver. A lethal arrow tip winked in the sunlight. The woman's face changed. For a moment she had Kim's face; and then Nikkie's; and then she was the hook-nosed huntress again.

Nonsense. It's hallucination. Go on. You have to go on. It doesn't exist. It's in your mind.

Mike repeated this to himself like a mantra. He goaded himself on, but he couldn't get one foot to move in front of the other. He was paralysed. He looked again at what he took to be hallucination. He saw the hounds twitchy with anticipation, and he could sense their excitement. A cold light gleamed in the eye of the huntress and he felt the tension of her arm drawing back the arrow. The tension transmitted to him. Even at this distance he could smell the sweat of her armpit. It was not the smell of illusion.

His chest constricted. He began to panic. He found his breath coming shorter and faster, and then in reaction, almost against the instincts of his fear, he found himself taking up a dance position. It was a dance Manoussos had taught him. The dance of war with spirits. The very posture released the constriction of his chest so that he could breathe freely again. He remembered to scoop at the earth with his toe. He heard the sound of the shepherd's *lira* in his head, and executed the dance. He was able to roll the path towards him an inch at a time, moving it like an escalator under his feet while the rest of the landscape remained still. He heard the dogs begin to howl, before the woman released her arrow.

The silver-tipped arrow flew directly at him, but in a motion astonishingly slow. Mike continued to draw the path under him with his dance, but as he did so he drew the arrow upon himself. Mike stopped dancing and the arrow stopped in mid-flight, butted against his chest. He could feel the sharpness of its tip pressing against him, threatening to puncture his skin. The woman gave a signal and the dogs raced at him, filling the air with yammering and howling.

The dogs flung themselves at him, but none would break into the lime mist of the path he trod. Their jaws snapped around his ankles and they barked and snarled with frustration, but they would not or could not penetrate the path. The huntress lowered her bow, her black eyes gleaming.

He heard words echoing inside his head. The lips of the huntress moved, but out of synch with the words:

The arrow is sincerity. These dogs, the dogs of anger. Speed the arrow. The sincere need not resist.

Mike began his dance again. At a crucial moment he began to paw the ground to roll the path underfoot. As he did so he felt the arrow penetrate him, but without pain. It passed through him, dissolving in the air behind him. The dogs continued to snarl and fling themselves around his feet. He increased his step until he had almost drawn abreast of the woman. Her face was expressionless.

Then in one miraculous moment, there was no huntress and no dogs. There was a tall brown bush surrounded by mossy rocks. Nothing else. Mike relaxed his dance position. His heart was pounding and his hands trembling. He was tempted to step out of the path to examine the bush. He waited, collecting his breath, half expecting it to change again.

There was nothing. Only an eerie silence. Even the cicadas and other insects had been silenced. He had terrified himself, he decided, with monstrous visions out of his own brain.

He sat down and lit a cigarette with shaking fingers, gazing at the bush, almost willing it to transform again. The illusion had gone. When he finished his cigarette, he stood up too quickly and felt a moment's giddiness. He pulled on his rucksack, collected up his crook and set off down the path. As he did so, the bush exploded into white flame.

Hallucination. If I passed my hand through that flame, I would not be burned. He was sorely tempted to leave the path and try. *I must test what is real and what is not, or lose my sanity.* He made to step off the path when something overhead distracted him. He looked up and saw a goshawk hovering high above. It reminded him of Manoussos singing. He left the bush burning and crackling under the brilliant sun, and hurried on.

He was nearing the top of the valley wall. Paliohora would be just the other side, he surmised. But now there was a new obstacle in his path.

It was a snake.

The creature, a brown serpent with green markings, lay under the mist and was stretched across the path before him. Mike stamped the earth, expecting the creature to slither away. Most snakes would slip away at the first approach, but this specimen seemed content to lie sleepily across the path. Mike reached out with his crook, nudging the snake's belly. It failed to respond. Then he tried to brush it from the path with the crook, but the crook seemed to pass through it. *Another hallucination.*

Another trick, he decided, to get him to leave the path. He stepped over it, and the snake bit his leg.

44

It was the fourth day since Mike's departure. Kim was having to check a rising panic that she might never see Mike again. At no other time had she felt so far from home. Never before had this country seemed so alien. She didn't know to whom she should confess her worst fears, or what she might say. She had placed herself in a foreign land, where things were understood differently. The lonely implications hung over her like a set of swords.

She worked hard at trying to maintain an air of normality, to smooth over her sense of impending disaster. After eating a spartan lunch, she took her plate over to wash it under the pump. But the pump was dry. She tried priming it, but it spat out nothing but air and insolent sucking noises. Perhaps it had dried permanently. She abandoned it and washed her dishes in the sea.

The white pigeons, heads cocked, watched her working. When she'd finished with the dishes she straightened the furniture on the patio. She wanted to brew coffee but there was no drinking water, and even the gas bottle was nearly empty. The air of neglect around the place was almost tangible.

The dream had visited her again in the night – the dream of crazed women conducting wild rituals in the hills, streaming down the mountain path, holding aloft their blazing torches until they came to the house – this house – and when they reached the gate she would always awake in a freezing sweat, with a cry of protest on her lips. What was the meaning of the dream? And why did it always begin with the cluster of flickering lights, like the candles in the beautiful graveyard of Paliohora? What did it mean?

A few tourists passed by the bottom of the garden. She looked up to see them watching her, and they turned away quickly. English, Mike would have said. How could she forget anything? The nights they'd sat out on the patio under an oil lamp, talking quietly, relaxing in each other's arms, watching night fishermen cruise silently by. What had happened to those times? The globe had turned since then.

She felt her eyes pricking. She needed something to distract her and saw the snorkel gear lying beneath the bench. Choosing the best snorkel and mask, she decided to swim to the rock and back again. She also took the spear gun and the flippers.

As she waded backwards into the water, it seemed the days spent swimming here with Mike represented another life. She fixed her mask and turned her head under the water, breathing through the snorkel tube. The green-jelly world. The world where all the rules were different.

The heavy, laboured breathing through the snorkel mask could be either calming or unnerving. Today it was calming. She swam towards the island, passing over the sea-bed kingdom of urchins and anemones and striped fish without registering them. If the rules of this underwater world were different, what were they? There weren't any rules: you just moved slowly, watchfully, seeing the world go by, feeding or becoming food. She wished the world on the land could be as simple. At least here there were no moral rules, no complications of relationships, no messy, confused emotions to contend with, no responsibilities, commitments, ties, no sense of loss or remorse.

There was only the cold, slow, green-jelly world, where creatures swam back and forth, hither and thither. She had forgiven Mike, but was finding it harder to forgive herself. Not that her offence was of the same order as Mike's: but she needed to forgive herself for having believed in a simple, uncomplicated world, like the one which existed underwater. Her crime had been to believe there was one big fish swimming around in the water, against which nothing else mattered. That fish was called love, and you got on its back and rode it like a girl on a dolphin, waving at the world.

Manoussos sat on the ridge overlooking the crone's house, awaiting Mike's return. Dusk would soon come, and if Mike did not come back then he, Manoussos, would have to go back down to Kamari alone. He could not tread Mike's path; he could not fight Mike's battles; he could not live Mike's life. He had already decided that if the Englishman had not returned within an hour after sundown, then he would not be coming.

But he was unable to free himself from intimations that something had gone badly wrong. He had no way of guessing what mishap might have occurred. Already he was wondering if he had made a mistake. Perhaps it was not appropriate for an Englishman to undertake this arduous work. Perhaps the Englishman lived in a world of different spirits; spirits requiring other methods of confrontation.

But all that was too late. Mike had set out on the path. Manoussos had given what help he could. The rest was in the hands of fate.

He closed his eyes and thought of Mike making his progress to the graveyard at Paliohora. Something in that thought made him think of a swarm of tiny lights. And the swarm of tiny lights reminded him of what had happened that night at the house.

Of course, he had not told Mike the complete story. How could he? Mike would not have believed him. He would have told Kim, and Kim would in turn have been recruited into the village women's conspiracy to hide the truth. And if twenty people agree you are a liar, then what is the value of the truth?

How hot it had been that evening it had all happened. The sirocco. Never before nor since had he known that wind be so hot and vile as it was that year. Driving people crazy. Tormenting people, turning their skin inside out, speaking in their ears like a demon, urging them to acts of folly and madness.

It was just as he had told Mike. All the men had gone to the other side of the island for the Festival of the Horse, to get away from this filthy wind, to get away from their wives, just to get away.

But not Manoussos, because he had heard about this house. He had seen the parties, and he had seen the woman Eva. He had spied on her from the hills behind the house. And this Eva was a beautiful woman. Confident, laughing, inspiring as a figurehead on a ship. And like all the men in the village, he envied the stupid donkey Lakis, who never merited her affections. He had wanted this woman. More than that, he thought he knew how he could have her.

Had he not waited for his moment? Waited until all the men had gone away to the festival, before going to that house. He took his brother there with him, too, his younger brother Dimitris.

Brother Dimitris was about to leave for Thessaloniki, for the seminary there, to become a priest. Why did Manoussos take him? He had asked himself that question many, many times. Maybe it was spite. A kind of jealousy because he was about to become a holy man. Who knows? Anyway, he persuaded him he should see something of life if he was to become a priest. Come and see something, Dimitri! Learn something! What good will you be if you know nothing of life!

And they had arrived there to discover her sitting under the yellow light of oil lamps, reading a book. She was always reading, this Eva. Like Kim. Eva was educated, literate. She provoked men by saying the pleasure they gave her was short; but the pleasure she derived from books lived on after they had gone. Meanwhile, she would take both.

Go away, you boys, she said when they got there. Go away. Go to the horse festival with the others. Give me some peace. Dimitris, the shy one, was easily discouraged, but he, Manoussos, had persisted. They stayed, doing everything to ingratiate themselves. Manoussos had made her laugh. Make a woman laugh, his father had told him, and everything else follows.

Then he had told Eva he would dance for her.

It was his plan all along. He knew how he could take preference over her damned books. And he had danced. It was one of those dances he'd refused to teach the Englishman. It had almost finished him. It was the dance of sexual arousal.

Mike felt the bite inject the fleshy part of his calf muscle like a needle. When the snake slithered away under a nearby boulder, it occurred to him that the creature was no hallucination. For a moment or two he felt nothing before a hot flush raced through his lower leg. He understood too little about serpents to know whether the bite was dangerous or even fatal; but it did occur to him that he should make all haste to reach Paliohora and get help.

The sun was dropping quickly, but it was still quite hot. He figured it was about four o'clock in the afternoon. He hoped the village wasn't more than half an hour away. His leg and his foot began to swell up fast, and he was compelled to walk with a pronounced limp. Within ten minutes, his left leg had almost completely seized. His temperature rocketed and he felt feverish. He was sweating profusely.

His journey was made more difficult when the path reached the top of the valley; for here it ascended a steep incline to reach a dirt road. Mike figured that the road must lead to Paliohora, but the visible mist crossed the road and continued over rocky terrain. The incline he had to climb comprised soft white dust: his feet sank into the dust, retarding his progress. His left leg was, by now, almost useless. When he reached the dirt road he had to haul himself across its lip, where he lay for a moment or two, panting heavily.

He lay on his belly in the white dust of the road, unable to move. He was too weak. He was exhausted. He felt giddy and his head swam; he could almost feel the poison circulating in his veins. *Get up!* he told himself. *Get up! You can't just lie down here and die!* But his body failed to respond to his brain's commands. *Manchester! I'm supposed to die in Manchester, not on a dirt road on a Greek island.*

Then he heard footsteps approaching him. *Manoussos! It's Manoussos! You were following me!* Manzesta!

Manoussos the shepherd. For a moment he saw a swirling island in the sky, brilliantly illuminated. Manoussos the shepherd was waving from the island. The footsteps drew nearer and came to a rest close to his head.

He opened his eyes. His lips were dry with dust. The air rising from the road was quivering with heat. Through it he saw a pair of shoes.

Metal shoes.

Kim saw the underwater shelf come up and realised she must be approaching the rock. She swam up to the tiny beach and sat on the sand, where only days ago they'd enjoyed barbecues and picnics.

She dried off in the sun, taking little pleasure in sitting alone on the rock. She could see their house across the water, whitewashed and singular. It looked lonely and sad and uncared for. The tiny rowing boat bobbed on the water in ruinous, orphaned silence. Kim stood up and fitted her mask over her head. She picked up the spear gun and waded back into the water.

She swam deliberately slowly, and after ten or fifteen minutes neared the shoreline and the house. As she approached the shallows she saw something wave from beneath a rock. She turned, swam back and examined the thing more closely. It was a decent-sized octopus. It spotted her with its strange, bulbous eye, and retreated further under the rock. Kim found she could stand up in the shallows, the water just reaching her chin. She bit a lungful of air and went down to inspect the creature. She could see it coiled under a large, weed-encumbered boulder, two of its legs trailing behind. It could have been three feet long from its head to the end of its tentacles: a good lunch for anyone who wanted a leg.

Give me my husband back, she thought, joking with herself, and I can make a present of this to him.

She surfaced again, cleared her snorkel and dived a second time. The octopus eyed her cautiously, backing under the weeds on the rock. She lined up her spear gun and fired. The spear grazed the boulder and was deflected into dense weeds a couple of yards away. Kim went after it, and coming behind the rock saw two or three of the octopus tentacles exposed. She made a grab.

Kim pulled hard on the tentacles, but the octopus had too tight a grip around its hiding place. She tried to get in closer, jabbing at the thing with the spear gun to dig it out from the rock. Dropping the gun, she reached in under its belly, tugging at its legs. At first the octopus shifted, but then succeeded in renegotiating its grip under the stone. Only three tentacles held it glued to the rock. Kim was going to have to leave it. She was running out of air. She released her grip and backed away.

But something was wrong. The lithe tentacles of the octopus had wound themselves around her wrist after taking up its new position. She tugged again but felt the grip tighten. For a moment she panicked and took in a mouthful of water. Then she pulled again, hard this time, but was unable to release herself.

She felt her legs thrashing behind her. Her flippers were out of the water. It seemed ridiculous: she was only in five feet of water, yet she couldn't break free. The weight of the boulder gripped by the creature was holding her down.

His brother Dimitris had played the *lira* – they were both musicians – and he had danced. It was hot. So hot. But he danced himself into a frenzy that night. Never before had he danced this dance in pursuit of a woman, but now he understood its true purpose! He felt a demon wind rise up inside him. He called up a wind. It had to be seen to be believed; both Eva and his brother, they were mesmerised. He danced for an hour without stopping. Dimitris played like he had never played before.

Then Manoussos had seen the spirit released in Eva's eyes. He felt the thing change in her.

Manoussos brought all this back to mind, and he spoke quietly to the dusk. 'This dance, Mikalis, is a powerful dance. It is a *terrifying* dance. This is why I will never dance this dance again.'

Yes, he had seen it in her eyes. He knew he could have her. He could scent her arousal. When he finished dancing, he smashed down a wineglass and she applauded with great gusto. Bravo, Manoussos! Bravo! It was won! She was won! He was about to send his brother away when they appeared at the garden gate.

They came just as he had described them to Mike. The village women with torches, pouring into the garden. They were drunk; they were wild. Their eyes were on fire. They looked like wild horses, there was no stopping them. They were mad for blood. Cruel! Vicious! They stripped that woman and they beat her senseless. And Manoussos and his brother cowered behind the house, too afraid to lift a finger, as the women hung her naked from a tree.

But still they were not satisfied. Their rage was unstoppable, and they turned it on Manoussos and Dimitris. There were nine of them, each with the strength of nine. They were maddened with drink. They hauled him and his brother into the garden, and he thought they too would be hanged. But first they were stripped naked. The women stood over them with their burning torches.

* * *

Mike looked up from the metal shoes. 'It's not happening,' he whispered. 'Not happening.'

The man was wearing the same habit of rough cloth, looped at the waist with hemp rope. He was leaning on his stave. His grey-black hair, hacked close to his skull, and his cropped beard were precisely as Mike remembered. Then there were the eyes: deep, black pools, like oil, no whites, bloodshot where they were cupped in their sockets. At first the eyes seemed angry; then they softened into an expression of pity. It was indeed the one Mike thought of as the saint. Here was the angel-militant; man or monster.

He reached down to help Mike up by the arm.

Mike struggled to his feet. He had to lean on Manoussos' crook just to stand. He glanced about him: there was no sign of the two acolyte-thugs who had attacked him before. The man, for so he now seemed, brushed a little dust from Mike's shoulders and said softly, almost inaudibly, 'Mikalis.'

Mike steadied himself against the man, barely able to stand. He felt the texture of the rough cloth of the man's garments; felt his warm breath against his cheek. His breath smelled both sweet and rotten. There was saliva on his lips. If he was a saint, or an angel, he reeked of mortality.

'Yes,' said Mike, almost weeping. '*Ne. Ne.* Mikalis.'

'Mikalis,' the man said again. His eyes brimmed with sorrow and pity.

'It's my leg. My leg.'

The saint took a step backwards and made a gesture at Mike's leg.

'Yes,' panted Mike. 'Yes. Yes. Please.'

The saint nodded thoughtfully. Then he lifted his staff in

the air, holding it aloft for a moment before bringing it down in a crashing blow on the back of Mike's calf. He followed it up immediately, driving his metal shoe into Mike's shin. Mike howled and went down. Pain rippled from his leg like an electrical charge.

When Mike opened his eyes again, the angel was leaning over him with an outstretched arm, offering to help him up. Mike spat dust from his mouth. 'Fuck you.'

The angel stepped forward and gently placed his shoe on Mike's swollen ankle. Then he ground Mike's foot into the dust. When Mike had finished screaming, he held out his hand again, beckoning Mike to his feet.

Mike cowered in terror. He knew if he got up, the angel would knock him down again. If he stayed on the ground, the angel would grind his leg. The angel beckoned. He allowed himself to be helped up.

Mike stood waiting for the blow. The angel raised a finger before his face and waved it from side to side. 'Mikalis,' he said again, almost inaudibly. Then he kicked Mike's feet from under him. Mike's head struck the road first, his teeth chipping on a stone. He spat out a gob of blood.

The angel offered a helping hand to lift him to his feet again.

Kim thought that if she thrashed with her legs, someone passing might see her. She thrashed. It was a stupid idea. No one might come by for half an hour.

Her lungs were straining as she fought desperately to free herself. She attacked the thing with her free hand, but it was useless. It had a tenacious grip on the underwater boulder. Her mouth filled with sea water again and her lungs exploded. The water was stirred up and now she could see nothing but swirling mud as she writhed, frantically and uselessly. Then the water cleared again, and the eye of the octopus seemed to be staring back at her. Kim saw everything in that oil-black eye. She saw Mike, she saw Nikkie and Chris, and she saw herself. She saw Lakis, and the women of the village, and the House of Lost Dreams. In the eye of the creature, the house was sealed in the same dissolving, milky lacquer that had come so frequently to haunt her.

She was going to die. She took in another mouthful of salt water. In desperation she looked around her. There was the spear from the gun, lying under some nearby weeds. She thrashed the water trying to reach it, flexing her fingertips. It was too far away. She was unable to reach it by an inch or two. Her fingers tore at the sand on the sea bed, digging frantically to dislodge it. At last the spear shifted and fell into her hand. She plucked it from the weeds and brought it round, plunging it into the bulbous eye of the octopus. The creature belched a cloud of ink and released her immediately.

She surfaced, coughing and spluttering, and went under again. Then she managed to stand, gasping and retching. She waded out of the water, hacking for air and weeping with relief, still clutching the spear. When she reached the shore she fell on her knees.

The yoghurt man was passing by on his donkey, making his return journey. '*Kali Mera! Kali Mera!*' Kim didn't answer. She was kneeling in the sand, gasping, shaking, weeping. 'What are you doing?' said the yoghurt man.

'I'm not,' she said, struggling for breath, 'I'm not going to let it pull us under.'

They were the first proper words she had ever spoken to him. 'Quite right,' he said, refusing to look baffled. He flicked his donkey on, and the beast trotted him away along the path. 'Quite right.'

What he had seen in their eyes! Monsters! Vile spirits! Demons had laid hold of every one of them! The things he saw in their burning eyes were to this day unspeakable! Unspeakable! Then with a mounting horror he understood what had summoned them, and the fearful demons inside them.

It was the dance. His father had warned him never to misuse the dance for selfish purposes. Demons will tear you to pieces, his father had told him. Demons and spirits will flay you. He had summoned them all with his abuse of the dance of power.

Dimitris was dragged away by a cohort of them. Those that remained fell on him and excited him with their hands. 'Does it sound like good sport, Mikalis,' he said to the encroaching darkness, 'to be preyed upon by these lusting women? Believe me, Mikalis, it is not good sport.' He had thought they would strip the flesh from him with their fingernails. But they aroused him despite himself, even against his terror.

And then he heard his brother screaming. Dimitris' terrified cries told him what to expect. One of them had found a scorpion trap, a bottle on the patio. They brought it and put to his genitals. The scorpions stung him again and again.

But he himself was treated differently. He had never understood why. He assumed the dance which had punished him had also protected him. And there was another matter, since he was tied to one of the women with a silver thread of affection, and it was she who had begun on him. His immoral use of the dance had summoned them and excited them beyond all restraint. Four or five of them shamelessly used themselves on him, one hot after the other. To this day he was not entirely certain which of them it was. And then when he was of no use to them any more they rained exhausted slaps and blows on him and cried abuse, and beat him until he almost lost consciousness.

With his dancing he had dared the volcano, and he was burned.

When he recovered, it was to find his brother weeping in agony, out of his mind with terror. In his anguish he had thought Manoussos one of his tormentors, still coming at him. He had to be carried home.

This was what happened that night at the house, under the light of their flaming torches. Since that time, they had promised that if he ever told a single word of this story, they would testify that it was he, Manoussos, and not they, who killed the woman Eva.

Manoussos blinked at the gathering darkness. It was one hour after dusk, and Mike had not returned.

Mike thought he would pass out. He could see the heat rising from the road, wavering around the metal shoes. He looked up at the sky and saw, far above him, a goshawk hovering directly overhead. It could almost have been the same goshawk who had followed his progress along the Path of Souls; the same bird which hovered high in the sky the evening Manoussos had offered up his song from the rock.

The angel took a step closer, raising it as if to bring it crashing down again on Mike's swollen leg. 'All right,' said Mike. 'All right.' He groped around for Manoussos' crook, and accepted the outstretched hand. As the angel leaned back to haul him to his feet, Mike looped the crook around the other's bare ankle, whipping it suddenly towards him. Caught off balance, the angel fell heavily.

Mike was on him in a second, lashing at his head with the crook. The angel reeled under the blows. Mike screamed, raining blows on the face that had haunted him for months. But his own fury, which should have strengthened his arm, made it tremble and weakened his blows. Still wide-eyed from the shock of the counterassault, the angel reached for Mike's throat. Together the two rolled in the dust.

Mike was being gripped and held tightly by the windpipe. He was choking, though he continued to rain weak blows on his antagonist's skull. Averting his head Mike saw one of the metal shoes shed by the angel in the struggle. He dropped the crook and made a grab for the shoe, lashing his assailant across the face with the hard heel. The grip on his throat weakened. The angel was staring back at him with wide-open eyes, like black mirrors. Mike saw his own distorted face in the mirror of those eyes.

Now he was kneeling on his adversary's chest. He angled the point of the shoe and pressed it in the left eye of the spread-eagled saint. Then he let the weight of his body collapse on to the shoe.

The angel's scream sounded from on high, way, way above him, where the goshawks flew. Mike was left panting and weeping in the dirt.

When he looked to see if his enemy was dead, there was no angel, no corpse, nothing. But beneath his chest was a metal shoe. He could barely recover his breath. He looked around the dirt track. The other shoe lay a few feet away. He picked up the second shoe and began to crawl, on his hands and knees, in the direction of the village.

When Mike recovered consciousness, he found himself in darkness, surrounded by a million tiny flickering lights.

He was unable to move. He lay in the dark, completely paralysed.

The place was utterly silent, and the only movement came from the dancing lights. By turning his head fractionally he worked out that his face was lying alongside an upright black marble slab. There was an inscription on the slab in gold lettering. One of the tiny lights close to his face illuminated the lettering.

As he looked, he saw that each of the tiny flickering lights was placed under a similar black marble slab. Finally it occurred to him that he was in a graveyard. He tried again to move, but was unable.

I'm dead. This is what it's like to be dead.

There was a shuffling sound of someone moving amongst the gravestones. An old woman in widow's black limped by. She stopped a short distance away, and peered straight through Mike.

She can't see me. I'm dead and buried. This is what it's like.

The old woman shuffled by, and Mike gave a groan. She turned suddenly, shuffled back a few paces, and peered again without seeing him. Mike groaned a second time. This time the old woman screamed, and, hitching up her skirt, dispensed with her limp and ran from the graveyard. Mike heard her screams diminishing in the distance. Somewhere a dog started barking.

After five minutes, four men returned with the old woman, who was still wailing and sobbing, and gesticulating towards the place where Mike lay sprawled. They were armed with a torch, and they approached him cautiously in the darkness.

'A doctor,' said Mike. 'Get me to a doctor.'

He managed to describe the snake to a local man, who

drove him immediately to the same hospital at Potami where he'd been treated for his broken arm. There he was administered an antidote to the venom. He was told that a bite from this particular snake had resulted in deaths. 'Not always,' they said cheerfully, 'but sometimes.' The swelling reduced almost immediately, and later in the evening, when the only signs of his mishap were the massive black and yellow bruises on his leg, he was allowed home. He ordered a taxi to take him back to Kamari.

In the village of Paliohora they told the story of the Englishman whose faith in the saint had saved his life. He was bitten by a snake and was found in the graveyard clinging to the saint's shoes. He had the shoes, they pointed out, the shoes. He wouldn't let them go. Not for anything.

'*Agios Mikalis,*' they said to each other in reverential tones. 'The saint. Again the saint has intervened to save someone's life.'

45

It was after midnight when Mike got out of the taxi and retraced the beach path to the House of Lost Dreams. His heart quickened when he saw, through the bushes, an oil lamp burning. He hesitated at the garden gate, gazing up at the patio.

Kim was there. She hadn't noticed him; she was lounging in a chair, reading a magazine under the lamp's weak yellow light. He opened the gate, and as it closed behind him, she heard it click, and looked up.

'Hi,' she said softly. 'I've been worried about you.'

She looked beautiful. The lamp lit one side of her. All trace of bitterness and confusion had gone from her face. The light played in the dark curls of her hair and flattered her deep caramel tan.

He hovered on the edge of the patio, as if he were a visitor. It had been swept and cleaned and restored to order. 'I brought you a present,' he said, holding aloft his pair of metal shoes.

'Lovely,' she said. 'Though flowers would be more traditional.'

'Can I be traditional tomorrow?'

'Is that a promise?'

'Yep. Flowers tomorrow.' He placed the shoes by the door.

Kim looked at them askance. 'Have you suddenly become religious?'

'No. No, I don't think so. I don't really know what to do with them.'

'Mike, are you limping?'

'Yes. I had another accident.'

'Oh, Mike!'

'But I'm back now.'

'Yes.'

'What about you? Are you back? I mean, have you come home?'

'Come home? Yes, I've come home.'

Mike kneeled in front of her chair and buried his head in her lap. He cried like a baby, and felt no shame. Kim stroked his hair and rocked him, and looked out across the sea at the shifting, impenitent black waters.

They went to bed. Mike showed her his wounds. She traced his bruises with her cool fingers. 'A snake did this?' she asked. He shrugged. He decided not to tell her about the Path of Souls, or the angel, or the crone, or the hawk or any of it. At least not for the moment. It was all in the past. Everything that was not happening between them at that instant was in the past, and had no bearing. They made love carefully and with dedication. Afterwards Mike fell asleep with no fear of sleepwalking.

In the early morning they swam naked together. The cold water shocked them awake. They kissed, and the salt water and the sunlight fizzed on their lips. They swam in the water like two dolphins reunited. They breaststroked out to the rock where they made love half in the water, and where they rested before swimming back again.

As they were walking out of the sea, in water up to their knees, a sudden pulsation threw them off their feet. The water drained quickly away from around their ankles. They turned in astonishment to see it run away so fast. As they got back on their feet they saw a huge wave lash the rock where only an hour earlier they had been making love. The wet sand trembled beneath them.

'It's an earthquake,' said Mike.

They ran up into the garden. The waves came after them, racing over the beach and into the garden itself, foaming around their legs. The ground was still trembling. The white pigeons were flying around frantically and the chickens and ducks were chasing up the garden to keep clear of the water. The donkey brayed and galloped in circles around its tether. The foaming wave drained off again, and the sea resumed its previous level, but the ground didn't stop trembling. Kim untethered the donkey and it immediately leapt the hedge, galloping across the neighbouring field.

'It's a long one,' said Kim.

Then the canopy pole in front of the house sagged towards them. They thought it must fall, but it steadied. The door of the house flew open, as did the shutters.

'Are we all right here?' Kim said.

'We can't go anywhere else!'

There was nothing to do but wait for the tremor to subside. The outhouse wall lurched to one side, but remained upright. Then the water pump fell through the earth. It completely vanished.

The tremor subsided, and everything was deathly quiet.

The white pigeons began settling in the trees. Mike and Kim stared at each other, looking for confirmation that the quake was over. Mike approached the hole where the water pump had disappeared.

'Don't go too near!'

He could see the pump. It had slipped six or seven feet. Steam and sulphurous odours were issuing from the hole. Mike drew back.

They went up to take a look at the patio. The concrete base had broken in six or seven places. Ants and centipedes were pouring out of one of the cracks. A narrow crevice had opened up in the ground running under the patio. Steam billowed out of it. The canopy pole swayed as Mike touched it.

'I don't fancy going inside. We should go up to the village.'

'Dressed like this?'

It hadn't occurred to Mike that he was still naked. He stepped on to the patio, dashed inside and returned with some clothes. Then he had to go back and pick up some money. 'We can get the rest later.'

They walked up to the village. There was much commotion, and more than a little damage, but it seemed no one had been seriously hurt by the tremor. A wall had collapsed on Lakis' taxi, which was uninsured. No one except the owner seemed unduly concerned about this mishap; after all, they had their own damage to think about.

Kati had lost some of her stock in the shop, but Mike and Kim found her sitting at a table with Vassillis outside the shop, drinking wine with neighbours. They insisted Mike and Kim join them. The two were in high spirits, as were most of the neighbours, frightened, stimulated and massively relieved at the experience.

'What can we do?' Vassillis shouted, pouring generous measures of wine. He waved the bottle at the heavens, as if everything was in the lap of the gods. 'What can we do?'

46

Manoussos walked his sheep down the hill, past the house abandoned by the English and up the beach. The end of summer was approaching. He smelled it in the air, in the wind. A shepherd sensed these things several days before anyone else. The temperature hadn't yet changed, but the season was already turning.

He clicked his teeth at his flock, directing them off the beach and up the path which led over the hill and behind the village. Two figures sat waiting for him on the brow of the hill. It was Mike and Kim. They stood as he approached.

'Manoussos! We knew you would come this way.'

He was pleased to see them together. He hadn't seen Kim in several days, and Mike not since they parted up in the hills three days ago. *'Yia! Yia!* How are you?'

'Good, Manoussos. And you?'

'Good! Good! Let's call it good.' He rubbed at the stubble on his chin and looked critically at Mike. 'I see you abandoned the house.'

'Yes. After the earthquake. It wasn't a good idea to stay there.'

'Earthquake? It was no earthquake. Just a little dance. But you are right. It was not good to stay there. I think the house is falling down. And the earth is still smoking. Where are you living?'

'We've been staying in one of Kati's rooms for the last two nights.'

'Kati's rooms, eh? Kati's rooms.'

'Manoussos, we came to say goodbye to you. We are leaving.'

The shepherd turned and looked out to sea. 'Leaving, is it? Yes. Leaving.' There was a moment of silence. He flicked at the dry earth with a new crook. His old one still lay discarded by the road to Paliohora. Then he turned back to them and said, 'Where will you go?'

'We haven't decided. Maybe to another island. Maybe home to England. We'll travel. We take the ferry the day after tomorrow.'

'It's soon! The day after tomorrow.' He looked at them, and again he said, 'But it's soon!'

'Yes. Look, tomorrow is a festival day,' said Mike. 'They are having music and dancing in the *platia*. It would be a great thing for us if you would come and eat with us. I will dance. I want to show Kim what you taught me.'

'It would be a fine thing to be in your company for the festival. I'm honoured you invite me. But I have to say, it is not for me, these festival days. I don't feel comfortable in crowds.'

'Oh, please come,' said Kim.

'No. I must say no.'

'Really?'

'No.' There was a long and difficult pause as Manoussos gazed out to sea again, leaning on his crook. He looked as though this disappointing parting was paining him. 'Tomorrow,' he said at last, 'I go to the monastery. You remember the old fool who looks out to the sea every day? You remember him?'

'Yes, of course.'

'He too would like to say goodbye to you.'

'But—'

'Yes, he would like to say goodbye. I know it. Tomorrow I go to take him some food. I would be very happy if you would walk with me.'

'We'll come,' said Kim. 'We'll be happy to come with you.'

'Good. It is settled. Now I must take my sheep.'

That night Mike told Kim everything that had happened to him up in the mountains. He recounted it all like a dream. She understood it as much more, and in time would interpret it for him. She was deeply impressed that his trail had ended in the graveyard at Paliohora, the scene of her own vision and revelation. Yet she seemed not to be surprised.

'The Path of Souls,' she repeated softly, falling asleep. 'The Path of Souls.'

In the morning they waited for Manoussos on the beach. He came with his canvas bag packed with cheese, olives, fruit, bread and water. Mike and Kim had also packed some food to take to the hermit. Manoussos nodded. 'He will have his own festival, that one!'

After they had moved on, Mike discreetly pressed into his hand the twenty-five thousand drachmae. The shepherd looked relieved. 'I didn't want to ask you; but I am glad. I did not have it myself, and I did not want the *mageesa* to be angry with me.'

'Don't you want to know what happened?'

'No; I don't want to know.'

'Anyway, Kim came back to me. Whether it had anything to do with it or not, I'll gladly pay.'

They walked through an avenue of quince and pear trees, through olive groves and under huge fig trees laden with fruit. Manoussos called to Kim, who had gone ahead. 'Kim, now your husband is a famous dancer. He could almost be Greek.'

'So he tells me.'

'Believe it.'

They passed above the hot steam bath, though Manoussos warned them not to try to use it since the earthquake. He said it was now hot enough to strip the flesh from the body. It would not be tolerable again, he pronounced, for six months.

When they came to the field of snakes, Mike asked if they might circumvent it instead of walking straight through. Kim agreed.

'I was bitten by a snake after we parted,' said Mike to Manoussos. 'I'd prefer it not to happen again.'

He consented to walk the long way round the field of snakes. Out of Kim's hearing, Manoussos said, 'But was it a snake?'

'I thought you didn't want to know.'

'You are right, Mike. I do not want to know. Hey, Kim! Not so far ahead!'

They approached the brow of the hill, and the monastery hove into view. The hermit was away from his usual observation post. They looked in the monastery courtyard. It stood exactly as they had last seen it. The church was locked. The clapperless bell resonated with unmarked time. The only difference was that the fig tree was now laden with bursting, ripe fruit. Most of the tree's harvest had already fallen to the concrete floor of the courtyard, where the sticky, blood-coloured figs had exploded out of their skins.

They went behind the church, and there, murmuring softly to himself, was the mad hermit. He smiled when he saw them approach.

But something else had changed. The hermit had shorn his hair and had shaved off his beard. His appearance was completely altered. Mike thought something around the mouth – indeed the entire face – looked rather familiar. The hermit muttered a few incomprehensible words.

'God has been,' said Manoussos. 'He says God has been.' The hermit laughed and asked something of the shepherd. 'He wants to know if you felt the earth tremble when God came by. He wants to know if you saw it.'

'Yes,' said Mike in Greek. 'We both saw.'

'God has been,' smiled the hermit. Then he began chanting softly to himself.

Kim had also noticed the detail of his features. It was obvious both to her and to Mike, and it was when she was placing beside the hermit the provisions they had brought that she was unable to contain herself from saying, 'But Manoussos, is this man your brother?'

Manoussos looked at Kim coldly.

'It's just that he looks so much like you.'

Manoussos smiled. Then he sat behind the hermit, embracing him. The hermit relaxed into the shepherd's strong arms, closing his eyes and chanting almost inaudibly.

'*Ne. Ne. Adelphos mou enai.* You are right. My only brother.' Manoussos rocked him gently, like a baby.

'Sit. Sit! I will tell you how this came to be. It cannot harm to tell you this story, because you are leaving and you cannot harm anyone by knowing more. Mike, I told you never to tell the whole story. Well, I am going to break my own rules.'

And he told them what had happened that night.

'And this,' said Kim solemnly, 'was the ordinary women of the village. Kati, and Maria and—'

Manoussos raised a hand to halt the litany. He continued to rock his hermit brother in his arms. 'That night,' he said, 'my brother's mind was driven into the sea. It has never returned.'

Manoussos kissed his brother's cheek, and closed his own eyes. He continued to rock him gently in his arms.

Kim and Mike looked at each other. They got up and went round to the courtyard in front of the monastery, to leave Manoussos alone with his brother for a while.

'Do we believe him?' asked Mike.

'How can we believe him? And yet how can we not?'

They walked back to Kamari with the shepherd. A boiling red disc set over the ocean, spinning the waters lilac and gold. Manoussos talked freely and asked them a lot of questions about England, and about the life there. He'd been to Liverpool and Bristol in the time before he quit the merchant navy, and claimed he liked both places. He told them he had no further inclination to travel. This was, he said pointedly to Mike, both his place of birth and his place of death.

When they reached the village and it came to parting, Kim flung her arms around him and kissed the rough silver stubble of his face. 'I love you, child,' the shepherd said. 'I did from the first. I love you both.' Then he embraced Mike, and his eyes were wet.

He looked around and picked a white gardenia from a hedgerow, thrusting it into Kim's hands. Then he found one for Mike. With the words 'Go to the good!' he turned and walked up the hill towards his lonely house.

'*Sto kalo!*' he shouted again. 'Go to the good!'

The next day Mike and Kim had to leave for Palioskala to catch the ferry to Kavala. They got up early to say goodbye to everyone. The tomato lady gave them a hug and a large bag of tomatoes. The butcher's wife insisted on wrapping them a cheese and a bag of sausages. Riga at the restaurant poured glasses of brandy and offered cigarettes. Maria cried and wanted Kim to choose a dress from her shop. Kati gave them a bottle of home-made jam and a pair of ceramic candlesticks.

It was at Kati's shop that Vassillis clapped Mike on the back and complimented him on his dancing at the previous night's festivities. 'Like a Greek!' he said. 'Just like a Greek, and better than some!'

'Yes,' said Mike, looking at Kim. 'I thought I showed real *kefi*.'

The men stood outside the shop in the sun, enjoying a cigarette together. Kim and Kati drank a last coffee inside.

'Kim, I want to ask you something.' Kati put down her cup. 'Did Manoussos say anything at all to you while you were with him?'

Kim coloured. 'What about?'

Kati hesitated. 'Anything. Any strange stories.'

'If he did tell me anything, I mean, any strange story, should I believe him?'

'So he has said something?'

'I didn't say that. I said, or what I meant to say was: what reason would he have for lying?'

Kati was about to reply when the men came back inside. They all kissed each other. Kim thanked Kati for all her kindnesses, large and small. Before Kim got into the car,

Kati walked round to give her another kiss on the cheek. As she did, she whispered, 'No reason. Manoussos would have no reason to lie.'

They exchanged a confidential look as Mike drove off. Everybody waved.

As they left the village on the road winding up into the mountains, they saw Manoussos standing alone atop a hill. He was leaning on his shepherd's crook.

'Stop the car!' Kim shouted.

She jumped out and Mike followed. They thought he would come down from the hill to speak to them. But with the sun behind him, he waved at them. Then he turned and disappeared behind the other side of the hill.

More Compelling Fiction from Headline:

DEAN KOONTZ

FROM THE No 1 BESTSELLING AUTHOR OF *COLD FIRE*

THE DOOR TO DECEMBER

Six years ago, Laura McCaffrey's three-year-old daughter Melanie was kidnapped by Laura's estranged husband, Dylan, and seemingly vanished from the face of the earth.

Now Melanie has been found, a nine-year-old wandering the Los Angeles streets with blank eyes and a secret in her soul she will not or can not reveal.

Dylan has been found too – or at least his mangled remains.

Melanie is home again. But can she ever truly be safe – as the floodgates of terror open and the bloody torrent comes pouring through...?

Also by Dean Koontz from Headline Feature

HIDEAWAY	WHISPERS
SHADOWFIRES	NIGHT CHILLS
COLD FIRE	THE HOUSE OF THUNDER
THE BAD PLACE	DARKNESS COMES
MIDNIGHT	CHASE
LIGHTNING	THE VISION
WATCHERS	THE VOICE OF THE NIGHT
THE SERVANTS OF TWILIGHT	PHANTOMS
THE MASK	TWILIGHT EYES
THE FACE OF FEAR	SHATTERED
STRANGERS	THE KEY TO MIDNIGHT
THE EYES OF DARKNESS	

This book was originally published under the pseudonym Leigh Nichols. This is the first British Commonwealth edition under the author's real name.

FICTION/GENERAL   0 7472 3705 0

More Horrifying Fiction from Headline:

THE PARASITE
RAMSEY CAMPBELL

"One of the scariest, most important novels of horror and the occult that I've read" STEPHEN KING

'Easily the finest practising British horror novelist'
Daily Telegraph

It all began with a little game – for children to amuse and frighten each other. A seance in a dark, empty house. And don't tell the grown-ups.

But something unexpected happened that night – some awful evil awoke in the foul darkness. Something each child sensed and fled from.

All but one of them…

Poor little Rose, shrieking with terror in that upstairs room, as some quivering form approached. Poor little Rose, unspeakably invaded…

Now, twenty years later, she has discovered unearthly powers she never possessed before, and has witnessed horrors no one else can see.

The gruesome presence that claimed her in childhood is ready now for the ultimate evil consummation. And Rose will learn at last the monstrous truth about…

THE PARASITE

Previously published as *To Wake the Dead*.
Winner of the British Fantasy Award for Best Novel.

FICTION/HORROR   0 7472 4061 2

More Compelling Fiction from Headline:

**WINNER OF THE 1991 BRAM STOKER AWARD FOR
BEST SHORT STORY COLLECTION**

PRAYERS TO BROKEN STONES

DAN SIMMONS

Demonstrating the incredible breadth and power of Dan Simmons's writing, *Prayers to Broken Stones* is set in worlds of dark imagination that only the author of such award-winning novels as *Carrion Comfort*, *Hyperion* and *The Fall of Hyperion* could envision.

Encounter an old man and a young boy for whom the ghosts of the civil war will not rest in peace... Driven mad by guilt, a scientist dooms himself with a final effort to administer poetic justice... Could the shadowy, deformed beings only half glimpsed by a coma patient be responsible for so much misery and death in our world...?

Ranging from the chill of deep space to a cold wind rising from an open grave, *Prayers to Broken Stones* is a transfixing collection of short fiction from a remarkable writer.

WITH AN INTRODUCTION BY HARLAN ELLISON

'This book is an architectural plan for a major literary career'
Locus

Also by Dan Simmons from Headline Feature
SONG OF KALI
Winner of the 1986 World Fantasy Award
CARRION COMFORT
Winner of the 1989 British Fantasy Society Award
Winner of the 1990 Bram Stoker Award
Winner of the 1990 Locus Award for Best Horror Novel
HYPERION
Winner of the 1990 Hugo Award
Winner of the 1990 Locus Award for Best Science Fiction Novel
THE FALL OF HYPERION
Winner of the 1991 Locus Award for Best Science Fiction Novel
Winner of the 1991 British Science Fiction Association Award
PHASES OF GRAVITY

FICTION/GENERAL   0 7472 3816 2

A selection of bestsellers
from Headline

THE PARASITE	Ramsey Campbell	£4.99 ☐
GAMEWORLD	J V Gallagher	£4.99 ☐
SCHEHERAZADE'S NIGHT OUT	Craig Shaw Gardner	£4.99 ☐
THE GIANT OF INISHKERRY	Sheila Gilluly	£4.99 ☐
THE HOODOO MAN	Steve Harris	£5.99 ☐
LIES AND FLAMES	Jenny Jones	£5.99 ☐
THE DOOR TO DECEMBER	Dean Koontz	£5.99 ☐
HIDEAWAY	Dean Koontz	£5.99 ☐
MIDNIGHT'S LAIR	Richard Laymon	£4.99 ☐
HEART-BEAST	Tanith Lee	£4.99 ☐
CHILDREN OF THE NIGHT	Dan Simmons	£4.99 ☐
FARNOR	Roger Taylor	£5.99 ☐

All Headline books are available at your local bookshop or newsagent, or can be ordered direct from the publisher. Just tick the titles you want and fill in the form below. Prices and availability subject to change without notice.

Headline Book Publishing PLC, Cash Sales Department, Bookpoint, 39 Milton Park, Abingdon, OXON, OX14 4TD, UK. If you have a credit card you may order by telephone — 0235 831700.

Please enclose a cheque or postal order made payable to Bookpoint Ltd to the value of the cover price and allow the following for postage and packing:

UK & BFPO: £1.00 for the first book, 50p for the second book and 30p for each additional book ordered up to a maximum charge of £3.00.

OVERSEAS & EIRE: £2.00 for the first book, £1.00 for the second book and 50p for each additional book.

Name ....

Address ....

....

....

If you would prefer to pay by credit card, please complete:
Please debit my Visa/Access/Diner's Card/American Express (delete as applicable) card no:

Signature ....Expiry Date ......